# THE
# WRONG MADONNA

# THE
# WRONG MADONNA

a novel

# Britt Holmström

The Canada Council | Le Conseil des Arts
for the Arts | du Canada
since 1957 | depuis 1957

ONTARIO ARTS COUNCIL
CONSEIL DES ARTS DE L'ONTARIO

The publisher gratefully acknowledges the support of the
Canada Council for the Arts and the Ontario Arts Council
for its publishing program. We acknowledge the financial support of
the Government of Canada through the Book Publishing Industry Development
Program (BPIDP) for our publishing activities.

Printed and bound in Canada

**National Library of Canada Cataloguing in Publication Data**

Holmström, Britt, 1946–
The wrong madonna

ISBN 1-896951-37-6

I. Title.

PS8565.O639165W76 2002    C813'.54    C2002-900032-7
PR9199.3.H5817W76 2002

Cover and text design: Tannice Goddard
Cover images: Dolores Pitcher
and Tannice Goddard

**Cormorant Books Inc.**
895 Don Mills Road, 400-2 Park Centre
Toronto, Ontario, Canada M3C 1W3
**www.cormorantbooks.coM**

*For Anita Lundh Davidsson*
*and lasting friendship*

"As we grow older and see the ends of stories as well as their beginnings, we realize that to the people who take part in them it is almost of greater importance that they should be stories, that they should form a recognizable pattern, than that they should be happy or tragic."

— REBECCA WEST: *BLACK LAMB AND GREY FALCON*

# Zagreb

**F**rom the tram stop the long wall looked more than twenty feet high. Splashes of vivid green poured down its side. The girl crossed the street heading towards it, past the flower vendors, over to where the wall curved inwards in an oval by the front entrance. The green was the new growth of tangled vines draping the wall from top to bottom. Above it a pillared balustrade ran like a lacy edge.

Tall arched gateways led to what lay beyond, flanking the church directly inside, built of the same stone as the wall, becoming one with it. Its round tower was crowned with an enormous verdigrised dome. A cross at its center stretched towards the gray sky. Similar towers, their cupolas smaller, dotted the wall, which appeared to go on for miles in both directions.

Such splendor could easily fool a visitor, especially a naive one, into thinking that this was a fortification that sheltered some fabled palace in a garden lush with rare flowers.

There was no palace. Mirogoj was a place for the dead. Up on the rim of Kaptol hill in Zagreb, it spread across the northeastern slope, a foothill of Medvednica mountain where bears had once roamed.

The young girl felt small and insignificant as she entered under one of the arches. The infant in her arms felt smaller still, weightless almost, but not insignificant. Despite everything, it would never be that.

Going through, she saw that the wall was the outside of an arcade, a corridor full of statues. The park-like grounds beyond the arcade lay shaded under a thick canopy of plane trees. Beneath it stretched out a vista of flowers and flickering votive candles in windproof red glasses. She wondered who had lit them all. There weren't many people about.

The young girl wandered up and down tree-lined alleys, reading gravestones as she went along, not understanding a word, not knowing how to pronounce any of the names. It was a particular name she was searching for, the familiar name of a certain stranger. She had lots of time and read each stone carefully, but found none with the name Sterić. Was it an unusual name?

In the branches above blackbirds sang without cease. For a while she got lost in the sound. She traversed the cemetery. On the opposite side a low wall marked the edge of the hill. Below it, a soft green landscape opened up. She sat down with her back to the cemetery and looked out over red tiled roofs dotting the slope, over forest-covered hills rolling north towards the part called Slovenia. Ahead of her stretched the fertile fields of Slavonia, as the eastern part of Croatia was called, all the way to Hungary. Was that the section of Serbia called Vojvodina further down in that direction? This country had so many pieces in its puzzle. There were even puzzles within the puzzles.

From the northern horizon a gray curtain of rain was gliding southeast.

In this city, where the image of Madonna and Child cropped up everywhere, the young girl ought to have fit right in, sitting silent on the stone wall, a sleeping infant on her lap, an ageless landscape for backdrop.

Suddenly a brass band erupted somewhere under the trees behind her. Craning her neck, she barely made out what looked like a group of people standing still by a graveside. She wondered where they'd come from. After a while, the music stopped and was replaced by the singing of a hymn, somber and slow. It was followed by the faint voice of a man talking. A priest, she presumed. At the end of the service a lone trumpet played the Last Post. It echoed throughout the cemetery. Through it all the chorus of blackbirds never stopped their serenade.

When the people had dispersed, the girl got up and drifted in under the canopy once again. Down the path she passed a priest who, apart from a curious glance, paid her no particular attention. He looked young and walked with his feet turned in.

Stupid pigeon-toed witch-burner, thought the girl, for she was in an irrational mood. She was also very frightened.

She was an outsider in this faraway country, which may have been why she was badly in need of a sense of inclusion. When she found a little three-legged stool left abandoned by a grave, she made the bold decision to sit down. This way, anybody seeing her would assume she was visiting with a loved one. Hopefully the owner of the wobbly stool would not arrive and feel outraged at the trespass.

For a long time she sat listening to the birds. If she killed herself this very day, in this city, at this cemetery, would they bury her here? Would they let her lie on the edge of the hill sloping east, under the protective foliage of ancient trees, birds singing for all eternity above her grave? The baby — her baby — the great-great-great grandson of an officer of the Habsburg Imperial Navy, might come and visit when he was older.

That, of course, would not happen. She was an outsider. If she died in this spot, the authorities would probably ship her home in a cardboard box tied with string. She wondered to whom they would address it.

"One day you will rest here," she whispered to the infant. "Your children and grandchildren will come and visit you. They will light votive candles in little red glasses and put armfuls of fresh flowers on your grave. Clear away old leaves and make it look pretty. Say a prayer and shed a tear and remember what a lovely man you were. You will have lived your life knowing that you belonged. That's all I can offer you."

The infant wasn't listening, the birdsong and the soft breeze rustling the leaves had lulled him back to sleep. He was a contented baby, easy to please. Sunlight slanted through the branches of the overhead tree and fell onto his sleeping face, lit the red fire of his hair, threw shadows on his round cheeks. The girl couldn't bear to look at him.

"Child," she said out loud, startling herself. "Oh, child. You picked the wrong Madonna!" She would not say his name.

Then, being a child herself, she drizzled runaway tears onto his face in a private, unplanned form of baptism. "Tomorrow's the big day," she went on, sniffling, feeling he ought to know. "Are you ready?"

The infant slept peacefully.

It was April 17, the day before Easter Sunday, 1965, overcast and gray, but not cold.

# London

# 1

**Lisa Grankvist arrived in England** via boat from Calais looking disheveled, having traveled for a long time without proper rest. Her white blouse, once a pristine symbol of respectability, had a crestfallen look. The prim pleats of her skirt had given up. Her shoes needed polishing.

The overnight train trip from Vienna to Paris had left her with a stiff neck from trying to sleep sitting up. Opposite her on the train had sat a serious young woman with thick glasses, who had spent most of the night reading a forbidding book with the title *Les Grands Mariages des Habsbourg*. Hour after hour the train had hurtled west through a nocturnal alpine landscape, hour after hour the woman had read. Not until two in the morning had she put her book down, removed her glasses, leaned back and closed her eyes in a fluid gesture of great contentment. The woman's silk blouse had blazed as white as newly fallen snow.

Lisa thought about the woman and her book the next day as she watched the fabled white cliffs take shape where a dull sea met an indistinguishable graphite sky. One day she too would read serious books in that same self-contained manner, at home in body and soul.

Then the ferry arrived in Dover and there were more immediate problems to deal with. Clamping her suitcase in a sweaty grip she went and knocked on the door of the damp isle called Great Britain to see if it would deign to let her in. You can do this, Lisa, she lectured herself. They don't know you. Stiff upper lip and all that. It's what the English say. It's what makes them respect a person.

At customs an elderly guardian of the realm looked over the young girl before him. Not in a hurry, he took in the dyed red hair and the serious blue eyes, the silver swallow in flight on the soiled collar of her blouse, the tired way she rubbed her neck, her chewed fingernails. Unsure of what this all meant, but having a general idea, he demanded proof of solvency.

Her friend Mimmi had warned her about the suspicious nature of the guardians of the remains of the British Empire. She hauled out of her handbag a wad of twenty-pound notes big enough to pay the man's salary for the foreseeable future.

The guardian of the realm quickly changed his tune. Shabby-looking and monied, the girl might well be a foreign aristocrat. "With all that money, miss, why the sad face?"

"Oh, I'm just tired. It's been a very long journey. I sat up reading a book about the Habsburgs all night."

Educated as well as monied. After that it was, "Welcome to the U.K, miss! Have a lovely stay, miss." Little did he realize how long that money was supposed to last, little did he know that she was not staying at the address she had given, The Mayfair Hotel. She was not averse to lying.

Safely inside the country she stuffed the pounds sterling back in her handbag, right next to the piece of paper where she had listed the few items she had brought from what had been her childhood home. The list read: "Silver spoon with my name and birthdate on it (Lisa Ann-Kristin 8.10.1946). Dad's things: passport, beret, tools, reading glasses, false teeth (wrapped in embroidered handkerchief)." These mementos were tucked in the bottom of her suitcase. These she must never lose. The photo in her father's unused passport showed a man with an expectant smile, hoping soon to go on his first trip.

Her own passport photo showed a young girl, eyes wide with fear, staring into the camera like a primitive member of a newly discovered tribe, fearful lest the photographer's magic machine might capture her soul.

Grabbing her suitcase, she boarded the train destined for Waterloo station, pleading with her undisciplined thoughts to focus on the new existence that lay waiting for her down the track. Her upper lip was so stiff by then it made her fellow passengers uncomfortable. A woman ushered her small child out of the compartment to a safer environment.

I'm going to London, she thought. Nothing else matters now, April 27, 1965. London was swinging like a pendulum out of control, or so they said. She imagined the vast metropolis up ahead rocking and singing as if life were a musical, Lord Nelson tapping his foot atop his column, the Queen shimmying around Buckingham Palace in a miniskirt, the streets crammed with glossy people in the latest fashions from Carnaby Street, famous bands playing in every club, every night, all night.

This will be fun, Lisa, promised the voice in her head. It sounded like a plea.

But it was certainly possible. The London she was about to arrive in was undergoing profound change. History was in the making daily, and what better distraction than social upheaval to take a person's mind off things?

London had become a city ruled by music and pop stars, "the new, classless aristocracy" as they, whose job it was to analyze, called them. New bands formed nightly in dark cellar clubs and went forth to conquer. London was where it was at.

Mimmi was waiting for her at Waterloo station. It was the second time in a month she had gotten off a train to find Mimmi's reassuring presence on the platform. This time she stood huddled in a green raincoat a size too big, her hair in a bun, drizzle-damp and lackluster. She was smiling, but her smile remained tentative as Lisa ran up to embrace her. It was the kind of smile reserved for a loved one who has just been released from the asylum and who is not ready to be incorporated into the community. Her left foot moved as if to take a step backward, but she didn't. She stretched her arms out to welcome her friend.

After hugging her for a long time Mimmi stepped back to look Lisa long in the eye, still with that same reserve. She took Lisa's hand, played with her fingers as if about to read her fortune, and then, biting her lip, but unable to stop herself, asked if Lisa was okay. Had it been anybody else asking, the question would have been an admonition. Lisa assured her she was fine.

"Are you really, really okay?"

"Why do you keep asking? Do I look demented? Am I drooling?" She *would be* all right eventually.

"I'm sorry, Lisa. It's just . . . I've been worried sick about you all alone in Vienna for a whole week. We didn't even know if you got out of Yugoslavia safely."

"Mimmi, please don't go all teary on me. I've been just fine, I promise. Nothing happened. I'm here, aren't I? I stayed in a great place in Vienna, by the way, a storage depot full of furniture." She stopped babbling. "I missed you something awful though."

She smiled at Mimmi, a big insincere smile, and everything was okay, the way it always was when beautiful Mimmi smiled back. As they left the station Mimmi started to relay what had taken place after Lisa had left Zagreb on the train. Nothing much, as it turned out. She and Mick had only stayed on for half an hour before they got the car and headed for Venice.

Lisa said she didn't want to talk about that business anymore. Not now, not ever. Mimmi blushed and apologized profusely. Lisa felt bad and asked her how Venice was.

"Oh, we had such a wonderful time in Venice," sighed Mimmi, her cheeks pink, happy again. It didn't take much. "It was just like a honeymoon. So romantic."

"Did you lie entwined in a gondola?"

"Yes we did. The very first evening. How did you know?"

"Just guessing," said Lisa. "I'm elated you had such a marvelous time. I had a marvelous time too. I bought a tea cup."

The street outside the station was lined with black taxis. Real English taxis like the ones she'd seen in movies. As soon as she saw them she asked, could they take one of them to Piccadilly Circus, so she could get a glimpse of London as it swung? Mimmi thought it best to indulge her. The rain fell gray and soft. There were crowds of people, cars and buses. The air smelled of exhaust fumes, the pavements were full of litter. Lisa kept her eyes peeled for famous pop stars but didn't see any. Most people looked disconcertingly ordinary, drab even, their heads bent in the drizzle, collars up, dashing in and out of traffic.

Piccadilly Circus lived up to her expectations. It looked just the way it did on a postcard Mimmi had once sent her. Here they got out and Mimmi led Lisa down a flight of stairs to the tube station, then onto a very long escalator that plunged headlong into the underworld. The downward travel made Lisa nervous. How far below were they going? She had some knowledge of Hell, having recently studied its pictorial images as envisioned by the old masters.

Ahead of them, as well as behind them, throngs of people were descending towards the earth's core, unperturbed, as if it was quite the normal thing to do. Others were rolling upwards towards the street, looking bored and unscathed. Whatever they did to you down there, they obviously didn't force you to stay.

"Don't be nervous," said Mimmi, noticing Lisa turn pale. "We have to go down. That's where you catch the tube. There's nothing to worry about." Mimmi had that look again, as if thinking of taking Lisa out to buy her a nice rainproof straitjacket.

"I'm not nervous. I'm just tired, that's all. It was a long trip."

"Don't worry, it's all over now. You did it."

"*We* did it."

"We did it. Everything will be okay. You're safe."

"Thank you, Mimmi. I love you."

"I know that, Lisa. I love you too."

They walked through an unpleasant tunnel to a platform called Piccadilly Line Westbound and caught a train for four stops. It was very crowded. A man in a bowler hat kept breathing down Lisa's neck. His breath was hot. At South Kensington they changed trains and took the District Line. This train was half empty. Nobody breathed on her.

"Whether it says Richmond or Ealing Broadway, it doesn't matter, both are fine," Mimmi taught her for future reference. Both went to Chiswick, and Chiswick was the place Lisa would call home from then on, a semi-detached three-story house on Airedale Avenue. It sounded bright and happy as if kindly elves lived there.

The people on the train were gray, damp shadows, void of glamour. No Carnaby Street here either. London might be swinging, but there were glaring discrepancies. Mimmi said, "Well, that's how it is." While the dirty old train rushed past ugly brick houses with triplet chimney pots, she chattered on, teaching Lisa how to interpret the different colored lines on the London Underground map so she'd be able to get around in this new life.

They got off at a station called Turnham Green. It was a much nicer place than the station so precariously close to the earth's core. Here was fresh air and a monotone song of rain falling on the weeds that grew on the track. There was ivy crawling down the dirty brick wall on the other side of the track. Lisa stood and looked at it through the rain, remembering another wall, until Mimmi took her by the arm and turned her towards the stairs leading up to the exit.

Outside the station stood a flower vendor in a blue apron and transparent plastic coat, shouting at passers-by to buy flowers. The flowers, unlike the people hurrying past, were gorgeous.

"Mimmi? Can I buy you some flowers?"

"That's okay, Lisa. You don't have to do that."

"I want you to have flowers, okay? Please?"

"Why?"

"Because it's bad luck to visit somebody empty-handed the very first time. You know that."

"Well, it's not an English custom, but it doesn't matter. That will be very nice."

Lisa put her suitcase down and bought an armful of wet blue and yellow flowers. Instantly she felt better.

The station was at the dead end of a small street, Turnham Green Terrace. It was full of little shops that were just closing for the day.

"This looks so English!"

"That's because we're in England."

It was a short walk down to Chiswick High Road, which went on forever in both directions. It too was full of shops. They crossed the High Road at what Mimmi called a zebra crossing, and after that it was only a skip and a hop before they stood by the entrance to the house on Airedale Avenue. There was a slender copper beech growing on one side of the gate, a tall spruce hid the view on the other. The house was a three-storey red brick semi like all the others. They all had large bay windows sticking out into their front yards. Pregnant bellies, thought Lisa. The front door was painted a glaring red. The door to the house on the left was black, the one on the right was lemon yellow. The one right across the street blazed a vivid purple.

This is what you will call home now, she told herself. Don't forget. It might look unfamiliar, but this is where you live. The house with the red door, tucked between a black and a yellow one.

Mimmi led her up a long staircase to the second floor, saying this was called the first floor in England, and showed Lisa to her room.

"I'll go make us some tea and sandwiches," said Mimmi. "Mick won't be back from the studio until after midnight. You make yourself at home."

Not having much of a choice, Lisa did just that. She put her Viennese Imperial teacup on the shelf by the bed and admired it for a bit, feeling a growing attachment to the one and only possession that was truly hers. She had bought it because it reminded her of the Empress Maria Theresa swathed in a blue lacy dress, looking down at her from the painting in the gallery in Vienna. And because it reminded her of sitting in that same gallery day after day, wearing her father's beret, absorbing every

15

detail of *The Last Judgment*. How she had nearly curtsied the first time she stood before it.

The room she was to live in was gloomy and uninviting, unused to human occupancy. The bed, her bed now, stood under a tall narrow window with a thin lace curtain that looked like it needed washing. It was a narrow berth with a pink nylon bedspread, once shiny but still slippery to the touch. The window faced something referred to as "the garden," a barren square of concrete with a weather-beaten table and two chairs where nobody ever appeared to sit. At the very back squatted a small toolshed with a rusty lock.

That night she sat down to write a letter to her favorite aunt, one of four, but the only one on her father's side. It was a short letter; she was tired. None of her aunts had heard from her since March. Her previous letters home, all sent from England via Mimmi, had been filled with lies. Though this was the first letter she would mail from England herself, it too held no truth. "Dear Aunt Margit: My first year in art school is almost over. Already I feel like I've lived here forever . . ."

There were no elves residing on Airedale Avenue, though the house contained a peculiar enough ménage. Mimmi and Mick Barker, her English boyfriend, a recording studio technician, were the normal ones. The house, christened "Tad Hall" by Mick, was owned by Mrs. Emily Wicks, a 72-year-old woman married to a Polish ex-fighter pilot named Tadeusz, twenty-two years her junior. Tad of Tad Hall they called him. Mrs. Wicks lectured every lodger, loudly, as if the entire human race were stone deaf, that she called herself Mrs. Wicks because, "First of all, I am a married woman. This makes me a missus. Secondly, I cannot conceive of having a foreign name, so I'm sticking to Wicks. All right, dear?"

Mrs. Wicks spent most of her time propped up in bed like an invalid, dressed in a fluffy scarlet bed-jacket, her face ruddy with ill-concealed health, vigorously brushing her dog's teeth.

She brushed and brushed and still the yappy beast had putrid breath. Whenever anybody ventured in with the rent money, treading lightly as if at a wake, there she sat like a faded prima donna, wedged in a gully between hills of pillows, Pekinese pinned firmly under one arm, toothbrush at the ready.

"He's got such bad breath today, poor darling sweetie. Just put the money on the dresser, will you? No, no, no! Not there! By the powder box! By the *powder* box! *That's* it, there's a love. Now then, off you go."

According to Bridget, the char, Mrs. Wicks was "as barmy as they come and should be in one of them institutions in one of them padded cells where you can't do anybody an injury." Bridget was Irish and prayed daily to a host of incompetent saints for this to come true. "Jesus, Mary and Joseph," she chanted every Thursday when she came upstairs to clean but instead stopped for illicit tea with the girls, "that Wicked Witch will be the death of me."

"Why don't you just quit?"

"The work's too easy, dear. You should see some of the other fecken harridans I have to suffer." As far as Lisa could tell, the harridans kept Bridget hopping, Bridget kept saints hopping and everybody was happy.

The Old Tad came marching around the corner from Chiswick High Road at 5:32 promptly every evening, out-Britishing the British in bowler hat and polished shoes, neatly folded newspaper tucked under his arm. He always carried an umbrella, no matter what the weather, because that's what an English gent of a certain class did. Judging by his gait, he might have had another one rammed up his posterior.

"What's his problem?" Lisa had never met anybody like the Tad and the Witch.

"Who? The Old Tad?" He was a daft bugger, according to Mick. "Ever so harmless, mind you, but as daft as the day is long."

The Old Tad might have been daft, but he was careful. He marched down the sidewalk like a rigid wind-up toy, looking neither left nor right. Every step was of equal length, his polished black shoes reflecting the sky, the crease in his trousers like a razor's edge. It was easy to imagine Old Tad as a fearless fighter pilot, sweeping over the ruins of Germany in a ramrod straight line, dropping equidistant bombs, dapper in his bowler hat and umbrella, breaking for tea at five o'clock sharp.

Mimmi and Mick's floor had a large, out-of-date kitchen at the back where a thriving community of silverfish had settled ages ago, during the Roman occupation, if Mick was anything to go by. Unlike the Romans, they were now in the process of taking over the world, immune to poison and stomping feet. The sink had a cold water tap that dripped with Old Tad-like regularity into an enormous porcelain sink with astounding acoustics.

But the most serious drawback was having to share the bathroom and toilet with the two young blokes renting the top floor. These boys were of the ever-so-British public school variety with hair short back and sides, always dressed in suits and ties. The arrogant sods were bank clerks, warned Mick, and thus best ignored. The lads in turn shunned Mick who had long hair, played loud music and sang out of tune. Class distinctions were alive and well.

The bank chaps were the reason Lisa never had a proper bath. It took strategic planning to produce a full tub of hot water in an English bathroom dependent on a Victorian gas-heater. It required the substantial addition of extra water boiled in kettles and pots on the two-ring gas burner and the carrying of brimming vessels from the kitchen down the long hall. This time-consuming and labor-intensive affair was not undertaken lightly. Every time she sunk into a hot bath to scrub London grime and black exhaust off her skin, there was a discreet knock on the door, followed by "I say! Will you be finished ever so shortly?"

New in the country and uncertain of its customs, Lisa found it baffling the way the bank chaps started every sentence with "I say!" Was it really necessary to say "I say" when you were already in the process of saying whatever it was you were going to say?

It was an unfortunate affliction of toffs and those pretending to be, informed Mick, ever delighted to further Lisa's education. Mick hailed from Brixton, but claimed extensive knowledge about everything related to the upper classes. During a brief history lesson, he drew Lisa's attention to a little known law that had come into effect in 1783. This law stated that if you did not have a chin you had to preface all communication with the words "I say," as otherwise people would be unaware of your attempt at verbal interaction. "Because if you don't have a chin, people can't see your jaw move, can they, luv?" Such unintentional ventriloquism had caused many disasters, wars even, through simple misunderstanding.

This according to a man who spoke without bothering to pronounce the letter T, unless it occurred at the start of a word. The letter H suffered even worse neglect. Mick said it was because his family was very poor and couldn't afford the "'ole alphabet."

It was among these people and their assembled peculiarities, in Tad Hall, Airedale Avenue, Chiswick, London, England, that Lisa Grankvist, through strange circumstances, found herself living. It was an existence designed to help her forget what she badly needed to forget. It was to be time out, a time when she could do whatever she wanted. Never in her life had she been in such a position. Never in her life had she ever dared to want much, for fear of repercussions.

Lisa fell cautiously in love with London. London was indifferent towards her and she was grateful for that. It wasn't a nosy city. Nobody questioned why she was there, where she'd been or what she'd done. Nobody cared. In London you were on your own. As Lisa had been on her own for quite a while, that worked out just fine.

She had turned eighteen the previous October. It had been her first birthday with both of her parents dead. Now her entire past was gone as well, so she might as well try to have some fun. When people asked what she was doing in London, she said she was an *au pair*. The city was teeming with Swedish *au pairs* seeking their fortune in the shape of a pop star.

It was the year that started with P.J. Proby splitting his pants at the Ritz Theatre. The Rolling Stones went on their first European tour. Men wore frilly shirts. Girls wore less and less. The Beatles were filming *Help!* And all over there throbbed new music, red-blooded wild music-as though the poor anemic country had been craving it for so long it suddenly could not get enough. It was not only music, it was a phenomenon that united a whole generation. Lisa was deeply grateful to be united with something.

*Satisfaction* gyrated up the charts in August when Lisa bought her record player. The Kinks sang *You Really Got Me* and she felt she had. The Who explained their generation, Donovan tried to *Catch the Wind*, Dylan revisited *Highway 61*. The Hollies felt *Alive*. The Spencer Davis Group kept on running, the Turtles were happy together and there was always something there to remind Sandy Shaw. After *The Eve of Destruction* came *The Midnight Hour*. And still, Tom Jones felt he had to ask *What's New, Pussycat?* The Rolling Stones declared, a bit too prematurely, *It's All Over Now*, and Mary Hopkin, nostalgic already, remembered *Those Were The Days*.

Going with the flow, Lisa Ann-Kristin Grankvist from Sweden turned into Lisa from Chiswick, one of the innumerable, inter-changeable, groovy birds crowding the new clubs that opened up where clubs had never dared. The Scotch of St. James became the hotspot for the moving, grooving legends the spring she arrived. Not just anybody got into such a club, but for young and nubile girls nothing was impossible. Lisa was young and nubile in that anonymously generic way: she was a pretty face atop a slender body.

Anonymity in London was effortless to attain. Like everybody else, she painted onto the blank canvas of her face whatever appealing features inspired her. A smile or a frown to reflect her mood. Long black eyelashes. A pale, pale brow, blushing cheeks, big sad child-like eyes. When she tired of the face in the mirror she rubbed it out and started over. Anonymity was convenient in that it made her invisible even while she was being stared at. Being stared at what was a young bird was supposed to aspire to.

Reverting back from dyed red to her natural dark blonde, she grew her hair long and straight. She lost weight and became very thin because, like most girls, she could not be bothered to eat very much. And like every other young thing, she wanted to wake up one morning and discover that she had turned into Jean Shrimpton or Julie Christie.

But the city was a jungle. Vulnerable and nearly naked under their mini-garments, Lisa and the other thousands of nubile bodies fell prey to the pitiful middle-aged predators who hunted at night. In the clubs, hanging around bands, it was the business end of the music scene, the managers, the wannabes, that they had to look out for. That's what most of them were, those men with a sweaty sheen, wolf-wannabes on the prowl for tender young lamb. A modern form of hell, less Bosch than Carnaby Street. As Lisa had scrutinized certain works by Bosch, she knew what she knew.

Standing in a club she would sometimes feel a hand slide up her leg. She would find, not Mick Jagger, but a leering mask belonging to somebody old enough to be her father, with a glass of whisky and a pathetic bulge in his pants. Greased-down thin hair, debauched bags under lewd eyes, an oily grin dressed up as jovial. All this atop the pinstripe suit reflecting total confidence in the power of money and the good cut of expensive cloth. Some, convinced they were still young, hunted with their pasty flab dolled up in frilly shirts and velvet jackets. Men like these never took kindly to being turned down. The thin veneer of good-time-Charlie disappeared, and something unloving and unloved was left: the loser at the core.

These sights made Lisa want to go home and hide in her room. Often she did.

If being a tender lamb was a liability, it at least saved her from having to develop a personality. She found this a relief; it made her existence less awkward. It was so difficult to know who to be. She remained a blank surface upon which she drew suitable features with her Mary Quant makeup. Pale, pouting lips, huge dark eyes with fake lashes, going about town in a different persona every night, a swinging chick in fab little miniskirts, looking groovy in swaggering bellbottoms, a sexy seductress in a crocheted dress and Courrèges boots.

She could have sparkled, she really could. She rubbed shoulders with people who did. She could have gone places, but never did, because she never had sex with the men who counted. For the longest time she didn't have sex with anybody at all, and that was no way to become popular. At times she considered not being so fussy and showing a bit of ambition. It wasn't as if the opportunities were not there. And what did she have to lose?

Late one night a friend of Mick's at EMI studios introduced Lisa and Mimmi to John Lennon downstairs at the Scotch of St. James. Mick had been learning how to mix sound at EMI and had made some useful contacts. John wore a striped jacket and a washed-out beige T-shirt. Standing below the stairs he looked Lisa deep in the eyes and squeezed her hand. Then he leaned forward and whispered something in her ear, looked into her eyes again and smiled a lewd smile. She couldn't make out a single word he had said, but her ear felt deliciously moist from his breath. As soon as she could discreetly get away with it, she rubbed her finger over her ear and licked it. She imagined it tasted like the whisky she had smelled on his breath.

Perhaps she should have seized the moment and licked more than his breath, but never having licked anybody she wouldn't have known where to start.

A few weeks later she went to a party at a house in a quiet Chelsea lane. It belonged to Brian Jones of the Rolling Stones. The other Stones were not there. There weren't many people at all at midnight when they arrived. The famous Stone himself was slouching around in a bathrobe and clogs he said he had bought in Mimmi and Lisa's hometown on the Stones' recent tour. His bangs covered his eyes, but he was so stoned he couldn't see anyway, boasting he had recently been voted the youngest alcoholic in London. If this was cause for jubilation, he didn't look ecstatic. A while later he insisted on showing Lisa a stop sign, informing her with pride that he had leaned out the window of the limo and grabbed it right out of the hand of a traffic copper on a street in Berlin. He told the story twice, giggling each time. A minute later he crashed to the floor unconscious, still clutching his stop sign. He looked so young lying prostrate in his striped terry cloth robe, a sad, ruined, filthy rich child. In less than four years he'd be dead.

Rubbing elbows with that many of the rich and famous in so short a time soon stopped being a misplaced sense of privilege. Most of them turned out to be disappointingly human, generously endowed with flaws and acne and bad habits. Burping and farting and puking, they were drunk and stoned, disorderly and self-centered. And most astoundingly of all, not very interesting. None of them had any noticeable mark, no odd-shaped moles to designate them as the chosen ones.

When the horn of plenty overflowed in this new existence, Lisa fled the excess and stayed home, sitting alone on the slippery bedspread in her room, or with Mimmi in the big front room, knitting and crocheting like somebody's grandmother, not a bit groovy. In truth, it's what she did more often than not as time went by, at first in an earnest attempt to save money. She soon discovered that she liked the occupational therapy aspect of it, so every week she walked down Chiswick High Road to buy more cheap synthetic yarn at Woolworth's on Turnham Green near the Wimpy Bar. Sitting cross-legged on her bed, she knitted striped sweaters to match her little miniskirts and to help keep her bum from turning frosty and red in the unkind English damp. Some of the sweaters were longer than her skirts. She was content with her knitting and her mug of PG-Tips, listening to Radio Luxembourg. It gave her time to grapple with her thoughts.

While knitting was soothing, she did not for a minute forget what had happened that Easter. But she never talked about it, not even with Mimmi or Mick, though they had been with her at the time, had helped her go through with it. The memory sat inside her like a superfluous clumsy organ, larger than an appendix but equally useless. And like an appendix, were it to burst, it might kill her. Until it did, she might as well enjoy herself.

Mick frequently worked nights, as a lot of bands preferred to record after hours during the studio's down time, leaving Mimmi and Lisa private evenings to play music and talk in their own language. And every week they watched *Thank Your Lucky Stars*, *Jukebox Jury*, *Top of the Pops* and, "where the week-end starts," *Ready, Steady, Go!* Right in the swing of things, they were still children. With music instead of toys, wearing the dolls' clothes themselves.

# 2

Time had passed without calling attention to itself. Already it was September and Lisa had been living with Mimmi and Mick for more than four months.

"I'm so sorry," she apologized, feeling parasitic, the unnecessary third member of a happy couple.

The happy couple didn't see it that way. "Why be sorry? Stay as long as you like." Mimmi liked having a friend around when Mick worked late, which was most of the time. Mick concurred. He didn't like to show it, but like Mimmi, he worried about Lisa. She had a strange past. He and Mimmi had talked it over more than once and agreed that she was not strong enough to cope on her own yet. There were nights when she cried out in her sleep. Assuming she was asleep.

They were wrong. Lisa may have been misguided, but she wasn't weak. Back in early April, on the day she left Sweden for good, she had discovered her strong side. It was a side that could get nasty, should the occasion demand it, because deep inside her there sloshed around an untapped well of anger. Anger and fear are not mutually exclusive.

⊷

She had run into this source of strength by accident at the central train station in Copenhagen, of all places. It was there, with time to spare before the train was due to leave, that she had decided to call Mimmi and Mick in London to make sure they were standing by the door packed and ready, and not sleeping in, forgetting this was not just another day. The three of them were supposed to meet up in Brussels the following day and needed to synchronize their watches, talking in code in subdued voices. This, she believed, was the protocol when undertaking illegal activities on foreign territory.

Off she went to find a phone. It was when she looked through the door to the crowded telegraph and telephone room that she encountered Hell as depicted by Bosch. Well, she reasoned, it was only a matter of time.

She may have finished high school with mediocre grades, but she knew a work by Bosch when she saw one. She had her father to thank for that. One of his few pleasures in life had been to browse through art books that he could ill afford but felt the deep need to own. The works by the fifteenth and sixteenth century masters were the ones with the greatest power to hold his attention. He would sit in his chair in the living room, and study every page for a very long time, longingly, the floor lamp beside him spotlighting whatever masterpiece was busy seducing him. Lisa would sneak a peak during these moments of private rapture, so as not to miss the fleeting instant when he would smile to himself, the only covert expression of his pleasure, shaking his head in amazement over what his eyes beheld. Observing him she could tell he was in a place far away.

For a long time Johan Grankvist had been unaware that his little girl used to borrow the books when he was at work, never saw her standing on tiptoe on a chair to pull them off the top shelf. Bosch was her favorite artist by the time she was five. She was too young to have the vocabulary necessary to attempt to describe the perverse details of the phantasmagoria before her, but all those repugnant images never failed to keep her enthralled. Nor was she aware what that hotbed of fear and guilt called religion could do to a person. Lying on the floor in the bedroom she contentedly taught herself to draw monsters. She became quite the expert on creatures with bird beaks and webbed feet and deformed bodies. She thought funnel hats were the cutest invention she'd ever seen. What a glorious time this man Bosch must have had painting such figures! And what a delightful time she had had copying him! Until the day her father discovered what she was up to and took to hiding the books for fear of medieval superstition traumatizing his innocent daughter. Considering that they lived with her mother, this was a useless precaution. Maybe Bosch had lived with his mother. If she had been anything like Lisa's mother, it would explain where he garnered his ideas.

By the time Lisa left for good, her father's art books had sat wrapped in plastic in a box in her friend Sonja's attic. She had a list of the contents: Dad's books, ten yellow and black art deco teacups, the big herring jar (for putting flowers in?)

The scene before Lisa that day in the train station Communications Room was instantly recognizable from the triptych *The Last Judgment*. Here hordes of condemned people, all foreigners who knew neither Danish nor English, shouted in various languages, waving hopeless arms to emphasize their desperate need to get to a phone before it was too late. Some didn't move at all. They were long dead, she could tell. The sinners still alive kept pushing and jostling. They weren't naked and did not have spears piercing their bodies in soft, yielding places. Not yet.

The swarthy faces of the horde also brought to mind another Bosch painting, the one called both *The Carrying of the Cross* and *The Ascent to Calvary*. There was another one with that theme, but the one Lisa recalled depicted a Christ who looked exactly like Sverker, the oldest son of the Petterssons who had lived on the floor below when she was little. Mr. Pettersson had killed himself one Midsummer's Eve and his wife and children had moved up north. Sverker had been feebleminded and people teased him.

The faces of the mob before her were those surrounding

Christ (or Sverker, depending on how she looked at it). They
were ugly, vicious and coarse. There was a woman in that painting as well. Saint Veronica. Her eyes modestly downcast, she
looked neither evil nor ignorant, yet Lisa as a child had been
convinced that she was just smarmy, sucking up to Christ to get
into heaven and wear one of those nice white gowns. There were
tiny balls dangling on threads from the wrap around her head.

In the crowded telegraph room there was no Savior in sight,
and the saintly ladies behind the counter, all hatless, were not
about to admit any repentant old sinner through the pearly
gates. The wretches clamoring for salvation were to be transported *en masse* to Satan's palace for their final torment, and
they looked like they didn't relish the prospect.

Lisa had stood shocked in the doorway of the waiting room
to the pit of hell. Was it Judgment Day already?

There were strict rules in hell. Everybody had to line up to
place a call and pay for it, only to wait for the time in the far distant future when a phone booth became available. By the looks
of it, this might take several years, what with half a million
damned clamoring for attention ahead of her. Still, there might
be time. By then she craved to hear Mimmi's voice assuring her
that everything was as it should be.

Lisa's best friend Sonja waited outside the door, dragging
violently on a cigarette, anxious and depressed. Lisa asked her
to keep a keen eye on the suitcase, the totebag and the picnic
basket, then marched forward and joined the damned before her
friend could exhale a cloud and answer. Sonja was dead against
what she called Lisa's fanatic insistence to risk life and limb in
unknown territory.

The line moved faster than she had hoped. Either that or she
had lost track of time, concentrating on trying not to sweat in
her crisp white blouse. It wasn't easy. The hell-fires burning
beneath the floor generated strong heat. Soon green monsters
with yellow eyes would slither up her legs, up under her pleated
skirt, to fondle her flesh before ripping it to shreds. All around
her there would come screams of anguish as people were hurled

into the pit, one at a time, like herrings to a trained seal.

She was preparing to be humble when her time came, with only seven more lost souls ahead of her, when she was rudely shoved backwards. A little weasel in a frayed suit jacket had forcefully rammed a bony elbow into her stomach and squeezed in front. As if she didn't exist. Was he demon or damned? Anybody that lamentably threadbare had to be human.

Staring down at the oily waves atop his impudent head she was overcome with an outrage so cold and sudden that, before she knew what she was doing, she had tapped the puny marauder hard on a dandruff-laden shoulder. He turned around and stared up at her with the effortless indifference so freely bestowed on lesser creatures. Staring down at his unshaven snout she felt her eyes turn to icy marbles. As they did, his condescending gaze began to flicker and look for a way out. As if she had power. It was a strange, heady sensation. She'd felt a flicker of it when dealing with a waiter on the ferry, but not nearly as potent. This eruption of cold fury turned her into the She-Devil of the Queue. Feeling the snug fit of the role she realized she had the gift, should she choose to accept responsibility for it. She flicked her thumb and hissed "Beat it" in English. It was an excellent flick, masterfully understated, but straight to the point. It said, "Out of my way, you worm-eaten little prick!" The swaggering She-Devil power made her invincible. Lowering his head, the grubby weasel scampered out of her life and disappeared. Resuming her place in the queue she stretched ten feet tall, giddy, tingling, with the cosy confidence of superhuman strength.

Of course. That was it. That's what she'd be like from now on! Sporting She-Devil courage in capital letters! Better a larger-than-life demon than one of the damned.

She made her three-minute call to England where her team stood ready to spring into action, compass in hand, rental car at the ready. Everything was going according to plan. Confident and cocky, all ten feet of her strutted out of the Communications Room. By the time she got back to the bench where her picnic basket sat, she'd shrunk back to the three inches that had lately been her mental stature.

Still, it was good to have discovered that she was not without courage.

~◆~

Lisa was strong enough to move on. It was high time to get a place of her own. A simple room. Four walls to enclose her. Small enough that her thoughts and her footsteps would not echo. That's what she wanted. A room in a house, where she could have a hot bath once in a while without an hour's preparation followed by an *I say*-assault.

The other reason for moving was Sonja. She had written to say she had finally saved up enough money to come for a visit soon, if she was able to stay with Lisa and not in a hotel. There simply wasn't room for her at Tad Hall.

The following Sunday Lisa checked the papers and made a list of possible places for rent in the Chiswick area. Chiswick with its striped steeple church on the old village green had become her new hometown. This was where she wanted to stay.

Good intentions aside, in the end it was Mimmi, pretending to be Lisa, who had to make the calls to ask when she could pop around to see the room. Lisa had succumbed to shyness. She was not like extrovert Mimmi, whose English was fluent, who could call up complete strangers while sitting in her underwear and a floppy hat, painting her toenails. Mimmi would start by inquiring about the room for rent and end up talking about some movie she'd seen. Every landlord she spoke to was dying to meet her. Hopefully they wouldn't be too disappointed when Lisa Grankvist with her worried face popped around instead.

The first room on the list was the one closest to Airedale Avenue. Mick agreed to come along for male support in case somebody tried to get fresh. To be on the safe side Lisa wore boots, bellbottoms, a bulky sweater with a matching hat and scarf, exposing no bare flesh, taking no risks on that unseasonably warm Sunday afternoon. She looked like *The Invisible Man's* twin sister.

The room was in a house on Burnaby Gardens. They timed the walk to see how long it would take, down Chiswick High Road past the Green, along Sutton Court Road to the underpass, a *pissoir* by the smell of it, that led to the maze of quiet little streets that continued down to the river. The house sat a brisk twenty-two minute walk away from Tad Hall, at the very end of a row of red brick terraced houses. There was a weedy fragment of front yard where a stunted shrub had died long ago. The house had a deep blue front door, a shade similar to that of Lisa's imperial teacup. She stared at the bell. It stared right back.

"You have to ring it, luv."

"You ring it. You're English."

"Lisa?"

"What?"

"Ring the bell. Okay?"

Mick stared at her until she did.

A very tall black man in a yellow caftan tore open the door. A big grin split his face when he saw them. He grabbed their hands and pumped them vigorously while dragging them inside. Did he mistake them for long lost friends? Was he a raving lunatic? "Come in, come in, please! I just now arrive myself. Follow me, please!" By then they had no choice, he was already shepherding them down the hall and around the corner to a room on the left.

Lisa stopped dead in the doorway. It was Hell's waiting room all over again. The room was stuffed to the rafters with thousands of dark-skinned men, a teeming crowd of maleficent faces with whites of eyes gleaming, scheming in her direction. As she turned to flee a short round-faced Indian popped out of the menacing midst like a happy popcorn, declaring how pleased he would be to show them the room. "It's right here on the ground floor at the back. Please come with me." He courteously held out an arm. Lisa did not want the room. She planned to never again set foot in this deceptively plain but pleasant-looking neighbourhood, but was too big a coward to say so.

Mick was thoroughly enjoying himself and blithely responded. "Thank you very much, sir. We would be overjoyed to see the room!"

The little Indian, who didn't look much older than Mick, said to please call him Ram. He led them to a door at the back where the hall turned left, unlocked it, and ushered them into the room. It was bright and spacious. Two large windows occupied most of the back wall, one on each side of French doors that opened onto a garden grown wild. A mossy stone wall contained the rampant spread of weeds and grass grown so tall it was lying in waves like a green lake. Here and there ivy trailed down the wall and crawled into the weeds. In the center of the garden an arthritic apple tree stood bent over a stone bench. Its drooping canopy shifted in green and gold and flecks of blue shadow. It was heavy with apples. Rotting apples littered the bench and the green waves of grass.

There was a smell out in that garden, a smell as sweet as a long forgotten dream. A smell of not only apples, but of the earth itself. The afternoon sun poured golden light into the room, a light so warm and tangible Lisa became convinced she could wrap herself in it. This was a room she could have a relationship with, knowing that if she loved it, it would love her back. Here angels sat on guard.

She was already lost in a captivating vision of herself sitting on the stone bench, a motionless figure, silent in an autumn idyll of russet and gold. A chilly wind would rustle the branches above as she sat there, a pale sun light her face. Oh, she wanted that bench, that tree, that wind, that autumn sun, that serene refuge, like the walled garden of a nunnery. Had Bosch lived in this room he would have been the first impressionist.

"Would I be allowed to use the garden?" The sound of her voice was unexpected, and so calm it surprised her.

If Ram did not recognize her voice as the chirpy one on the phone earlier, he didn't let on. "Oh, my goodness, yes!" he gushed. He flung both arms towards the open doors in an expansive gesture, as if to lift up the garden and place it in her needy hands. "It's all yours. Do whatever you please with it. Nobody ever goes there. Too much bloody work."

"I'll take it. The room, I mean. And the garden too. If that's all right?"

Mick's eyebrows shot up into his hair, but he kept his mouth shut, concentrating on something fascinating high in the sky above the apple tree. Ram was so delighted he clapped his hands. "Jolly good!" he shouted, and dragged them back to the room by the kitchen.

There were two men sitting at the table having a quiet cup of tea, another Indian and a skinny black guy. Opposite them sat an anemic English girl warming her hands on her cup, her bony elbows resting on the table. She was so colorless in comparison she was in danger of fading from sight. The black man who had opened the door was nowhere to be seen. The thousands of sinister dark-skinned, gleaming-white-of-the-eye fiends that had crowded the room had disappeared. Had she had another demon-infested hallucination?

She asked if there had not been more people when they arrived.

Yes, confessed Ram, there had been three more chaps, a friend from Calcutta and two African students who had been visiting Jackson.

"This chap here is Jackson."

"Hello, Jackson. I'm Lisa."

"Very pleased to make your acquaintance." Jackson stood up and ceremoniously shook her hand. He was a student from Rhodesia and he rented the room on the first floor, directly above hers. His friends had been banished so as not to frighten the possible lady tenant. Looking at the way she was dressed, he politely inquired if she had arrived straight from Sweden where he had heard it was always extremely cold.

The tall Indian introduced himself as Amrit. He too had a room upstairs, as did the girl whose name was Beryl. Beryl sometimes slept with Amrit, it would soon become clear, a quiet domestic arrangement nobody ever mentioned. Lisa asked Beryl what she did for a living and was told that she was a student like the rest of them. She studied English literature, she said, expressing a vague interest in the poetry of Byron. Lisa was never to see her reading a book, but books might have been too heavy for those thin transparent hands to hold. Unlike the rest of them, Beryl did not venture out much. Perhaps hers was a correspondence course.

Lisa explained that she was an art student, but was at the moment taking a break. She had recently returned from studying in Vienna.

On the top floor, in the attic room, lived old Mrs. Parkinson. She suffered from arthritis and had difficulty climbing up and down the stairs. As she didn't like to leave her room, she was more or less invisible. Every other day Ram took up a bottle of milk for her tea and once a week Jackson helped her out with the shopping.

Lisa moved in that same afternoon, unpacked her meager belongings and placed them in strategic spots to make the room look lived-in. The result was pathetic. Her cup and jar of tea took up less than a fifth of the mantelpiece. The rest of her stuff, a few balls of yarn, knitting needles, some books and magazines, didn't manage to fill the small bookshelf beside the bed. She got out the bag with her father's tools and lined them up on the shelf, but a set of tools at the ready beside the bed did not create the right ambiance.

She had too few belongings to put her mark on the room. It was as if she didn't yet exist. The mirror of her loneliness cast no reflection. She had nothing to put on the bed, no pretty pillows, no bedspread, nothing to hang on the walls or in the windows, no carpet to cover the drab linoleum floor. There would have to be some improvements made. She would ask Sonja to bring the old herring jar left in her attic. Filled with flowers it would look a work of art on the mantelpiece, bathed in the afternoon light.

She spent the remainder of the day glued to the edge of the

bed gazing out the French doors at her new niche, thinking about what to put on the list of things needed to put her stamp on the room. She pondered and gazed, pondered and gazed, but all she came up with were four things: "Herring jar. Colorful bedspread and some pillows, and a carpet. She'd never furnished a home.

Still, it was peculiar how right it felt to sit in this unknown corner of the world. She had traveled since she left her childhood behind, both in distance and in time. Even the last four months in London had been a trip through one hundred and twenty odd days, each one another step from the starting point. But here, in this room, in this garden, here she would take a break. Here everything would be all right.

In the evening Ram invited her to share an Indian dinner with the rest of the tenants. He said she had to, it was an established Sunday tradition. She couldn't figure out what the food was, and was afraid to ask. It was so beyond spicy even the Indian lads kept dousing the fire by sluicing jug after jug of ice water down their gullets. Tears streamed down their faces. She asked why they made the food so spicy if it made them cry. They said they liked it that way and kept on crying. She smiled at their self-imposed torture, wondering if they did it to impress the girl from the cold north.

"Look. She can smile!" This to each other, clapping their hands. And to Lisa, "You should smile more often. It takes the sadness out of your eyes."

The tearful meal made a nice change from tinned spaghetti and beans on toast. Afterwards she excused herself, fetched a towel, shampoo and soap, and went upstairs to sink into a long and luxurious bath. Nobody knocked on the door. It inspired her body to relax. Her muscles started to ripple and tremble, unsure of how to go about it.

Scrubbed pink, and with a feeling of tentative contentment, she wrote another letter to Aunt Margit, a one-page letter starting, "After almost a year at Airedale Avenue, I have moved to a different house. This one is cheaper and closer to the school.

I was very lucky to find it. There is a beautiful garden outside my room."

She put the letter in an envelope and crawled into her new bed in her new room in her new house. Through the French doors she discovered a crescent moon perched in the apple tree. She heard the wind rustle its branches, but didn't know why it made her smile.

⊷

The very next day she went out to sit on the stone bench, determined to try out a nunnery garden persona. It was late Monday morning and as far as she could tell, nobody was around. To perfect the look she shrouded herself in her black shawl from Portobello Road.

The bench turned out to be not at all comfortable. Lichen had established territory and it was scratchy. There was only the crooked tree to lean against, and its rough bark hurt her back. Ignoring these setbacks, she assumed a suitably enigmatic position, stared into the distance, feeling her eyes droop with an appropriate amount of obscure pain. It was important to get the look right, as if by doing so she would learn something about herself that she badly needed to know.

It was a cloudy day, suitably gray for melancholy posturing. A book of poetry lay open in her lap. It was a paperback anthology of Japanese poetry by Lafcadio Hearn, translated into Swedish, one of Mimmi's books that she had borrowed the previous afternoon with this very posturing in mind. The haikus were easy to read, being only three lines long. Back home she had tried to read other kinds of poetry now and then, heavy stuff loaded with clever symbolism and sophisticated metaphors, under the assumption that it would ennoble her soul. It had never worked out. After an ennobling line or two her thoughts would stray and next thing she'd find herself debating whether or not to change her nail polish, or if she'd get zits if she ate a whole chocolate bar. Or she'd fall asleep.

Perhaps Beryl would read her some Byron one of these days and explain all the clever bits.

She did not move. Autumn leaves fell to her feet, as if on cue. The September sun peeked out once, checking that she was awake. In the end, though she very much looked the part, being an enigma required far too much effort. Her back ached.

There she sat, reducing her inherent melancholy to amateur theatrics. After fifteen minutes she was bored stiff. Still, she refused to give up.

To pass the time she scrutinized the overgrown mess that had once been a garden. That was when she proudly identified the two bushes with the large shiny leaves growing by the back wall. They were rhododendrons. The Billings next door to Tad Hall had a rhododendron filling their little front patch, obscuring their ground floor bay window. One day Mrs. Billings had come out the door as Mimmi and Lisa arrived home and Lisa had asked, "What's that bush with those beautiful red flowers by your window?" Mrs. Billings had looked at her askance, if not unkindly, and replied, "Why, they're rhododendrons, dear," as if any idiot knew that.

But that's what did it. The moment she recognized the rhododendrons, a tidal wave of energy washed an exquisite treasure onto the deserted shore of her ambition. It was so powerful it nearly knocked her off the bench.

She was going to grow a garden.

Her phony guise faded like a ghost at sun-up. She shed the despondent black shawl, got down on sturdy knees like a practical peasant and started to pull weeds. It took hours to clear the former flower bed by the south wall alone. Her only helpful tools were a pair of scissors, a wrench and a knitting needle. When she finished it was early afternoon and she was sweaty with honest labor, arms covered in dirt to her elbows. Her nail polish had chipped together with four of her carefully filed nails, but it didn't matter, she no longer gave a damn, because she was going to grow a garden, a lovely garden full of flowers and bushes and shrubs and trees and vines.

The next door neighbor had a garden of sorts. Color-coordinated flowers huddled in repressed clusters of six between a row of over-pruned shrubs. Some of the flowers were still in bloom. It was an unimaginative arrangement, but it *was* a garden, and looking over the fence would be an inspiration. Two beautiful bushes full of flowers that hung like bells in shades of red and purple grew by the neighbor's back door. She meant to find out what they were. Perhaps the woman next door would become her friend and they would have tea and thinly sliced fruitcake while talking gardening like equals. Mrs. Wicks had tea and fruitcake every day at four, according to Bridget. It would be a very English thing to do. The woman would give her useful tips on planting flowers and lend her the appropriate tools.

The next morning Lisa saw a woman, tall and bony, enter the garden next door. The woman was wielding a pair of pruning shears in her gloved hand. Grabbing the opportunity, Lisa rushed outside. "Excuse me, may I ask you a few questions about gardening, please? I just moved in two days ago." She smiled a neighborly smile over the dividing wall. The woman went rigid, stared in horror, and, apron flapping, scurried back into her house like a timid woodland creature. Lisa imagined her in there, quivering in a dark corner, nose twitching.

Had she said something wrong? Ram assured her later that it was nothing she had said or done. Mrs. Mortimer, or Mrs. Mortified as they called her, was like that.

"She doesn't like darkies. And you live in a house full of darkies, in case you hadn't noticed."

So she did.

"Why doesn't she like darkies?"

"The English are like that," he explained. "They like to think they are superior, you see. God knows why. Also, they like to keep to themselves. It's the climate, I think."

That Mrs. Mortified would think herself superior to anybody was unimaginable, unless it was to dumber, more timid woodland creatures.

Mrs. Billings was far less superior when Lisa dropped in for an impromptu visit. She gave Lisa a rigorous lesson in gardening, heaping upon her a variety of seeds collected from her own flowers. She pointed out the difference between annuals and perennials, and instructed her pupil as to what she might plant in the autumn and which plants would fare better in the spring. She was fairly sure that the bushes in Mrs. Mortified's garden were fuchsias and that yes, they were ever so lovely. "There's one out back, dear, come have a look." Lisa followed her out to admire the fuchsia. Much larger than Mrs. Mortified's, it was more like a small tree.

Lisa wanted one in the worst way. She wanted a whole forest of them. If she had a fuchsia or two she would never ask for anything else.

Mrs. Billings invited her back inside for tea and a biscuit, and never stopped talking. She made a list of things Lisa would find useful when starting out. Tools, peat moss, manure, fungicide. "And gardening gloves, dear. You don't want to ruin your lovely hands." She recommended a nursery, drew a map of how to get there, showed her brochures full of large color photographs. Leafing through them Lisa discovered gardens of almost hallucinatory beauty. Bushes dripped with flowers, pink, orange, yellow, purple and blue. Throngs of blooms cascaded, exploded, poured out of the earth. Here existed a world where beauty was actually attainable and where soil and soul need not lie barren.

"Are you all right, dear?"

"Pardon?"

"You look a bit peaked, dear. And you're breathing oddly."

"Oh . . . no . . . I'm fine. It's all a bit much, is all. Is it all right if I write down some of the names in this book? To take to the nursery?"

"You go right ahead, dear. I'll fetch you paper and a pen, shall I?"

"Oh yes, please."

Mrs. Billings didn't bother to hide her amusement. But Lisa could not explain her strange urge to this woman, she had only just encountered it herself. All she knew was that this was an indulgence she would not deny herself, no matter the cost.

"Can anybody make a garden with all these shrubs and bushes growing in it?" She pointed to the pictures, not convinced that they were of this world.

"With the right amount of light and good soil, yes. You plant them, dear, you don't make them yourself, do you?"

"Holy sh . . . Oh, I'm so sorry."

"That's quite all right."

"It's just . . . I never realized ordinary gardens could be so beautiful. My grandpa had a garden of sorts, but it was very small. The outhouse took up most of it, and he didn't have any flowers, only four gooseberry bushes at the back."

"I see. You know, you must try to find a book with pictures of Moe Nay's garden. You'd enjoy that."

"Moe who?"

"Moe Nay, dear. The French Impressionist?"

"Oh, him. Yes, of course." She knew of the Impressionists, thanks to her father, but had never heard of Moe Nay. He must have been a painter her father had not approved of, or the name would be familiar.

"Surely you have seen his paintings at the National Gallery?"

"Of course."

"In fact I might have a . . . " Mrs. Billings trailed off and came back with a small book. *Monet's Garden* it was called.

"Oh, him!"

Her father had called him Cloud Monétt. Like Mrs. Billings, he had not spoken French. Lisa turned the pages of the book, remembered images of water lilies, turned another page and craved a flood of nasturtiums drowning her path. She didn't have a path, but never mind.

"Thank you, Mrs. Billings! I'll be in your debt forever." She embarrassed the woman by spontaneously hugging her. They both blushed.

"That won't be necessary, I'm sure."

Up on the corner of Chiswick High Road she caught a bus

straight to the nursery. The man there insisted that the shrubs on her list should be planted in the spring for best results, but she bought three fuchsias and a laurel anyway, unable to wait a minute longer.

It was while daydreaming in the moist air among the temptations of the nursery that a black mulberry sapling reached out and snagged her sleeve with a slender branch, as if to shyly ask, could it please come home with her? Its leaves trembled. She imagined it was in anticipation and didn't have the heart to let it down.

The excess didn't end there. After she had spent far more than she could afford, two large potted hibiscuses caught her attention. One was unfolding its wrinkled orange petals into the light, the other one boasted three deep scarlet flowers, sultry and seductive in the warm humidity. Lisa, entranced, remembered something. She felt the flowers beckon, languid and flirtatious, wafting secret perfume. Or was it the memory? They were too expensive an indulgence, these beauties, but she bought them anyway, including the large clay pots they were displayed in.

By then she had spent her allowance for the next few months. Her financial situation was growing more precarious by the day, but that would have to work itself out, this was important. There was still plenty of money in her account back in Sweden. There had to be.

In her ambitious fervor she had not given a thought about transporting the loot back to her garden-to-be, so she asked the man at the nursery to please call a cab. The nursery owner fell about himself laughing. "No cabbie'd take that lot, would he, luv?" But, he added, seeing her face fall, as she had spent half a king's ransom he would be ever so happy to deliver it all in his van after they closed for the day. Miss needn't worry.

⊷⊸

The two hibiscuses took up residence inside her room, one by each window. The following summer when her new garden was in its first bloom and the hibiscuses had grown larger, she sat on her bed one afternoon, on her beautiful emerald bedspread, gazing, like a woman in love, at her paradise. Birds sang as though they'd just now mastered new songs and couldn't wait to show them off.

Something was fluttering over by the pink honeysuckle and the purple-leafed hebes she had planted that spring. When she stepped outside she discovered two red admiral butterflies gamboling as if they owned the place, hiding chameleon-like among the mixed dahlias when she got too close.

The butterflies were not the promised purple ones she remembered from long ago, but she said to herself, surprised and yet not, "Lisa, you know what this is, don't you? This is your tropical island." She must have known that all along. That was why she had bought the hibiscuses, that's what had nudged her memory when she first saw them. There was no ocean lapping stretches of white sand in Chiswick, but, appropriately enough, Jackson upstairs helped solve that problem by constantly playing Harry Belafonte's *This is my island in the sun*. It was his only record.

This was as close as she would get to that chimeric island in the Pacific. The original plan had been for her and her father to travel there together. She had been too young to distinguish between wishful thinking and future plans, needing for there not to be such distinctions.

Remembering all this when looking at her garden, she sometimes sensed that, almost within reach, there was allowable joy.

# 3

**A**n island far away.

That was how Lisa and her father had survived all those scorched years when her mother's rage burnt out of control. Spinning their farfetched dream of a tropical island in the blue Pacific that only they knew the way to. This dream, gossamer fragile at first due to a lack of basic facts, had grown increasingly solid as they studied maps and consulted books.

Tenuous at first, as their fantasy grew bolder, they dared to embellish, invent the island detail by detail. It was as if it had been shrouded in early morning mist that had at long last started to clear. They grew familiar with it in their imagination, learned their way around.

Then one day it was too late.

Lisa's father took ill in the middle of the night. It was a week before she turned twelve. She woke up when the ambulance men arrived and banged the stretcher in the doorway. As soon as she realized what was going on, she rushed off a request and a promise. "Dear God, please don't let him die before my birthday! If you let him live I will do anything. I'll even try to love my mother." A minute later the ambulance men suggested to her mother that she and her daughter get dressed and come to the hospital.

As his last morning dawned, her father looked very small in the hospital bed. He was wearing his faded striped pajamas. His hair was tussled, making him look a bit unkempt, but there was a peaceful smile lighting his face, as if he had finally received word that everything was going to be all right. His eyes were calm when they looked into his daughter's. Then they closed, and that was good, because he needed to sleep, he'd been awake half the night. His hand was still clutching Lisa's when the nurse said, "I'm sorry, dear," and dislodged it. God, following some private agenda, had ignored Lisa's request.

His death certificate stated the cause of death as a heart attack, but Lisa knew better. Her mother had nagged him to death, only that can't be written on a death certificate. It was her mother's madness that had forced them to flee to an island in a faraway ocean.

What illness Lisa's mother had suffered from nobody knew. Ordinary people did not have their heads examined. If a woman was prone to fits of violent rage and persecution mania, then that was the way she was. A royal pain in the neck, but a pain to be endured.

Presumably her mother had been different in younger days. In their wedding photo she looked quite slender, her hair nicely waved for the occasion, her smile sweet and radiant. Then, at some point, she had changed and, step by step, started driving her husband and daughter away, while simultaneously going hysterical if they tried to leave.

When dementia took hold of his wife, Johan Grankvist had quietly slipped into the hall to put on his coat and shoes, Signe Grankvist pursuing him, throwing herself flat against the door to the apartment, arms splayed like a crucified harpy, whimpering like a small child, eerily shrill and petulant. Her method had been to pinch him if he got too close, sharp painful little stabs that left scars. He had opened the door with gentle determination, every time, forcing her to move with it, closing it behind him, hurrying down the stairs to embark on a very long trek all over town, keeping his thoughts to himself.

As a small child, Lisa had been so terrified of being alone with her mother during her fits that she had grabbed hold of her father's leg and stood on his foot, making him unable to move without taking her along. At times like that he had closed the door after them like it was the last time, because he was harboring a secret plan he would at long last put into action. They had fled down the stairs, out into the street, around the corner as fast as possible. There were times when the wretched woman felt inspired to hang out the window and make a public display of her paranoia, her voice ripping through the neighbourhood like a sonic boom.

Safe and out of sight, Johan Grankvist and his daughter strolled the streets hand in hand, ever farther away from the misery of the hearth, slowly as if they had not a care in the world, never once mentioning the woman sitting broken at the kitchen table chewing on her knuckles. These had been the times when they perfected their dream, when the tropical island took shape, palm tree by palm tree, so vivid that the wind at their back had grown warm and flower-scented. They were going to move there one day, yes they were, just the two of them. As soon as they had enough money. Johan Grankvist had promised.

The islanders would be expecting them. They would be gathered on the beach waving garlands of red flowers, their bodies cinnamon against the white sand, when Lisa and Johan showed up. Songs of welcome would fill the air. The people would lead the visitors in victorious procession to a grass hut built especially for them. It's what people lived in there. They had neither windows nor doors; they didn't need them. Pretty soon the two of them would be cinnamon brown, too. Johan would go fishing with the men while little Lisa went swimming with the children in a blue lagoon with a waterfall. Every day they would feast on strange and wondrous fruits and the bounty of the sea while the wind rustled the palm fronds overhead.

At night the sough of the Pacific against the sandy shores of the island would lull them safely to sleep. The interior of the island was covered with the deepest emerald jungle, festooned with unimaginable flowers every shade of the rainbow. Mainly hibiscus, Johan Grankvist had added, because they were the most beautiful flowers he could think of. Red ones and orange ones, yellow and white ones too, but mostly red ones. Butterflies the size of his hands held out flat, tumbled and played in the gentle breeze.

"Purple ones too?" Lisa had asked when badly in need of promises.

"Oh my, yes," he had assured her. "Especially purple ones." There were no snakes and no spiders, so she would never have to be afraid. "But do you know what there are plenty of? Parrots. And they're all tame and can talk."

"Really? Can we have a pet parrot?"

"Absolutely! A red and blue one, how's that?"

"A red and blue one with green wings and a yellow head!"

"Wonderful! And we'll teach it Swedish and everybody will be impressed."

"Dad? Will we go there soon?"

"As soon as we have the money, Lisa. It just takes a little while."

She had realized that it cost a lot of money to travel that far, so she saved all her coins in a piggy bank. She had never understood why her father blushed every time she proudly rattled it for him to show that her funds were building up; they would soon have money for the tickets.

⊐◇⊏

She thought of this during summer days when her gardening efforts had started to pay off, when she had created, to quote Ram, "A jolly well topnotch garden." The cheeky sod then had the nerve to boast about it, playing sahib to his Swedish gardener. He started to entertain ideas about putting out a table and chairs so his friends could all sit and have a drink and enjoy the magnificence. "Right here, I think, would look fine."

The next day Lisa dug a flower bed in the spot he had chosen. She didn't want anybody out there. The garden was *hers*, *hers*, *hers* alone. It was her island. Her refuge. It was all she had and nobody had a right to set foot there. There was only one way to prevent anybody using it: to fill every inch with so many flowers and bushes and trees there would be no room for any people apart from herself and a few friends. And even then, only right outside the French doors, in her private spot where nobody else could possibly sit without intruding on her privacy.

Ram started to let loose hints that he might increase the rent now the garden looked so bloody marvelous. He was bossy sometimes, but Lisa was taller and could tower over him if need be. And she remembered that she wasn't only a fugitive, a fifteen-minute enigma and a gardener, but also a girl with She-Devil courage, who could rid the world of annoying little men with a flick of her thumb. She shared with Ram her opinions about increasing the rent to reward a woman's unpaid labor. A heinous crime, she called it, pleased with the phrase. From that day on she never paid rent for the month of May each year. It became her modest reward for creating a garden she had completely forgotten wasn't hers, convinced that if you plant a seed, then what grows is yours.

It brought her something akin to peace of mind when she strolled through her small domain, lady of the manor, anticipating the magic of new growth, a tender green shoot poking out of the soil, something that she herself had planted. Small baby leaves, fragile and new, that would one day become big boastful flowers. Beauty sprung out of nowhere in this place. Growing such beauty out of tiny seeds made her feel clever, as though she knew secrets nobody else did.

When the weather was mild, flowers still bloomed in October. The buddleia would be full of purple plumes, lording it over the gold and scarlet polyanthus that sat like worshippers at its feet. The dahlias, begonias, lithodoras and gladioli lasted the longest, together with the calla lilies and yellow mimosa. In late fall, when the last flower died and the last splash of color faded, she wanted to go out and cover her beloved garden with a blanket until spring. Sing it a lullaby as it fell asleep, her arboreal infant. Some of the more tender shrubs she did cover with boxes. During the winter months when it was too cold and wet she stood with her nose against the window making sure the garden was sleeping comfortably. If it snowed, she was pleased that it had a blanket to keep warm under.

⊷

One afternoon when she was out pruning the forsythias that threatened to stop the light coming through the left window, it started to rain. The shower soon gathered strength and turned into a torrential downpour, but she finished what she was doing anyway, trying not to trample the throng of white and blue campanulas spreading beneath the shrubs. Her bare feet had grown heavy boots of mud, her clothes and hair were plastered to her body, when Jackson leaned out his window to yell to the madwoman squatting in a flower bed below.

"Hey, Lissa! De rain be coming down!"

"Thank you, Jackson, I hadn't noticed."

"You crazy, woman?"

"Yes!" She smeared mud on her face, let out a blood-curdling war-whoop and stomped an unbridled dance of wild abandon. Jackson slammed his window shut and pulled the curtains. Lisa continued cavorting in the monsoon slush, not wanting the moment of freedom to end, hoping Mrs. Mortified was observing the spectacle.

Torrential rain or not, dance or not, there was work to be done. She still had to deadhead the climbing roses and trim down the penstemons that looked like they were crowding out her beloved mulberry tree. It required discipline to keep a tropical island. Only when the work was finished did she allow herself to go inside, sneaking in via the kitchen door where the clematis climbed higher and higher up the wall behind the delphiniums and the lavender.

Entering the house via the kitchen, she stole several spoonfuls of leftovers of what Ram called *sabzi dam* from a pot, then moved a pile of plates out of the sink so she could clean her feet in it. Nobody saw her, which was just as well. It wasn't the kind of thing Ram looked kindly upon but, as her room now displayed spotless white rugs over the plain linoleum, she had to be careful. She got her soap and towel and plodded up to the bathroom on clean feet, humming like a Pooh-Bear in honey heaven. As she passed Jackson's door she heard him quietly lock it. She stopped outside his door, but in the end resisted the temptation of letting off another war-whoop through his keyhole.

After a hot shower she headed back to the kitchen and helped herself to some more *sabzi dam* while making a pot of tea. In her room she got out her tin of chocolate biscuits and curled up on the luscious emerald bedspread beneath the framed Monet reprint where the water lilies never wilted. She made a nest among the exotic orange and turquoise pillows with little mirrors in the fabric. They came from a store owned by a second cousin of Ram's, who had given her twenty percent off. Burrowing in the middle of the bed she had a perfect view straight out into the garden through the open doors. There was not a more satisfying sight in the world. The heavy branches of the apple tree dripped onto the stone bench, watering the hostas and pink busy lizzies growing in a red ring beneath. She listened to the music of the rain falling steadily onto her fecund jungle and realized that she was experiencing joy.

The joy wasn't what she had expected it to be, the playfulness of it, the unadorned simplicity. Nor had she dreamt of having her first date with it so soon.

She sprang up out of her nest, plucked a red hibiscus flower to put in her hair, walked up to the mirror and looked into her father's blue eyes. She noticed how they sparkled, and said to him, "This is our island, dad. See the hibiscus flower in my hair? Remember?" And he said he did. She felt his smile on her lips. There are butterflies in the garden, she told him. They're not purple, but they are beautiful. He said he was very happy for her.

Lisa did not invite many people to her island. There were not many people that qualified. Her reasons for not letting just anybody into paradise were purely selfish. How could she let just anybody disturb what she had worked so hard to create? Sonja came to stay, of course. Mimmi and Mick visited often, as well as her new friends, Pru, Melvin and James.

And much later, towards the end, Len, the Canadian.

But first, Pru.

# 4

Lisa and Mimmi met Pru in the Greek restaurant close to Turnham Green Terrace. It was conveniently close to Mimmi's, but better still, it wasn't English, so they decided one day to give it a try. Going for lunch was a tradition they had established after Lisa moved into Ram's. Once a week she walked over to fetch Mimmi to go for lunch like grown-up ladies and talk of whatever was new. Usually they caught the tube into town and went somewhere in Soho, to take in a movie after, but not that day. It was November already. The London sky hung more leaden than ever, touching the tops of their heads.

They were sitting in a booth at the back talking to Dimitrios, the owner. They didn't have much of a choice, he was a man who loathed neglecting his female customers. He was offering them another glass of ouzo, on the house, when the door was flung open and an English thoroughbred trotted in. Her long red mane was similar in shade to the one Lisa had briefly sported earlier that year, but unlike Lisa's, the color was genuine. Its natural waves sparkled with a bright golden sheen that made the young woman's face glow. She was not chinless, she had a lovely chin, but Lisa could tell she was descended from aristocracy. She was also a part-time waitress at Dimitrios'. It was her day off and she was just visiting. Uninvited she made herself at home beside Dimitrios and hauled a red-stained brown parcel out of a plastic bag. She plopped it down on the table and opened it up to reveal a bleeding slab of meat. Wasn't it lovely? She had decided to cook dinner that night, she reported, as if they had been dying to find out. Helping herself to a piece of moussaka from Lisa's plate, the young woman continued. The thing was, she was not an experienced cook, having tried it only twice before and failed both bloody times. Anything might happen. What did they think, should she rub her rump roast with garlic before shoving it in the oven? She prodded the meat with her finger. It looked like she was trying to get its attention.

"You rub your lovely rump with whatever you wish, my pretty darling. I'll still adore you," said Dimitrios, thrilled to be the brain behind such wit.

The young woman, whose name was Pru, looked at the two Swedish girls and rolled her eyes. They rolled theirs back. It was to be the start of a great friendship. Pru had a strong upper-class-twit accent, but considering her beautiful chin, Lisa wasn't too surprised that she did not start her sentences with "I say."

Pru revealed in later conversation that she had forsaken the values of her pinnacled class to come down and roam among the common people, the real people, as she referred to ordinary working stiffs, in order to do real things. Waitressing was something real that real people partook in.

It was the indulgent nonchalance with which she presented this claptrap that enabled her to get away with it.

The girls left the restaurant together and she invited them up to "The Flat," located on the corner across the street. It was up on the first floor of what could be described, more or less, as a mansion. A decrepit former mansion at any rate. Lisa had walked by it many times, unaware of the importance it would have in her life. The Flat was enormous and had a large balcony perched over the pillared entrance. "Used to be ever so posh," said Pru as if this was somehow amusing.

Rooms lay concealed behind a rainbow of doors. There were bedrooms behind the blue, green, red, and orange doors, but the room behind the yellow one stood empty. The purple door led to the living room, a shrine to the times, missing not a detail of the necessary dope-smoking paraphernalia. Posters of Che Guevara, The Beatles, The Rolling Stones, and The Who covered the wall in between reproductions of paintings by Dali and Magritte. Dirty plates, glasses and cutlery grew in piles between the pillows on the floor. Amidst the detritus stood three sofas, a dining table with four chairs, brick-and-board shelves holding a record-player and two huge speakers, piles of records, and obligatory literature such as *IT*, *Melody Maker* and a second-hand copy of Ginsberg's *Howl*.

Two young men were lounging around in the mess talking profoundly about the state of French cinema. They were Pru's flat mates; two jaded, purposely scruffy upper-class brats named James and Melvin. James, coiled like a long thin snake among the pillows, was blond and pale and spoke slowly, lazily, his elocution precise. You could tell he'd been practicing. His quest for life's offerings on the wild side would not last. Soon he would seek his pleasures in more exclusive surroundings. Melvin had long dark hair that curled slightly. He was fey and flirtatious and always horny, but a sociable, friendly sort of horny. He lay stretched out on one of the sofas in a state of ready availability.

Lisa asked Pru later, were they, you know, poofters? Pru said she didn't think so, as she had slept with both of them, though not at the same time. "Mind you, I'm not altogether sure about James. He gets a bit distracted during climax."

The trio, togged out in the latest retro finery from Oxfam, was in the vanguard of the Love Generation. They were already ambling, if and when they felt like it, towards a future that would soon be a long psychedelic cartoon. In a few years everybody would dress exactly like them. Lisa, intent on escape, was seduced from the start. This supremely confident trio epitomized the social refinement of the times, they knew the way to where it was going to be at next without having to look.

Their second-hand glad rags and what-year-is-it? languor hid their Cambridge educations and the fact that they were not nearly as poor or simple as they made out to be.

They sat down, seance-like, around a coffee table buried under cigarette papers, ashtrays and bags of grass. Melvin rolled a joint. It was the first time Lisa smoked dope. She got stoned, or thought she did. They said she did. It could have been balancing on the cusp of delicious danger that made her dizzy. Danger, when delicious, had a tendency to have that effect.

"Take me away to this new future you've discovered," she begged.

"It's straight ahead, darling, can't miss it. It's that great big bloody thing looming on the horizon."

How could they afford such an enormous place, and how did they get away with turning it into such a festive slum? The answer was surprisingly simple. Pru's grandfather owned the building. His plan was to demolish it as soon as he could make a "lovely bit of profit" by doing so. Should he die before property values shot high enough to tempt him, Pru would inherit the entire bundle. Lisa was amazed. Suddenly she had a friend who assumed it a natural condition to be endowed with nabob relatives and real estate. And who found it amusing to wait on proles in a Greek restaurant.

"Pru," said Lisa, not sure if it was a compliment, "you're incredible."

"Oh, I know, darling," Pru purred. "And I dare say, you have incredible insight into a person's character."

The way she said it made Lisa smile and when she did Pru gazed at her, lovingly, as at a favorite child. "Oh Lisa, you must smile more often. It makes you a whole different person. It quite lights up your face."

People kept telling her that, not realizing it took far more than stretching your lips to make a new person.

The sleek creatures in the Flat were fascinating to behold. At first she envied them the carefree arrogance that buoyed their existence, their pathological lack of moral restraint. Emotions like guilt or regret were phenomena they could not pretend to comprehend.

Pru and the boys in turn admired Lisa's ability to live alone on an island refuge, or so they said, though admittedly they would never dream of trading. The following summer, Pru and Melvin would lie around in the serene grace of her room, the doors open to the earthly delight of her garden, secure that trust funds, country mansions, and family traditions waited patiently for the prodigals' inevitable return. Though, as Melvin pointed out, his country mansion was teeming with alcoholic inbred half-wits, so what was there to hurry back to?

Lisa tried to despise them, but couldn't manage. She tried to adopt their carefree life philosophy. That too was beyond her means.

><>

Shortly after they became friends, Pru persuaded Lisa to work part time as a waitress at the Greek's. She had noticed that Lisa was never burdened with an excess of cash. "Why not *earn* some money, darling?" Pru asked the question as though earning a living was just eccentric enough to make it an acceptable pastime. Acquiring an income was certainly a practical idea. Lisa's inheritance had by then shrunk an alarming degree, but she didn't tell Pru this, not wanting to sour a beautiful relationship by revealing that she actually *needed* to work in order to survive. She'd been meaning to get around to it, but the garden had taken up too much time. In November she no longer had that excuse.

She started on a Monday, working the daily lunch shift. She lasted until Saturday afternoon, and that was the extent of her career in the service industry. Pru kept at it; she was a star, because she didn't give a damn. She was, as she put it, an upper-class masochist doing penance for centuries of oppressing the peasantry. This view had nothing whatsoever to do with generations of accumulated regret, it simply sounded rather superb. To Pru it was all a game.

Lisa, on the other hand, descendant of the downtrodden, was free of that kind of dishonest moral drivel. Nor was what anger she harbored dormant. She couldn't for the life of her see why she should have to put up with people who fussed about not getting roast potatoes with the lamb, about the lamb tasting a bit funny, lemony almost, rather queer that. She took pains to point out to three such patrons during the week, that if they did not wish to consume foreign food, they should not be sitting in a goddam Greek restaurant. Though one would have thought, she added as an afterthought, full of She-Devil thumb-flicking anger, that they would be grateful for the chance to eat food that actually tasted of something. The patrons left outraged, and despite all the free advice, did not leave a tip.

She quit on the Saturday at 2:26 p.m. as soon as the last customer was out the door. Dimitrios was sitting in a booth at the back going through a stack of receipts when she threw herself down opposite him. Conscious of the cheap drama of her gesture she wailed, "I can't take anymore!"

"Thank God!" Dimitrios was swept away with relief, thinking he would otherwise have had to either fire the hopeless girl or shoot her. Being a gentleman, he was not looking forward to either option. She was, he assured her, leaning forward to plant a kiss of pity on her furrowed brow, the most appallingly useless waitress he had ever laid his suffering eyes on.

"I wasn't that bad, was I?"

"My pretty, you could kill my business single-handed." Her eyes were too expressive, for one thing. To look at his dear patrons with such naked contempt did not do much for customer relations. If somebody wanted a detailed analysis of moussaka, only to turn it down because it sounded ever so odd and didn't come with peas, you had to put up with it. "This is England," he explained, his patience not as endless as it seemed. "You have to be kind to these poor people. Let the customers think they are the embodiment of culinary refinement. Tell them the moussaka is Shepherd's Pie if you wish." By the way he shook his head, it was clearly weighing him down with terminal sorrow. "But you do *not* inform the customers that there is a goddamn fish-and-chip shop down the road!"

"Why not? People are so tiresome, Dimitrios, I can't help it. They don't deserve to be treated nicely."

It was a defense that did not count for much. The Greek sighed dramatically, turned his randy eyes to heaven, where no help was to be found. "Whatever can we do with you?"

"I'm sorry. I wasn't cut out to be a waitress." Lisa wanted badly to cry but it was a weakness she did not allow herself. A stiff upper lip, not a lower trembling one.

"I noticed. But tell you what I'll do, my beautiful darling." Dimitrios threw the receipts into a box and slammed the lid. "I take you gambling tonight. Yes? We celebrate that I get rid of the world's most useless waitress. Hey, Pru! You come too! Wear your sexy dress, okay?"

Lisa looked at Pru who said, "Well, what the hell." Lisa had never been to a casino. Remarkably, neither had Pru.

When the restaurant closed at eleven they went to pick up Dimitrios. Pru was looking casual in what Lisa assumed was a Saint Laurent Mondrian collection knock-off. It turned out to be the real thing. Lisa, of modest means, wore a homemade crocheted white number with the netted midriff, and was more insulted than flattered when Pru marveled over her incredibly "in" dress and how she ought to use her talent and go into the fashion business. Lisa asked her not to be such a patronizing upper class bitch. Pru wanted to know why she didn't just be a dear and relax.

"Smile, darling."

"I'll smile when damn well I feel like it."

She didn't feel like smiling in Dimitrios' car as it rocketed through the orange sodium-lit labyrinth that was London at night. In the face of his blatant disregard for all other traffic, it being English and beneath him, they soon gave up any hope of survival. Only when he crash-landed in a posh, quiet residential street in Kensington did they dare open their eyes.

Having felt the breath of death ruffle her hair, Lisa realized that she wanted to live, very much, whatever the setbacks. She was smiling by the time she got out of the car. Pru smiled back and gave her a brief hug. They clasped hands and shivered in the damp December night.

The casino was located in one of the elegant terrace houses, at a suitably discreet distance from the nearest lamppost. There were no signs, no vulgar neon lights pointing the way, only a diminutive brass plaque under the door bell. Dimitrios rang the bell, two short signals and a long one. A man opened the door four inches. When he saw who it was, the door opened wide to swallow them. Grinning, the man pumped Dimitrios' hand, slapped his shoulder. Dimitrios grinned, pumped and slapped right back in a manly ritual of brotherhood. The two young birds batted adorable lashes and, toes pointing inward girly-fashion, followed the menfolk into a quiet hallway richly decorated in burgundy and gold. Roulette and baccarat were through the doors to the left, their guide informed them, chemin-de-fer and blackjack to the right. Upstairs, Dimitrios whispered, there were poker games, but these premises were off limits to young ladies. He was expected to join a game very shortly and they would have to amuse themselves. This he knew would be no problem for his pretty darlings. Five minutes later he was gone.

The casino had the hushed dignity of a funeral parlor. There were no clattering one-armed bandits, no loud music, no half-naked dancing girls, only the seductive whisper of money convincing the patrons that everything was right as rain in a luxurious world. The food and the drinks in the casino were free. Once the pretty darlings realized that, they spent the first hour washing down toasted ham-and-cheese triangles with a steady stream of gin and tonic. The drinks had not been watered down. Eating and drinking they wandered from room to room watching rich people throw their money away. It looked dead easy.

The more gin and tonics, the more positive Lisa became that this was a movie set. Everybody else was far too elegant, for one thing. Look at all those men standing about pretending to be David Niven. One of them probably *was* David Niven. Look at those expensive suits, those manicured hands, those silver cigarette holders, that confident posture.

They could not be real. Real people didn't look like that, including herself. The slender girl in the tiny scrap of a white dress that stared back from every mirror was not Lisa Grankvist. Her hair was too long. She was too skinny, her cheeks gaunt. And she'd never dress like that in public. She'd never dare.

Dimitrios had disappeared. When Pru decided she wanted to play chemin-de-fer she found out that sugar daddy had left word with the management to the effect that if his beautiful darlings wanted to gamble, they could do so only for fun, not for money.

"Oh, screw that!" Pru sat down and gambled anyway, her Saint Laurent original riding high on delectable thighs. Around her several aged gentlemen went into cardiac arrest. Lisa left Pru and the gentlemen to their fate and wandered off to seek her own fortune.

Everything was going splendidly until she got too drunk and started to make a fuss at the roulette table. Free gin and tonics will give a girl a different outlook on life. The croupier finally had to yield to her demands in order to avoid a scene. All right, then, she could gamble with money, he said, but "only once, young lady, only once, is that absolutely clear?" He said it in a very quiet, jaw clenched, why-don't-you-put-a-bob-on-black-then-you-dumb-bint? manner.

"Fine." Lisa took out the hundred pounds she had cashed the day before. She got some chips, the whole hundred pounds worth, and stacked every single one on number 18 in a tidy little tower, taking her time just to irritate, trying to look like she'd done this every day since she was tall enough to reach the table. The croupier shook his head and figured the loudmouth slut deserved her loss.

She was eighteen years old. She had left Zagreb on the eighteenth of April, on a cloudy Easter Sunday, running a detour from Strossmayerov trg, the square beneath the plane trees by the Palace café, all the way to the train station. Compared to that, putting her livelihood for the next few months on a number with one feeble chance in 37 to win did not seem at all rash. It may have been masochism or plain stupidity, but at that moment she was in no mood for analysis. The croupier looked like he wanted to rip her head off and spin it in the wheel.

The table by then was surrounded by yet more tense men, their reptilian eyes discreetly observing her, their groomed faces revealing nothing. Lisa was one of only two females in the room, and the only person under forty. Opposite her sat an old woman, dowager-like and pearl-bedecked, placing stacks of chips on corner bets. Her hair was the same shade of blue as her satin dress. In the past half hour she had lost every time.

The wheel spun and the little ball whipped around and around so fast it disappeared. Then it slowed down, slower and slower, and bobbed about for a bit before finding a permanent home in the number 18 slot.

"The lucky bloody bitch!" yelled the dowager. Every pair of reptile eyes slid from the wheel to Lisa. Lisa's eyes turned to the wheel.

"Thirty-six hundred pounds sterling, darling!" whispered a fat man with a distinct Stockholm accent.

It slowly entered Lisa's gin-pickled neocortex that she'd won.

The croupier mumbled a curt command to a waiter who slithered off like an eel through a marsh of tailored suits. A minute later Lisa's cautious euphoria was interrupted by a vicious hiss in her ear. Dimitrios, too, had turned into a reptile. He kept hissing until she managed to grasp what he was on about. She had jeopardized his standing at the club with her reckless behavior. Things were not good. His forked tongue flickered like he was about to bite her. "Now you will have to leave. Right away. This is no joke. Unless . . ."

Unless she agreed that it was all in good fun and did not demand her winnings, that is. Would she do that, like a good darling girl? Did she not owe him that?

She thought not. "I won fair and square! Give me my money!" Her voice was shrill. She felt outrageous and rich. It was a larger than life feeling. Feelings that size, she noticed, are powerful. Pru heard the siren of her voice and came running.

"Give the girl her bloody money!" The dowager banged a liver-spotted fist on the table in a fit of female solidarity. Stacks of chips fell about. All the David Nivens nodded.

"Hear, hear!" yelled Pru.

It was the kind of scene that happens only in far-fetched movies, though had it been a movie, a handsome multimillionaire would have rushed to Lisa's aid, rather than an old woman with electric blue hair. Lisa and the millionaire would have fallen in love, hopped into his Lamborghini parked at the curb, and driven straight to his villa in Antibes.

That didn't happen, though the fat man voiced his support after she said to him in Swedish, "I won this money honorably, didn't I?"

"You're right," he replied and switched to English. "I say you pay her." The David Nivens concurred.

"Bloody right!" The dowager banged her fist some more. It was clearly a habit of hers. She wore two large diamond rings. People like that get listened to.

In the end Lisa was handed her winnings. In cash. It wasn't as if the casino could not afford to pay what they owed her. When they got up to leave, Pru was as elated as Lisa, if less guardedly so. Dimitrios refused to accompany them. They were no longer his beautiful darlings. He refused to even sully his eyes on them, but only until Lisa whispered with hot breath in his greedy ear that he could have ten percent if he stopped hissing. After all, she would not have won, had he not invited her.

It was a temptation his mercenary soul was unable to resist. Everything sorted out, the three of them left together, a happy man and his little harem. Feeling generous, Pru and Lisa allowed him to take them to a nightclub to celebrate. It wasn't the kind of place they would normally frequent. The tuxedoed orchestra and the pompous chandeliers made them laugh out loud. The patrons consisted of old men with much younger women. At least they fit in. Pru pointed out a Member of Parliament. Lisa pointed out a Swedish *au pair* Mimmi had once introduced her to, sitting with a man old enough to be her grandfather. The girl looked like she couldn't decide whether to be impressed or cry for help. Lisa fell into her role as a rich woman and snapped her fingers, demanding champagne. Dimitrios insisted on cognac. Had the waiters had forelocks they would have tugged them right off. Drunk beyond giving a damn, the girls ignored it when Dimitrios let spill to everybody within earshot that they were his devoted mistresses.

As they got ever more bleary-eyed, Pru began babbling on about how eighteen was obviously Lisa's lucky number, and how they must do this again, and wasn't it fun?

Lisa started to brood. "Tell me something, Dimitrios," she said as the night began to fray at the edge. "Why do men rape women?"

"Only men who hate women rape them, my pretty darling," explained their wise womanizer, swirling the Napoleon cognac in his snifter. "Men who love women never resort to such barbaric tactics."

"Thank you so much for that bit of profound insight," said Pru, who knew how to make sarcasm sound impeccably polite. "What brought that on?" She stared at Lisa. There was a suspicious gleam in the pink of her after-hours eyes.

"I've no idea. Something I read in the paper, I suppose. Some girls that got raped. It just upset me. You know how sometimes things get to you?"

"In the wrong place at the wrong time," concluded Dimitrios. "Happens all the time. Girls must always be very careful. They should never trust men. You are very lucky to be with me, my darlings."

"Why don't you go home to your wife and tell her that shit?" asked Pru.

Lisa no longer felt drunk. "Let's go home," she said, "This place makes me feel cheap."

"Okay, my darling. But first you give me my cut, eh?"

Lisa gave him his cut, counting out the bills quickly, before she changed her mind. As Dimitrios tucked the money away he made sure that the pretty darlings were aware of two important facts: one, that his wife was a *very* fortunate woman, and two, that he would *never* take them gambling again as long as he lived.

He did offer Lisa another job cleaning his restaurant after hours when his beloved patrons would not have to be exposed to her odd ways. Lisa, despite her recent windfall, was about to accept when Pru with surprising force demanded that she turn it down. Pru had other plans. She refused to say what those plans were, only that they would have a lovely chat in a day or two when they were once again in a state of cold daylight sobriety. Dimitrios waved a waiter over for another Cuban cigar, putting it on Lisa's bill.

The girls chose to take a cab home. The Greek got into his car, sped through a red light and disappeared into a frosty night that was almost over.

⊷

The following Monday morning Lisa went to the bank down by the green to deposit £3000 into a new savings account. She was referred to a junior manager who turned out to be one of the sods from Airedale Avenue. "I say," she said, waving her windfall, "I need to deposit a spot of cash."

She couldn't bring herself to tell Mimmi and Mick about her win, it seemed too obscene. Only Pru and Dimitrios knew and Dimitrios preferred to pretend it never happened. Pru promised not to breathe a word to anybody. Well-brought up people never mention money. Besides, Pru had something else nibbling at her peace of mind. It was quite unlike her. Monday night she paid Lisa a visit.

"There's something I wish to know, darling," she said, standing in the middle of the room, arms crossed, as if many things depended on the answer.

"What?"

"What were you really on about the other night when you asked the Greek why men rape women?" There was still a tinge of pink in her scrutinizing eyes.

"Nothing."

"Don't lie."

"I'm not lying."

"You bloody well are."

"Well, I'm not very good at talking about stuff like that." The excuse was true. Her body was growing awkward and stiff. It felt like the onset of sudden paralysis.

"Tell it to me like a story then. I want to know" Pru was persistent. There was something intent in her eyes that evening. In anybody else's eyes it would have been called somberness, but Pru had never been officially somber in her life.

"Why? What do you care? Why can't you just leave me alone?"

"I truly don't know, Lisa, but I can't. Now tell me." Pru was not going to let it alone.

"Like a story?"

"If you wish."

"A once-upon-a-time story?"

"You choose the format."

Tell Pru a story? Yes, she could try and do that. In a strange way she even wanted to, if only to see how it would feel. It might help. "You won't interrupt?"

Pru somberly shook her head.

"That will be a first."

"I promise."

"Not even if it's a long one?"

"I've got all night, darling." Looking at Pru, Lisa realized how much Pru cared about her. It made her feel strong. And grateful enough to want to give something back.

"All right then. Like a fairy tale. But I must warn you, there is no prince."

"That's quite all right. I met a real prince a while back. He was the most pompous buffoon you could imagine."

"Let's make a pot of tea first, all right?"

"If you insist. I'll go make the tea. You dig out the chocolate biscuits."

They put the tea tray by the fireplace and sat down on the pillows with little mirrors in them. The mirrors reflected the flames. Lisa fiddled with the sugar and the milk. Tea was the farthest thing from her mind.

She kept fiddling. "I've never revisited that night. It might take a while to dare go through it."

"So you said. Better get started then." Pru's voice was patient.

"Can I close my eyes and read it to you like out of a book?"

"Go ahead. Just stop babbling and get on with it."

"Okay then. Here we go."

# 5

It seems like ages ago, but it happened in June last year. It was one of those nights when it doesn't grow dark and the air turns blue instead. Summer evenings at home sometimes were like that. Still are, I suppose. And when the air turns that shade of blue, you see, there's enchantment in the air. It gives you bold ideas.

I was with Sonja, my best friend since childhood whom I've told you about. We were seventeen and the indigo-tinted world was ours, whispering sweet promises.

We had started out around six, in no particular hurry, walking from where Sonja lived in the suburbs into the center of the city. It was Saturday night and it was going to be a night to remember, we could feel it, so we needed to approach it slowly to savor every moment. Wearing brand new dresses, having done each other's hair, taken our time with a forbidden amount of makeup, how could our dreams not come true? Both our dresses were of cotton gingham, very popular. Brigitte Bardot wore cotton gingham when she married Jacques what's-his-name. Remember? Sonja's was green and white with a flared skirt, and she looked very pretty, being tall and thin. Mine was orange and white and straight with three flounces at the hem. It was the prettiest dress I'd ever owned, and I had paid for it myself with my first paycheck from my very first job. I'd just got a job as a receptionist in a cosmetics firm.

We arrived downtown and looked around for a bit, checked the lay of the land. The city was full of people, everybody was dressed up, looking expectant, milling around as if they were all at a big party, waiting for the host to pop the cork and festivities to begin. By then we were alert, prepared for whatever treat fate had in store for us.

We sashayed along the summer sidewalks, Sonja and I, arms linked to show we were best friends, that was the custom, flaunting our pretty dresses, backs straight, chests straining outward until it hurt. Well, I mean, look at my chest. Not Bardot exactly.

The dream was to meet some really cute guys. You know, the delicious romance of it all? This is how it would happen: Prince Charming would appear, his eyes meet mine, and bang, there'd be lightning. We would drown in each other's gaze and the world would be a new place. We'd float in slow motion to the nearest café that, needless to say, would have candles on the tables, the softer to illuminate true love.

After a suitable length of time we would marry our princes, Sonja and I, and live in mindless bliss until the end of time. We were young and naïve and foolish.

It was down a long narrow street winding from the main square through the old town down to the harbor, that we found them, in the cobblestone charm of that come-hither blue dusk. There was a pawnshop close by and a porn shop with weird stuff in the window. Penis-shaped candles and handcuffs, not the stuff of romance.

But there they were, those gorgeous guys we'd fantasized about! Two laughing faces popping out of a second story window, just like that. The timing was perfect. We froze in our tracks.

Imagine gypsy violins, blushing cheeks, fluttering hearts, the lot. We sighed at the sight of those tousled blond mops! Was it *this* easy? Snap your fingers and your dreams come true? Was Fate was so considerate? We turned our starry eyes upwards and sighed our helloes.

The dream boys helloed us back, but they sounded funny. It turned out they weren't Swedish. This marred the perfection, briefly. Luckily one of them, the one I had picked out as my future husband, spoke passable Swedish. The other one just smiled and nodded, smiled and nodded. He did so most ardently, you could tell he was dying to communicate.

Foreign or not, we staked our claims. Sonja murmured without moving her lips that the nodding one was hers. He had a dimple in his left cheek and Sonja had always been a sucker for dimples. I indicated with a squeeze of her arm that it was an excellent choice. I was going to live happily forever after with the other one whose blue eyes were to die for. Sonja squeezed my arm back. We sighed some more. Our feet lost touch with the cobblestones. We hovered and waited to be transported into some parallel world where fairy godmothers would sprinkle us with pixie-dust.

Oh, that blue blue air, Pru. If you could only have seen it. Such a mild and cunning aphrodisiac. Gentle but teasing. It was the kind of night when dreams came true, but we'd known that all along. A *Bella Notte* when Ladies meet their Tramps.

Next our happy heroes informed us that they were Yugoslavs. Sonja said, oh no, and all the gypsy violins fell silent.

You see, back home Serbs and Croats are always going at one another downtown, it's an ongoing war. When they aren't hurling homemade bombs to settle ill-defined grievances, they have a habit of shoving knives into each other on crowded sidewalks like it's a form of greeting. Those guys have strange customs.

And there I was, already so happy I wouldn't have thought it possible. What to do? Surely, we reasoned, anxiously, desperate not to lose out, they couldn't *all* be bad. It was presumptuous to assume that they were all the same. I mean, there are some very nasty Swedes about too. These two looked so adorable and sweet, so terribly open-faced and earnest. How could they not be?

We lingered for a while, fought off disappointment. It was not part of our dreams coming true, so we conveniently concluded that it was in all likelihood safe to ignore our prejudices. Doubts flickered. We kept dawdling, coy and giggling, resisting tempta- tion, not wanting to resist. We were good girls. Virgins still. But in the end those ear-to-ear infectious grins disarmed us and led us up a wooden staircase, step by step, to a small apartment under the eaves. I still remember the sound of those creaky stairs. They sounded like new shoes.

It was a daring thing to do, only by then we felt so brave we had stopped fretting. We were grown-ups, we figured, we could handle it. We entered a small dark room, illuminated only by the smiles of the two young men. They welcomed us formally, a whiff of aftershave in the air, so close we could touch them, feel the heat off their bodies. They shook our hands and bade us to please come in. Sonja squeezed my arm as we stepped into the main room. We were now *in* the adventure. The large room with its sloping ceiling had claimed us. It was very quaint in a candle-in-a-wine-bottle bohemian way, like a French movie or something.

We looked around the room, shy and awkward, unsure of the protocol, wishing we were more experienced. Right inside the door was an old porcelain sink with only a cold water tap and a bunch of dirty dishes. Beside it, under the window facing the courtyard, sat a hot plate on a small table. There were two beds, neatly made, head to head by the longest wall of the room, separated by a shelf. At the other end of the room, by the win- dow from which they had disarmed us, stood a sofa, a coffee table and some chairs. A couple of floor lamps threw a cosy glow. The room was L-shaped, I noticed. At the hidden arm of the L was a door. The door was shut.

I don't remember any specific details, but it couldn't have been a messy place, or we would never have stayed. A grubby dump reeking of dubious aromas, piles of dirty underwear, would have set off an alarm. We would have turned and fled like sensible girls. This I know. But there is a certain assurance in tidy surroundings. They reflect the pleasant personalities of the people living therein. I had read that in a magazine, so I knew.

We were cordially invited to sit down on the couch while our young suitors took a chair each. They introduced themselves, Juraj and Stanko, and were as courteous as can be, alert to our every need, as eager as puppies to please. Would we like a cup of coffee? Or did we prefer tea? Alcohol? We said coffee would be very nice, thank you.

Shortly after we sat down, the door to the adjacent room opened and an old man came shuffling out in a pair of sheepskin slippers. He greeted everybody with a curt nod and eased himself into a chair. There he sat and didn't say a peep. We assumed he didn't speak Swedish. I wondered if he was the grandfather of one of them. Our new friends acted as if no clarification were necessary. We started to relax. It was reassuring that the old man's patriarchal demeanor was probably due to the fact that he was a grandfather. Who else would he be? It also explained why they were so well-behaved.

They proudly showed us their record collection. It consisted of four singles. Which one would we like them to play first? Sonja chose the Elvis one. They crooned along in painful English, bustled around making coffee and cheese sandwiches. It was all so domestic and ordinary. They even paid proper attention to the details of setting the table, putting a carefully folded paper napkin on each plate, polishing the spoons with a towel, all the while clowning around, making us laugh, smiling their lovely smiles. We spent an hour or so trying to make meaningful conversation in Swedish, German and English. Outside the night turned a deeper shade of blue. Life was perfect.

Later on, when we had played their four singles several times, we made arrangements to go to a movie the next day. Some Western playing at the Palladium. They admired tough guys like John Wayne and that new guy, Clint Eastwood, and kept pulling imaginary guns from imaginary holsters to indicate that they too would like to be cowboys and sit tall in the saddle.

Then it started.

There was a loud crash downstairs. It was followed by the sound of bad tempered feet thumping up the stairs. Our hosts exchanged a look. Their smiles became strained. They quickly lit cigarettes. My future husband developed a sudden fascination for his feet. There was further commotion as the front door opened. Somebody roared and it slammed shut again. An ominous tremor ran through the building. There was more banging around as if whoever had arrived had got lost in the dark, then two men stumbled over the threshold. They weren't giants, but they seemed to take up an awful lot of space. Either that or the room had shrunk. We shrank too as we were introduced to them. This is Ilija and Drago, mumbled our hosts, not looking us in the eye. Their smiles were gone by then. The introduction went ignored by both visitors.

We recognized the guy named Ilija. He was a notorious troublemaker downtown. How to describe him? He was a one-man paramilitary unit constantly on the prowl, craving battles, needing to prove who was the real man. His pose was that of The Mean Hombre. That was how he wanted to be perceived. He was only a bit taller than me, and he had these strange slanted eyes and flat cheekbones that made him look like a Mongolian tribesman. I read later that around the fifth century or so, Mongol-Turkish Asiatic Huns migrated down into the Balkan Peninsula. Perhaps he was a descendant of those Huns. He was not unattractive; he simply didn't appear human. His face looked like somebody had hammered it out of a slab of granite and painted human features on it. He was either born that way or spent his formative years in front of a mirror perfecting his lithoidal persona. It wasn't a face designed for laughter. I had once seen four policemen struggle to haul him into a squad car.

The man called Drago was taller, a shapeless bulky sack of turnips. Dark hair sprouted out of his shirt, which was open down to the waist, and all over his arms where his sleeves were rolled up. He looked like he had been tarred and rolled in pubic hair.

Both were as void of human warmth as inanimate objects.

Instinct implored us to run. But we were seventeen, intent on romance. We still mistook our illusions for reality. Life was supposed to be a simple affair. Our system was straightforward: there were cute guys and there were ugly guys. Cute guys were the good ones and ugly ones were bad. We had no desire to discover that there existed those to whom our sweet hand-written labels did not apply.

Our hosts had deflated for good. They did nothing to prevent the intruders from making themselves at home. Boozy fumes wafted as they prowled about. The last record had finished playing and the room was silent. We waited for our heroes to heed their protective instincts and demand the trespassers get lost. They never did. Nor did the old man, he sat as before and never opened his mouth.

It turned out they were in no position to do anything. The apartment belonged to The Mean Hombre. Of all the tens of thousands of places in the city, this was the one we had blundered into, hearts a-flutter. God, Pru, we felt so stupid. There we were, drinking his coffee and eating his sandwiches. And he did not look like a generous man.

The Mean Hombre slithered about like a black shadow. The man named Drago kept lurking in the shadows. Sonja said the next day that he reminded her of one of the big dumb Bear Brothers in Donald Duck magazines, the ones that always try to steal uncle Scrooge's money.

That's how I will always think of them. The Mean Hombre and Brother Bear. Not to make a joke of it all, but to demean them. It makes it easier, having at least the power to belittle them retroactively. Like sticking your tongue out behind somebody's back. They don't notice, but it makes you feel better.

The atmosphere in the room had changed. A cold front had swept in. Dark clouds were gathering. There were smattering bursts of conversation in a language Sonja and I did not understand. We signaled to each other that it was time to go. We were thoroughly polite about it. "It's been a lovely evening," we said, smiling as we got up. My smile was so nervous and insincere, my lips stuck to my teeth. Sonja lied and said we were expected at a birthday party at a friend's house. "We're already late," she apologized. "Thank you so . . ."

That's when The Mean Hombre stopped dead. He twirled around and acknowledged our presence with a suddenness so jarring it stopped us dead in our tracks. Acting as if he had been deep in thought the entire time, and had only this minute had a penetrating insight, he held up a hand. Not as a blessing, but a stop signal: Halt! He issued an order: we could not leave without having partaken in a glass of slivovitz, party or no party. It was the polite and proper thing to do where he came from. Traditions must be respected.

An invisible wall slammed into place behind him. We had little choice but to sit down again. We could have said, *No, thank you,* and marched out, except nobody had ever accused us of bad manners before and it was a bit confusing. We had been brought up to behave politely in company, to try to make a good impression. And we were scared.

Besides, marching out the door would never have worked. I tried it later and it was useless. It was an impenetrable wall, you see. The outside world was no longer within our reach.

We knew then that something bad was going to happen.

They poured plum brandy into dainty little glasses that looked like thimbles in their hands. Raising their glasses, mimicking a toast, they drank with us, saying nothing, never looking us in the eye. I wasn't used to alcohol and took only a careful sip. It burnt my throat. I don't recall if we had a second glass. There is a no-man's-land where my memory is unable to tread between drinking plum brandy and what happened later. That remains in sharp focus.

The lights had been turned off at some point and the room lay peaceful in the semi-darkness, all black and white, the only light coming from the streetlight outside, the softer to illuminate Sonja being raped. One of the cute guys, the one with the dimple, was on top of her.

It's so very strange, you know. I had always imagined rape as a violent act, loudly shouted obscenities, brutal behavior, slapping and beating, the shrieks of the victim. But there was nothing of that. Apart from the discreet creak of the bed there wasn't a sound to be heard. The demeanor of the three men, who had pulled up chairs to the bed to watch, was that of supreme calm. The old man sat at the head of the bed, chin in hand, leaning forward with clinical fascination, as if about to take notes or point out mistakes.

Why was I standing in the middle of the room like that? I was being led to the other bed. The Mean Hombre had me by the back of the dress. He shoved me onto the bed. Towering in front of me like a black monolith he handed me the bottle of slivovitz. He used words sparingly. *Drink.* Even his gestures were pared down to a minimum. When I refused the bottle and he raised his arm, it was so fast and efficient that I at first didn't know what had propelled my head against the wall. The shock of the impact stunned me more than the pain. He looked as if he hadn't moved. His eyes never met mine when he handed me the bottle again, patiently adding three more words to ensure I knew he meant business and wasn't merely acting the gracious host. *Drink for me, baby,* he said. Just like that, in bad English, a line from some B-movie.

What puzzled me was his utter indifference. He was not overcome by desire to have sex with me, or hurt me even. I don't know what he wanted. It must have been about power. That's what it's about, isn't it? Only he seemed more bored than anything. He was going about what he was doing like it was a necessary routine, perhaps to prove some point, something he could do in his sleep. That had to be undertaken because the occasion called for it. A man's gotta do what a man's gotta do. Is it possible, do you think, that men rape simply because they're bored? Because they're too unintelligent, too unable, to ease their own boredom?

That time I accepted the bottle. I took a very small sip, tried to make it look like a greedy gulp, and handed the bottle back. He shook his head fractionally. I kept taking tiny sips. When he decided I'd had enough, he grabbed the bottle and indicated with his hand that I was to remove my dress. Not a word did he utter. It was beneath him to waste language on the likes of me. But no way was I going to take my dress off. And I was not going to stand naked before the stone monster who had just launched a fist into my face. And I was not going to get raped. I was under the impression that I still had a choice, you see. So, using his economical method of communication I shook my head.

He didn't bat an eyelid. This was no big deal. Grabbing the front of my dress he lifted me up, his gesture as swift as it was effortless, explaining with another sparse movement that, if I didn't obey, he would rip my dress from the neckline all the way down to the flounced hem. His cold eyes conveyed nothing. They didn't see me.

I pretended to give up. While I fiddled with the zipper at the back, I planned my escape. He just stood there, this cold black shadow, showing no emotion at all. He took a swig of plum brandy. The room was so quiet I could hear him swallow. Then I scooted. Just as I was about to grapple with the old-fashioned lock my head exploded. It was amazing. Gravity lost its pull and I zoomed like a canon ball straight back into the room. I had not heard him follow me, so feline and swift were his movements, so used to hunting at night was he. But he must have exerted himself that time, because when I crash-landed I lost consciousness.

When I came to, I was lying on the floor inside a semicircular fence, a fence made of five pairs of inanimate legs dressed in uniform black. Three of the pairs wore black shoes. One was barefoot. The pair of feet in sheepskin slippers belonged to the old man. There was a steady trickle from my nose. I thought, I better not drip on their shoes.

We live by certain rules, don't we? That is the way society functions and we all know our place. Suddenly there were no rules. Events happened regardless of our behavior. We had lost control over our lives.

That was when I decided to throw some sort of fit. All that

was left by then was the terror. I had nothing to lose. Never having had a fit of any kind, I just plunged into it, hoping for the best. It was a stellar performance, full of raspy moans and labored breathing. I got so involved I forgot I was faking it. I rolled my eyes like a dying animal. My nosebleed added drama. Then, at some point, there was prude Sonja squatting by my side, stark naked. Her features had gathered in a tight bunch in the middle of her face. I didn't recognize her. She put her arm around my shoulders until I calmed down, wiping my face with a serviette.

She told me the next day, that when she had seen me thrash about on the floor she had fully believed that I was having some kind of seizure triggered by the terror. It's what had convinced them that I wasn't faking it.

At one point a pair of fence posts left and came back. A hand offered me a cup of water and a small white pill. A quiet voice said, *Take it.* I took it.

We hoped that it would be over by then, that they had had their fun. It was clear that they had lost interest in us, but even so, they had no intention of letting us leave. They acted tired and listless, but held onto their power by ordering us to go to bed.

⊱✦⊰

There are many hours unaccounted for here. I have no idea what went on. Somebody must have taken my dress off, because at daybreak I woke up in my underwear in one of the beds. I had no memory of going to bed. Had the pill put me to sleep? Had Sonja slept? I asked her the next day, the only time afterwards that we ever talked about it, but she just shook her head in persistent denial.

I lay with my eyes closed for the longest time trying to ignore the fact that I badly had to pee. Would I be allowed to go? It wasn't the kind of party where they doled out favors, but I finally I became desperate, sat up in bed, raised a hand to get their attention, and begged to go to the toilet. Hearing my plea, Sonja sat up in the other bed and repeated it.

Our captors were lounging around the coffee table with their feet up, shoes on, looking relaxed, smoking and drinking coffee. They gave us a cursory glance, poured more coffee and proceeded to discuss our request in their own language. At least we hoped that's what they were doing. It took considerable time to analyze the pros and cons of our request.

As I sat there waiting, I noticed a photo of a young girl on top of the dresser. She had watched everything that went on from a cheap wooden frame on a crocheted mat, her face as fresh as a rose, innocent and empty. A girl of no opinions.

At long last they arrived at a unanimous decision and turned to us. Somebody lifted an eyebrow in my direction. *You first.* I was allowed to leave the bed and get into my dress while they all watched, but they drew the line when it came to wearing shoes. Shoes were *verboten* in this new existence. There was no indoor toilet, so after I got dressed I was led down the stairs, through a back door, across the yard to the outhouse.

My guard was Juraj, the one I had been supposed to live happily ever after with. Who had sung and laughed and made us sandwiches. He tried to be friendly, though his eyes did not meet mine when he smiled at me. I looked away. Cute had been redefined. All the old labels with their little hearts and arrows had been discarded. Like any good soldier, he stood guard while I had a pee in the smelly old outhouse. There was no toilet paper, only an old phone directory. I tried to look up my number, but somebody had used up the G-section.

I didn't try to escape. He held me by the arm as we walked to and from the outhouse, a firm grip just above my elbow, bending my arm backwards. He was a lot stronger than I was. Besides, when reality has been suspended you behave differently. All reference points disappear. The old rules no longer apply.

When we crossed the little yard we met another guard leading his prisoner. Sonja's feet were bare like mine. Her hands

were twisted behind her back where her rapist had them in
a tight lock. He knew his job, that one. You could tell it was
painful by the way her shoulders were hunched up. Our paths
met halfway across the yard.

I don't know why this moment stands out in my mind, but I
will always see clearly this picture of two captives, arms bent
behind their backs, their paths crossing, eyes downcast. A pair
of feet with pearly pink toenails, another pair with bright orange
nails, except the left big toe where the polish is chipped off.
Uncombed hair. Faceless guards by their sides.

Sonja and I didn't look at each other. That would be to
acknowledge our degradation and that was something we had to
avoid at all costs. So we passed like strangers with bowed heads.

It must have been after four o'clock because it was getting
light. A new day was breaking. Starlings were busy singing.
Right in the center of the yard by the bicycle stands, there were
flowers growing. Pretty flowers in a neglected flower bed. Funny,
I can never recall what kind they were, or what color. Sometimes I'm convinced they were delphiniums, at other times that
they were only weeds. I can't picture them. But at the time I
thought they looked so innocent growing there, so misplaced in
that concrete yard, deserving a better place.

⊳◇⊲

Upstairs the rules had not changed. We were ordered back into
bed. As if they were thinking, *let's store them in the beds until we
decide what to do with them.* I lay as still as a corpse, eyes closed,
until I had to go to the bathroom again. This time the request
caused no debate. Only Brother Bear and my guard were left
awake. The old man and Sonja's rapist had disappeared. The
Mean Hombre lay snoring on the couch.

Brother Bear himself honored Sonja by doing guard duty. She
got to go first. I had my regular escort. The early morning sun
dazzled, the blue sky was without a cloud. It was going to be a
beautiful day. I thought, *Today we can go to the beach.* You have
to think like that, like you still have a future. It helps a bit.

Sometimes I wonder what those flowers were if they were not delphiniums or weeds. Were they foxgloves or gladioli?

We returned to our jail again. It smelled of stale smoke and sweat. It was late enough in the morning to dare assume that we would now be allowed to stay up and keep our clothes on. There were just the four of us awake.

It was almost as if we'd overstayed our welcome and didn't know how to leave. Maybe we were going crazy. I stood huddled by the sink when Brother Bear loomed before me, demanding attention. He filled my entire field of vision, it was hard to avoid him. He ordered me to take my clothes off. He actually used words, so it was no use pretending to misinterpret a gesture. *Take all clothes off. Right now.*

It was never going to end.

I shook my head. Another pointless gesture of defiance. Brother Bear's beefy slab of an arm rammed against the side of my head. I stumbled towards the sink and a glass fell to the floor and broke. My head was spinning like a top.

Brother Bear was no longer indifferent. He was happy, because now he got to be the boss. He intended to make the most of it to prove himself worthy of the title. When I stood back up, he raised his other hand. Not to hit me, but to point to the big bulky ring he was wearing. It was a tasteless object with a sharp black jagged stone rising out of the center. A lethal weapon. He pointed first to the ring, then to my face, and followed his explicit gesture by a flick of the hand. My clothes were to be removed. At once. His wordless language was far too eloquent to be misunderstood.

I gave up again and started to undress. Brother Bear supervised, impatiently scratching my shoulder with his ring when I was too slow getting unzipped.

When my clothes lay on the floor, Brother Bear pointed to the bed where I had slept. I got back in. He then began barking in his own language. My prison guard was receiving orders to get into bed with me. He undressed and complied. It didn't take long. Brother Bear was beaming affably. I could tell he just loved being the kingpin. I expected him to clap hands and jump up and down and whoop. Instead he indicated to my guard to help himself. My guard hesitated at first, but Brother Bear was persuasive, so he quickly got on top of me. Brother Bear, pleased with the way things were progressing, disappeared behind the shelf into the other bed to tend to Sonja who had already done as she'd been told.

Losing my virginity was a bizarre experience. My guard was aroused, yet reluctant. He tried to be gentle. He stroked my hair and whispered very quietly, so Brother Bear wouldn't hear, *I not hurt you*. As if we were in it together. I kept my eyes squeezed shut, except at one point when I opened them and looked straight at him. His face was less than an inch from mine. Our noses briefly touched. I noticed how his eyebrows turned down almost at a right angle. Below his right eyebrow was a small triangular birthmark. His cheekbones were high and finely chiseled. His forehead was damp. I could smell sweat mingling with aftershave.

He must have felt my stare, because he opened his eyes. They were blue. They reflected his shame. But the shame didn't stop him doing his job. I felt him move inside me.

It was such an intimate encounter. We both closed our eyes.

Sonja said afterwards that Brother Bear didn't rape her. He made a few attempts, but couldn't get it up. And through it all The Mean Hombre snored, and his girlfriend stared at us with her bovine eyes from the frame on the dresser. I know it was his girlfriend, I saw them a few weeks later at the movies. He pretended not to see me.

A sunbeam took its time traveling the length of the room. The starlings had moved on. The city lay early Sunday silent.

Suddenly we were allowed to get up and get dressed. They didn't even prevent us putting our shoes on that time, which brought the first glimmer of hope. We tried to make as little sound as possible, dreading The Mean Hombre waking up with renewed energy. The sun was shining.

How long had we been held there? About fifteen hours. That's why I'm going through it step by step, trying to figure out how all those hours passed.

Now comes an even more unbelievable part. Standing around fully dressed, shoes and all, still not hopeful, I decided to do the dishes. *I think I'll help you with the dishes*, I heard myself say. It shocked our captors. It shocked me too. I sounded so normal. But I had to do something tediously, ridiculously ordinary just then or I would have broken down and hurled myself at their feet, begging for mercy. Which would have been a bad move. I knew that if I went crazy they might kill us. We were of no importance to them.

So I did the dishes. First I swept up the pieces of broken glass with my hands, then I asked politely if they had any detergent. *Use the cigarette ashes.* Brother Bear was being helpful. *Is what my mother she use in my country.* Like an obedient girl, I lit a cigarette and used the ashes to clean the dishes. Sonja, who smokes, rushed to partake in this bizarre tableau of domestic normalcy. She puffed away and rubbed plates with a dirty towel as though there was nothing she loved more.

Meanwhile our captors sat on the beds in their underwear, shaking their hung-over heads in amazement. Brother Bear, idly scratching various body parts, repeated what strange and wonderful girls we were. After such a busy night, here we were, scrubbing their dishes like it was a real privilege.

Warped? You don't need to tell me that. But it worked, you see. We stayed sane, we avoided becoming victims in our own eyes. That was important. And so impressed was Brother Bear, he announced that he would take us out to a café and buy us breakfast.

My rapist sat silently smoking, studying his feet again, while Brother Bear presented his bribe like it was an irresistible treat.

I handed Sonja another rinsed plate and we exchanged a quick glance. There was hope in that glance. We didn't dare think about the humiliation of being seen in public with our captors, but we quickly mustered up some enthusiasm. We'd be able to go back into the free world. We'd be able to go home and pretend nothing had happened.

*Go home.* You have no idea how sweet those words sounded. I was staying at Sonja's for the weekend. Her parents had gone to visit her older brother in Trelleborg. No one would ever know what had happened.

But first, our Sunday treat. Sonja pointed out that I had blood all over the front of my dress, but Brother Bear saw this as no hindrance. He handed me my white cardigan thrown on a chair and told me to put it on and button it. And the bruises on my face? *You put on the powder*, was his solution. So I put on the powder. I told Sonja that she too had blood on her face. She had bitten her lip so hard she had drawn blood. Sonja, always meticulous about her appearance, shrugged.

We were too frightened to feel relief as we descended the staircase. Brother Bear was in the lead. What if he got to the door only to lock it and laugh at us, pleased with his joke as he forced us back for another round?

Then we were out in the street. Just like that, nothing to it. This way, ladies, through the front door, that's it, mind the step.

The feeling of freedom was still guarded. It was overshadowed by the embarrassment of being seen with those two in public. They walked beside us like devoted boyfriends, Sonja and Brother Bear in front, the other one and I behind, so close our shoulders touched. I felt faint at the thought of running into somebody I knew. Whoever it was would smirk and know whom Lisa Grankvist had spent the night with. That's why we never went to the police. People would have found out. The shame would have annihilated us. We went up to their place of our own free will. People would have laughed and scorned us. *You went for coffee with two of the guys the next morning?*

Why didn't we cut and run? We were no longer ourselves. Some spring had broken and hampered natural movement.

There were a few people out and about, but nobody we knew. Our captors took us to the Mitt-i-City cafeteria, which lies between a small round fountain and a large square fountain up on the main square. Sonja and I made a beeline for the far end, sitting with our backs to the outside. The cafeteria has glass walls and anybody strolling by can see in. A scattered handful of people were having coffee. They were all strangers. Our secret was safe.

The waiter kept staring at my face while our escorts ordered ham sandwiches and Danish pastries. He knew what kind of girls we were, that waiter. Whores that deserved what they got, yes sir. Sonja and I ordered coffee, not looking him in the eye.

And there we sat saying nothing. It wasn't like there was anything to talk about. Brother Bear wolfed his sandwiches and pastry, slurped his coffee, burped like a damn caricature of himself. He stated with paternal pride, once again, what good girls we were. Sonja bitterly asked for a letter of reference. My heart stopped. But he didn't reply. He stared at her and got up, so abruptly his chair fell over, and indicated with a grimace that he had to deprive us of his company. Then he sauntered out. He didn't pay.

The relief at seeing the back of him was acute. As soon as he was safely out of sight we got up to leave too, but the other one, my rapist, grabbed my arm and said, *Please, you sit. I speak.* His voice came at me, unexpected and loud, like another slap. I stared at those tilted eyebrows, that birthmark, those cheekbones and those blue eyes that in a previous life had been to-die-for. Sonja glared first at him, then at me, and made for the ladies' room.

*I very sorry.* He looked genuinely distressed. *I not know you are virgin.*

I couldn't bear to look at him. I stared at my coffee cup and saucer. They were white. The waiter had spilt brown puddles in the saucer. I had put sugar in the coffee, but never touched it.

*I like you much. I want we be friends*, he went on as his hand came crawling across the table. It stopped beside my left hand, which recoiled and slid into in my lap. There was no point telling him that we were never going to be friends, or that I hated him.

I was so busy studying the details of my coffee cup, I never noticed Sonja standing by the table until she snapped, *Let's go!* I automatically got up and followed her out. *Please!* he called out as we left. I didn't turn around, not even to spit in his face.

We headed straight for the bus stop, walking with our eyes to the ground like two people searching for something valuable they'd lost. We didn't talk, but on the bus, as we crossed the bridge, Sonja took my hand and held it all the way out to her place. She had gashes on the side of her neck, crusted with dried blood. I never asked her how it happened, not then, and not when she sat on the edge of the bathtub and cried until she couldn't breathe.

Later that evening when I had to go back home, I told my mother that some drunk at Club 54 had slammed a door in my face as we were leaving.

My mother, not easily fooled, stared at me with cold contempt for a long time and said in her knowing voice, *You were drunk weren't you? You got so drunk you didn't know where you were going! Didn't you?*

So I confessed that, yes, that was indeed the case. She had found me out again. I apologized for my behavior and for thinking that I could get away with lying to her. The manic gleam in her eyes reflected the triumph she felt as she confirmed what she had always known: that I was no good.

# 6

**Pru, who had stared into the fire** the entire time, turned around then and let her eyes rest on her friend's face. Such a young face it was, with cheeks rosy from the fire still burning. Innocent, except for the eyes that shied away from Pru's, still imprisoned, still looking for a way out.

"Tell me something, Lisa," said Pru after a while. "Did you ever think of killing yourself afterwards?"

Only when Pru repeated her question did Lisa answer it. "Yes. Yes, I did. Twice. Once sitting on a train and once sitting in a cemetery. But never seriously, I don't think. I couldn't have been, could I, or I'd be dead. Sometimes I think that perhaps I should have."

"No." Pru shook her head. She rubbed a finger on one of the mirrors in the pillow. "I had an older sister," she said after a hesitant pause, gazing back into the fire as she spoke. "Her name was Miranda. When she was fourteen, home from school for the hols, our uncle, our mother's younger brother, raped her. He was thirty-six. Two of his friends watched and made comments, criticizing her performance. She told me this because she wanted me to be careful so that it wouldn't happen to me too.

Like you, she told nobody else. And like you, she was the one who felt guilty. A week later she slit her wrists in the rose garden, on the stone bench by her favorite yellow roses. I thought of that when you mentioned those flowers growing in the yard. To this day I can't bear to look at yellow roses.

"The gardener found her lying on the bench dressed in her nightgown and rubber boots. She'd downed most of a bottle of rare vintage of Jerez de Anada before cutting herself. The rest of the sherry had poured onto the path where she'd dropped the bottle before she curled up to die. Not only was it a rare vintage, it was the only bottle left. I swear on my sister's soul that our dear old pater was more upset about the sherry than he was about Miranda. I was ten at the time.

"Uncle Sebastian was cast from the bosom of the family, but he went free. I stabbed his left cheek with a pair of scissors after she died, but that was the extent of his punishment. They cast him as far as Australia, where he bought a sheep farm, got married and had three sons, the spit and image of their dear papa. They send horrid photos every Christmas of them grinning perfect-family grins under a cheerfully bright sheep-farming sky."

Miranda had been a blonde, quiet girl, artistic and dreamy. "Much like you," said Pru, turning towards Lisa.

"Is that why you like having me around?"

"I don't know why I like having you around."

"I like being around. I need being around."

"I know." Pru reached out and let a strand of Lisa's hair flow through the palm of her hand. "Her hair was this shade exactly, long and straight like yours." As she let go of the wheat-colored strand, she leaned forward and put her arms around her friend. Leaning forward, Lisa placed her arms around Pru and that's how they sat for a long silent time, warmed by the fire, not talking, foreheads touching, hair hanging around their faces like a curtain guarding a critically ill patient.

When they became two people again, Lisa said, "Isn't it

strange how when we share our stories of horror, they sound so trivial?"

"I know."

Pru, choking on a private rage, turned her face back to the fire and sat very still.

# 7

**L**isa decided not to touch the easily gained money from her casino windfall unless there was an emergency. It wasn't really her money and she knew it.

Sonja would not have approved. She had written once again to hammer into her errant friend's head that she was slowly but determinedly approaching pauperhood. Sonja wished to know when Lisa planned to grow up and start earning a living like the rest of the human race.

At once, as it turned out. This was what Pru's scheme had been all about. An acquaintance of hers, Estelle, had recently opened a boutique just off the King's Road in Chelsea, selling cheaper versions of "*Le style Anglais*; fab designer clothes, hats, shoes, the lot." The boutique consisted of one not very large room, and demand was already more than she could keep up with. Pru had told Estelle about Lisa's copycat crocheted dress, assuring her that it looked exactly like the real thing, whatever the real thing was, and Estelle had said in that case she was definitely interested. She asked to be introduced to "this Lisa, by all means."

The three of them met in a pub a few days later. It was twelve days before Christmas, a damp and cold evening. Lisa wore her crocheted dress to the meeting to advertise it. Her legs turned red on the way to the tube station. Pru wore one of Lisa's sweaters, a striped affair in various shades of purple and green. Estelle said the dress and sweater were *très* fab, and offered to sell Lisa designs on consignment.

"Ta-da! There you go, me old love," said Pru, the never-been-somber-in-my-life Pru, on the tube going home. "You're now in the fashion industry. Is that bloody enterprising, or what?"

"Thank you, Pru." Lisa was scared witless at the prospect of having to live up to her friend's expectations.

"That's quite all right."

Lisa stared at her to make sure she wasn't about to grow long black ears and webbed feet, plop a designer funnel on her head and put an end to this deceivingly pleasant dream. Pru demanded to know why she was being stared at. Lisa explained, hoping to confuse her.

"Darling," Pru said, "I shall have to extract the stone of madness from your head."

"Pardon?"

"*The Cure of Folly*, my dear. Hangs in the Prado. Did you think I did not know my Bosch? For your information, darling pet, the surgeon in that painting also wears a funnel on his head. A very funnelly person was our Bosch. Some claim the funnel hat to be the symbol of deceit. But trust me, I would never wear one around you."

Lisa's self-administered education had neglected that particular work. Nor had she realized that Pru, who was a few years older than her, had a degree in art and art history. Busy waiting on tables, she had never bothered to mention it.

"You never told me." Lisa felt the extent of her ignorance and didn't like it. Pru, unlike herself, was in possession of real knowledge, the clever kind that knows how to analyze and decide what symbolizes what, and why. The kind of knowledge that was like a whole other language that she did not understand.

"It never occurred to me that you might have an interest in

the works of Bosch." Pru sounded surprised.

"Well, I do." It was a short defensive statement.

"I had no idea. You never told me. Which is your favorite work?"

"*The Last Judgment*. The triptych, not the other one. I saw it in Vienna in April."

"Lucky you. I've never seen it. Care to tell me about it?" Pru, as usual, sniffed out when there was more than met the eye and ear.

"I'm not an art expert."

"Oh for fuck's sake, Lisa, don't be annoying."

"Well, it's long story."

"What's it about?"

"About *The Last Judgment*."

"I gathered that. What else"

"Vienna. And the empress Maria Theresa. And a teacup."

"Is that the teacup on your mantelpiece?"

"That's the one."

"I've often wondered about it."

"Well, now you know."

"An intriguing mix, judgments, empresses and teacups. Shall we go to a café and eat pastries while you tell me all about it?"

"It's what I used to do in Vienna actually. Eat pastries, I mean."

"All alone?"

"Of course I was alone. I didn't know anybody."

"Well, you're not alone anymore. Let's go. My treat. Your story."

"My stone to be extracted?" The idea appealed. She would get to relive Vienna one more time, eat pastries and talk of the details of the triptych. This story would be a pleasure to tell.

# 8

This was back in April. I had been traveling around with Mimmi
and Mick, as you know. Somehow, we ended up in Zagreb. From
there Mimmi and Mick went off to Venice to schmooze in gondolas. I didn't want to go to Venice, so I took the train to Vienna.

After the train crossed the border into Austria I fell asleep.
One moment there were peaks and valleys with little villages
and church steeples, the next I woke up and the train was standing empty by a platform where a sign read *Südbahnhof Wien*,
same as on my ticket. That's what made my visit so unreal. I
simply woke up in Vienna one evening. As if a ghost train had
transported me out of some dream and deposited me there.

I was the only one left on the train, so I got my stuff and hurried off. Forward, oh brave one, I cheered myself on. Off you go,
down that escalator into that cavernous hall below. I was scared.
Then I remembered that they spoke German in Austria. I would
be able to communicate.

We were forced to learn German for four years in high school,
you see. Our class had the misfortune to be taught by a large
ungainly woman named Mrs. Dahlgren. An odd creature, never
quite there, permanently floating in a dream world blessedly

free of students. She always perched on the edge of her desk, unaware that it gave us an excellent view of her of knee-length bloomers, the kind that nobody had worn since the turn of the century. She taught straight out of the book, ignoring the class, chanting every lesson like a sermon, with eyes half closed. When she pointed to you, you never knew whether to say amen or bend a verb. And German verbs are not very pliable. Hopefully the Austrians would not be as meticulous about grammatical correctness as old Mrs. D.

*Gehen, ging, gegangen,* I said, and down the escalator I went. In the terminal below I bought a map, checked the direction to the center and walked bravely into the hub of the dead empire that was Vienna on Easter Sunday. I crossed over to where a street-sign informed me that I was on the corner of Prinz-Eugen-Strasse and Landstrasser Gürtel. In front of me, across the grass, behind a wall, a palace sprawled in a vast garden. Kitty corner from the big ugly train station it didn't look quite real. The ornate wrought iron main gate was closed but one of the smaller gates stood open and welcoming. It looked truly magnificent. On each side of the central gate, a vampiric stone lion held up a golden coat of arms and a crown. Cherubs with raised arms offered gilded garlands.

I went in. There were other people strolling about, so I figured it must be all right. It surprised me that they let ordinary people like me walk around in that place. And what an amazing place it was, Pru! I was blissfully ignorant of the fact that this was the *Oberes* Belvedere, you see, the Upper one, I was enamored by the grandeur of it all, it was so haughty and so approachable at the same time. It was a moment ripe for a gushing commentary about baroque splendor, had I but known what "baroque" meant. I didn't learn that until a few days later in a guidebook.

On the other side of the palace was another spread of garden, full of statues and fountains and spring flowers. At the farthest end there was another, smaller palace, the *Unteres* Belvedere. As if one palace wasn't enough. Over on the horizon I could see the *Wiener* skyline full of spires and domes and columns. It looked like they were poking through the fabric of time from centuries long gone. Beyond the skyline stretched a shadowy outline of mountains. I had never seen anything like it. The sun was setting somewhere to the west of the largest dome, the one that would turn out to be the Hofburg. Carting my heavy suitcase like a refugee, I exited the palace gardens at the other end, reluctantly.

I continued down to the circle of streets called the Ring. Just before it sank from view, the setting sun lit up the golden ornaments on a roof ahead of me, spotlighting a performance that has been ongoing for centuries. Roofs in Vienna, I discovered, were crowded places, full of all kinds of goings-on. Who sculpted all that stuff? Do you know? How many artists had plunged to their death from those heights? Or did they do their work on the ground and have the finished product hoisted up? Those opulent roofs teemed with cherubs and putti and gargoyles, naked men and women with sheets draping their private bits, heroes on horses, suffering martyrs, winged creatures, wingless creatures, soldiers in plumed helmets, shields and swords at the ready, chariots, angels blowing trumpets, urns and eagles, you name it.

I felt as though I'd left the real world behind and entered a gentler place where every detail held profound meaning. I trotted on in the middle of it all, heading west, small and humble beneath all those architectural peacocks. Over to the right the spires of Stefansdom stood silhouetted against the evening sky. Behind its spire a cloud cover was heading my way. I hoped it wouldn't rain, I had no place to stay. All around me the Viennese went about their business. They seemed a richer, more self-satisfied lot than the people, of the city I had just left. Better fed, better dressed people, confident of their place in the scheme of things in the seat of the former Empire.

I wish I knew how to make you understand what it felt like to be as completely alone as I was walking the streets in a place where I had arrived an hour earlier. It subdued sound, that feeling.

My suitcase was getting heavier by the minute. At Rathausplatz I got off the Ring and headed further west, following some instinct perhaps. I had no idea where I was, or where I was going, but I crossed a street called Landesgerichtstrasse, mainly because I could pronounce it. A minute later a small sign halfway down an unassuming street caught my eye. *Pension Bauer* it said. I knew at once it was the place meant for me. Don't ask why. I went straight there.

A big heavy wooden door led into a long dark entranceway. I groped around for the light switch and found it by a sign pointing to *Pension Bauer, 3:e Stock*. It was up three flights of cold stone steps. It echoed down the stairwell each time I banged the suitcase against a step. I knocked on the door and a woman in her sixties wearing a bright red housecoat opened it, a napkin in one hand, a wonderful smell of food wafting out behind her. I realized how hungry I was. I had not eaten all day.

When she heard my carefully pronounced *Haben Sie bitte ein Zimmer?* she smiled a jovial smile and nodded. *Kommen Sie doch herein, Fräulein!* She waved her napkin about and seemed delighted to see me. It wasn't tourist season, perhaps business was slow. Maybe she'd invite me to dinner? I wished I'd known how to say *Please feed me before I faint.*

I stepped into a long hallway. It was pleasantly uplifting to discover that my high school German was functional. I could actually communicate with this woman. We would never exchange profound philosophical insights, but we did discuss the price of a room and the length of my stay. In days to come we would also swap pleasantries about the sights of Vienna, the weather, the museums, how my day had been, and did I eat properly?

Frau Bauer glanced at my passport, handed it back and asked, a bit perturbed, *Sind Sie doch ganz allein?* I confessed that, yes, I was all alone, that I had no parents. Such is life. Hearing this, she let out a sigh so deep she deflated a size or two. She patted herself on the cheek and waved the napkin about some more, shooing away all the sadness of life.

And what was I doing in Vienna all alone on Easter Sunday? I told her I had traveled there in order to visit the many art museums. Rumor had it they were quite magnificent. *Ganz prächtig* were the words that came to mind, and they did the trick. She nodded in profound agreement. I explained that I was an art student studying in London and that this was an educational trip. The information made Frau Bauer look very serious, for she had, as it turned out, immense respect for *Kultur*. I can be quite a proficient liar when inspired, in case you didn't know. Then Frau Bauer brought me down the hall to the most peculiar room I had ever seen. It was enormous and stuffed with furniture and odds and ends. Three tall windows faced the street and each windowsill was crammed with old books, one row atop another. Intricate moldings curled around the door and the high ceiling. It looked like a ballroom turned storage room for a theater, filled to the brim with massive old furniture that would have looked spot-on in some festive operetta. There were no less than five beds placed like they'd been thrown in blindly and left where they landed. Everything was very ornate. I thought, Frau Bauer must like to hoard things. Maybe she was stark raving mad and planned to store me there too. Maybe nobody left her *Pension* alive. I suggested that the room was maybe a bit big for only one person? A cubicle with a hard cot would suffice. She said *Asch!* and waved her napkin like she had a thousand rooms just like it.

The room was remarkably inexpensive, so I settled right in. I soon grew very attached to my eccentric boudoir. It suited the chimerical state of my existence. I should have stayed there, dressed up in nineteenth-century costume and become part of it. There were four cracked plaster statues of famous composers keeping me company. I recognized Beethoven at once, and later on, Mozart and Schubert, but I was never sure about the fourth one, so to make up for it I let him wear my father's beret at night. As it made him look French, I called him Pierre.

Apart from the five beds and four statues there were two large armoires of dark wood, four ornate dressers with brass handles and elaborate fittings, one with a marble top. On an oak chest covered with an embroidered tablecloth with fringes, sat an ancient lace-making apparatus with spools still full of silk thread. There were half a dozen mirrors on the walls, making sure I would never lose sight of myself in that particular chamber. There were shelves full of more books, many written in old German, a spinning wheel, several small tables with empty vases, and a dining table holding an assortment of tasseled lamps. The remaining space was fought over by a posse of fat cherubs, children playing violins, flutes and accordions, soldiers on horses charging into battle, not to mention a coterie of ladies and gentlemen of the court. They were scattered over every available surface. On one of the beds lay a shepherdess holding a baby lamb. Her head had broken off and she lay staring at her own butt. I picked up the pieces, fitted her head loosely to her body and put her on top of some books in the nearest window. Five minutes later her head crashed to the floor and broke in half. I left her there.

Each bed was decorated with velvet pillows, embroidered pillows, satin pillows, brocade pillows, all of them dusty. That night, trying to forget that I was starving, I did a bit of redecorating, putting lamps in strategic spots on dressers and tables where the cords would reach. I had to push some of the furniture around. Then I lit all the lamps and watched their pools of light create shadowy corners, intimate little bedrooms.

I decided to spend the first night in the bed nearest the window, hoping I would wake up in a different age and hear horse-drawn carriages go by in the street below.

I seemed to be the only guest, apart from an elderly gentleman, who was dressed as if it were indeed the nineteenth century. Sometimes he came hobbling down the hall tapping a cane. When we first met he bowed his head and said *Grüss Gott, Fräulein*, so I parroted *Grüss Gott, mein Herr*. I wasn't sure if that was the correct way to greet a gentleman from a previous century, but he seemed happy enough. Late at night there came the faint echo of a soprano hitting the high notes in his room. He kept either a gramophone or a gifted mistress.

The next day I discovered that the floor above was also part of the Pension. It had been taken over by a group of black musicians from the States. They were constantly humming or singing whenever I met them, always doing the boogie-woogie up and down the stairs. Now and then one of them would come bouncing past me on the stairs carrying a saxophone or a trumpet. They called me honey and offered me sticks of gum, as if I were a homeless orphan in some country they had just liberated.

I spent the first day walking the streets, studying an old guidebook Frau Bauer had lent me. There were three facts in the guidebook that fascinated me. One was that the Turks had introduced coffee to Vienna during the siege of 1529, which made me wonder, not only what the Viennese drank before that, but what would have happened if the Ottomans had not been in the mood for a scrap that time? I bet you never thought of that. What if the Turks had been a mild-mannered lot that preferred to stay home and potter in the garden, giving rise to expressions like "as timid as a Turk"?

The second intriguing tidbit was the fact that Empress Maria Theresa had given birth to sixteen children. Or archduchess Maria Theresa, as had been her title during her childbearing years. Sixteen children! I became obsessed with her teeth after learning about that excess. One of my aunts told me once that every time you have a child you lose a tooth. If this were anything to go by, the good Empress would not have had too many pearly whites to chew her schnitzel with, would she? I tried to find out if my hypothesis was true but discovered, studying various portraits in the hushed rooms of the citadels of *Kultur*, that imperial folk kept their lips clamped shut when being rendered immortal on canvas. The brush strokes depicting Maria Theresa showed a powdered wig, a plump and pleasant face with a double chin, her eyebrows thin elegant semicircles, a smile on her cupid's lips. But her mouth was firmly closed. Now I knew why: she had very few teeth.

You have an art degree, you must have noticed? No?

Never mind. It was the third piece of information that grabbed me by the shoulders and shook me till my eyes popped. The triptych *The Last Judgment*, Bosch's original work, was located right there in Vienna. At the *Akademie der bildenden Künste* on Schillerplatz. I would be able to see the real thing! I'd had no idea. It had never occurred to me that these works actually existed in the here-and-now. You see, I grew up trying to draw images from the works of Bosch and Bruegel, but I won't go into that right now.

Frau Bauer instructed me how to get the *Akademie*. I was at the gallery when it opened in the morning, breathless with expectation. It wasn't really a gallery, it was an art school. The *Gemäldegalerie* itself was unassumingly tucked away on the top floor like it was no big deal. I paid a few *Schillings* and walked in. And there it was, sitting in the middle of a small room, lit up with spotlights. *The Last Judgment*. Oh, Pru, it was such an incredible sight! I think I curtsied before it. When I stepped back to look at all three panels at once, I couldn't, it was too overwhelming. I had to divide it up, travel through it slowly, panel by panel, demon by demon.

That first morning I studied the left side panel where Christ creates Eve and she and Adam eat the forbidden fruit only to be chased out of the Garden of Eden. My study raised a string of unanswered questions. Maybe you can answer some of them?

Why does the sword-wielding angel chasing them have black wings? And what about all those black rebel angels falling like manna from heaven? Considering how many of them there were, was heaven left empty after their eviction? And if they were so bad, why were they let into heaven in the first place? Did they metamorphose into the demoniacal hybrids of fishes and birds and humans in the center panel? Is that black cat-like creature atop the cliff sitting with its arms stretched towards heaven welcoming the black angels? And what is that nasty-looking owl on the naked tree branch supposed to represent?

And why is Christ wearing a red robe?

Something else struck me. Despite its Christ and the Garden

of Eden, and despite its heaven and hell, the triptych did not seem to me a particularly religious work. It couldn't have been or it wouldn't have fascinated me. It was more a depiction of the cold indifference of cruelty. It reminded me of The Mean Hombre and Brother Bear. And only an indifferent God would be able to sit on his comfy cloud and do nothing while all that evil went on below. Consequently God is cruel? Thus religion is the source of evil, and there you go? I don't know, I'm a Lutheran who never went to church.

Maybe Bosch did not believe in God. Could that be? Was my initial impression as a very young child not far off the mark? Had Bosch had lots of fun painting those pictures? You smile, Pru. Does that mean you agree?

I devoted the next three days to the center panel and the day after that to the right panel. The guard came to check on me the second day, but he could tell I was in a state of slack-jawed awe and an unlikely candidate for trouble. I wasn't disturbing anyone, there was almost no one around to disturb. Still, by the fifth day I was afraid the guard would frisk me, or kick me out, before I was finished with the right panel. I'd go up close and study every morbid detail, every hairline crack in the paint, back up and sit down at a distance and stare at it some more, up and down like a yo-yo.

And every day I was pained by the knowledge that my father had missed out on this, every day I wished he had been able to use his passport at least once, to sit there beside me and gaze in wonder at his favorite work of art. It would have made him so happy. Bosch was one of his favorites, you see.

No, it's okay, I'm not really crying.

Only my father's beret got to be part of the experience. I wore it, you see. I could have brought his teeth along too, but was afraid, in case I got frisked.

Yes, I have his false teeth, wrapped in a handkerchief, if you must know. I thought once that that they looked like the smile of a Cheshire cat and figured if the cat could join its smile, then so could my father.

But never mind that.

I sat before this judgment pondering, day after day, which punishment would be doled out to me. Sautéed in a frying pan? Boiled in that cauldron in the room where the damned hung from the ceiling waiting their turn? Thrown into a water barrel where dragons went bobbing for sinners? Shoved directly into the teeming pit by pecking birds?

Judging by Heaven in the center panel, I would not be sent an invitation. It was not a crowded place. There was Christ in his red robe, the Virgin, and St. John, heaven's regulars, four angels with white wings busy trumpeting, but only a mere handful of saved souls. It looked like one of those intimidating exclusive boutiques where ordinary people never dare even window-shop, where there are always more snooty sales clerks than customers, and you wonder how they manage to survive charging prices ordinary people can't afford.

It's a bit how I feel about my garden, come to think of it. Few are worthy to be let in. Maybe God is a private sort of person. A loner.

I think guilt is like a sixth sense, stemming from some part of the human Ur-psyche that has not had the courage to evolve, that still crouches in the scorched scrubland where witchcraft and devilry stoke the fires of fear.

During my studies I discovered something. There was a lack of terror in the faces of the sinners, a lack of any emotion at all. Was it due to resignation or indifference, or had the sinners reached a destination beyond fear? Were they already dead and therefore immune to ordinary pain? Did they not scream in fear because they knew they were guilty and had it coming? Remember the naked men speared by the bare branches of a dead tree? Their faces are utterly void of expression. The young boy being barbecued on a spit by that blue-faced crone, his face is as calm as if he's sleeping. Yet these sinners are all trapped in a torture factory. Not even in the third panel do the damned look too perturbed, waiting to be hurled into the pit. Only one sinner in the crowd is wailing in terror. The face of the naked woman being carried by a slavering ape-like demon towards the pit shows no emotion. I would never be able to take punishment looking that detached.

In the right panel, is that head devil watching over the proceedings Satan himself? Remember his turban and glowing night-light eyes? He looks kind of silly, doesn't he? He really ought to be more imposing, sitting in the center of that fiendish place where nothing remains but eternal night and hellfire, don't you think? And how come there is a ship in the background? What does it symbolize? Why does everything have to symbolize something?

You know that demon with a trumpet coming out his butt? What's he tooting?

Oh Pru, there was so much I didn't know, that I still don't know. But until then I had never wanted to know much, you see. All I had ever wanted was to be a little bit happy.

On the third day I had to get up and take a walk around to see what else was in the gallery. That's when I discovered that there were two paintings on the back of *The Last Judgment*. To the left the rich merchant Bavo of Ghent stood straight and powerful, a hawk perched on his hand. To the right St. James of Compostela was on a pilgrimage in a simple sackcloth robe, a staff over his bent shoulder. They were almost life-size, two apparitions drained of blood, as pale as if all the color had been sucked out of them by the hell on the other side.

If you folded the side panels the two would stand side by side, one rich and one poor. Like you and me.

It was in one of the other rooms that I came upon another portrait of my favorite royal. She looked older in that one, a dowager Empress with three chins. Her smiling mouth was still shut. She was dressed in frothy clouds of lace that looked so real I wanted to touch it, straighten bits of it out, tidy her up. There was a blush of red about the nose indicating that the good lady was not averse to swinging a goblet or two. I had grown quite fond of the woman, especially after finding out, leafing through a book in a bookstore, that she had put a stop to witch burning in her empire.

After studying *The Last Judgment* in detail for five days I promised myself not to go back again, but I did anyway, on my very last day in Vienna, saying a brief *wiederseh'n* to it and the Empress. It seemed good manners.

I was very proud of myself for studying art.

When I left the museum I always had a *Weisswurst* at some *Wurst*-stand, eating it on the sidewalk in the spring winds, pretending to be Viennese, then I spent the mid-part of every afternoon in a *Konditorei*. There was one close to the *Votivkirche* that I especially liked. It was an old fashioned room, all dark mahogany, with stained glass windows, high ceilings and a quiet private atmosphere. White-haired men reading books, that kind of place. A woman wearing rings and bracelets always sat at the same table by the door, always with a piece of *Torte*, playing with her little fork. I thought if she could sit alone, so could I.

Having nobody to talk to made me feel mute so I made up for it by eating pastries. I had *Mohnkuchen* and *Pariser Spitze*, *Nusskuchen* and *Linzer Augen*. I ate *Sachertorte* and *Esterhazy-schnitte*, *Kardinaltorte* and my favorite, *Biedermeiertorte*.

You may smile, Pru, but I'm telling you this because pastries were a very important part of my experience. They consoled me.

When I was up to my ears in empty calories, I spent the rest of the afternoon walking off the excess. This was my big walk of the day and it lasted well into the evening. I walked out to Schönbrunn Palace and back the first day. The second day I made it out to the Prater where I spent fifteen minutes staring up at the giant Ferris wheel, having a *Wurst* before retracing my steps.

I liked to think of my friend, the Empress, and how she had once traveled those streets in a royal carriage pulled by white horses, on her way from Hofburg to Schönbrunn, smiling at her subjects with closed lips.

It was one afternoon on the Graben that a cup in the window of a tea shop caught my eye. It sat perched on its saucer on a high shelf, as on a throne, surrounded by a court of fancy jars of tea. I heard it calling my name, this beautiful, very regal teacup, deep blue with a gilded rim and a small rose pattern in a band below the gold. It was quite large and had a nice round shape as if brought up on cakes and cream. An imperial teacup it was, reminding me of the amply rounded Empress in her frothy lace.

Well, you've admired my cup and saucer, so you know what I mean.

I shivered as I stood staring at the cup, like an urchin pressing a snotty nose against the window of a rich man's shop. The sun had huddled in a cloudmass all day and it felt like winter. Cold, gray, what did I care, as long as that cup became my very own. I had no idea why, but it was going to be the first of my possessions, the first objects to define my new existence, whatever it would turn out to be. One day people would say, *Yes, I remember Lisa Grankvist. She had this beautiful teacup she bought in Vienna when she was young.*

So I entered the shop, propelled by my sudden urge, and said "*Grüss Gott*" the way I had learnt from my nineteenth-century gentleman friend. Pointing to the window I said, *Die blaue Tasse, bitte.* I felt rather clever when I was rewarded with a friendly smile from the woman behind the counter. *Eine elegante Tasse, nicht war?* I could tell she approved of my choice.

After she removed it from the shelf she let me hold it. The cup sat in my cold hands, surrounded by my bitten nails, looking haughty, very *Wien*, very expensive. It was perfect. *Angenehm*, I said, like I was some kind of connoisseur, hoping the woman had not noticed my ragged nails. She packed the cup and saucer in a sturdy box, wrapped gold paper around it and tied it with ribbons. Anything simpler would not have been good enough. I also bought some fancy tea in an attractive wooden box painted with Chinese motifs. The idea was that when I found a home I would drink fancy tea out of my regal cup every day. When the fancy tea was gone I would buy new tea and store it in my beautiful jar. Only I don't dare use it for fear of breaking it.

I carried my new treasures home to my theater storage depot and placed my imperial teacup on one of the dressers where the evening sun would highlight it and inspire royal dreams.

I stayed at Frau Bauer's for eight nights, picking a different bed each night until I tried them all, then starting over. My original plan had been to stay only a night or two, but I found it impossible to leave. It was mainly *The Last Judgment*. You have no idea how much my father would have appreciated my detailed study! Or how good it felt to be able to do it for him. For that was part of it, I think, giving him this delayed gift.

But it was the city too, my eccentric storage depot and Frau Bauer. She always came running to the door to see if I had had a pleasant day. Had I eaten good Austrian food? Which museum had I visited? Which paintings had I liked the best? I never told her about my special relationship with Bosch. It was too private. Instead I told her that I liked the portraits of *Die Kaiserin Maria Theresa* the best. *Schön!* She'd sigh and nod as if she'd known her well. *Schön!*

Still. I had known all along that I would have to leave at some point, so on the seventh morning I forced myself to go out and buy a train ticket for the following day. Onwards, brave Lisa, kind of thing. Then I left and came here.

# 9

**L**isa left out the details that did not add to the lightness of the tale. No point bothering Pru with details that lack charm, vignettes that had nothing to do with art, Empresses and teacups.

The last afternoon in Vienna she had been restless, sitting in the silence of her ballroom-size storage depot. In order to tire herself out, she had walked all the way out to Grinzing on the northwest edge of Vienna where the hills and the vineyards took over. It had been a long, long walk, and early evening by the time she had found herself on the old main street lined with *Weinstuben* and *Weingartens*. It had been too cold to sit outside in the wine-gardens, but through the open windows of the *Stuben* she had seen people stuffing their faces, drinking wine out of glass mugs and listening to *Wienermusik*, looking jolly, many of them singing along to the music.

Every *Stube* had been full of people sitting around large tables, surrounded by family and friends. She had not gone inside anywhere. She would have liked to, but would have felt foolish sitting all by herself, swinging a mug, trying to look festive. Standing out in the street of the once country village, she had listened to a violin and an accordion play La Paloma, remembering how they used to play that song when she went dancing at the open-air dance pavilion at home on Saturday nights. Back in another life, two years earlier, when she was sixteen.

She too had danced the tango once, usually on the toes of some pimply drunk.

For a long time she had stood rooted to the spot. It had grown dark by then, and chilly, still she had stood there, like H.C. Andersen's poor little match girl. Then the violin and accordion had struck up Du Schwarze Zigeuner and all at once she had seen her mother sitting at a table laid with a white tablecloth, a table covered with plates and glasses, at some party in a distant past. Her mother looking blissful, humming along with the music, swinging from side to side on spreading thighs squeezed into a shiny party dress, her cigarette burning in its wooden holder. Beside her, in his best suit and tie, Lisa's father sitting quietly smiling. It could have been a smile of indulgence, seeing his wife in a rare moment of good cheer. It could have been a smile of embarrassment and shame. Lisa had closed her eyes for the vision to pass.

Eventually a stingy wind from the hills had swept the length of the street, cleaning it of unwanted debris. She had left in a hurry with a lump in her throat, like an unyielding piece of Torte gone bad, catching the last tram back into the city. The night had grown colder still by the time she got off. The streets between the tram-stop and the Pension had stretched deserted into darkness. She had expected to hear a hollow echo of her steps as on a stage, where no matter how real the set looks, everything is illusion.

She had decided to spend her last night in the bed by the window where the streetlight fell on her feet, the window where the body of the headless shepherdess had come to its final rest, thinking, "Tomorrow will be my last day in Vienna. In the evening I will catch the overnight train to Paris and this will all be over."

She had fallen asleep at some point, but woken up again at three o'clock in the morning, desperate to pee. The hallway was a dark and unheated tunnel. She had tiptoed through it fast, the floor was cold, into the lavatory, where she had fiddled with the switch to no avail. The bulb had burnt out. While fumbling in the dark for toilet paper, there had been a discreet but demanding knock on the front door. It was a big wooden door, even a timid knock echoed magnified down the hallway. She had nearly fallen off the toilet in fear.

Had they caught up with her? Were they coming to get her? Could they do that in Austria? Was it the Yugoslav police or demons in funnel hats, hags with blue faces waiting out there?

Footsteps had hurried past the toilet. There had come the sound of Frau Bauer's hushed voice, not sounding at all frightened. It had been answered by the voice of a man. Lisa had strained to hear what they were saying, glad the toilet door was locked, and had heard Frau Bauer ask the man if he had had any trouble crossing the border, understanding the words *Probleme* and *über die Grenze*. The man had replied that *alles* had gone *ganz gut* all the way from Budapest to Vienna. Frau Bauer had inquired where he was planning to go next.

He was heading for America, he had a *Schwester* in New York, although he wasn't sure about his sister's whereabouts in that large city. Frau Bauer's voice had sounded optimistic, reassuring. She had a contact over there, she would give him the address. Did he need *Geld*? No, he would not take money from her. Frau Bauer said she had a room ready for him. Would he like some food, perhaps a cup of tea? He had eaten, thank you, but a cup of hot tea would be *wunderbar*.

As their footsteps passed the lavatory, Lisa had overheard something she had not quite understood, catching only part of the sentence before the voices had disappeared into Frau Bauer's private quarters and the night had grown silent once again.

She had not dared flush the toilet before scurrying back to the safety of the furniture storage depot to get out her dictionary and look up the words. The man had worried about leaving his grown-up daughter behind in Budapest. *Meine erwachsene Tochter*, married with a small child.

He had escaped from Hungary into Austria and come to this *Pension* where he had been expected. He had had to leave his daughter and grandchild behind. He was on his way to the United States to look for his sister in New York.

Lisa had realized that it was a destination for people traveling an illegal underground route through the Iron Curtain. They had something in common, Lisa and that faceless man, but she did not want to think about that. She had lain awake in the third bed thinking what a tauntingly peculiar world it was. Over on the nearest dresser a band of cherubs had laughed and frolicked in the light from the lamppost outside. The old man had long since turned off his gramophone and the night would have been free of any noise at all, had it not been for the sound of Lisa wailing with her face stuffed into a dusty velvet pillow.

The following evening she had locked her suitcase, grabbed her beret off Pierre's plaster head and gone knocking on the door to Frau Bauer's private apartment. She had expected the good lady to look secretive or preoccupied, distant, as she was harboring a fugitive, but she had been her same jolly self, patting Lisa's cheek several times, fondly. She had wished her well and made her promise to come and visit again soon. Lisa had assured her she would, if she could stay in the same room.

"*Immer, mein Kind.*" Always. But, she had indicated, putting her fingertips at the corners of her mouth, Lisa must learn to smile.

Then had come time to leave. She had walked through the spring evening, her suitcase heavier now it held an imperial cup and saucer and jar of fancy tea. The chestnut trees in Vienna had been in full bloom, the flowers the same blushing pink as the ones in Zagreb, not white like the one in the park across from what had until recently been her home.

At *Westbahnhof* she had stopped to remove a letter from her handbag. She had torn into many small pieces, dropping them like a sudden snowfall into the wastebasket inside the entrance to the station. They had fallen leisurely onto a half-eaten apple, an empty beer bottle, and a crumpled *Die Zeit.* Some of them had stuck to the apple.

*Auf wiederseh'n!*

Leaving this hand-written last remnant of her old life behind, she had gone in search of the train to Paris, not to stop there, but to continue straight to London. Not to go to art school though. At the time she had had no idea what she was going to do.

"Whatever it turns out to be," she had told herself, "I have not only dad's tools, his beret and his teeth, but my imperial teacup and Viennese education in Empresses and demons to get me started. I'm not entirely without means."

The following afternoon she had arrived in London.

# 10

↓

**N**ow that she was a *bona fide* designer, mere synthetic yarn from Woolworths would not suffice. She took the tube into the city and went upmarket to where prices were more forbidding. To celebrate her change in status she also splurged on a pair of celebratory purple suede boots.

The following day she spent alone on the new soft white carpet in her room, matching colors and drawing pictures. Both hibiscus bushes were in bud. In the garden a southern wind was twirling the fallen leaves from the apple tree in a last dance. Later that afternoon it started to rain. Soon the rain turned to sleet. Lisa, too busy to notice the weather conditions, skipped first breakfast, then lunch, nibbling chocolate biscuits as she played with her new toys. By evening she had to force herself to take a break and walked through the freezing dusk over to The Bedlington Café on St. Mary's Grove to grease her innards with fried eggs and chips.

She was in her pajamas and thick knee socks at ten o'clock that evening when Pru, Melvin and James appeared unannounced at her door waving three bottles of cheap champagne. They had decided to help celebrate Lisa's change of status, whether she wanted to or not, and there was no stopping them. They got drunk and sang along with Harry Belafonte upstairs until Jackson got peeved, stomped on the floor, and turned his record off. It was the first time Melvin ended up staying the night. Lisa felt awkward with the arrangement, but Pru insisted she keep him. From her demeanor Lisa suspected she had planned it all along, and did not understand why until later when she and Melvin lay curled like twin embryos on her bed, fully clothed, giggling, talking of nothing in particular, Melvin kissing her nose. This was what it was like to sleep in the same bed as a man and not fear for your life. To feel a little bit good, being with a friend. This was Pru's message to her.

In the very early morning while it was still dark, they made love. It was the first time she had had sex since she was raped. It was pleasant. Sex with Melvin was a relaxed exercise. "Let's do it again," she said, shy but eager, and he laughed and complied. Afterwards they dozed off, children, safe on the island.

The lusterless morning light inspired Melvin to talk philosophy during tea and toast. This was after Lisa mentioned her incomprehension regarding life's inexplicable plan for her. Melvin was of the firm opinion that this was nothing to fret over, whatever it was. Kierkegaard, the Danish philosopher, her fellow Scandinavian, he reminded her as if she already knew, wrote in his diary once that life, although it has to be lived forwards, can only ever be understood backwards.

"So you'll have to be patient, old girl. Years from now you'll be able to look back and check what it was all about and say, bloody Christ, I wish I'd known. Until then, darling, don't take it too seriously or the joke will be on you."

⊷◆⊷

Mulling over what Melvin had said, Lisa immersed herself in cautious bliss. But only knee-deep. No sense overdoing it. The thing was, as she had told Melvin, it had all been too simple, had all come about with such ease. Ease was unfamiliar, it made her suspicious, so, to make her days harder, and to feel more deserving, she got up at seven every morning, made tea and toast, crocheted and knitted, sketched and worked with patterns, color and texture combinations until early afternoon. Sometimes, if she was good, she allowed herself to listen to her favorite music. This routine was accentuated by the repeated question: Why were so many nice things happening to her? What was the catch?

Just before the Christmas holidays she took a sweater and two dresses to Estelle's boutique. "Fab!" was the verdict. "Make more, okay?" Two days after Boxing Day, Ram came knocking to say there was a phone call from "what I think is a French woman." Estelle was calling to say she had some lovely money waiting, and did Lisa have any more groovy clothes for her?

Lisa went at it with fury. She became a one-woman production line, getting up at half past six and working until five with only a half-hour break for lunch. Working hard agreed with her. She had labels made that said *la Lisa*. Now if people asked, "And what do you do?" she would have an answer. She would say, *avec* nonchalance, "I'm a fashion designer. How about you?" Hopefully Mary Quant would not be the first person to inquire.

One day she took time out to pop up to the Greek's for lunch and to announce that she was now a businesswoman. "Good for you, my pretty darling," said Dimitrios. He ordered Pru, who was serving wench that day, to give his business colleague an extra large portion of Greek lamb and okra on the house. Business people look after each other.

Mimmi wasn't at all surprised. "You see! I told you everything would be all right, didn't I?" Her very best Mimmi-smile never left her face. It was as if some burden had been lifted from her fragile shoulders. The next time she visited she was wearing a *By la Lisa* sweater.

Having had such luck never ceased to be a worry. Would devil hunters eventually sniff her spoor and track her down? She told herself this was paranoia, the result of having grown up with a mentally ill mother, and that paranoia is a punishment in itself.

# 11

**Sonja came for her first visit** in April, 1966. She stepped off the train and shoved the Grankvist herring jar into Lisa's hands, pretending to be resentful for having had to cart it along. Lisa knew better and hugged her hard, making sure she was real. Sonja didn't let her go for the longest time.

The white jar with its blue pattern stood on parade on the mantelpiece the same evening, full of flowers from the vendor outside the tube station. It added a dimension to the room that only Lisa knew about, this jar of long ago adorning the present. Well, Sonja knew about it too, to a degree, but she was stubborn. Sonja refused too see as nostalgia what she preferred to think of as a steady reminder.

Now and then, when she caught Lisa staring at the jar in that wide-eyed way she had when determined not to cry, Sonja looked away. Eight months older and two inches taller, Sonja always had a domineering streak when dealing with Lisa, but it was love for her friend that made her act that way, a misplaced sense of mothering. With Lisa she had always had to step in and set her straight, she was so clueless at times, that girl, so without direction, like a part of her had forgotten to grow up because nobody had guided her along the way, showing her what turns to take.

Watching that look in her friend's eyes, Sonja also knew when to step back and wait for the difficult moment to pass.

It was the year that, according to one headline, saw "Working Class Cultural Supremacy of TV, Stage and Film." Miniskirts shrank to an all-time short. Predators were having a field day. Fashion became more decorative and outrageous, trying to see what it could get away with, though Lisa never saw anybody wearing Paco Rabanne plastics and chainmail.

Pink Floyd became the house band at the Marquee. Donovan smoked pot on TV and the Establishment expressed suitable outrage. The Rolling Stones had their nineteenth nervous breakdown. The Kinks became dedicated followers of fashion. According to John Lennon, busy dropping acid, The Beatles were now more popular than Jesus. The statement was elegant in its simple truth, but the Americans took exception to it. Not that it mattered. As Melvin brought to their attention, Americans were a bunch of wankers anyway, so their opinion wasn't worth a bucket of piss.

And there was Lisa Grankvist, smack in the middle of it all, made to feel like she belonged, was part of the scene, fitting right in. She was deeply grateful for that. It had only been a calendar year since she had said good-bye to Sonja at the train station in Copenhagen before embarking upon an ill-planned and dangerous journey.

Now here stood Sonja, a mythical creature stepped out of a favorite tale, her honey hair darker after a long winter. Lisa, having stepped through some looking-glass, not quite as clueless as she used to be, presented her friend with this brave new world, heaped it upon her like a gift, asking, do you like it?

Sonja loved it. But she drew the line at meeting Pru, Melvin and James, and Dimitrios too, anybody she suspected having usurped her prominent position in Lisa's life, any deviant who was purposely keeping her friend from returning her rightful place. Sonja rested assured that she knew what was best for her friend. Quite likely she was right.

Leading a willing Lisa by the hand she retreated with her into a safe cocoon. Once again they were what? Twelve, thirteen? Laughing at everything, gossiping and playing records, as if any minute Sonja's mom would knock on the door and say, "Are you staying for supper, Lisa?"

There were moments when they happened to look at each other and their eyes, of their own accord, would mention the forbidden subject before they had time to turn their heads and pretend everything was as it should be.

The first week they saw Pink Floyd, the Spencer Davis Group and John Mayall's Bluesbreakers at the Marquee, keeping to themselves in a corner of the club, looking and listening from inside their cocoon, speaking only their own language. During the day Sonja marathoned Lisa up and down Carnaby Street and the King's Road, snapping pictures of every shop she spent her money in. After two days she needed another suitcase.

"Take mine," offered Lisa, convinced she'd never use it again.

At Estelle's, sensible Sonja lost control and bonded with a pair of knee-length silver boots half a size too small, deciding the next minute that a grotesque chrome necklace would complement the boots. She ended up looking like a spaceship-in-flight dominatrix.

"Where do you plan to wear that?"

"Come home and you'll find out. Your hometown's pretty wild these days."

"It is? Don't tell me you got a job in one of those 'massage parlors'?"

"Don't be disgusting. But guess who does? You know that woman with the big boobs who lives beside Yvonne? She works in one. It's true. And she's at least forty. She told Yvonne. They make movies there."

A dubious flavor of home.

What other news?

Time had not stood still to await Lisa's return. That came as a bit of a shock. It seemed so inconsiderate. Sonja had run into

Aunt Margit at Tempo department store. Aunt Margit sent her niece a message, "How come you never write anymore?"

~~⋅~~

Lisa had stopped writing because she felt bad about always lying. Her relatives, an unimaginative and gullible bunch, were under the impression that Signe and Johan's only child, Lisa, was going to art school in London. She had fed them the lie, served it up as an official document, and they, with their ingrained respect for authority, had swallowed it. She had not told them a true word since she left home.

She had four aunts. Apart from Aunt Margit on her father's side, there were her mother's sisters, Bojan and Gulli, and her mother's brother's wife, Aunt Stina. Three of them had seen her off at the ferry in October, 1964.

It had been a clear crisp morning with gulls shrieking loudly over a sea that had stretched a cold gray all the way to the horizon. Dark clouds had started to sweep in from the north as they stood on the quay getting ready to say good-bye. "It's gonna rain," Aunt Margit had said and started sobbing. Lisa had not let the tears move her, recalling that her aunt had cried harder still the previous spring when her neighbor's budgie died.

She had hugged the aunts hastily and boarded the ferry, a gust of wind shoving her up the gangway. Putting on a brave face, she had gone up on deck to shout a final farewell to the aunts, a brave adventurer jauntily waving her beret, but they had already left for the bus.

In Copenhagen she had stopped in at Magasin du Nord to buy several items that she would need in the coming months. A green winter coat, a pleated skirt and a white blouse, a bottle of perfume and a supply of Mary Quant make up, all according to plan. Afterwards she had gone for a stroll up and down Strøget, wafting perfume, before catching the ferry back home where she had headed straight for the station to hop a train destined for Hälsingborg where her friend Barbro lived. She had not left the country until March the following year. Her aunts had had no idea. They still had no idea.

There were a great many things her aunts would never know. The first of Lisa's letters had slid through their mail-slots dressed in English stamps, postmarked in England, all mailed by Mimmi who sent them on in a different envelope when she received them from Lisa in Hälsingborg. And the aunts, with the same sense of duty, had responded, though they never had a lot to say.

Aunt Gulli had written to inform her that little Inger had broken her ankle when she fell off the bicycle Lisa had left behind. "The tires weren't very good." Her tone had been reproachful. "On a cheerier note, uncle Henning is a new man since taking up the accordion." Lisa's accordion.

Aunt Stina had managed only one letter. The written word had never been her forte. Two pages torn from a notebook had informed Lisa that Stina's sister Emma's daughter, who was "only seventeen for crying out loud," had been "taken pregnant." Beware of boys, had been her dire message, or you will *for sure* get pregnant too. "Trust me, English boys are no different from Swedish boys."

Aunt Margit had written to say how much she missed Lisa, but only in her first two missives. Both had been rather short. The third one had announced that she had landed a new job in that shoe store near Triangeln and was real busy. Her fourth letter had contained big news. A widow for fourteen years, she had finally met a new man. His name was Evald. "Neither a drunk nor a pervert! How about that!" Evald was a taxi driver, a bit on the scrawny side, though nice enough. He was a widower with two grown sons, liked hockey, and danced a mean waltz. Post-Evald Aunt Margit had soon become preoccupied with her love life and her correspondence had fallen behind. She was a fine one to talk about not writing.

Aunt Bojan had written three times, mainly about the weather and chronic constipation.

By Christmas 1965, all correspondence had died what appeared to be a natural death. By then Lisa already had already begun to think of her aunts as a far distant memory.

Girlfriends were getting engaged and married, Sonja reported. One after the other.

"What about you?" Lisa had delayed asking the question. "Have you met anybody yet?"

"Me? You're joking!" Sonja's tone remained light, her laughter carefree. They didn't look at each other, in case their eyes would brush by the forbidden subject.

"So everybody's getting married and settling down except for us." Lisa laughed too, matching her friend's carefree tone.

"Seems that way."

"Well, we're only nineteen."

Sonja had cut her hair into bangs. They covered the premature lines on her teenage forehead. The lines she blamed on her irrational friend Lisa.

On May first, two days before Sonja was due to leave, Lisa, Mimmi and Mick treated her to a belated birthday present, "with love from London." They took her to the New Musical Express poll winner's concert at Wembley's Empire Pool. The Beatles, The Rolling Stones, Bob Dylan and The Who were all featured.

"This is too much!" screeched Sonja, stomping ecstatic feet in her dominatrix silver boots, chrome necklace thudding against her chest, tearing her hair out at the sight of Paul McCartney. It was a grand finale to her visit. Lisa triumphantly claimed the success of it as a personal accomplishment.

Sonja left on a rain-sodden evening. It was Lisa's turn to stay behind. Before getting on the train Sonja asked for the seventh time that day, "Why won't you come home?"

Lisa's response was vague and insufficient, but "not yet" sounded better than "I don't know how."

Sonja shook her head. As she boarded the train, she turned around and said, not without effort, "You should never have left. You've let them win." *Them.* The way she pronounced it gave the simple word a jagged edge. It tore at Lisa. *They* did not exist in this world.

"No," she said. She knew Sonja had not meant to leave her with a wound, and hid from her the fact that she had drawn blood. "You're wrong."

Sonja did not reply. Lisa watched her board, hoping she would never come back. There was something disturbing, something not right, about watching the back of a friend exit your precarious existence, telling you the enemy had won. It was like watching one of the walls of your room come tumbling down over your head.

When the train pulled out of the station in a cloud of steam obscuring Sonja's crying face in an open window, Lisa was already counting the days to her next visit. She took the escalator into the netherworld and caught the tube back to Chiswick where her room gaped empty. Sonja's chrome necklace was still lying on the bed waiting to be packed. Lisa picked it up and put it on. Then she got her yarns out of her two new baskets, spread them over the white carpet, sat down cross-legged and got to work matching colors. Sonja's necklace hung heavy on her chest.

# 12

Early on a Tuesday morning, two months after Sonja's departure, Lisa was in her garden weeding. In the summer she mixed work with gardening and liked to get an early start. Her tropical Chiswick island lay dewy and sweet under a mild sun. The scarlet and yellow columbines were extravagant that July, so exquisite she wondered if there wasn't some kind of God seeing to the details after all, some higher being secretly fertilizing spots of beauty at night. The asters were bloated with the goodness of the earth, the flowers on the rhododendrons hung so big and heavy they were in danger of breaking off their stems. In its special place, the mulberry sapling was undergoing a vigorous growth spurt.

She was telling it what a good little sapling it was, stroking its slender trunk, babbling baby-talk under her straw hat, when Mimmi appeared at the kitchen door. She waved and told Lisa to keep working, watching her from the doorway, her hands deep in the pockets of the same ratty cardigan she had worn on the trip to Yugoslavia. Her hair, tied back with a rubber band, looked greasy, her face was pale and unpainted. Only Mimmi could manage to look beautiful in a state of neglect.

"Say, Lisa, how about some tea?"

"Sure. Go fix it while I kill off these weeds. If I don't, my nasturtiums won't grow and cover my path."

"You don't have a path."

"It's a pretend path."

They had tea on the stone bench, sitting on two of the Indian pillows with little mirrors.

"I love it here so much." Sitting with Mimmi in the warm sun with birds twittering, flowers covering the garden like a crazy quilt, was surely paradise. Lisa's toes curled with pleasure. She leaned back in what might one day become a fluid gesture of great contentment.

"Your garden looks wonderful," said Mimmi and burst into tears. They were wild and sudden tears, making Lisa splash hot tea all over her legs. Mimmi never cried without a good reason, and she seldom had one, blessed as she was with that famous sunny disposition of hers. But no more. She had become homesick, she confessed, it was eating her up from the inside out. She wanted to go home, she had to go home, but the problem was Mick. He was going to be very hurt. Mimmi sniffled and hiccuped and cried some more. Mick loved her. To be loved was a terrible thing.

"I thought you loved Mick."

"I do. I did. I don't know . . . it's like I've started to grow up and he hasn't. It feels like I've already left him behind." Mimmi blushed at the admission of her treachery.

"Well, you were only seventeen when you met him."

"And he was nineteen. His mum had just died. We've been playing house ever since. Messy house, with ugly furniture that isn't ours."

"And now you're tired of it?"

"I just want to go home! I need to be with mom and dad and my sisters." She missed going with her parents to visit grandma and grandpa outside Skillinge, swimming with her sisters at Sandhammaren. "The water's always cold, but remember how white the sand is? And soft? How the sand dunes go on for miles and miles? The purple crocuses in the spring? How the sea stretches forever? Remember freshly smoked fish?"

"I do." Lisa had never been to Sandhammaren.

"I want to sit in grandma's garden and eat herring with sour cream and chives."

"With those tiny new potatoes with the skins still on?"

"Yes!" Mimmi hiccuped a trembling smile. "And dill. It's what we always have on Midsummer's Eve. They have a flagpole in the middle of the lawn and grandpa always hoists the flag that day. I missed it again this year. You understand that, don't you, Lisa?"

"Yes, of course." She turned her head towards the sun, pretending that's where her blush came from. Idyllic family life was an alien concept.

The day was already sadder, the sun less bright. All over the garden, flowers hung their heads while the girls smiled wistfully at each other, thinking separate thoughts, already creating distance. While Mimmi dreamt of white beaches and dill, Lisa thought of not having the goodness of Mimmi close by. Another wall would tumble. She asked her, could she at least leave her tatty old cardigan behind? To be remembered by? The request made Mimmi laugh in mid-sniffle, but she folded it and put it on the bed when she left, patting it like a faithful pet. Lisa wore it on chilly evenings until it fell apart.

⊷

A week later Mimmi was gone. She could not bear to face Mick and that terrible love of his, so she left him a note taped in the center of the TV screen where he'd be sure to find it: *Mick, I had to go back home. Please forgive me if you can. It doesn't mean I don't love you. I do. I'm so very sorry. Your own Mimmi.*

It was very unlike her.

Mick's cocky Cockney persona did not stand up to the loss of his beloved Mimmi. He slunk into the Greek's one night and sat whimpering in his beer, every bit a sad sod without pride. Pru, who was working the evening shift, phoned Lisa and begged her to come over and do something. She arrived to find

Mick slouched in a corner. He looked pitiful.

"Hello, Lisa."

"Hello, Mick." She wanted to pat him on the head and say, There, there.

"Did you know then?"

"Sort of."

"Bleedin hell, Lisa."

Mick downed his pint, calling it funeral ale, and grabbed Lisa's arm across the table. "Explain it to me."

"Explain what?"

"About Mimmi. About women. I'm a simple bloke. Happy with me work, me woman, a pint now and then. It's all the meaning I need in life. It's not asking for much, is it? I've still got me work and as many pints as I want, so how come all the meaning is gone then? Can you tell me that?"

"No, Mick, I can't."

"I catered to her every wish, only she was never very demanding, which made it difficult. But I always assumed she knew that I worshipped her."

"I know she did."

"Well, it was so bleedin obvious! Wasn't it? Or maybe she did know and just didn't give a toss? Is that it?" He let go of Lisa's arm and slammed a fist on the table. "Is that it?"

Lisa, not used to the drama of young men displaying broken hearts, told him that Mimmi did care an awful lot, she was Mimmi after all, but that when you are overcome with home-sickness, there's bugger-all you can do about it. You have to return to where your roots are. "It's in your blood, Mick, it pulls at you the way the moon does the ocean." The same moon that would reflect in the sea by a white beach when Mimmi sat eating herring and new potatoes with dill. Night would come to that part of the world, but in the summer it would never grow dark. The air would turn blue instead.

How could she make Mick understand that? The air never turned blue in London.

"What about you then, luv? Why aren't you overcome then?

How come there's no fucking moon pulling at you? Exempt, are you?"

"I have nothing to go back to. You know that." She didn't tell him how badly that moon pulled at times.

Mick muttered that it didn't make any fucking sense, banged his glass against his forehead and yelled for another vat of lager; he was that vulnerable. At closing time Lisa and Pru and Dimitrios had to drag him around the corner to Dimitrios' car and deliver him back to Tad Hall. When they carted him into the house he screamed. "No! Not up there!" before passing out with a whimper. They heaved him up the stairs all the same. The room exuded bitter neglect. Mimmi's note was still glued to the TV screen. Pru and Lisa read it and removed it.

"Poor bastard," said Pru.

Lisa called Mick several times over the next few weeks but he was never home. A few months later she ran into him at the Cromwellian. He was sitting in the bar with a girl named Ilke, a bottle-blonde Fräulein with nipples the size of Cuban cigars. She wasn't half as beautiful as Mimmi, and not a fraction as sweet.

Whatever fleeting happiness Mick found with his German blonde, or the subsequent series of nameless beauties, did nothing to lessen the shock when he learned that Mimmi was getting married to a good Swedish boy named Lasse. Rumor had it he hurled an amplifier through a window in a recording studio and went broke paying for the damage.

Shortly after that outburst, Lisa ran into him again at the Cromwellian one night. She had received a letter from Mimmi two days earlier announcing her upcoming nuptials and invitation to the wedding. As she was going up to the bar, there was Mick haunting the staircase, pale and restless, looking ready for a fight. He had lost weight, though the thin face rather suited him.

"Want to go outside and smoke a joint?" was his sullen greeting, so they did, sitting on the front steps watching the night traffic roll by. "Heard from Mimmi lately?" was his next question.

"Why?" She asked. "Have you?"

"She sent me an invitation to the wedding."

From inside the club, in a thoroughly insensitive bit of timing, came the sound of Percy Sledge wailing *When a Man Loves a Woman*. Mick gave up. He leaned his head on Lisa's shoulder and cried, quietly soaking her dress. She sensed that he, too, half way gone already, was slipping out of her life. Another wall was about to tumble.

And she hugged tighter the Mick she had met in Brussels two and a half years earlier. Mick, who had been there in her hour of need, who had helped her commit what she perceived to be an unforgivable crime.

# 13

It had been an interminable train trip from Copenhagen to Brussels. When she had finally escaped the train, struggling with her shoulder bag, her suitcase and her picnic basket, there on the *Bruxelles Midi* platform had waited Mimmi and Mick, just as they had promised. Angelical Mimmi, sweet beautiful Mimmi, grinning from ear to perfect ear, waving both arms in Lisa's direction. When men walked by Mimmi, they slowed their pace, their hearts softened. You could see it in their eyes.

Mimmi had run up to Lisa and hugged her hard. In her footsteps had followed the young man Lisa assumed was her boyfriend, Mick Barker, a cheerful one-man celebration of bad taste. His newly shorn head had been hidden under a garish, checkered peaked cap that perfectly matched his vest. The plan had been to look as respectable and middle-class as possible, and this had been Mick's idea of how a respectable gent traveled in Europe. For all Lisa knew, never having traveled, he was right. He had stuck his thumbs in his vest, looking lordly and pleased, rocking on his heels, beaming at her. Momentarily forgetting why they were there, she had allowed herself to laugh.

"Yer carriage awoits, miloidi." Determined to keep things

light-hearted, he had turned cockney porter, grabbing her suitcase, already her friend.

Holding on to her fancy picnic basket, Lisa had linked arms with Mimmi and they had followed their worthy gentleman companion outside, down the street to where a green tin can on wheels stood parked by the curb. It had clearly been built to hold no more than half a dozen eggs, and then only if two went in the trunk.

"This Dinky toy is our car? We'll never fit into that!"

"Nonsense," Mick had assured her, putting her suitcase in the trunk beside theirs. "It only looks that way cos it's a bleedin Renault. The French don't know how to build cars, do they? There's plenty of room, mind you, only you can't see it. It's a bit like the Tardis that way."

"The what?"

Mick had explained about a famous English doctor named Who, a man with unusual travel arrangements. Lisa, intrigued to be learning foreign culture already, had crammed the basket, the shoulder bag and herself into the back seat of the tin can. Mick and Mimmi had folded themselves into the front and slammed the doors. It had been very crowded.

Or, as Mick had put it, ever so bleedin cosy.

"Ready?" He had sounded jolly enough, but the gray eyes meeting Lisa's in the rear-view mirror had been somber. They signaled that he was as frightened as she was, and that if she wanted to change her mind he'd very much understand, but that now was the time.

"I'm ready."

"You sure now?"

"Yes. Yes, I'm very sure."

"All right, luv." He had started the car.

It had been a long trip down south. Nerves had grown more frazzled by the day, the border-crossing had been a torture. By the time they had arrived in Trieste, Lisa had been ready to fall apart. The effort of keeping in one piece had absorbed too much energy. Mick, more on edge than his male ego would ever admit, had asked the girls, Did they mind if he popped out for a quick pint?

By three in the morning he had not yet returned. They had had a run-in with a traffic cop earlier that day, a Mafioso-looking thug in black shades, who had menaced them with a traffic ticket and verbal abuse in Italian. Remembering that incident, they figured anything could have happened. By three thirty they had been sick with worry, convinced that Mick had had another encounter with corrupt gangster authorities and was rotting in jail. What if the police were to come to the hotel to check up on them?

A minute later Mick, in exuberant spirits, had stumbled in, wearing a pair of football shorts over his pants. In response to their question about his whereabouts he had erupted with heartfelt enthusiasm that Italians were his absolute favorite dagos. He had run into some football fans in a bar, see, where over several drinks they had managed to resolve their imagined differences and become brothers unto death. To celebrate this, "Mario, Carlo, Guido and a 'alf-breed named Donatello Perkins" had invited him to a restaurant to continue the brotherly love-in over large plates of seafood, bleedin shells and all. Mick had by then decided to stay in Trieste, to hang out with his mates and take in a game or two. Because, and here he had lit up, Juventus were playing in Turin next Sunday! Or was it the Sunday after? Whenever it was, his mates were going up on the bus and had invited him to come along.

Lisa had commented that she had never heard of that particular group and Mick, staggered by such ignorance, had made her endure a tedious lesson in the history of European football. "For you own good, luv."

At that point a bell had struck four and Lisa had pointed out that they were moving on the next day and that was that. They were getting this trip over with. He might be having a terrific time, but this was not a goddam pleasure trip. They were not here to watch football, and the sooner he got that through his thick English fish-and-chip skull, the better.

While listening to her, Mick had removed the football shorts and put them on his head. He had stood before her like a cheerful garden gnome. But he had not understood. "Why not make it a pleasure trip?" A bit of pleasure would make everything so much easier. Here he had performed a little dance to illustrate how joyous life could be given half a chance.

It had been only a matter of time before Lisa started cracking. "Fuck you, you stupid asshole!" (Her English had improved dramatically.) She had screamed and cried, sobbed and yelled. Mimmi, too, had burst into tears, and somebody had hammered on the door for them *per favore* to shut up or the *polizia* would come and straighten them out.

Mimmi had said, of course they should get this over with, of course it was driving Lisa mad. It was driving her mad too. Calming down, Lisa had sniffled how sorry she was, how very, very sorry. It had been selfish of her to drag them along on such a crazy caper, she should have known better, and could they ever forgive her? Should they split up in Trieste? Mick had clutched her in a brotherly embrace, and assured her that they should go on together, that he was a stupid bastard, and to pay him no mind.

"Crazy as it is, we're here for you, luv. I haven't forgotten that. And we've had a good time, haven't we? I don't regret a minute of it."

"Me neither," Mimmi's nodding had been a bit too emphatic.

Lisa had apologized again and again for having talked them into coming along. She had been truly selfish and insane to expect friends to take such risks.

Never mind that, she had not twisted their arms, had she?

They had made up. Lisa had padded back to her room and crawled into bed. It had been getting light by then. Somewhere out in the unknown city named Trieste somebody had been singing. She had felt equal parts stupid, guilty, horrible and scared. Listening to the unknown singer, she had tried to pray, out of sheer desperation, but little conviction, "God, if you exist, please let me die during the night."

She had forgotten she was in a Catholic country. Why on earth would a Catholic God listen to somebody born Protestant, raised heathen, a hypocrite sinner looking for an easy way out?

# 14

**Yes, she thought, as Mick sniffled,** his forehead pressed against her shoulder, when she had badly needed him, he had been there for his heathen sinner friend, trusting her blind conviction. He had carried her picnic basket every day on their forays in Zagreb, along the winding streets up in the old city on the hill. He had kept watch near the Palace Café while she stood on Strossmayerov trg shaking hands with a strange man who smelled faintly of alcohol. A man with a tooth missing.

Too many, still too recent, memories made a fragile dam burst. Lisa put her arms around Mick and joined in the crying. People stepped carefully around them. The joint got soggy, but they smoked it anyway.

During the week Lisa spent her days from early to late working in her room, or studio, as she referred to it, and tending to her garden, but on Friday night she and Pru dressed up and went out to play. Sometimes Pru dragged her out in the middle of the week.

On Friday nights they usually they went into Soho, to

the Flamingo or Les Cousins. Both clubs held all-night music sessions on the weekend, which meant they were able to stay in town all night and take the first tube home in the morning. Lisa preferred Les Cousins where the music, not as loud, tended towards blues and folk. Alexis Korner did the all night stints regularly and all kinds of people dropped in.

One night in September 1966 they were making their way down the stairs to Les Cousins. It was close to midnight and getting crowded. In front of them stood a black guy under a cloud of hair grown wild. He was carrying a Fender guitar. It kept poking Pru who finally gave it a healthy shove. The black guy twirled around and looked them up and down before treating Pru to a lewd wink. Pru looked highly amused, as always when ogled by the common man. This one was quite ugly to boot.

"Hey babe. What's your name?" For an ugly guy he did not lack confidence.

Pru introduced herself, countess-like, from far above. "My name is Prudence Spankmebottomhard. What's yours, my good man?" Only Pru could make moral lassitude seem like a virtue to strive for.

"Dick. As in Suck My."

"Pleased to meet you, mister Asinsuckmy. Is that an Armenian name?"

The black guy rolled his eyes and turned his back on the countess, who immediately forgot about him. There were several American blues people jamming that night; the place was hopping and sweating in thick clouds of smoke. Later on they saw the ugly black guy get into conversation with Alexis Korner. Next thing he had plugged in his Stratocaster and was playing. It was as if he had plugged in the whole jolting audience. Nobody had ever seen a guitar handled that way, never heard that kind of sound created by anyone. Les Cousins wasn't equipped to handle it, it felt ready to explode. The ugly guy, suddenly irresistible, said he had recently arrived from the States. He was a simple guitar-man, he said. His name was Jimi Hendrix.

Pru was transfixed. She looked so simple-minded she was

in danger of drooling down her purebred chin. She sidled up to him before he left, beating the crowds, and slipped him her phone number, doing something with her tongue in his ear.

A week later she called Lisa to report that she had spent the night having the most incredible sex with the guitar man. His real name was Johnny, which she thought utterly sweet, and adorably American.

In no time at all the guitar man became world famous and Pru declared her bed hallowed ground.

In March 1967 Jimi Hendrix set his guitar on fire at the Astoria. Pru heaved an orgasmic sigh watching the flames. In April, together with ten thousand other people, they attended the benefit for IT magazine that was "one of the defining moments of the hippie era in Britain" at the Alexandra Palace. When the spring morning dawned, Melvin carried Lisa piggyback along the littered pavements to the tube station.

Spring was followed by the Summer of Love, a parallel world where everyone was a hippie swathed in ethnic clothes of Indian cottons and brocade, headbands and tassels and flowing scarves. Everybody looked like ragtag gypsies, wishing they were. It was slow-motion romantic; at least until the scene went into freefall and drugs expanded minds until they popped like balloons. Life became *A Magical Mystery Tour* in a *Purple Haze*. To the question *Are You Experienced?* the answer was a self-indulgent affirmative.

In this parallel world, time was a series of historical cultural events, each trying to outdo the previous one. Lisa took note of these milestones, sensing she would not be coming this way again.

She was an excellent flower child, so thin and ethereal, gravity nearly lost its hold over her. Her hair flowed long and silky. Like everybody else she floated mindlessly along life's path towards some day-glo acid sunset, layers of transparent Indian cotton fluttering about her like so many psychedelic wings.

The scenery kept altering, becoming yet more unreal. They sat, the entire generation, suspended in that purple haze, swaying dreamily, striving for a higher level of consciousness as Ravi Shankar played another mind-numbing two-hour raga that everybody pretended to understand.

As a groovy person, Lisa had sex occasionally, in a pointless sort of way, and only with the odd male flower child that struck her fancy. Gentle boys with long hair and smooth hairless bodies. Off and on with Melvin, handily. He was safe and comfortable. Always with her eyes closed.

Pru nearly lost her job at the Greek's that summer. She was so stoned at work one day she insisted on force-feeding a customer who refused to eat his moussaka. Grabbing him by the hair, she yanked his head back and hooted, "Open wide, you yobbo bastard!"

James met a young man and fell in love. It came as no surprise to anybody. He had often mused, during bleary-eyed nights that, "You know, I wouldn't be the slightest bit surprised if I turned out to be a total poof."

Melvin got up most mornings and smoked a joint for breakfast. He turned twenty-four that year and, as he was fond of putting it, was busy watching his trust fund go up in smoke. "Inhale, darlings," he advised. "This is bloody expensive shit."

Had they kept their eyes open long enough, they would have noticed that everything was not fun and games. In May the Beatles stopped touring. Mick Jagger and Keith Richard went up on a drug charge. Brian Jones got busted. Late August the Beatles and Jagger ran off to Wales with the Maharishi.

"If the cultural heroes of our time are ready to believe in the pseudo-religion of some giggling con-artist in a nightgown," reflected Pru, "how precarious is the situation for the rest of us?"

It was a valid question. In three years Hendrix would be dead.

⊳◇⊲

Sonja came for another visit in mid-August. This time, as per request, she brought Lisa's father's art books. They looked smaller than Lisa remembered them, the pages not as glossy, but she clutched them to her heart, demons and all, and inhaled their musty smell. Again the two girls regressed into their cocoon. Lisa became the old Lisa for a while, pleased that she still remembered how.

But time had not stood still. Their eyes spoke less of forbidden subjects. Sonja never mentioned *them*.

On the Sunday before Sonja was due to fly back they went to a Jimi Hendrix concert. Lisa spotted Pru and Melvin in the first row, Pru's wild red mane pulsing in the strobe lights. Lisa and Sonja were tucked up on the second balcony like mice in the attic. Midway through the performance the lights went out, and in the darkness a voice announced that Brian Epstein had been found dead. As Epstein was Hendrix' manager, the concert was to be cut short, out of respect. They reluctantly got up and jostled with the slow-moving crowd. It was drizzling outside and the street was full of people. A television-crew had already arrived to film the audience exiting the concert, as though death might be cause for great excitement.

Sonja waved regally at a camera, jumping up and down like it was Mardi Gras, thrilled with this terrific, significant end to her holiday. Her face, preoccupied with getting the attention of a TV-camera, told Lisa that her best friend was a happy girl, and for the first time since leaving home, she felt an uncomfortable sting of resentment. It was a small sting, but a sting nevertheless. Sonja was leaving in two days, flying this time, going back to where she belonged. She had given up nothing.

Everybody had expected the Love Generation, gentle and sweet as it was, to dance forever on the dirty sidewalks leading towards new sensations. Seeking yet farther-out music, drugs more mind-blowing than the stuff of the night before, secure in the knowledge that this brilliant generation had found Truth in all its elegant simplicity and hung it around its neck among the cheap Moroccan beads. And being on the side of peace and love, how could they not be right?

There was a free concert in Hyde Park in June 1969. Donovan and Blind Faith were top billing. The papers said 150,000 people milled about. Melvin got stoned and fell down, almost crushing a toddler. The toddler had red hair. It stared at Lisa, mistaking her for the culprit, and burst out screaming. "He hasn't had his nap," apologized a freckled young woman and scooped him up. Lisa turned away without a reply.

On July 2 Brian Jones drowned in his swimming pool. Three days later Lisa joined her friends at the next free concert in Hyde Park. Mick Jagger read Shelley and pranced around in a little white dress. On stage, freed white butterflies escaped over the crowd. There weren't very many, most were already dead. It was a bleakly dishonest moment. Something wan and sad threw a shadow over the hot sunny day. It was a goodbye to what would never be again, only nobody knew it at the time.

Lisa didn't enjoy it. "That was downright weird."

Melvin agreed. "Things aren't the same, are they?"

All that love, and this was how it ended. In August the Manson Family went on a rampage in California. It wasn't their first one. In the fall the ugly truth about My Lai unraveled. In December the concert at Altamont ripped the mask off beautiful Truth and exposed a cheap Halloween trick, suitably decked out in orange and black. Lisa watched it on television and scanned the crowd for funnel hats, crones with knotty skin.

Thus, despite all the initial confidence, the sixties ended, putting up a notice saying: "Sorry. Fun discontinued. Please return to what you were doing." There were no more distractions. Nothing more to do but empty the ashtrays and wash the dirty glasses. Time out had come to an end. Lisa was grateful to have been included, and hoped that one day it would all make sense, that she'd be able to look back and see how it had helped shape her, if at all. In the meantime it was time to head for the exit, wherever it was, to whatever lay beyond.

"Well," said Pru, resigned already, "we should have bloody known, shouldn't we?"

They bloody well should.

~⟡~

The seventies began with a sixties icon having a breakdown. The man in the nightshirt had not brought John Lennon eternal peace after all. In March the US National Guard killed students at Kent State. It was an ugly start to the decade, but there was no going back.

Fashion changed and the gypsies disappeared. Lisa missed not being able to hide behind a costume. The silhouette of the new fashion was too rigid, too revealing. Estelle, going with the flow, continued to flourish. April 1970, she opened another one-room emporium, this one on Portobello Road. Lisa was still making enough money to live on.

Both Pru and Lisa continued to have sex with Melvin until Pru, already bored with the seventies, decided to go back to university and begin a post-graduate degree.

"In Art History? That's stupid." Lisa was jealous. She didn't want to lose her.

"It's not as stupid as you think, darling," corrected Pru. She suddenly fancied herself owning a posh gallery one day, selling whatever passed for art at outrageous prices to pretentious fools. Monied fools, she assured Lisa, are as gullible as poor ones.

"From now on," Pru declared upon departure, "Melvin will have to amuse himself. Either that or you'll have to shag him twice as often. Must keep our boy happy, mustn't we?"

"I don't see why. He's a grown man."

"No darling, he's not."

Germaine Greer published *The Female Eunuch* and Pru wrote from Cambridge to say that she had become a feminist. She was doing her best to grow up, she confessed, but was having a hard time of it. Lisa's theory was that Pru had been grown up all her life and just faked the rest. Pru said she had a point.

Lisa's hardworking existence on her island refuge became one of solitude. It took a while to come to terms with this new version of life. It didn't make sense to her, and it was not what she wanted, it was no longer time out, but she was doing all right. At least there was some consistency. The house still smelled of spicy food. Harry Belafonte still sang, if not very often.

The garden thrived.

Melvin stayed on in the Flat. Pru's grandfather passed away that summer and she now owned the building. But Melvin found no light-hearted amusement in the brand new decade; he had already tired of it within a month. He became involved in left-wing politics and protest marches, everything controversial his ancestors had sought to suppress. This he found meaningful. It made him truly happy to be able to rebel for a worthy cause and still annoy his family. He met a black girl sporting a big Afro and high-heeled hooker boots, who assured him she didn't take no shit from no man. Her name was Zoe, but he called her his Afro-babe. She agreed to move into the Flat, but not before Melvin cleaned it up. To everybody's surprise he did.

In September Jimi Hendrix played his last concert. He died the same month. Pru, in town the following week-end, looked pale and widow-like, pumping her shallow grief for all it was worth, sitting in the Flat, on the bed where "he shagged the daylight out of me." In October Janis Joplin died. The Beatles were falling apart.

Lisa, looking over her shoulder, wondered, what next?

# 15

he end of the world came in January 1971. The break-up of the Beatles became final on the first. And then, as if that wasn't bad enough, Lisa fell in love. It was something she had not counted on, nor hoped for.

It happened in a pub in Chelsea, somewhere off the King's Road. To say that it took her by surprise would be too feeble a description. Had she known it was going to happen she would have stayed home and hidden under the bed.

Estelle invited her for a drink one evening to talk about some ideas she had been toying with. The pub was one of Estelle's regular after-work hangouts and a fairly quiet place. It was to be a couple of drinks, a friendly discussion, then home to an early night with a cup of tea. It was Lisa's first and last visit. She never set foot there again.

These were new times, different times. Swinging London no longer swung. Glam rock was on the rise. Lisa looked at the new scene and told herself what she already knew. "You're getting too old for this."

Mick and Mimmi were long gone. Pru spent most of her time in Cambridge. The wild and crazy tide had ebbed, leaving behind a barren stretch littered with debris people no longer wanted. She only saw Melvin and Zoe when they were not at some rally or other. Sometimes she had lunch at the Greek's, Dimitrios sliding into her booth with a bottle of ouzo. His hair was thinning and he had grown fat. They talked about the good old days. A sad pastime at age twenty-four.

She was fiddling with her gin and tonic, pushing the thin slice of lemon through the crowd of ice cubes. Estelle was drawing a detailed depiction of a vest in her notebook, short quick lines joined together. "Now look, this is what I had in mind," she said, tapping her pen on the drawing. "Look closely at the cut in the front part here. Are you paying attention?"

That was when life ended. At the exact moment when Estelle's pen went tap, tap in the notebook, Lisa felt a force grab hold of her face and lift it. She looked up and there he was, a lone wolf with melancholy eyes. A gentle soul, had it not been for the tension in his jaw. But whatever and whoever he was, her fate lay in his face, this she knew instantly. He smiled when their eyes met, as if they'd made a date and here she was, right on time. The room disappeared, leaving her feeling faint in the thin air of whatever planet she was now on.

Primitive urges, sensing their time had come, awoke and emerged from inside her, dressed in animal hides and carrying clubs. They were grunting, single-minded creatures, shaking their shaggy heads. She was at their mercy.

Estelle, who was French and practical in affairs of the heart and the crotch, took one look at Lisa, one at the lone wolf, closed her leather-covered notebook, tucked her pen away and said, "Call me tomorrow. Good luck." She sounded amused. A second later she was gone.

Lisa never stopped looking at the man. It was pre-ordained and she had no control, she wanted no control. She watched as he grabbed his glass and made his way to her table, as she knew he would. He was wearing jeans, a sheepskin jacket and ugly workmen's boots. Not a dedicated follower of fashion, this one. He had long legs and did not look English, his eyes were too dark, his gait too relaxed. The closer he came the less she was able to breathe. She needed a doctor, she was paralyzed. No. Too late. She was dying. This was what dying was like. He did not say, "Mind if I join you?" He simply sat down and said "Hi. I'm Jimmy." His accent was American.

"I'm Lisa." So overwrought was she that she pronounced her name the Swedish way with a very long *i*.

"You're not English." His eyes never left hers. She would have sobbed if they had.

"Neither are you." Her voice sounded weak, the way a voice does when its owner is about to expire for lack of oxygen.

There they were, thrown together in a Chelsea pub on a strange planet, a woman from Sweden, and a man from the USA. They did not talk much at first, there was no need to hurry. They looked at each other, and it was an unimagined luxury. His hair was almost black, straight and not very long, but it touched his collar at the back, as if he had not had a haircut for a while. His face was angular, there were shadows in the hollows of his cheeks and in his brown eyes. He said his mother was Anglo-Cuban and his father Irish-Italian.

"Do you want to go for a walk?" Lisa asked, not caring what he was. She had to be alone with him, even on a cold winter street.

"Yes." She liked the way he exhaled the word, as though he had been holding his breath waiting for just that question since the moment he was born.

Outside the pub he took her hand and she felt she had finally arrived home after a long voyage. Here was the place where she had been expected. They walked up the King's Road towards Sloane Square. He was staying in a hotel close by Victoria Station, he said, on his way back to the States, having finished a contract in the Gulf. So that was why he had a tan. He was in the oil business. Ah, she thought, that explains the work boots. Hard labor, he confessed with a half smile.

"What about you?" He made the question sound so discreet.

She started talking. Words came toppling as out of an over-stuffed closet. She told him about traveling with her friends, about Vienna, going to the casino, about making clothes for Estelle's shop, about her work which was play, her garden, and the quiet turn her life had taken. About her mother, her father. Their make-believe island. She told him about her guilt, vaguely, so as to not have to pinpoint a reason, for there were a few details she left out. It was the most she had ever talked in her entire life. It made her breathless, it flushed her cheeks in the cold, but as long as he held her hand she was capable of anything. When she was finished his face had softened and she was, not drained, but full. Then it was his turn.

When he was twenty-one he drove off the road to avoid an oncoming car and hit a tree and killed his sister. She was his only sister. Her name was Stella. He had picked her up from a friend's house. She was sixteen. He was familiar with the concept of guilt.

"Can we go to my hotel room?" It was a straightforward question. His eyes were on hers, his face serious.

She should have said, "Come to my garden of earthly delights instead. Let's be Adam and Eve and let's never eat apples." But she didn't. She was too busy gazing at every detail of his face, grateful for this gift. This was what love was like. "The sooner the better," she replied.

He sighed with relief and smiled a big smile and in that smile she was lost forever. They ran the whole way to his hotel. By then it wasn't very far, but it would still have been pathetic had it not been so urgent.

It was the first time Lisa ever made love. And the second time. And the third time. Three times in a single night, life made sense both backwards and forwards. His body had hard edges and shadows, in his face especially, as if he had recently lost weight. She touched those edges, traced them with her hands and her thoughts, and they yielded and softened. She ran her fingers through his hair and prayed that she would die doing it. Never had she guessed that human emotions could be so intense. They could obliterate. They ought to. They did. He looked into her eyes and whispered words to her, about her, about them. She was of great significance now. She whispered words back, unsure of what they were or what language they were in.

And their eyes never stopped talking.

When she woke up, hours later, he was still sleeping. She looked at him for a long time, stunned to be allowed such a sight. It would be her most treasured memory, the sight of Jimmy sleeping, legs tangled in a sheet, the duvet on the floor, arms stretched out.

She sat up, trying to inhale all of him. She wanted to tear out her hair and scream in joy and despair, of love and hate, of birth and death, a scream so loud it would shatter windows and derail trains for miles around. When she ran out of air, she wanted to fall down dead on top of his naked body. Make this the end-station.

But death is never that considerate.

Looking at his naked body she was struck by a piercing insight and knew what this was all about. *The Last Judgment* again. Of course it was. This was the scene in the center panel of the triptych, the libidinous hussy up on the roof, snakes slithering up her body, her lover waiting on the bed, a dragon for a pillow. She looks like she's blindly pushing away a larger dragon hissing by her side.

Lisa's mistake had been thinking that she deserved to be loved. She realized that now. This mistake had made things so much worse, but they could be put to right before it was too late. There was a scraping of webbed feet under the bed, barely audible. Another dragon perhaps, or a gray gargoyle playing a lute on top of his head. Whatever they were, they'd be carrying sharp wooden stakes to ram through her flesh now it was the most tender it would ever be.

There was still time. She took a deep breath and concentrated very hard on what had to be done. Compared to this, she thought, anything else in life would be a breeze. Very quietly she slipped out of bed and got dressed, hating her clothes for shielding her body from him. On the bedside table lay his passport.

Jimmy Daniel Sullivan it read. Born April 19, 1942 in New York. Not quite her lucky number.

There were two snapshots tucked into the passport. One was of a group of men, some young, some older, somewhere by the sea, all of them laughing with the wind in their hair. Blue sea, blue sky, white sand, white sun. The other snapshot was of Jimmy alone, wearing jeans and nothing else, a half-smile on his lips, a Frisbee in his hand. His eyes looked into the camera. Behind him there was only his shadow in the sand and a band of blue sea meeting blue sky.

She put the snapshot in her bag, making it hers. How could she be expected to go on living without the image of her beloved's face? The creatures under the bed could impale her to their hearts' content, she was taking that photo with her. In return she left a photo of herself that Pru once took. It had been stashed in the side pocket of her bag for ages, in an envelope with some other photos of Pru and Melvin and herself. In the photo she sat cross-legged on her emerald bedspread, dressed in her skimpy little crocheted number, holding her imperial teacup as if to take a sip. It was one of Pru's attempts at being artistic. It represented, she had explained, Lisa's talent and dream, and how the two would always clash. The idea was pretentious, but it was a good photo.

She got out the small embroidery scissors she always carried in her bag. They came in handy whenever she found an interesting fabric or yarn and needed to pinch some to match with her stash. It was time to snip another sample. She cut a strand of his hair from behind his left ear, where it was longest, and tucked it carefully into her wallet. Then she cut a ribbon of long dark blonde hair off her own head and left it on top of her photo beside his passport.

She thought, if her scissors had been a gun she could have shot him straight through the head. She could have lovingly put the gun right on the spot where she'd cut his hair, and very gently pulled the trigger. Then she could have shot herself firmly through the temple, to fall dead beside him, dying happy in a moment of perfection.

There was a plane ticket tucked into the passport as well. She did not check the departure date, did not want to know when he would be gone from London. Not that it mattered, it was she who was departing, thumbing her nose at the powers that be. She sat on the floor with her back against the bed and started to pull on her new black boots, forcing herself not to turn around and look at him one last time.

Lisa, she said, her voice desperate in her head, heavy with sorrow, Lisa, you can do this. You knew there was a catch. Now it's time to pay. Just be grateful that you have known love.

This was true. She had known love.

She grabbed her jacket, stroked the sheepskin collar of his, felt how soft it was, rubbed her nose against it, let it wipe her cheeks dry, and then, soundlessly so as not to wake him, she left room number 41. She had paid the price.

This is what love is like, she told herself. It makes you strong as well as weak.

She stopped in the hotel corridor and searched her bag for a piece of paper and a pen. She had to leave a message. Tearing the back off an envelope she squatted down in the hotel corridor, outside the room that held her one true love. Leaning against the pale blue wall she pondered what to write.

In the end she scribbled, "Thank you, thank you, thank you. Forever. Lisa."

She slid the note under the door to the room where Jimmy Daniel Sullivan lay sleeping, leaned her head against the wall thinking, he's in there, on the other side of this wall, naked in bed. If I slipped in beside him he'd put his arms around me in his sleep.

If she had the strength to leave him, she could do anything. So she left the hotel, running through an empty lobby smelling of bacon and toast, and walked all the way back to Chiswick. Down towards Sloane Square, on to King's Road, through several side streets up to Cromwell Road. It took hours. She couldn't walk very fast, it made her breathless. She was still on the planet where the air was thin. And she was falling to pieces.

It started to snow when she reached West Kensington, the kind of snowfall that paints the world white anywhere else but London, where it creates only brown slush and traffic chaos. Snow and slush, through it all she was experiencing euphoria for the first time in her life.

Her long skirt was soaked, slapping wet and cold against her legs. Her hands were red and frozen, she could not bend her fingers. There was a pair of warm gloves in her bag, but she'd forgotten they were there. Her hair was drenched. By the time she reached Hammersmith icicles had formed. They rattled around her head as she walked. Her new boots were made of ice too. So were her extremities. Icy pearls gathered down her cheeks. It was morning by then, traffic was growing heavier in the slush. Her earlobes must have fallen off somewhere along Chiswick Mall, she could no longer feel them. She imagined them like two icy pink chunks in the snow by the bend in the river. Despite all that she didn't feel the slightest bit cold. How could she, with such fire burning inside her? The few people out and about on foot stared at her, confounded, as if she had just crawled out of the Thames, a mermaid in search of feet.

She had lived an entire life in less than eight hours. Perhaps when life is so intense and so concentrated it has to be short. Either way, it had been worth it. Nothing would ever go wrong between her and the one she loved. This is what she told herself. Over and over.

When she arrived home it had stopped snowing. Soon it had melted.

⊷⊣

She worked through the following days with the mindless concentration of a captive digging a tunnel to freedom. She was too exhausted to sleep, too hungry to eat. Every time she ran into Ram he delivered the same diagnosis. "I think you are catching this bloody influenza thing going about. You look like you have a fever. How about some hot soup?"

A week later she took a couple of vests to Estelle's. She woke up one morning and there they were, ready and waiting. Unless elves had turned up at night to work their little fingers to the bone, she had to assume they were the result of her own labor. The vests were exactly what Estelle had in mind. She held them up, turned them around, inside out, squealed over the texture combination of the patchwork. They were magnificent, the best *la Lisa* had ever produced. Lisa stared dully at the vests and did not recognize them.

Estelle did not comment on the amazing fact that Lisa had undergone a successful lobotomy without interrupting her work schedule. Instead she handed the feebleminded woman two sealed envelopes. One contained a most welcome check, the other one was an envelope Estelle had got from Eddie, the bartender at her usual pub. It had Lisa's name on it. The folded sheet of paper inside read "Thank *you*, thank *you*, thank *you*. Forever. Jimmy."

Lisa wanted to boast to Estelle, "Not many relationships are this perfect," but didn't.

She continued her zombie-like existence, filling the hollow at her core with a sustaining form of pain. It was astounding the amount of pain that fit into a single hollow core. In an antique shop in Kensington she bought a silver frame to honor Jimmy's photo. It was hugely expensive, but not nearly expensive enough. His lock of hair was tucked in a gold locket on a chain around her neck. The enigmatic part of her was pleased to have something to be enigmatic about.

Without bossy old Pru, Lisa did not venture out a great deal. It made her realize how much she had depended on her friend, how much she needed her, how much she missed her. These days Pru only came into town only once a month. The first time they met after Lisa's post-Jimmy life, they shared a bottle of wine at the Flat, which Pru still called home when in town. She sipped some wine and glared at her absentminded friend.

"Darling? I'm bloody *talking* to you."

"What?"

"Christ, Lisa! What's the matter?"

"Nothing." Jimmy was nobody's business. Not even Pru's.

It was Estelle who told Pru how Lisa and "some American in a sheepskin coat and ugly boots" had hypnotized each other. When they next got together, Pru, like a protective mother hen, demanded to know every naked fact about this Yankee wanker. Who was he? What was he doing in London? What was Lisa not telling her, and more to the point, why?

"Darling, it's me, Pru. Talk to me!"

"It's nothing."

"You bloody better tell me, Lisa!"

Lisa told her it was only a one-night stand. Technically that was not a lie. Pru demanded to know if it was utterly delicious. Lisa did not deign to reply. Pru shrieked with laughter. Lisa didn't understand why until she felt the imbecile smile on her face giving her away. Pru would have laughed longer and harder had Lisa not lost control and slapped her hard in the face.

"You bloody bitch! You hit me!"

"Don't *ever* laugh at me like that, or I'll never speak to you again as long as I live! Goddam aristocrat-bitch." The last sentence delivered in a mumble.

"I'm sorry, darling." Something in Lisa's face pushed Pru into submission. "Oh my God! Is it that bad?"

"Yes."

"Is it death?"

"Yes."

"Oh, my poor darling!"

"Don't ever tell. And don't mention it ever again."

"My poor baby. Come cry in my arms!"

So she did, blubbering long and hard, thinking briefly of how Mick had once soaked the shoulder of her dress, the way she now did Pru's designer sweater. But Pru, being Pru, had not finished her interrogation.

"Why on earth did you leave him? That's the part I cannot for the life of me comprehend. You're not suffering from sudden profound stupidity, are you?"

"I was paying the price."

"What price?"

"The price needed to get rid of my guilt."

"What fucking guilt? Please, please, don't tell me it was guilt for being raped?"

"No, not that." Not exactly. She scrambled around in her head for a good answer and grabbed on to an obvious one. "The guilt for wishing my mother dead." This was no lie. And one day, she thought, she might tell Pru the whole truth. If she ever told anybody it would be Pru.

"You wished your mother dead?"

"Yes. For years. It was a daily habit. But the thing is, you see, the last time I did, the feeling was strong and it worked like a charm."

Pru looked dubious, as though having a mother was not quite fashionable in her circles. "You've never told me about your mother."

"You've never told me about yours either."

"My mother is an bland upper-class robot. She does as she's told, all according to etiquette."

"Well, mine was demented. She never did as she was told. Not that she was ever told."

"Tell me about her."

"Will you tell me about yours?"

"I spent most of my formative years in boarding schools and university, darling. I hardly know the bloody woman. She still calls me Prudence like we'd only recently been introduced."

"Poor Prudence."

"Poor Lisa." Sounding half amused.

"Never call me poor Lisa. It's what my aunts used to call me."

# 16

**It seems everything happened that year.** In mid-September, a few months after that night I told you about, my mother died in a freakish accident. It was really embarrassing. She fell off a bus.

It was a weeknight. She had dragged me along to my Aunt Bojan's, because it was Bojan's birthday and we had to go for coffee and cake and bring her flowers. My mother kept harping on about how it wouldn't hurt for me to act like a good daughter once in a while, and how it might stop people from talking. This was how she always went on, yap, yap, yap, making sure you felt like shit at least twice a day.

*People are talking?* I always replied. *I had no idea. About what?* And she would hiss back, *You know what I mean,* every time. I never had a clue and neither did she, but my survival instinct had long since taught me to comply or suffer the consequences. It would be safer to let the matter drop and get gussied up in *something decent for a change. And for God's sake, wear proper shoes.*

I had nothing against Aunt Bojan. It was her husband I couldn't stand. Uncle Ove was, still is I'm sure, a scrawny, shifty-eyed weasel of a man with large flapping pachyderm ears and a rodent snout. I swear, he's a one-man zoo. I had always hated him with a passion and if nobody knew that it was only because they conveniently chose not to. It started shortly after I turned twelve, right after my father died. Uncle Weasel started pawing me, rubbing up against me whenever he had the chance. He always found an excuse to follow me into the kitchen or any other place I tried to hide. He'd sneak up behind me and put a paw up my skirt while making some feeble joke to pretend it wasn't really happening, or worse, that I had actually encouraged it. His face was always sweaty and he'd giggle like we were sharing a terrific secret. The first time it happened I got confused and angry and started shoving and kicking him. He informed me with cold contempt that I ought to show a bit of gratitude, because I had such puny tits I would never find a boyfriend. He was, in his own magnanimous way, trying to boost my confidence.

Rather than thank him, I told my mother. Another fatal mistake. She started sputtering. *Oh, for God's sake! Who do you think you are? Ove's just being friendly. That's the way he is!* Next time there was a family gathering she went out of her way to teach me a lesson in much-needed etiquette. *Lisa, don't be so goddam ignorant! Give your uncle Ove a hug. It's Christmas! Don't you dare kick your uncle!* I got his knee cap that time. He had a bad knee.

That was my mother for you, defending my uncle against me.

That's why I didn't want to go to Aunt Bojan's that night. But, as ever, it was clear that my mother was going to work herself into a state of frothy hysteria if she didn't get her way. She always did and the repercussions were nasty. She would descend into a foul vindictive mood that would linger like poisonous gas for days on end. The world would grow dark and ominous and I would have to walk barefoot on the shards of her resentment until my feet bled. Because that's the way it was. Only blood-sacrifice appeased her.

It sounds dramatic, but you know, as a child I often dreamt that it was eternal night. Something bad had happened to the sun and it had died. I would be out playing with my friends at high noon in the glow of the streetlights, and there would be nothing in the sky but a vast darkness shunned by moon and stars. Our faces would be ghostly white as we played tag in listless slow motion among shadows that were there to stay.

I put on the dress she had picked for my high school graduation. It was an ugly green one with pink flowers. I forced my feet into the shoes that pinched my toes, and tagged along to Aunt Bojan's, refusing to sit beside my mother on the bus. At my aunt's I was a model of etiquette and good manners. I sat smiling at the table, sipped one cup of coffee after another, pinkie finger out. This was my mother's idea of lady-like behavior. Meanwhile she spouted tidbits like, *Well, Lisa never had any ambition, she'll be spending her life working in that office.* This from a woman who cleaned public toilets for a living.

I was good that evening; I smiled and had another piece of cake. And another one. That way I had an excuse to swallow regularly and was less likely to scream.

On the way back we had to change buses downtown. Number thirteen was about to pull out and my mother yelled an order for me to run. I charged after the bus, hurled myself on and asked the conductor to please wait. A minute later my mother caught up and started to clamber on, wheezing and panting and red in the face. Just as she made it up the steps her eyes bulged and her face flushed deep scarlet. She stared at me perplexed, like I had pulled some dirty trick on her. I returned the stare, embarrassed, wondering what she would do to humiliate me this time. Wishing she'd drop dead. It never occurred to me that something might be wrong, but in the middle of the staring match she let go and toppled right off. I'm sorry to say it looked a stupendously clumsy maneuver. I wished I wasn't there.

When she was about to tumble backwards her eyes met mine again for a brief moment, and she saw what I felt, she read my wish. I know she did.

A split second later the conductor screamed *STOP!* and I heard her skull crack on the pavement, felt the thump as one of the back wheels crushed what turned out to be her knees. I

thought, *Oh Christ! What will she think of next?* The reaction
was automatic, the question moot. They said later that it was a
massive stroke that had caused her to topple off like that. My
wish had come true.

I was very upset, facing the realization that I was now an
orphan, because my own evil thoughts had killed my mother.
Upset, too, for not feeling more grief. You're supposed to grieve
when a parent dies. I was inconsolable when my father died. But
as the days went by it became impossible to deny the relief I felt
to be rid of her. The apartment was quiet, a soothing sort of
quiet I had never before experienced, so soothing the air felt soft
against my skin. There was nobody to scorn and criticize. Never
again would I have to dread her steps coming up the stairs, the
thud as she put her bag down to open the door, the key in the
lock, waiting to see who or what would enter the hall that day
wearing her clothes.

She wasn't a very nice person. Several people had already
confided this, as if it might somehow have escaped my attention. Let me quote the close relative that came to fetch me at the
hospital after the accident: "That lunatic witch should have
been strangled at birth." Mind you, Aunt Margit was my father's
sister. They never got along.

I wasn't the only one who failed to grieve. The gathering after
her funeral was loud and rambunctious. It was held in one of
the dining rooms of an old inn near the chapel. My mother's two
younger sisters, Aunt Bojan and Aunt Gulli had arranged everything and, as they didn't have to foot the bill, had ordered a
never-ending supply of open-face sandwiches followed by
obscene piles of cakes and pastries. *It'll save us having to cook
supper tonight*, said Aunt Gulli. She was fond of cake, was Aunt
Gulli. Still is, I'm sure.

There was beer and schnapps with the sandwiches and three
kinds of liqueur with the coffee. At the end, Uncle Valle, my
mother's brother, the youngest of the siblings, felt moved to lead
us in a rousing chorus of the national anthem. His motive was
blissfully obscure, but we all stood at attention. Then he insisted

on treating us to his famous rendition of an old classic about a woman named Fia Jansson who had two one-eyed brothers, at which point the manager of that renowned establishment appeared in the doorway to deliver a vicious complaint. National fervor was one thing, but boisterous frivolity at a time such as this! He took aim with his steel barrel eyes and mowed us down with contempt. To him we were nothing but rabble dressed in black.

*That was Sigrid's favorite song!* hollered my uncle. He muttered something about setting his dog on the uppity jerk-off freak. Aunt Stina pointed out that he didn't have a dog. This observation deeply saddened him, and he fell silent. Five minutes later, drunk as a skunk, Uncle Valle announced he was off to buy a dog and, after another quick schnapps, got up and teetered out. According to Aunt Stina he came home later that evening with a male bull-dog pup which, he announced, he had named Sigrid after my mother, even though it wasn't nearly as ugly.

Some family, eh? But that's why my mother's funeral was a joyous celebration.

Another example of what she was like?

Okay, here's one. It was a Saturday morning, four weeks before my father died. I was still in bed, because on weekends I stayed in bed until she was finished breakfast to avoid having to sit at the table with her. There was going to be trouble again that morning. My father was misbehaving. His crime? He was making a cheese sandwich. She caught him red-handed, as she put it, opening a new package rather than finishing the dried-up wedge on the bottom shelf in the fridge. He said something to the effect of, *Oh, sorry dear, I didn't see it. Does it matter?*

God, did it matter! I was huddling under the covers, out of the hurricane, but I knew what she looked like when she accelerated out of control. Her face heated to a sickly crimson, her eyes shrank and went blind, and her tongue stuck out of her mouth and she panted for air like a dog. Her arms shook and her tight fists hammered the air. Then she started to sweat and her dry permed tufts of hair got all wet and sticky.

That Saturday her lunacy reached the height it had been striving for. The crime of the cheese was only a prologue to an endless litany of cruel crimes and abominations against her. When she ran out of unspeakable deeds committed in the present, she plunged into the distant past where she dug up any old dirt that could pass for unforgivable injustices, if dusted off and presented the right way. Then she resurfaced to fire off another volley of accusations. On and on it went.

My mother turned life into a grim and futile venture. She shrank our spirits and dried them, then hung them on her belt like trophies.

Eventually my father left the kitchen and put on his coat and shoes. He always did at times like that. He'd escape and go for a very long walk until she cooled off. But that day was different. He disappeared for two days. I was so frightened, Pru. The flow of time stopped and jerked forward and stopped again. I thought, what if he's finally so fed up he won't come home again?

My mother didn't dare call the police, because what could she say if they asked why he had disappeared? *Well, officer, not only did he fox-trot with my cousin's friend Vera back in 1948, but this morning he attempted to make a cheese sandwich! Here's the knife, officer, you can check it for fingerprints.*

My father didn't return until late Sunday night. He arrived home in a taxi around midnight. I was still awake, I hadn't slept since he left. It was a long two days. As he walked in the door she stood waiting, cloaked in that special bilious martyrdom of hers. It hung on her like a black robe on some high priestess. Where had he been? she demanded to know. Her voice was quiet and slow, the way it always was when she wanted to emphasize her suffering. She craved blood, that was the thing, but my father smiled and said nothing, refusing to climb onto the sacrificial altar, the way he had so many times. I'm pretty sure he'd been drinking. He didn't get drunk very often, maybe once a year, but when he did that was the way he smiled. Like he didn't give a shit. My mother, sure of her power, raised her accusatory dagger. Spill your guts, was her order. He ignored her. It was the first time I saw him shove her aside.

She kept quiet that time. I think she got scared.

Later I asked him where he had disappeared to. *Copenhagen.* It was a conspirator's hushed reply. Then he smiled, but it was such a sad excuse for a smile. I didn't dare ask anything else. I wondered for the longest time if he had gone to a woman. You know, to a prostitute. I hoped he had spent the night with a genial Danish lady bouncing with jolly bonhomie, who had shared a post-coital cigar with him and made him Danish sandwiches with roastbeef and remoulade sauce and fried onion. Those were his favorite, you see. I hoped that she had served them with a big glass of cold beer, just because he was such a kind man.

It was preferable to the unbearable image of him alone on a bench at Kongen's Nytorv as the clock struck midnight.

Of all the moral obscenities I could not forgive my mother, it was this image I forgave the least.

# 17

**A**s usual, Lisa left out chunks of the story. Some moments demand to be kept private.

After her mother's funeral, when she was getting rid of everything in the apartment, the props of their unassuming existence, she had made a disturbing discovery.

With her aunts and uncles busy scavenging in the apartment, she had fled the warfare. It was while sneaking out, not bothering to close the door, it had occurred to her that she had forgotten about the storage room in the cellar. It had been ages since she had set foot there.

Continuing straight down, she had unlocked the door to the Grankvist allotted space and stepped inside the dark room to flick on the switch. The light had blinked and she had stood face to face with her childhood. There it had been, neatly preserved, carefully tucked away. Her red Monark bicycle, leaning against the wall, waiting. Her father had bought it second hand one Sunday long ago. She had ridden it all the way home, zigzagging over the sidewalk, while he held on. Back home he had said, "Did you know I let go of the bike ages ago?" Full of pride she had got back on, knowing she could, riding by herself all the way down the bicycle path to the corner of the park where the chestnut tree was in bloom. She had turned around under the cloud of white flowers and waved to him. He had smiled and waved back.

He would always be standing there, waving and smiling, growing smaller and smaller over the distance of the years.

Next a net bag with yellow rubber balls and skipping-rope hanging over a handle bar had caught her attention. From long ago came the noise of rubber balls bouncing against a brick wall, the feel of the thawing sun of early spring against her back, puddles in the gutter reflecting her red shoes, boys playing soccer over in the park.

Her father's work jacket still hung on its hook. On the old kitchen table, once his workbench, had stood a brown leather case. She recognized it at once, shocked to have forgotten all about that cursed old accordion she had never wanted to play. The leather case had dried and cracked under a layer of dust. She had not opened it.

The accordion, too, had been secondhand. They had found an ad for it in the paper, the address a smelly old building downtown. She and her father had climbed a long flight of stairs to a room where an old man smelling of akvavit sat staring out the window as though utterly alone, paying them no attention. Beside three empty bottles on the table stood an open case with a small two-octave accordion, the kind with piano keys. She had heard her father say that, well, it looked like a fine accordion, and had observed as he discreetly put some money on the table. The man nodded as they left, a forgotten cigarette burning to ashes between fingers stained yellow.

For two years she had taken lessons with a teacher who was partial to polkas. She had hated every minute of it. After her father's death, her mother had not mentioned the accordion again, even though it had been her idea in the first place. It was as if she had forgotten its existence. Lisa, relieved never to play another polka, had conveniently forgotten about it too.

Behind the accordion case had stood a blue tote bag with

fake leather trim. Looking at it, it was instantly summer again, Lisa running barefoot along the endless beach outside the city, loud shrieks of children mixing with the sounds of the sea. There had been picnics with raspberry cordial and soggy sandwiches with melted butter. A long ago happiness reached out of the tote bag and touched her fleetingly.

So many things, old and worn and dusty. Under the workbench stood the old kick-sleigh. Had it always been so small? In between the long metal bars at the back of the sleigh, a pair of wooden skis and ski poles, tied together with string, the bars rusty, the skis bent. Once again she stood on top of the hill in the park waiting her turn to ski down the steep slope towards the pond, convinced that this time she would make it all the way to the big oak tree. She pulled her hat down over her forehead, snow crystals stinging her face, damp mittens chilling her hands.

And in a corner, tucked away in a paper bag, some of her mother's old housecoats, neatly folded as if freshly laundered. She smelled the soaps shaped like lemons she had always bought for her for Christmas. They had come in a box with lots of green tissue paper. Her mother had once said she liked them, so Lisa had kept on buying them, year after year, eager to please.

On a shelf two old hats had kept each other company. A black demure pot with a crinkled net, and a red one with a fake flower. She tried on the red one, which was too small. Underneath that hat she discovered her father's old beret, the brown one he had been wearing the time she biked all the way to the flowering chestnut tree. Throwing the red hat on the floor, she put on the beret.

In the blue cupboard attached to the outer wall hung a set of unused tools in a tidy row. Her father had got them at a sale, telling her at the time what a terrific deal it was for brand-name quality tools. Good tools always come in handy. He was going to bring them to their island to help people fix things.

Below the cupboard a pair of small rubber boots gathered

dust. One glance at them and it was Sunday in the forest; they were picking chanterelles. Lisa had her own basket, a small square one. It had been raining and brown and yellow leaves stuck to her boots. A strong smell of earth filled her nostrils.

There in the cellar storage had sat preserved all the seasons of her childhood, ready for her return, should she change her mind about proceeding forward into the future. Lisa had stared helpless at every item. Funny stuff, material possessions. She had forgotten all about these objects that had once been part of her life, that had helped define her for however short a time, only to rediscover them again when it had come time to get rid of them. But if this stuff evoked such powerful emotions in her, how could she possibly part with it?

More important, the careful organization of her childhood's seasons had been her mother's work. Lisa had been down in the storage room only a few times after her father's death, but at those times it had been a jumble of boxes and clothes and odds and ends. Nobody else had been there since. It had been her mother, who at some point had tidied, who had left her child's belongings in a place where they would be not only preserved, but easily found should time reverse itself. The cellar had been a dark forgotten museum, created to the memory of a child by somebody who wanted to remember. Remember what? It had not made sense. Had her mother, on her peremptory raid through life, secretly as if in shame, loved her child? Or at least the idea of her child?

Was it possible to love the idea of a child and hate the child? Did it work the other way around? Could you love a child but hate the very idea of it?

Lisa had felt bereaved. When the cellar door opened at the end of the corridor leading to the storage area, she was sitting on the old kitchen table crying shamelessly. Voices and shuffling feet had come her way, the unmistakable yapping of Aunt Gulli and Uncle Henning.

"What are you doing down here, for goodness sake? I thought you . . . oh dear, oh my, are you crying? It's okay. Poor

Lisa, you just let it out, there's a girl. A cry will do you good. Here, use my hankie, it's almost clean."

Uncle Henning hovered outside the range of the emotional woman-stuff.

"Aunt Gulli? Do you think my mother loved me?"

"What?" Gulli, too busy scanning the storage space for loot, turned around, puzzled. "Did she *love* you? Jeez, I've no idea. Signe was too damn peculiar to figure out. You know that. But if she knew how to love at all, I'd say she did. In her own way."

"Are you sure?"

"Yeah. I'd say so. She got a bit jealous when you were born, is all. Johan was too crazy about being a dad, he just loved you to pieces."

"I know he did. But . . ." She stopped crying, busy formulating a question that never got asked.

"That's better!" Aunt Gulli, having retrieved her soggy hankie, got down to business. "Now then, why on earth are you wearing that old beret? It's not clean. Jeez, I remember that one! It was Johan's, wasn't it? You should take it off right now, it's been lying around down here forever. You'll get cooties. Go on, take it off, it's not healthy."

"Are you saying my dad had lice?"

"No, you stupid girl, of course not! It's what happens when you leave stuff lying around in the cellar, things start to breed in them. It's in the dust, you see. That's where germs come from. Well, now. What have we here? Is that your old bike?"

"Yes."

"Well, now! It's just about the right size for Inger, isn't it, Henning? Henning! Get in here! Are you listening? Not exactly new, of course . . ."

"Hey, Gulli, look! Tools!" Uncle Henning, less discreet now, was reaching for the never-used hammers, screwdrivers and wrenches, breathing heavily, coveting them. "Say, I could use these!"

"I'm taking those with me." Lisa had surprised herself.

"What the hell for? You're a girl!"

"So?"

"So girls don't use tools!"

"Says who?"

"Oh, come on, for God's sake! Everybody knows that!"

"I need tools for the art school in London. For sculpting and stuff. Chipping at blocks of marble, that kind of thing. You need good equipment." Lisa got up and gathered the tools into the tote bag that had once held the wilted sandwiches of summer picnics. Had Henning tried to stop her she would have rearranged his nose with a wrench.

"You'd think an art school would provide proper tools. Huh, Gulli? Real art tools. Can't be much of a school, can it? Huh, Gulli? No real tools. What does that tell you?"

"There's a nice accordion," Lisa had offered. "Best you could hope to find. We bought if from that famous accordion player, you know the one I mean? Who used to play on the radio?"

"Oh yeah! I know the one you mean. He used to play in the park too."

They were impressed. Henning carting the dusty case, Gulli leading the red Monark bicycle, they waddled down the corridor, pleased with their finds.

Back in the storage room Lisa gave her childhood a parting glance and hurried out with her bag of tools through the side door up to the street. She ran several blocks to get away from what was no more. By the water tower, too out of breath, she had been forced to stop. The old tower had been a decrepit apartment building for decades. The cylinder hotel they called it. It was said to be teeming with criminals, thieves and murderers, sticking up like a sore thumb on the hill, on the spot where they had burnt witches back when fear of the Devil ruled the day. Big bonfires had blazed there long before then, every May when the people chose a *Majgreve*, the Earl of May, and crowned him with flowers so he could ride the summer into town on Walpurgis Night. They still had bonfires in the park on that night. A long time ago there had been bonfires on St. Hans' night at Midsummer as well. Midsummer's Eve had once belonged to the dark powers. That was why witches had held their biggest celebration on that night. It was said that only fire and steel could ward them off.

During witch-burning days they would without a doubt have torched her mother. "And," Lisa thought at the time, catching her breath at the bus stop, "me as well for what I plan to do."

# 18

As the seventies were so stubbornly different from the sixties, it came as no surprise when the termites of change started to nibble their way into the house. In the fall of 1971 Amrit received a summons back to Madras to get married. A bride had been chosen, the dowry was most generous, what was he waiting for? He did not go willingly.

In the spring of 1972 a great deal of fuss and commotion erupted over old Mrs. Parkinson's cat. Funny thing that, because nobody knew she had a cat. She was not supposed to. It was one of Ram's rules that pets were very much not allowed.

But one day Mrs. Parkinson up and died. Lisa was working in the garden that afternoon, pruning a shrub by the north wall, when she heard the sound of a small child crying. The sound wasn't sudden, it crept up on her before jerking her head upright. It didn't come at her from the past, it was not out to haunt her. No, it came from Mrs. Parkinson's open attic window where it had no business coming from. Ram was in the kitchen, so she ran inside and informed him that it sounded as if Mrs. Parkinson had just given birth. Ram grew alarmed at the thought of such a phenomenon occurring under his roof, no doubt against his rules, and scampered up the stairs with Lisa in tow.

Mrs. Parkinson got a bottle of milk every other day. The bottle Ram had taken up the day before sat untouched outside her door, a sure sign that something was not right. Ram knocked, but there was no answer, just the same child-like cry. He tried the door, which was unlocked, and that's when they discovered a large Persian cat mewling forlornly by Mrs. Parkinson's bed, rubbing against the liver-spotted arm hanging over the edge. He was hungry, poor thing.

Mrs. Parkinson had died in her bed, alone and without a fuss. A heart attack was later confirmed. She must have felt death on its way to fetch her though, because she had taken the time to scribble a last note that begged, *Please take care of my Prince.* The note had fallen to the floor. Unless she was referring to a member of the royal family, smiling down from a portrait on the wall, they could only assume that the cat's name was Prince.

Ram, in a blatant disregard for death, was furious to find one of his rules so rudely ignored. "'Madam,' I jolly well tell her a long time ago when she first ask me about this. 'Madam,' I say to her, 'there will be no pets in this house.'" Now he found out there had jolly well been a fluffy Persian residing on the third floor for perhaps ten years. He was not pleased.

A chill wind blew through the room and Lisa saw how she too might end up such a sad and desolate sight, a mottled arm hanging over the edge of a smelly bed, as if making a last attempt to escape the inevitable. An aged inconvenience, a bottle of souring milk outside her door announcing a demise that would otherwise go unnoticed.

Mrs. Parkinson's lonely death did nothing to soften Ram's fascist landlord heart. To show that he meant business he grabbed the cat by the scruff of the neck, dangled it in front of Lisa's face like a furry rag, and announced that he was going to have the bloody vermin put down at the vet's at once, wait and see, and that he thoroughly resented the expense. Lisa said he could not possibly be nasty enough to do such a thing. He said he jolly well could.

"In that case, you pervert-murderer, you better hand over that cat right now."

Ram reminded her again that he did not allow cats in his house, that it was a Rule, and please, never to call him a pervert-murderer. Lisa retorted that it didn't matter whether he allowed cats or not, because she was taking poor Prince to live with some friends of hers, kind and good people, so Ram better keep his killer hands off him. In Ram's opinion it was utterly pointless to keep such a useless creature alive. It wasn't as if there were mice in the attic. Sweeping the puss up from Ram's arms of death into the safe haven of her own, Lisa said that was an attitude typical of a pervert-murderer.

And speaking of useless creatures, she went on, did they not have holy cows in India? All over the damn place? Starved scrawny things standing on railroad tracks for hours on end stopping the trains from traveling, leaving people to suffocate inside? Holding up traffic on the roads and shitting all over the place?

Ram sharply demanded that she not compare holy cows with flea-ridden cats, adding that she was a very silly woman indeed. Prince meowed in protest. Lisa ignored Ram and carried the cat downstairs to feed him some milk, then put him in a cardboard box and took him to stay with Melvin and Zoe, where he lived out his golden years in peace (he had two left). He passed away one night on the first shelf of the boards and bricks bookcase, next to a stack of anti-war pamphlets and Ginsberg's *Howl*, which he pissed all over on his way to reunite with Mrs. Parkinson in heaven.

---

A year later Lisa's red hibiscus contracted some kind of hibiscus bubonic plague. Reddish blobs appeared all over the bark. She kept expecting it to sneeze. Neither fungicide nor pesticide had any effect. Soon the leaves began to yellow, one by one, and drop off. The other hibiscus followed suit and by Easter they were both dead.

It was a bad omen. Something was going to happen, though she couldn't for the life of her think what. The worst had already happened.

A month later there was great uproar in the social club by the kitchen. Ram and two of his friends were sitting at the dining table immersed in a wild shouting chorus. Ram was waving a letter about. It appeared that from Bombay had come a decree that he was to get married whether he liked it or not. The letter said he had dawdled long enough. He had finished his degree, was now an engineer with a good job, and he had a house as his uncle had died the year before and left it to Ram. Thirty was shamefully late for a man to get married. A man needs a wife; he needs to produce heirs. What kind of man was he that he had not yet accomplished this task? For how long should his parents live in such shame? To help speed up the process they had found him a suitable wife. The middle daughter of Mr. Prakash of Prakash Exports. Remember Shakuntala? Ram did not. Would he please return home as soon as possible and make his aged parents proud? His wife-to-be was beautiful and had an extremely alluring dowry. Both his friends were very sympathetic, patting his shoulders and pouring him yet another cup of tea.

Ram, who already had two part-time girlfriends, was deeply vexed to be ensnared by tradition, but knew it was what fate had always had in store for him.

The homeland beckoned. It was Ram's turn to make good.

But Ram would go only if he could return to England. This, he said, was very much his stipulation. He had a house and a good job. He loved London. His life was here. While he realized that traditions were not to be taken lightly, only on this condition would he follow orders. A long distance call settled the matter. Mr. Prakash's middle daughter could not wait to move to England.

The pale Beryl, Amrit's sometime sleeping partner, was long

gone. She had left shortly after Amrit. Nobody knew what had happened to her. More than likely she faded into the woodwork. Jackson and his Harry Belafonte record had left early that year, clutching their hands hard, tears in his eyes, saying what good years these had been.

In May Ram left for Bombay, showing an impressive flair for swearing in English as he dragged a big suitcase to a waiting taxi. He was to be gone for three months.

Lisa was left in command of the household, only there was nobody to command, not even hibiscus plants. There were two new students from Tanzania named Nelson and George, and an Irish lad named Joe who had taken over Mrs. Parkinson's attic room, but none of them was ever around. She had the small kitchen to herself, which should have been a relief, had there still been leftovers to try out. Apart from all the Indian dishes, Jackson had often conjured up interesting concoctions involving bits of goat and coconut. If either of the new students ate, they did not do so at home.

The house succumbed to the dusty silence that reigns in homes that have sat empty for years after the owner's mysterious death. Lisa clattered around the ghost mansion with only Jimmy's photo for company, telling him daily how strange life had become. When she heard the front door late at night she never knew if it was Joe, George or Nelson, or an ax-murderer craving fresh victims. She lay rigid in bed until she heard the footsteps continue up the stairs. A voice would shout softly in an African language, doors would slam. There would be movement and noise in the room above. Sometimes she heard female giggling.

It was during this time of suspended animation that Sonja called from Sweden. Lisa sat on the dining table in the empty communal room and listened to the voice in her ear tell her that she was getting married. His name was Andreas Niklasson and he was an engineer. He was tall and blond and wonderful. It was going to be a Christmas Wedding in the small country church not far from Sonja's maternal grandparents' farm. They were hoping for snow to make it Christmas-card pretty. Sonja demanded Lisa come home, finally, for this special occasion.

"Remember when we were thirteen and stayed at my grandparents' for a week in the summer? When we went to Kivik to the big market? Eating ice cream in big waffle cones with whipped cream and jam?"

Lisa remembered it well.

"Please, Lisa, will you come? For me?"

Finally she gave in. "Yes, Sonja. I will come to your wedding. Of course I will." Thinking, if Sonja wanted to marry an engineer, she should have married Ram and moved into the house.

Lisa would have gone back for Sonja's wedding, she had every intention, but something happened, a disaster she could not have imagined possible.

But before that she met another man, only this time it was different.

When Pru was in town they spent time together, especially if Pru came alone, which she often did, if only to please her friend. This is how Lisa met Len McTavish, escaping the dusty echo of the house to go with Pru to a concert in some park.

She was at a loss, she needed somebody to acknowledge her existence, and Len was there. His eyes had that semi-vacant look that in the sixties had been interpreted as proof of having reached a higher plane. Lisa found it convenient to interpret it that way too, though in truth, his look was merely semi-vacant. He had yet to discover that the sixties were over.

It was a Saturday and Pru was in town, unfortunately with her newly acquired posse of pretentious intellectual friends. They were a nasal group of conceited nitwits, constantly putting each other down with remarks like "Oh, don't be cunty, Lucinda. That kind of post-modern viewpoint might be controversial, but it doesn't go with your shoes."

Compared to Pru's friends, Len seemed steeped in quiet wisdom. No wonder Lisa took to him. When they first met, she pretended to mistake him for an alien. She asked him how he liked hanging out with earthlings. He was stoned and found the remark incredibly witty.

Pru pronounced him "harmless, if a bit daft" and dismissed him.

Later that night Len invited Lisa back to the mothership. It was parked somewhere near Earl's Court and looked suspiciously like a cramped bedsit, done up in a previous century in tones of sepia that had long since faded into shades that didn't warrant even a rude name. It turned out Len was not an alien, but a Canadian from Hamilton, Ontario. He was of Scottish parentage, but having spent two months in London already, considered himself more or less an English bloke. He was quite the philosopher at times, though what he said never amounted to much. At least we have that in common, thought Lisa, chalking it up in his favor. Len, for his part, sensed deep and clever thoughts in her enigmatic silence. He became enamored with her Giaconda smile.

The most important aspect of Len was that he was not threatening. He lacked that shield of testosterone hardness that so easily bruised whoever touched it. He meant well. His body was smooth and hairless; the way he tossed his head of flowing brown locks out of his face almost girlish. He looked with admiration in the mirror where he saw a gentle stud, a flower-power-hippie kind of guy, though flower power had by then dropped its petals. Needing to impress her he told her that girls sometimes mistook him for Rod Stewart. From far away, he added when she raised her eyebrows. He made her nostalgic for the good old days of make-believe.

But she could not abide this Canadian bloke's dingy bedsit, so she shared a secret: she lived on a tropical island in Chiswick. After a brief description and history of this legendary refuge, she invited him to come and stay. Perhaps it was careless, but why not? She was alone in an empty house. Maybe Len could bring the vitality of his alien life form to it. He had his bag packed within minutes.

Having been lonely for too long, Lisa appreciated his presence to such a degree she mistook her relief for something else. He loved her room, he loved Chiswick. He loved her garden. Len loved everything about Lisa, including her quiet self-reliance. When he was with her it rubbed off on him so much that he mistook her strength for his own.

With the perfume from the honeysuckle as their aphrodisiac, they had leisurely sex with the French doors wide open. Birds twittered in the apple-tree, flowers nodded in the breeze. When it was sunny they had picnics in the garden. Lisa told Len about the weedy neglect of eight years ago as he admired the flower-spangled tropical paradise he'd grown fond of lolling about in. That summer she had planted a swelling cluster of primroses with golden centers that paled into a gentle lilac, then turned dark purple at the edges. They were so stunningly magnificent Len assumed they were artificial blooms on metal stems. The black mulberry sapling was growing up strong and healthy out of a bed of nasturtiums. The apple tree was heavy with fruit, the air sweetly perfumed. Flies hummed, bees buzzed, butterflies flitted.

Lisa was happy having somebody there, somebody for her alone, an Adam to her Eve, somebody to admire her creation. Sometimes when she watched Len float about in her garden in his white Indian shirt and long brown hair, she thought he might be mistaken for an elf, had elves been tall. He was ethereal and otherworldly, but in paradise that was not out of place. She plucked an apple off the tree and offered it to him. They played ball with it for a while, throwing it back and forth, then he ate it.

Other times she failed to see him at all. These were moments when her flesh and spirit grew suddenly weak, her bones liquefied, and she imagined Jimmy Sullivan over by the rhododendrons, naked to the waist, throwing his Frisbee at her. At moments like that, time kindly stopped and waited for her to catch up.

Before Len arrived she hid Jimmy's photo in a shiny fire-engine-red box she'd bought to keep her imperial teacup and saucer safe. It was made of cherry wood and had a lock. Jimmy's note was wrapped in plastic and tucked under the cup. Len wanted to know what was in the locket hanging around Lisa's neck. She told him it was bad luck to open it and that if he did he would die.

He said he respected that.

⊷

One Thursday afternoon in August she went alone into the city. She had no specific purpose for doing so and her walk was aimless. She was turning from Curzon Street down Half Moon Street, when a man exited a narrow white building up ahead and shouted her name. The voice sounded familiar. She looked over and there stood Mick. An older, better dressed Mick with short hair, but Mick all the same. Lisa nearly wept with joy to see this figment of her imagination materialize in the middle of Mayfair. It had been such a long time. They embraced on the corner, clung briefly to their shared memories, then asked what was new.

How time had moved on, how far they had journeyed down different tracks. Three years earlier, Mick had married a lass from Glasgow named Jennifer, and was now the father of two little nippers named Timothy and Eleanor. He proudly produced a photo of a curly-haired little tot grinning a toothless grin beside a pretty woman with long brown hair holding a small baby. His wife didn't look anything like Mimmi. Jennifer had a face very much her own, pretty and freckled, with a glint in her eye. Mick said he'd got a job at the new EMI studios that spring. She remembered that it had always been his ambition. They'd just bought a semi in Putney. Lisa could tell by the width of his smile that it was a happy man standing before her.

While he didn't mention the past, she read in his eyes that he had not forgotten. She told him she had met a Canadian and that the relationship was getting serious, having no idea how true this really was. Mick asked if she was happy. She said she was.

"So luv, this love of your life, does he have a name?"

"Jimmy Sullivan is the love of my life."

"Well, Lisa, I hope you and Jimmy will be very happy."

"I hope so too."

They walked down to Piccadilly together and parted. Mick headed down the stairs to the Green Park tube station. Lisa watched the earth swallow him up, feeling a pang of loss. These days he looked like a man who could afford the whole alphabet. He was walking tall, this older Mick who had embraced suburban bliss; wife and nippers not an added burden but a crowning achievement. Looking at him she knew that this was the role he had been meant to play all along: the family man. He'd always been great with children.

The knowledge that she would probably never see him again weighed on her. She would have liked to take him home for a keepsake. Instead she escaped into the park and sat on a bench for a long time, reflecting under the shady canopy. Thinking many thoughts about many things was a suitable pastime in Green Park, a place conducive to the aloneness of quiet reflection. The trees in the park were plane trees, like the ones on Strossmayerov trg in Zagreb, and the ones shading Mirogoj cemetery.

Len called them sycamores.

Many musings later she got up and wandered towards Buckingham Palace and its throng of tourists crowding the gates, then onwards down the Mall to Trafalgar Square. Later in St. James Square she stood irresolute on the pavement, then crossed over to the center and circled the fenced-off park several times, feeling restless, simultaneously nostalgic and premonitory. Round and round she went while her heart played xylophone up and down her ribs, a haunting and ominous tune. Two American polyester tourists stopped to stare unabashed. "Drug addict," concluded the woman. "London's full of them."

Lisa turned her back on their disapproval, faces and continued up to Piccadilly Circus to catch the tube back to Chiswick. She descended into the earth's core, remembering how it had frightened her eight years ago when she arrived in the rain with her imperial teacup.

If she didn't know that this was a farewell stroll, she sensed it in the tune her heart was playing.

〜◇〜

Len was cooking spaghetti that night. Melvin and Zoe were coming for supper to help liven the place up a bit. It had been a while since she had seen them. They had been busy with letters and meetings and marches, protesting France's intention of testing another nuclear bomb over the Mururoa Atoll in the Pacific.

For the first time she broke her ingrained habit and did not change at South Kensington. That day she went two stops further and caught the Ealing Broadway, which continued to Chiswick Park, and that's where she got off, staying put in her seat and closing her eyes, when it stopped at Turnham Green.

The road from Chiswick Park station led straight down to the green. She sat on a bench again and reflected on how for eight years the striped steeple of the church had been a landmark, the center of what had once been a village that she had made hers. She had not been inside that church a single time. The insides of churches made her uncomfortable.

She got up, turned her back on the church and walked home.

# 19

In August, the day before Ram was due back with his new bride, Len moved in with Melvin and Zoe. Live-in guests were against Ram's rules. Len was leaving for Canada in a few weeks anyway. His imminent departure worried Lisa, who had got used to his unobtrusive presence. Already they had the habits of a couple, the established comfort of a domestic routine. She liked having somebody to sleep with and didn't want to think about would happen when he left.

He hadn't left yet when her life fell apart again.

She had envisioned Ram's bride a shy doe-eyed beauty floating through the door in a shimmering pink silk sari with gold trim, greeting her in a soft lilting voice. Shakuntala, the Prakash middle daughter, was dressed western style in a navy blue two-piece suit. Her English was heavily accented, and peppered with what she assumed classy Anglicisms, delivered in a piercing tone of voice. "I say, vhat about this bloody veather!" was her favorite. She was pretty in a pudgy sort of way, her gestures elegant and graceful, her painted nails flawless, indicating hands that were seldom used. The gems in her many rings looked real. Her western business-like outfit led Lisa to think that she was one of those modern Indian women, a lawyer or a doctor. (Amrit had written to say that his wife was a doctor.) But Ram's bride's occupation was that of being waited on. She liked to lean back in a chair and sip tea. She was helpless without servants. This meant she was helpless.

"Oh," she said, on being introduced to Lisa, "You must be the Swedish gardener." Treating the gardener to the kind of empty half-smile bestowed on servants, she swept on, lady of the manor already.

In a matter of days Shakuntala let it be known that she would much prefer if Lisa refrained from weeding and watering and doing "vhatever it is you do, dearie" while she, Shakuntala sat in her garden enjoying the air.

Those were fighting words, but Lisa thought it wise to ignore the challenge. For now at least. A waiting game ensued while she, feeling threatened, thought of ways to rid the manor of its lady. Pesticide in her tea came out tops. The insertion of a sharp gardening tool up the good lady's cushiony behind would not work as well, though Lisa liked the Bosch aspect of such an act.

One afternoon there was a knock on the door and in swept the bone-idle chatelaine, uninvited. She had taken to wearing saris again, having realized that dressing English was not uncommon in England. Her right arm was so full of bracelets it resembled a metal pipe. Stopping in the middle of the room she gazed about appreciatively. "Mm," she mused to herself, ignoring the dust in her air that was her gardener, "I think I shall like this for my bedroom. I think I shall like to vake up to a wiew of the garden. It vill remind me of home."

"This is my room!"

The statement amused Shakuntala a great deal.

"My husband is the owner of this house, dearie. If I vish to live in this room who are you to stop me, may I ask? Now, these brass shelves belong to the house, yes?"

"No, they damn well do not!"

"Don't you dare speak to me in that tone of woice. This is my husband's house, please you remember that."

Fear woke up Lisa's She-Devil temper. It reared its furious head and barked. "Get the hell out of my room before I kick you out on your fat ass!"

Out swept the indignant Shakuntala, her sari going swish-swish, her bracelets going clink-clink. Lisa fell on her bed, stunned. Never once had it occurred to her that she did not own this room, that it was not her garden, her refuge, outside those French doors. Shakuntala was right. It was her husband's house. She could sleep in any damn room she pleased. All day, should she feel like it.

Still, thought Lisa. Still. To think that I will be booted out like Prince the puss. Put down at the vet's, if Shakuntala has her way. This could not be. She would talk to Ram. Make him see reason. They went back a long way. He was bound to see her point.

In the evening there came another knock on her door, a softer one this time, and Ram slid shamefaced into the shadows of what was no longer Lisa's room. It was to be as the lady of the manor had ordered. The Swedish gardener, who had so greatly offended that lady, his new bride, was to be evicted without further ado. Lisa's services were no longer needed. Ram, embarrassed and downcast, could not apologize enough.

"I assume I am allowed to take what belongs to me?"

"Why, yes, of course! Don't be silly."

"Just checking."

"I am so very, very sorry, my dear. We have had many good times in this house, have we not?"

"It's okay, Ram. Really."

It was not okay at all. Lisa reasoned that if she had paid for her sins by giving up Jimmy Sullivan, why should she now find herself back in the left pane of Bosch's triptych? Why was she being cast out of the garden by a black-winged angel wielding an armload of bracelets in lieu of a sword? For feeding Len an apple?

The truth was, she could never belong to what was not hers. A solitary human animal can not belong at all. Everybody needs a family of some sort, a tribe.

While this was obvious, it was not what she wanted to hear from her own lips.

⊨◇⊲

She was cast out a week later, a fugitive once again, forced to join Len at The Flat. Only one thought enabled her to survive the devastating loss: the revenge she had planned on the sacred cow that had caused it, that bracelet-covered avenging angel, Shakuntala.

The weekend her marching orders came into effect, Ram and his Prakash middle-daughter-bride went to visit with some relative of hers up near Manchester. They left early on the Friday afternoon. Ram had arranged it that way, judging by the sheepish farewell he bade the Swedish gardener. His eyes were downcast, his feet a-shuffle. As they left, the chatelaine shouted a loud order in English to her husband, "Kindly tell that voman not to make a mess" while pointedly ignoring the woman in question, on her swish-swish, jangle-jangle way out the door.

"You just wait, dearie," Lisa thought. "You just wait."

Shortly after midnight Len, Melvin and Zoe came sneaking over, dressed in black, rebel angels cast down to earth to wreak havoc. They carried large garbage bags, boxes and shovels. It was important to be discreet, in case Mrs. Mortified or any of the neighbors suffered insomnia and stood looking out their windows. This was a vitally important job and it had to be completed before sunrise. They were going to erase paradise. Ram had agreed that Lisa was allowed to take with her whatever was hers. She was holding him to his word.

It was hard labor that took most of the night. Lisa wasn't sure if transplanting fuchsias would work, but was determined not to leave them behind. Melvin had borrowed an old van into which they loaded everything, except the poor annuals that became the innocent victims of massive bloomicide, as Zoe called it. The corpses were stuffed in bags for mass burial. Lisa hadn't realized quite how many bushes and flowers she had managed to crowd into her small paradise. She cried without pride as she pulled up nasturtiums, revealing the non-existent path underneath.

When they were done, apart from the apple tree and the rhododendrons, only the black mulberry tree was left. It had grown too large to dig up, and she didn't have the heart to cut it down. Crying, she hugged its trunk and stroked its leaves, thinking it needed to be calmed down, told it she had no choice but to leave it behind.

"Stop shagging the tree," whispered Zoe. "It's time to split."

Everything else that Lisa had planted, pruned, watered and tended to over the past eight years was gone. Paradise lay ravished, a trampled muddy mess. The branches of the apple tree hung as if in mourning, shedding apples like tears. It was a sad, barren place, a battlefield from which the corpses had all been removed, but where a scent of death still lingered.

When she stood in the doorway for the last time, looking into her refuge, her home, the place where she had assumed she belonged, she saw only the stripped bed and the ugly bookshelf she had hidden as soon as she got a nicer one. The white carpets that had covered the floor were gone. The brown lino, laid bare once again, was cracked and ugly. Dust danced in the sunbeams that lit up nothing but a drab emptiness as she closed the door for the last time. On the way out she hurled her key onto the table in the communal room. It slid right off and landed in Shakuntala's favorite chair.

There was only one thing to do with what they had salvaged. Later in the morning they drove over to Airedale Avenue to visit Mrs. Billings. The good lady was baffled to see Lisa and her black-clad companions lined up on her front path, and more than a little stunned to find herself appointed adoptive mother to a van full of garden. "Gobsmacked" was the word she used, twice. But she was too kind to turn her back on the poor uprooted orphans. "Not to worry, dear. There'll be plenty of room for everything in the back garden. It will look ever so lovely, I'm sure."

She looked older than Lisa remembered her. Then again, it had been a while.

She asked about the Wickses. Mrs. Wicks had passed away two years earlier. "All of a sudden it was. Dog's dead too, and good riddance to that savage mutt. But Mr. Wicks is still about. Punctual as ever, he is. Got himself a lady-friend too. Oh, yes. Bridget, the char, no less! Fancy that!"

Fancy that indeed. All those saints must have got off their lazy behinds if only to shut up the incessant noise of Bridget's daily prayers.

What smarted the most was that Lisa would not to get to see Shakuntala's reaction when she returned and found the garden of earthly delights gone missing.

⊷

Len kept telling Lisa she was beautiful as though it wasn't true but he wanted to boost her confidence by being kind. One night, a week before he was to return home, when they lay in bed talking about how they would have to part, he blurted out, "Let's get married!"

She could tell that he took himself by surprise, sensed him collecting himself, convincing himself that of course he meant it. He did it well, to the point of enthusiasm. Yes, he said, Lisa should definitely come with him to Canada, it was meant to be, couldn't she see that? He said he loved her, which she thought peculiar, as he didn't know her.

But she thought, if he's willing, then so am I. "Yes," she replied, convincing herself that she meant it too. She needed to replace her losses.

It's possible he asked her to marry him and come back to Canada because he knew she had nowhere to go and felt bad for her. Having lost her two homes, the sixties and her room, having no place to hide, she had sighed, "Where do I go from here?" enough times. He might have mistaken her despair for a hint.

There was also the fear of one day dying in one or another rented room like old Mrs. Parkinson, hastily scribbling a last plea. Lisa didn't want another room, it was the garden she needed. Without her refuge she was in an unfamiliar time and place. She could not get comfortable.

Why not move to Canada then? Where else did she have to go? Why not travel a great big whooping distance? What was that Buddhist saying? The journey is all? It was as good an excuse as any.

She consented, thinking about Sonja's Christmas wedding and how she would miss it. Something else to feel miserable about. But Sonja didn't really need bothersome old Lisa anymore, did she? Sonja had moved on. Sonja would wear white satin shoes and flowers in her hair when she danced the wedding waltz with her husband. Lisa preferred the image of her friend waltzing around with silver dominatrix boots poking out under the hem of her wedding gown, the ugly chrome necklace like a tiara on her head, still the Sonja that had been her friend for twenty years. Since they were seven.

Sonja would live happily ever after, that was the important thing.

"Yes, okay, sure, let's get married. Why not? Pour some more wine and let's celebrate."

"Hold out your mug, wife."

"Thank you, husband. And tell me about your family. Are they nice?" It would feel good to be included in a family.

"I'm sure they will be when they meet you."

She should have asked exactly what that was supposed to mean, had she not been preoccupied with visions of Christmas dinners, weddings, birthday parties. Aunts in their Sunday best gossiping, drunk uncles playing cards, ties loose, suit jackets off; children running around shrieking. She didn't stop to think, why in those visions, she was one of the children.

A week later Lisa was on her way to Canada with her husband-to-be. Traveling to this new country would bring her far, far away from what had been. Over time it would also bring her a lot closer to it.

# Canada

# 20

They left for the airport very early in the morning, without making a sound, letting Melvin and Zoe sleep off the previous night's farewell wine. They didn't have to leave that early, it was merely to avoid another farewell. After eight years Lisa was leaving damp and drafty London to travel thousands of miles to some country where she didn't know a soul, in order to get married to a man she was fairly sure she didn't love.

Having lost her island refuge, one shore was as good as another.

She slung her bag over her shoulder, grabbed the suitcase, and closed the door to The Flat for the last time. The red box, holding her teacup, Jimmy's photo and note, sat secure in her shoulder bag. In the nest of the cup, her father's false teeth lay wrapped in the same old handkerchief. The box rested on top of his beret. That was it. The rest had been shipped in a very large trunk with fake brass locks. She had bought it under the mistaken impression that she had acquired many belongings, having led such a full life, and was dismayed to find that, after lowering her bundles of stuff into the trunk, it had been only half full. Zoe had persuaded her to take the brass and glass shelf too. "Well, why the hell not?" she insisted. "It's yours." So they had dismantled it, wrapped the glass in sheets and towels, and packed it. Still the trunk wasn't full, so modest was her accumulated wealth.

"Should have packed your garden too," said Melvin. "All those shrubs and whatnot."

It was raining when they left, drizzling like the evening eight years ago when she had arrived. The orange glow of the streetlights, still on along Chiswick High Road, made it look like the middle of the night, except the birds were up and singing in the rain-sodden tree outside The Flat. It was late August and it was going to be another wet day. As they waited to cross the street she turned around and looked up, expecting to see what? Pru perhaps? Dressed in a Saint Laurent original, half asleep, her red hair damp in the rain, shouting, "Darling, don't leave! I still need you!"

A yellow towel hung limp on the balcony above the peeling pillars of the entrance. There were no signs of life.

Pru didn't live here anymore.

Lisa took Len's hand as they crossed the street. She had to hold on to something. His hand, like hers, was damp and cold. It was too early for there to be much traffic. Nobody was out and about. They passed The Greek's which wouldn't open for hours. She felt a twinge of guilt at not having said good-bye to Dimitrios. It had been ages since she'd been in for lunch.

Before heading up Turnham Green Terrace she stopped on the corner to allow herself a last look at Chiswick, down the High Road towards the green. The puddles along the gutters reflected the orange glare of the streetlights. A lone milk float clattered by. Lisa wanted a bottle of milk for her tea. She wanted to drink it while sitting on her bed, listening through the open doors to the music of the rain washing the petals of each flower in paradise.

She couldn't bear to leave.

Len pulled at her arm. He was getting irritable. "Don't just stand there, for fuck's sake, it's pissing down."

"I'm coming."

The flower vendor had not yet arrived at his stand by the tube station. This, for some reason, made her burst into tears.

⊷

Later that day, having suffered another onslaught of persuasive second thoughts, she forced herself to follow Len onto the plane that would transport them across the Atlantic. It was not a place of great ambiance. They had to strap themselves, still damp, into uncomfortable seats beside a strange man. It was horrible. The space was too confined. There was no way she could go through with it. She had to go and get her garden back.

"Excuse me."

Len watched his bride-to-be unfasten her seat belt and climb over the hefty slab of man in the aisle seat. "Where the hell are you going?"

Lisa was hurrying down the aisle. The plane was already rolling down the runway, there wasn't much time. She was stopped by a stewardess, who came storming down the aisle to force the rebel back into her seat, just as the plane tilted up and escaped into the washed-out English sky.

Higher and higher it rose through the dark leaking clouds. Lisa was no longer in England. She was doomed, stuck in a smelly metal tube, strapped into a straitjacket seat. Nobody deserved such a fate. She was trembling. Her heart pounded, gravity pulled. All the visions of hell she had suffered between Copenhagen and Zagreb and Vienna paled compared to this. She sweated in her damp clothes and wrote a letter to Pru in her head: *Now I know where Bosch got his ideas. He flew fifteenth-century second class cattle pen. PS. Oh Pru, dearest Pru, I can't stand it!*

The confined space pressed closer. To her right a stranger's pudgy elbow squeezed deeper into her upper arm. Her legs had nowhere to go except under her chin. The air contained more nicotine than oxygen. She was no longer on planet earth. *Terra firma* had vanished somewhere far below.

But there was an antidote to this torture. Gin and tonic. She had been drinking a gin and tonic the night she met Jimmy.

"Which button do you press for the stewardess?"

"That one. Why? You okay?"

"No, but I will be."

Hours later, Lisa was pleasantly drunk, amusing herself by digging her elbow into the stranger's fluorescent polyester arm. She was considering a little nap when Len pointed excitedly out the cabin window. Looking at his glowing face, she found that it wasn't Len at all, it was some beaming little boy wanting to show her something special he'd found. Puzzled she thought, "I don't know this boy."

"Look!" He was grinning. "That's Toronto down there!"

"Yeah?" Even Lisa found her response lacking. She mustered up some enthusiasm. "My goodness, it looks big!"

"Oh yeah!" The boy sounded like he'd built it himself.

Having bad-mouthed his homeland since the day she met him, he now couldn't wait to tear off the plane and kiss the soil of that very land. At the same time it occurred to Lisa that she was thousands of miles from anyplace resembling home. That she in fact did not have a home. That if she wanted to return to London she would have to get on another metal tube, and sit strapped in another straitjacket. Worse, upon arriving back in London she would have no refuge to escape to. She was a woman of no fixed address.

It didn't take long before they landed with a thud in the country called Canada, and were allowed to get off. Her legs were wobbly from gin and from having been folded up for seven hours. Inside the airport all the people sounded exactly like Len, including the customs and immigration officers. They didn't search her suitcase, and therefore did not need to inquire why she was bringing an old set of false teeth into the country. Should they have done so, she had her story ready: these were the imperial teeth that had once belonged to the Empress Maria Theresa.

Then she was sitting beside Len in the back seat of a pastel blue car that had been proudly introduced as a Brand New

Chevrolet Impala. Lisa knew nothing about cars, apart from the fact that they had four wheels and an engine. She had never had any use for one. Admittedly, this one was very roomy, almost like an English taxi. She could stretch her legs out and lean back. Better still, it was air-conditioned. She had never experienced air-conditioning, but it struck her as the height of ingenious luxury. The air in this country had the consistency of a wet blanket. "It gets like that in the summer," confessed Len in response to her shock at the tropical humidity. Despite what he had told her about his country, she had imagined an endless white expanse where people wore buffalo hides and plodded around on snowshoes scanning an empty horizon.

It was Thursday afternoon in Canada. In the front seat of the brand new Chevrolet Impala sat the two strangers whose cautious hands had shaken hers at the airport. One was Len's older brother Steve, the tall skinny man whose car it was; the other was Steve's wife, Lucy, a sturdy little blonde in turquoise shorts. Lisa had been surprised to see people wearing shorts at the airport.

They were traveling down a major traffic artery called the Cue-ee towards the spot on the horizon where the sky was doing a stellar imitation of pea soup.

"WELCOME TO CANADA," enunciated the sturdy blonde for the third time. Each time her voice grew louder to make it easier for the slightly bedraggled foreigner in the back to comprehend the intricacies of the English language.

"THANK YOU." The foreigner enunciated right back, putting on Pru's toff aristocrat accent. These people knew she had lived in London for the past eight years. People in England speak English. It's a known fact. They had exchanged a list of polite pleasantries back at the airport. All in English. What was wrong with these people?

Unperturbed, the brand new Chevrolet Impala sped down the Cue-ee towards the pea-soup cloud.

Len said his parents lived up on the mountain. She imagined a log cabin perched on a snow-clad peak.

"He means the escarpment," explained Steve. "It's not a real mountain or nothing."

Lisa, who did not know what an escarpment was, was not about to reveal the depth of her foreign ignorance to these air-conditioned people.

The city they arrived in was so unlike anything she was used to that she closed her eyes. She felt the car head up a hill, presumably the escarpment. A few minutes later the car stopped and she opened her eyes again. They had arrived in the driveway of the three-bedroom brick bungalow where Len had grown up. There was some kind of apple tree growing in the middle of the front lawn, but it looked nothing like Lisa's apple tree. Along the front of the house a military row of marigolds stood at attention. Len's parents were standing in the driveway, equally disciplined. Judging by their reaction to Lisa, they suspected her of having crossed the Atlantic for the sole purpose of embarrassing them.

Perhaps it was the smell of gin on her breath. Perhaps she should have worn a bra. These were the kinds of details one has to see to in respectable society, only such vital details had completely slipped her mind, it had been so long.

It was also glaringly obvious that they were in no hurry to fold their long-lost son to their eager bosoms.

"Hi dad," said Len, grinning a grin that didn't sit comfortably on his face. He received only a curt nod in return.

"Nice trip, son?" asked his mother. She looked as if she might have succumbed to a brief embrace had her husband approved of that kind of emotional exhibitionism.

Len's younger brother, Greg, showed up a bit later with his wife Patti. Lisa was happy to see him give Len a brotherly hug and call him Lennie. Greg and Patti had a brand new car too. Theirs was black and called a Capri. They made everybody troop out and admire it, inside and out. When the men buried their heads under the hood, Lisa expected incantations to issue forth. It was clear that cars were worshipped in this part of the world. Those with a brand new one were the blessed.

The fact that she had never owned a car proved incomprehensible to Len's family. That she did not even know how to drive one was deeply suspect. It made them so uncomfortable, they dared not look her in the eye.

Having admired the four-wheeled wonder for an appropriate length of time, they trooped back in to the fake-wood-paneled family room where they pretended to have a conversation, grabbing subjects out of the air, seemingly at random, while waiting for dinner to be served.

Lisa had lived alone in her room for far too long, developed odd if comforting habits, and had grown deplorably inept at family situations. She had never had a proper family to start with. Assuming the people before her made up such a unit.

Being part of this group of strangers was a physical pain. Len's mom tried to sound cheerful every time she popped her head out of the kitchen to report on the roast and the doneness of the potatoes, but Lisa could tell it was difficult for her. How many times did she need to ask, "I hope you like roast and potatoes, Lisa?" Len's mom, too, found this a bad dream. Lisa wanted to apologize for her intrusion and take her leave.

Len's father gave a deeper meaning to the word dour. He ignored all womenfolk on principle. He ignored Len too. Greg would later confide to Lisa that it was because Len had long hair. According to daddy McT this made Len's manhood highly questionable. That he had just dragged back a dubious migrant woman from overseas did nothing whatsoever to contradict that belief. Len's father never got over his first impression of Lisa. To him she would remain a gin-soaked foreign deviant without a driver's license.

Knowing what he knew, daddy McT sat firmly entrenched in his fake leather chair, ignoring a suspect world. Just as he would every Sunday after they had dutifully partaken of the weekly family dinner. Roast beef, Yorkshire pudding, roast potatoes, glazed carrots, and sometimes broccoli, sometimes cauliflower, always hidden under a layer of orange cheese-food product with an intriguing chemical tang. As soon as they were finished daddy McT would retire to his chair, light an Export-A and twirl it around slowly, staring at it with dull anger as if ready to knock the fiendish nicotine invader right out of his own hand.

If he bothered to talk, it was about fishing or cars or the job down at the steel plant, and only with Steve and Greg. They were the good sons who one day would turn into less rigid versions of himself. Len, who had failed his father by trying to march to a different drummer, went ignored.

One of the things that bound Len and Lisa was the way they had both failed to please a parental autocrat. That, and the hard-to-get-rid-off sense that they could do nothing right. It didn't take long to discover how much Len's upbringing had stunted him, how much it still hurt him, whether he admitted it or not, and mostly he didn't. Because of that Lisa forgave him a lot more than she otherwise would have.

Her sisters-in-law to be, Patti and Lucy, were friendly in the we-versus-you way of those who know best. The problem soon became apparent. They were both religious and that ruled out any closeness, especially after it became clear that they were hoping to make a decent Christian out of the new sister-in-law foisted upon them. They soon realized that she lacked all the required attributes. Working on this taciturn creature from overseas would take some doing.

It was true. Lisa's roots had absorbed nutrients in a far more pagan soil. She had never been exposed to good "Christian values," had been unfamiliar with the very term until meeting new relatives-to-be. It was a tempting notion, but it soon became obvious that these were the same values that had always been an excuse for the narrow-minded condemnation of everyone who did not share the same faith. An excuse to perform center-panel-of-the-triptych atrocities. She wanted none of that. Admittedly, she had acted irresponsibly at times, but never that irresponsibly. She wanted to tell them that whether knee-deep in shit creek, or in the dewy grass of paradise, she had always stood on her own two feet. Only it wasn't the kind of thing she would dare tell Lucy and Patti.

Lisa sat in their midst like a stranger who had mistaken their living room for a bus shelter, checking her watch, waiting for a bus that never arrived.

⊷

Until they got married she was given the room Len had once shared with Greg. It still had matching curtains and bedspreads full of chubby-faced cowboys frolicking around lewdly grinning cacti that looked like prickly green perverts with triple erections. Every morning when she tried her best to wake up in her island refuge, it was this strange place that greeted her, enfolded her within its baby-blue walls. On the wall directly in front of her hung a picture of Our Lord the Savior. Each new morning he stared down at the woman in the bed with blank eyes, not recognizing her as one of his flock. She glared back in defiance and stuck her tongue out. Our Lord the Savior did not bat an eyelid.

The days before the wedding she spent sitting on the bed, leafing through department store catalogues looking for affordable furniture. Len's mum had one from a store called Eaton's and another one from a place called Sears. The furniture looked foreign, too New World twentieth century rococo. Lisa couldn't relate to it. It alienated her, it was too ornate, not real wood but covered with something called veneer. She had to look up the word.

The McTavish's living room furniture, Len's mum proudly informed her, was Italian Renaissance from Toronto.

Lisa put aside the thick catalogues and next thing she knew she was married to somebody named Leonard Francis McTavish. Suddenly there they were, dressed up and awkward, Len looking so lost in his brother Greg's good suit it made her heart wobble. She wanted to comb his hair and straighten his tie and tell him what a brave boy he was.

The tying of this knot was a quick and simple affair, for which everybody was grateful, though when the Justice of the Peace asked, "Do you Lisa Ann-Kristin Grankvist take Leonard Francis

McTavish . . . ?" Lisa said nothing, not realizing she was being addressed. He was forced to repeat it. It wasn't only Len's name that sounded unfamiliar.

Afterwards she thought, "I've married a Francis, just like Maria Theresa. I could call him Franz . . . and may we not have sixteen children."

They had requested there be no post-nuptial merrymaking. As the word was missing from the McTavish dictionary, not a voice was raised in protest. The happy couple headed down to Niagara Falls in Len's 1962 Ford, festively decorated with a garland of rust spots. It didn't have air-conditioning, but there were little holes where the rust had eaten through. Besides, the weather had cooled.

This was something else they had in common; the incapacity to grasp the importance of a brand new car.

The trip was to be a weekend honeymoon only. They felt they ought to go somewhere, adhere to some kind of protocol. Niagara Falls had seemed the appropriate place. It was close and it was world famous, Lisa knew, she had seen photos. She had seen the movie with Marilyn Monroe, too, though unlike the Loomises, Len and Lisa did not stay in cabin B at Rainbow Cabins. While neither Rose nor Lisa loved the man they were there with, Lisa did not plan to kill her husband.

*Honeymoon.* How golden sweet and romantic the sound. But to Lisa in Niagara Falls it raised, for some twisted reason, the ghost of the honeyed moon showing off in the indigo air on that night long ago when she lost her childish illusions. She had no idea why it chose to illuminate her consciousness that particular afternoon.

"Come on, Len. Let's go sightseeing."

The Falls were spectacular, the town tacky. That was okay, she was not in a romantic mood. On the other side of the roaring waters the United States of America stretched out big and mighty and sure of itself. Somewhere over there a man named Jimmy Sullivan was going about his life in unfashionable workman's boots, shadows in his face that sorrow had etched there.

She didn't feel as if he could sense her standing there. Nor could she see him waving, though she did look carefully. All she felt was a fine mist of water on her face.

"Well," said Len later that night, grinning the grin she found so endearing.

"Well what?"

"What's it feel like to be Mrs. McTavish?" They were back in the hotel room after a honeymoon dinner in a restaurant where they each had been served steak the size of a small European country. It would have cost a king's ransom anywhere in London. The baked potato was so large she could have hollowed it out and taken up residence in it.

"Okay." Actually she felt nothing much at all, apart from gut-wrenching indigestion. She wasn't used to eating that much meat. Arms folded over her stomach, she stood looking at the view out the window, scanning the horizon for Jimmy. He had to be down there somewhere.

How inexplicable to love somebody with such ludicrous faithfulness.

It was all too much. She had this very day acquired a husband who was already turning out to be different from the bloke he had pretended to be when she met him in London. A man who visibly shrank when in the bosom of his family. He had flattened, but that was all right. If you have a pretend marriage, a cardboard husband is not unbefitting.

Len was starting a job in the printing department of the Hamilton *Spectator* the following week. During the drive down to Niagara Falls he had expressed hope that Lisa too would get a job in the near future, else he wouldn't see much of his paycheck. He was planning to buy this cool stereo from this guy he knew, just so as she was aware of it, so he needed to start saving right away.

Lisa had replied that of course she would get a job. She was used to supporting herself. How did he think she'd survived the last eight years?

"Hey, Lees!"

"What?"

"I said, what are you staring at?"

"Oh . . . America. It's so close you could touch it. I've never been to America."

"Forget it. You're in Canada now. Canada is way better."

"It is? In what way?"

"In every way. Trust me."

"If you say so." She turned her back on Jimmy and raised her glass of champagne. "Well then . . . cheers, Franz, me old lad. May we both keep our teeth."

# 21

**W**hy on earth did I marry Len?

This was the second disoriented thought to make it out of her consciousness when she woke up the next morning. The first one was "Where am I?" Answering that one was easy. She was in a king-size bed with a brand new husband in a room on the tenth floor of a hotel on the edge of a country called Canada. A late September sun blasted through the panoramic window like a searchlight intent on finding the truth.

Not far away the famous waterfalls roared, as they must have since the beginning of time. From the room next door came the sound of a vacuum cleaner. Down the corridor a woman with a strong accent was shouting to somebody to get more towels. It was Sunday. Just another day. None of this bothered Len, who looked sweet snoozing beside her, a leftover champagne grin hanging crooked on his face. She lifted up a strand of his brown hair and played with it, thinking that this person was her husband and that he had nice hair.

But why marry him?

A tricky question, it had several answers as well as none. One reason she had married Len was because she didn't love him. If love was the idiotic mindless obsession she had succumbed to in room 41 in the hotel near Victoria station, she was far better off without it.

The death knell of her existence had come when her island refuge sank under the weight of that bracelet-covered sacred cow. After that was gone there had then been nothing of importance left. She had paid her dues and still owed. Len had been the one who had been there for her, the bloke from over the sea who said he loved her because he wanted to, offering a convenient solution.

Going back home had not been an option. Sonja was getting married. Lisa would miss her wedding and hated herself for it. Sonja had missed Lisa's; she didn't even know she was married. Lisa felt wretched about that too, as though she had betrayed her best friend.

Would she have gone back if Sonja had not been about to get hitched? She thought about it, playing with Len's hair, but honestly, or dishonestly, didn't know. Mimmi was married too. She had called the day before Lisa left her island barren, to report that she had just had a baby girl. Her name was Emma.

Lisa's unacknowledged fear was that no one back home would have time for her. That she no longer belonged there. She still had no fixed address. She had married Len because she had been unable to come up with an alternative option. It was not something she was proud of. On the other hand, she doubted if Len's reasons for marrying her were any nobler.

When she had first laid eyes on Hamilton, she had thought, not too surprised, well, here's a fitting punishment for my sins. She had mistaken the steel mills for the third panel of the triptych.

⊨◇⊣

Living in Hamilton was too easy to qualify as punishment of any sort. People were friendly, non-judgmental, and had not the slightest interest in her foreign background. In the face of such indifference Lisa, with matching indifference, went on automatic pilot for a long time. Bit by bit her past fell by the wayside until it seemed like a story she'd once heard. Nobody noticed. Neither did she. Days and months went by, like unwanted gifts still in their wraps.

What she did notice was that she became heavy. She didn't gain weight, it was gravity grabbing hold of her, making up for all the weightless years. No longer able to float through time, she plodded, without hurry, towards whatever the future would spring on her.

In London she had spent eight years in a multiethnic household, a place pungent with spicy food and incense, a babble of incomprehensible languages, full of oddballs living various fantasy lives, from Swedish gardener to Indian sahib. To go from that to the bland conformity of life in Hamilton was too severe a shock. People were friendly to a fault and agreed with everything she said. They were decent and honest, cheerful and content, and liked to think well of other people. They all had families. They all had houses and jobs and cars and barbecues.

Lisa had had no idea that an uncomplicated good life could be so uninteresting.

To say that she didn't fit in would be an understatement. At the first family gathering, Len's cousin Janine sidled up to Lisa, smiled like a dear old friend to the new family member and asked, "So, Lisa, what's new?" Lisa, who had never before laid eyes on the woman, thought it a peculiar question to ask a stranger.

"Nothing that you would know anything about," she explained and that, for some reason, wiped the smile off cousin Janine's congenial face. Turning her back on Len's nasty wife, Janine walked off in a huff to tell Lucy that she was for sure right about that Lisa being something else.

Lisa later pointed out to Len what a weird cousin he had, begging him to explain what she had done wrong this time. He reminded her once again that it was she who was the weird one.

"It can't be that difficult, for fuck's sake," he sighed, frustrated.

A week after that episode, out of Christian compassion, her sisters-in-law invited her to a party. It was a very special kind of party that had a name, and it was in the middle of the week. Only women were invited. Lisa put on a bra and dressed up in a respectable dress to make a good impression. She was touched that they wanted to include her in the festivities.

They picked her up in the brand new Ford Capri. Patti's mother was with them, intrigued to meet the peculiar woman Len had dragged back from overseas. Never having met anybody from Switzerland, she was naturally curious. "I hear the Alps are real nice."

"Real, real nice." Lisa didn't bother to elucidate her place of origin.

They arrived at a suburban bungalow that looked like a mirror image of the McTavish bungalow, but on a different part of the escarpment. A woman opened the door and let them know that she was pleased as punch that they could make it, adding in the same breath that everybody was in the *wreck* room down in the basement.

People in Canada spent a lot of their lives down in their cellars, Lisa had noticed. They called them *wreck* rooms, but they didn't wreck them, quite the contrary, they put up fake wood paneling and carpeting and then spent most of their free time down there, even though they had a whole house upstairs. Some people built bars with barstools and beer on tap. It was very odd.

There was a whole bunch of ladies in the wood paneled cellar sitting around in a large circle. It looked like they were about to hold a séance. Lisa wondered if they belonged to a cult. Here and there stood card tables with trays of triangular little sandwiches full of gooey stuff. The sandwiches were covered with plastic wrap so presumably they were not meant for eating. At the end of the room stood a very large table full of plastic containers and bowls and things.

The ladies were not wearing party hats, nor were they especially dressed up. It had to be a cult. Lisa got worried and asked

Lucy what this was all about.

"It's a Tupperware party." The way Lucy slammed her tongue on the *T* informed Lisa that she was lamentably ignorant.

"A what party?" Lisa was every bit that ignorant.

"Tupperware? You've never been to a Tupperware party?"

"No." She sensed her probation was not going well. Patti and Lucy exchanged a look. Best to apologize. "I'm sorry."

"That's all right," said Lucy, though clearly it wasn't.

They sat down and a lady in pink stretch pants got up and said how darn happy she was to see them all, before proceeding to show them all the plastic paraphernalia, one item at a time. The woman revealed in a series of pleasant surprises all the clever ways you could use the various items. When she was finished, everybody nodded approval and got up and fingered the displays, making favorable comments as to the practical implications of this and that. One after the other, the ladies got out money and checkbooks and bought several pieces. It was what you were supposed to do. Proving that she was as worthy as the rest of them, Lisa made enthusiastic sounds and bought a pair of green salad tongs and four of the biggest rectangular containers.

After business was taken care of the hostess, whose name was Sandi-with-an-i, brought out pots of tea and coffee. Next she removed the plastic wrap from the trays and said, "Help yourselves, gals," and they all tucked into little triangular sandwiches full of gooey stuff. The ones with yellow goo and green bits were especially delectable. Downing a fifth one, Lisa asked what the stuff was.

"It's egg salad," said Patti and exchanged another look with Lucy and her mother.

"Egg salad?"

"You never had egg salad?" Patti's mother stared at Lisa in disbelief, as if here stood the missing link between *homo sapiens* and the chimpanzees.

"No," Lisa confessed. "We don't have egg salad in Switzerland." Smiling politely she helped herself to a sixth triangle and, because she was genuinely interested, asked how to make this delicacy.

"You chop up hard-boiled eggs and some green onions and mix them with mayonnaise. It's real easy. You like it?"

"Yes, it's delicious." That briefly redeemed her, until she asked, "What are green onions?"

By then she had attracted quite a crowd. The hostess went to the kitchen and came back with a bunch of green onions. They looked like malnourished leeks, but apparently they were not. Looking them over Lisa assured her that, no, she had never seen green onions before. They didn't grow in Switzerland, as far as she was aware, and she had never laid eyes on them in England. She didn't bother to reveal the fact that she had eaten precious few vegetables in her life, especially during the last eight years. Fruit and chocolate biscuits, yes. Beans on toast, stolen bits of goat and the like, yes. Green onions, no.

She was a true deviant.

Pru would not have liked goo-filled triangles. She would not have lasted a day in this place. Lisa let that thought console her. Compared to Pru she was doing just fine. Of course, Pru would never have agreed to move across the Atlantic in the first place. Not because she lacked the stamina, nor because of sheer arrogance, but because she would never have a need to relocate. Pru would have refused to go to drive-in movies, and eat French fries and popcorn in the front seat of a car with a crackling speaker hooked to the window. Lisa had taken a shine to this pastime; she enjoyed eating ketchup-sodden fries while watching a movie on a giant screen in the night sky.

Years later she wished she had kept a diary to help visualize what on earth she had been up to those first years on the new continent, when she wasn't at the drive-in or going to Tupperware parties. The larger brushstrokes of the various pictures were clear enough, but the details remained fuzzy.

Her mother-in-law said two decades later that what she remembered most about Lisa when she first arrived in Canada, was how much grape juice she used to drink.

"I never drank grape juice! I don't even like the stuff!"

"You did then, dear."

"It's true," said Len. "You did. Gallons of it. Your teeth used to be purple."

She had had no idea. "I must have been a real winner."

"No kidding."

During her first months in the new country she drank percolated coffee and ate bologna sandwiches made with sliced white bread, saying to Len, "This is disgusting!" He demanded to know what was wrong with his all-time favorite sandwich. Lisa insisted it was not real bread, not real meat and not real mustard either, thus it could not possibly be a real sandwich.

He said she was full of shit.

Soon Lisa discovered Denninger's where they sold lovely sourdough rye bread, fragrant hams, spicy salamis and real cheeses. Len proclaimed her a snob, and said he was very disappointed with the way she was turning out. His eccentric wife explained that this was basic working class fare where she came from, but he would have none of her pitiful excuses.

She watched reruns of *Bewitched* and learnt to wiggle her nose but could never make people disappear.

"What's the matter?" growled daddy McT one Sunday. "You got an itch?"

Life was so easy there was literally nothing to it. Lisa plodded through those first days and months like a sloth in lead shoes, absent-minded and iron-deficient, unburdened by dreams and ambitions. She had stopped making clothes.

# 22

As soon as they had returned from the two-day honeymoon with a view of the rim of America, Lisa called Sonja to announce her drastic change of marital status and country of residence. Sonja was shattered to hear not only that Lisa would be absent from her wedding, but also for not announcing her own nuptials. At first she fell silent. When she found her voice again, a trans-atlantic argument ensued, with Lisa, defensive, well aware that she'd let her friend down. The argument ended abruptly when Sonja burst into tears and hung up. She had never done that before. Lisa was left staring at a cold black receiver that had nothing further to communicate. Living without Sonja, if only Sonja's voice, was unimaginable. Without Sonja she had no link to her country of birth, nobody to confirm that she had existed before age eighteen.

She called back four times but there was no reply.

It took a month of wounded silence before Sonja reached out with an expensive gift of silver cutlery that Lisa didn't use for years because it was too nice. Responding at once, she sent Mimmi money to buy Sonja a set of Orrefors crystal wine glasses, her remembered idea of impeccable Swedish taste. When Sonja received them she called Lisa and they talked for three hours, both clutching the phone cord to hold on to the familiar voice, feeling the distance.

Len threw a fit when he saw the phone bill.

Lisa also had sit down to perform another delayed duty: write and inform her four aunts that she had moved to Canada and married a Canadian. She kept it cheerful, pretending it had not been two years since she had written a sentence that was not scribbled on the back of a Christmas card, hoping her light-hearted tone would prevent them from realizing the seriousness of the matter. Aunt Stina and Aunt Bojan eventually wrote back, in a combined letter, to congratulate her, but the tone of the letter was a stiff nod verging on frosty. Signe and Johan's daughter had disappointed them once again, though that came as no surprise from somebody who had studied art only to end up working in a one-woman sweatshop. All the same, they sent a dozen towels and a white tablecloth Lisa recognized as one of Bojan's second best. A post scriptum said, "And now our dear King has passed away," as if Lisa's erratic behavior was responsible for that too.

Aunt Gulli eventually sent a dozen spoons. One was bent. Her PS read, "A hole developed in the accordion. Henning says it couldn't have been very good. He had to buy a new one. It was expensive, but a much better quality."

Aunt Margit got in touch last. She sent Swedish money, two wrinkled hundred-kronor bills and a short letter. It was one of her last; she had given up on ever seeing her only brother's only child again. Her tone and her handwriting were resigned. Eight years is a long time not to see a person, she repeated twice in one paragraph. She wrote as if speaking for the entire country: "All of Sweden is mourning the death of our beloved King Gustav." "We Swedes don't know much about Canada." Why anybody would want to move that far away was beyond her. Had not living in England all those godforsaken years been bad enough?

Jimmy Daniel Sullivan, wherever he was, turned thirty-one the year Lisa got married. There was a coup in Chile. Lisa watched it on the evening news. She'd taken to watching a lot of TV, her window to the rest of the world.

"Where the hell is Chili?" asked Len from the doorway.

"Southwest of Burrito," she offered, feeling bitchy.

He told her to shove it. It did not bode well.

⌐◇⌐

They had moved into a duplex three days after they arrived back from Niagara Falls. If she had had to stay with Len's parents for any length of time she would have run all the way back to Niagara Falls and jumped in. When she offered to do the dishes, she was turned down. They had a dishwasher. When she suggested she help out with the garden, Len's mum assured her there was no need to fuss about the yard. The disciplined marigolds didn't need a commanding officer. The frost would take them soon enough. Lisa, in desperation, pressed on. Could she plant a variety of flowers bulbs then, add a bit of color come spring, that sort of thing?

"Whatever for?" Mrs. McT asked rather sharply. "Why spend money to create extra work?"

"I'm sorry."

"Don't fret about it."

She tried to make conversation. She asked what kind of apple tree it was growing on the front lawn. It was a crab apple tree. Were the apples tasty?

"You don't eat them, do you? You make jelly."

Lisa had never heard of apple jelly, green onions or egg salad. She didn't have a driver's license, and she walked around with purple teeth. Who could blame Len's mother for not wanting to talk to her?

The newlyweds looked at one apartment after another, in tall buildings and small, old buildings and new, cheap buildings and expensive ones. The apartments were all disconcertingly similar and none had a proper kitchen that you could put a table in. They were running out of options.

"What's a duplex?"

"It's a part of a house."

"There's an ad here for . . ."

It was the second story of an old house featuring a large kitchen, living room and two bedrooms. But it was on Fairholt Road in the east end of the city, a part of the city Len wasn't crazy about.

"What's wrong with it?"

"It's not the best part of town."

"In what way?" Having grown up in a "bad" part of town, she had difficulty with the concept.

"It's the east end." As this was hardly a sufficient explanation, Lisa insisted they go and look at it. Len said, fine, go ahead, you can see for yourself.

Fairholt Road lacked the blandness of the street where Len had grown up. It was a road full of three-story brick homes surrounded by mature trees, both deciduous and evergreen. As they turned into the driveway she spotted a squirrel spiral its way up the trunk of what looked very much like a plane tree. Loud birds were singing. A wooden staircase at the back of the house led to a separate entrance to the apartment for rent on the second floor. A marmalade cat sleeping on the landing did not stir. They had to step over it to get to the door that opened onto the large bright kitchen. The east and south walls had big windows with deep sills. She would be able to grow all kinds of plants there. In the backyard on the south side a large maple spread its branches. It was early October and the leaves were turning in shades of pumpkin and tangerine, lemon and cherry. She watched the colors shift in the afternoon light and wondered what Moe Nay would have made of it.

Lisa had already decided.

An L-shaped hallway led from the kitchen to an open space in the center of the house. Here she would put a telephone table and one of the Renaissance chairs from the Sears catalogue to curl up in while she spent a fortune on long distance phone calls. Her friends' voices would reach her from across the world and she would pretend they were calling from around the corner to say they were popping over for tea, to sit chatting in her big bright kitchen while the leaves of the maple turned the color of fruit.

The living room was spacious with a wide bay window facing west. She would try to grow hibiscus there. They might get enough light. If not, she'd move them to the kitchen. She would mist them with water to keep them fresh like she'd done on her lost island. There would be continuity.

"This is the place," she declared, giving in to her excitement. "This is where we're going to live. Bad part of town or not."

"Whatever," said Len. He was fed up with apartment hunting. A place was a place. "As long as you help pay for it. I'm getting that stereo system, remember?"

"I remember."

They moved in three days later, Len with his new stereo and his records, Lisa with two small hibiscus planted in Mexican clay pots and a catalogue Renaissance chair, but not much else. Her trunk did not arrive until two weeks later.

Then there was Lisa McTavish in her very first home as a married woman. It took a while to adapt to the role. In the beginning she had the notion that they must now invite people for dinner. It was what married people did. Lovingly prepared food, a candle-lit table, wine in shimmering crystal goblets. Bone china and her silverware, bent spoon, aunt Bojan's table cloth and all. Animated conversation about fascinating subjects, flushed cheeks, soft music in the background. A tasteful television commercial life, not a hair out of place, everybody smiling with a full set of straight teeth.

She tried it once with Len's family, to their immense discomfort, but had the good grace never to repeat this *faux pas*. Len's dad scrutinized her carefully prepared Swedish smörgåsbord, pointed to a plate and growled. "What's that supposed to be?"

"It's smoked salmon. Scottish salmon."

"Could have fooled me. What's that green stuff on top?"

"It's dill."

"Dill?" His dark glare confirmed her worst suspicions. He

would have made an industrious witch-hunter. *"Dill?* "

"Have some bread, dear." His wife patted his shoulder with a soothing hand.

"What kind of bread is that?"

"It's German bread. From Denninger's. This one here is rye with caraway seeds and the black one is pumpernickel."

"German bread with Scottish salmon?" From deep inside daddy McT came a rumble of outrage.

"What a pity you don't like it," Lisa said.

"What's a pity?" asked Len's mother.

"Your husband not liking Scottish salmon."

"Oh, he likes it, all right. He just doesn't like it smoked."

He ought to, she thought, considering he smokes like a goddam chimney. "How about some meatballs then?" Lisa was down to her last strained smile.

"He doesn't like Swedish meatballs." His wife answered for him.

"They're not Swedish. They're Cuban."

"Cuban?" They were all staring by then, some at the subversive meatballs, some at Lisa. Only Len was smiling at her, but he had returned from smoking a joint on the porch. Lisa smiled back at her husband. Times like that they were happily married.

"Yes. The famous Cuban meatballs from Fidel Castro's recipe book. You must have heard of them, surely?"

Shunning communist meatballs and other controversial offerings, daddy McT tried not to choke on a piece of Nazi bread with a slice of peculiar Danish cheese that didn't taste like no damn cheese he'd ever had.

Daddy McT never forgave Lisa. She never forgave him either. She gave up instead. From then on soirées *chez* Len involved people chugging beer straight from the bottle while passing a joint around. When they got the munchies they ordered pizza from Mother's, ignoring her plea for anchovies, because, as they explained, they were not dagos. Afterwards they were kind enough to leave their mess for her to clean up. They were Len's old buddies, Ben, Ted, Josh, Gordie, Susan, Linda, faces with attached names. Their conversation was uninspiring. "This guy I know scored some great dope from this dealer in Toronto last week. Down by Ryerson." "Yeah? I was in Toronto the other day, but I didn't buy nothin'." "I'm thinking of selling my car." "No shit?"

These were coma-inducing events, but who was Lisa to complain? She did not have the charm to inspire a more sparkling exchange of wit. She had nothing to offer, nothing that wouldn't make them look at her funny. "A dark angel chased me out of paradise," would not go over well, but such were her thoughts, more often that not. She joined them in the beginning, having delusions of wanting to be a good hostess, but there was nothing to hostess except to pass joints along. As time went by she withdrew into her room to play with her toys. Her boxes and yarns and fabrics. She unlocked the fire-engine-red box to sneak a peek at Jimmy playing with his Frisbee, to lift out the imperial teacup to admire it. What would they think of her if they knew she locked herself in her room in order to fondle a cup?

It happened once in a while that one of the women came knocking on the door and said, "Hey, Lisa, whatcha doing in there?" This was how she became friends with Jenny Henderson. Jenny was shy and pretty and had an irresistible smile. Her voice was soft, her Hi! when she called Lisa as breathless as if she'd been running to the phone, unable to wait. Lisa was delighted to discover that Jenny had, despite her softness, a stinging sense of humor. She had started showing up with Len's old buddy, Ben, after Ben dumped his other girlfriend, Susan, the young woman who once picked the only flower off one of the hibiscuses and put it in her hair.

Jenny spent the evening with Lisa in her room, confessing that, yes, she too was bored with the flock in the living room. She wanted to know what Lisa was up to behind her closed door. Lisa took an instant liking to this new person and showed her, opened up her pretty boxes like a market stall. The small oak sea chest she'd found on the Isle of Dogs. The miniature dresser full of little drawers with different flowers painted on each of them. "That's where I used to keep my flower seeds when I had a garden." The black lacquered Japanese box, the boxes painted with motifs of flowers, birds, moons and stars. She showed them all to Jenny, except for the fire-engine-red one, saying only that she had found it in a flower shop in Camden Town, that it was made of cherry wood and contained her most valued treasures. She did not reveal that those treasures consisted of a teacup, her father's false teeth, and a photo of the man she loved, with whom she had spent less than nine and a half hours in 1971.

Sometimes, holding her cup, she would imagine that maybe she and Len would one day have a child, who would grow up and one day tell his or her friends, "My mother bought this cup in Vienna in 1965 in a shop on a street called Graben." To which somebody might reply, "It's a very beautiful cup" or, "I was in Vienna once." Then the grown child might reflect, "It's funny, you know, she treasured it, but she never drank out of it." That child, if asked, would also say, "Yes, I'm an only child."

The red box remained closed.

But Jenny was curious. "What's so special about that one?"

"I can't tell you. It's my secret. Not even Len knows."

"One day you'll tell me." Jenny smiled.

Was that a challenge? "Don't count on it." Lisa said it more rudely than intended, but Jenny laughed, so she laughed too. It was from that moment, when the tension eased and laughter filled the room, she started to feel close to this new person in her life.

"What are all these pieces of leather and yarn for?"

"For the vests and sweaters I used to make. I designed clothes in London." Lisa showed her one of the vests she had kept as a memento. She kept it in a Tupperware container.

"Oh, Lisa! It's beautiful!" It flattered her the way Jenny's eyes sparkled when she held up the vest, the way her smile spread across her face as her fingers traced the texture of each detail.

"You think so?" Lisa asked, though she knew damn well that it was a gorgeous piece of work.

"Oh yes!"

"I made loads of them. It's what I used to do for a living."

"Wow! Are you ever talented! I had no idea! Ben never said."

"Ben doesn't know. I doubt if even Len has noticed."

"You must be so proud." Jenny stroked the soft suede with her fingertips, reflectively. "I just work in an office."

"It's quite easy, really. Anybody could do it."

"No way! Can you teach me to make something like that? I'd just love to be able to do that."

"Sure. No problem. It'd be fun. We'll need more leather though. You wouldn't happen to know where I could buy some?"

"In Toronto for sure. On Spadina probably. My cousin got some in a store there last year. She took this class in upholstery? She got the leather to cover a chair. It wasn't very expensive, I don't think, and it looked real good. Can I try this on?"

"Go right ahead. You can keep it."

"Oh, Lisa! It's too much!"

"I'll make another one, don't worry about it."

Lisa's life was blessed with another dimension after that. Two days later she went with Jenny to Toronto on the bus. It was winter by then, snowy and cold the way she had imagined Canada to be. The landscape outside the bus was black and white. In Toronto they walked up and down Spadina, a sadistic wind their persistent companion, but it didn't matter, they were in no hurry, they were looking for a perfect place to buy leather remnants. She was going to teach Jenny to make vests. She found what she was looking for in a big warehouse-like cavern of a store. A little Jewish man in a yarmulke sat perched on a stool, squawking like an ill-tempered parrot at nobody in particular. Lisa took an instant liking to the place and spent more than an hour nosing around. The store had an Old World smell to it. The leather was a lot cheaper than in London.

"Let's come back often," she said to Jenny, who was all for it.

Afterwards they had lunch in a Chinese restaurant where they ate with chopsticks and made a mess. In the afternoon Jenny showed her Yorkville and the club where she had seen Kris

Kristofferson perform. She said Yorkville was where it was at.

"What is it that is at here?"

"You know. Stuff. Anything that goes on?"

Lisa didn't see what the fuss over Toronto was all about, though she would have liked to hear Kris Kristofferson. Her impression so far was that this was an urban center without any distinguishing features. It reminded her of the strawberries they grew here. Big, but without flavor. Jenny was shocked by her reaction. It was not the kind of thing one said about Toronto, not if one came from Hamilton, she warned her dissenting friend, telling her to keep her voice down.

Lisa explained about the cities where she had been put in her place by the past and learnt to respect it. In Toronto she sensed no past. Perhaps its history was yet to be made. Not that she cared one way or the other. She had a friend now. Somebody to talk to.

꜀꜁ꜗ

Jenny continued to come around after she broke up with Ben. She introduced Lisa to two of her other friends, Lauren, a graduate student in sociology, married to a fellow graduate student, and Diane, a nurse who was divorced and lived with her seven-year-old daughter. Once a week the four of them went out for pizza and beer. The fog lifted and Lisa became visible. People called her on the phone and wanted to know when they could see her. That's what had been missing, being part of something. Such as when Jenny, lounging about Lisa's special room, absent-mindedly pulled up a pant leg and noted, "My legs are so gross, look at them! I haven't shaved them since I split up with Ben." Lisa replying, "You should see my armpits," which would remind Diane that her Aunt Geraldine had a hairy butt, and they would laugh and have some more tea, coffee, wine or beer. The little things, the points that connected.

Jenny was a good listener in her own way. After Lisa had finished telling her some story of her London life, Jenny was sometimes very quiet, then would blurt out a question unrelated to anything. "Did you ever feel lonely in high school?" "Does Len ever get on your nerves?" "Do you know what I like on hot dogs? Peanut butter. Is that sick or what?" It was an oddly child-like quality that appealed to something untouched inside Lisa.

When Lisa started working it was Jenny who helped her fill out her first income tax return. She did Len's too while she was at it. It was Jenny who guided her through the process of getting a learner's license, she and Lauren who tried to teach Lisa to drive. They both assured her she'd make a good driver if she'd consent to drive faster than four miles per hour with her eyes closed. She tried three times but, to her relief, never passed the test.

# 23

**Lisa and Len never had children.** Lisa was on the pill, convinced that Len would not cherish the idea of sharing center stage. Nor would he have wanted the responsibility. "One day Lisa and I are gonna have lots of kids," he'd tell people in those early days, and after a year or so she'd think to herself, "In your dreams, buddy. It's not like you order them from a department store catalogue. Little fake oak veneer infants."

There were times when she weakened and thought she might stop taking the pill, but she never did.

Perhaps her attitude was a factor in Len starting to screw around after a few years. It was to become his habit, confident that his wife had no idea, because she didn't care enough. She did have an idea, but he was right that she didn't care enough to confront him. Lisa suspected he would have continued even if confronted. If a man thinks of himself as a stud, then he will go about his studding.

They lived in the nice spacious duplex for two and a half years before they were evicted. The landlady's married son, home for a visit from Vancouver, enlightened his mother about the peculiar smell coming from upstairs. One evening he came upstairs to inform them that they were evicted, emphasizing how lucky they were that he didn't call the police. His mother was hurt, they had betrayed her trust, they were delinquents. Lisa wanted to protest, "It was my husband and his friends. Throw them in jail, but please let me stay so I can watch the maple turn russet and gold."

She missed the kitchen with all its windows, the bright light and her many plants, her new substitute garden that once again she had not been allowed to keep. It was in this kitchen that she had grown her first herbs, in tin cans she painted yellow and red and green. The kitchen, warm from the sun both summer and winter, had been fragrant with tarragon, oregano, dill and parsley.

She missed the beautiful maple the most.

They moved to another duplex on Aberdeen in the west end. Len was happy about that. Lisa liked it because it had a screened-in sun porch, which was a treat during the humid summer evenings. The hibiscuses thrived out there. She bought some large ferns to keep them company, and straw mats for the floor to pretend she was living in the tropics. Not paradise, and not quite a garden, but it looked good. She sat there alone, sometimes with Len, but mostly with Jenny and their friends. They drank chilled wine and had lazy conversations while the night wind cooled the film of sweat off their bodies. Sometimes they ordered pizza with anchovies or shared a bucket of ice cream.

The first summer in the new place, Jenny was still high from the Stones' concert in Toronto the previous March. She couldn't get over having seen Mick Jagger live. Len went, but Lisa didn't dare. The Stones belonged to another life. Brian Jones had been dead for seven years. It was 1976 already and she realized with amazement that she would turn thirty in October.

It was on the screened-in porch that Lisa told Jenny the story about Mick Jagger's sock.

It was in 1967. The Summer of Love. Is that what you called it here too? Already I think of it as the good old days. We were so damn groovy back then, my friends and I, we were the *crème de la crème*, or so we thought. Then there were the other people, the ones who wanted to be like us but couldn't quite manage, the ones who made an effort when it was required that you make no effort. The group I would have been part of, but for a stroke of luck.

A typical example was this tall, scrawny American in an ankle-length raincoat, who invited us for dinner one night. We didn't even know him and kept arguing afterwards if his name had been Milton or Wilbur. It might have been Wilton or Milbur, suggested my friend Pru, so we called him Milbur. The whole evening was so void of meaning it would have depressed me for years to come had Melvin not sold one of his socks.

We accepted the invitation after having talked to this character in a pub the night before. *Come for dinner tomorrow*, he said out of the blue. *I'd really appreciate it.* It was weird, strangers don't ask you to dinner, but we said, *Sure, why not? Where do you live?"* Maybe he had a lot of food to get rid of. Melvin thought it might be amusing. James, our other friend, refused, because in his opinion, Americans had too many teeth, and butts like the rear end of an English taxi. He blamed this on the over-consumption of peanut butter.

Milbur lived down in Lewisham, miles away from anywhere. We were already stoned when we trotted to the tube station. It had rained all day and there were large puddles everywhere reflecting the orange glow of the streetlights. We were splashing in them pretending they were puddles of acid-laced orange juice, getting soaked and laughing hysterically about the dinner we didn't want to go to, hoping against hope that it would be the usual sixties version of a dinner party. An Indian cotton bedspread for a table cloth on an upside-down packing crate, tripping people, candles and joss sticks, dope, music and, at some point, even food.

Milbur's place was a mailbox of a room that made mine look

like the entire Taj Mahal. A light bulb dangling on a frayed cord from the ceiling, that kind of ambiance. It was a sad sight. We three visitors sat lined in a row on the narrow bed, Melvin in the middle, wet feet, drinking red Italian anti-freeze out of yellow plastic mugs, trying not to laugh, waiting for the stuff in the two pots to get cooked. Whatever it was gave off a very dubious aroma. The American kept stirring the pots like a tall skinny wizard with a secret potion. Pru whispered, *As soon as we've sampled his slop, let's get the hell out of here. Feign death if need be.*

As he stirred, Milbur babbled non-stop about stuff he was convinced would impress us. He claimed to have met Jack Kerouac in Tampa.

*Where the fuck is Tampa?* Melvin wanted to know.

*It's in Florida, man.*

*Did you meet Mata Hari as well?* Pru piped up, looking as earnest as can be. This threw him, so she had to explain. *Mata Hari, darling. Kerouac has a cat named Mata Hari that he loves passionately. Surely you knew that?*

I've always loved the polished way Pru lies. The sheer lack of effort involved. You should hear her. She can fabricate something out of the blue and make you blush with shame for never having heard of it.

*Oh yeah!* said Milbur, and kept stirring grooves in his pots. *I forgot, that's all. Sure I did, man. Great cat, Mata Hari. Real friendly too, man. It had kittens one night I was there. Jack gave me one.*

Pru's response to that was, *You must have been ever so proud.*

*Yeah, man*, Milbur went on. *I sure was.* Round and round went the spoon in the wizard's cauldrons. We couldn't for the life of us figure out why he was so nervous.

Having exhausted the subject of Jack and his cat, Milbur wanted to get on to more important matters. Say, he asked, was it was true that I had slept with John Lennon?

You look shocked, Jenny. Well, so was I!

Where had he gotten that idea? Another one of Pru's stories, what else?

*Not for a few days,* I confessed. I must say I quite enjoyed the status it conferred upon me. *I often sleep with John Lennon,* I went on. *It's a regular sort of thing, really.*

This admission left him speechless and for several blissful minutes he shut up and stared into his mug of wine. For all we knew he was reading the future in the dregs. God knows there were enough of them. Whatever he saw there made him conclude that Pru was Melvin's girlfriend and that I was available, as John Lennon had been excluded. Milbur's eyes gleamed with sugarplum visions of shagging one of Lennon's girls until Melvin put him straight by informing him that we were actually both his birds.

*I always keep two, old boy, in case one gets sick,* was Melvin's explanation. He made it sound both plausible and practical. *Time of month and all that. I don't mind sharing one with Lennon, but after him I draw the line. One can't let go of one's morals completely, can one?*

This silenced the American for another few minutes. He continued stirring his pots. Melvin rolled a joint. Decades later, when our innards had rotted from the excess of anti-freeze, the food was declared perfect. It consisted of rice that after years of boiling managed to still be hard, lumps of strange-tasting fat mixed with the odd green something or other, swimming in bright orange grease.

It looked festive enough, sort of like an abstract Christmas decoration, but it was impossible to figure out what the hell it was pretending to be, and it seemed rude to ask. We chewed slowly and meditatively, one crunchy grain of rice at a time, until Milbur asked if we liked the beef curry.

*What bloody beef curry?* asked Pru, and that was it. We put our plates on the floor and bent double, screaming with laughter. Melvin kicked his feet with such abandon his left foot ended up in his food.

*Bugger me gently!* he yelled and we laughed harder still. He tore his socks off, leaving the curried one on the plate, looked at his watch and announced that if we hurried we could just about make it down to the Marquee. *There's a spectacular group playing tonight. Ever heard of the Savoy Brown Blues Band?*

*Yes!* we yelled, *Oh yes! You wouldn't want to miss them!*

*One of the blokes in the band is a good mate of mine,* lied Melvin. *He plays lead guitar. If I get a chance I'll introduce you. He loves Americans. Can't get enough of them.*

Hearing this, Milbur got all excited, forgot the food and grabbed his long scruffy raincoat shouting *Groovy, man! What are we waiting for?*

*Right you are, me mate,* said Melvin and got up. When Milbur reminded him about his socks, Melvin stared at the soggy mess on the plate and replied, *Oh, I'll just leave them, shall I? They didn't match anyway. No, come to think of it, I better keep the blue one. Mick Jagger gave it to me.*

*Jagger gave you that sock?*

*Yes. Well a pair actually. Last year at a party. We had a bet about something or other and I won. Turned out he didn't have any money, so he gave me his socks. Bit of a cheap bastard, is Mick. Can't remember what I did with the other one.*

*Your pet mouse lives in it, darling, remember?* Said Pru, catching on at once.

*Right you are, old thing, right you are. I forgot.*

*Jagger gave you that sock?* repeated the American. He stared at it as if it was the Shroud of Turin.

*Why, yes, old boy. What of it?*

*Can I buy it?*

*Can you what?*

*Can I buy your sock?*

Melvin was so baffled, Pru had to slowly explain to him that Milbur wished to purchase his sock. *He wants to buy my fucking sock?* he babbled. *The one swimming about in the curry?*

*That's the one.*

*How much do you want to pay for it?* It was Melvin's turn to catch on. *Considering it was Mick Jagger's?*

*I'll give you a hundred bucks.*

*A hundred bucks? Is that dollars you're talking about?*

*American greenbacks, man. I got cash. Is it a deal?*

*. . . Oh, I don't know . . .*

*Please?* Milbur looked like he'd sell him his mother if Melvin would have her.

*Oh, all right. But only this one. My mouse Wooster lives in the one other and knowing him he won't want to move.*

*That's fine, man, it ain't like I'm gonna wear it.*

So Milbur gave Melvin an American hundred-dollar bill and Melvin gave Milbur his blue sock that he'd bought at Woolworth's on Turnham Green. It had a small hole in the heel.

And then, not daring to look at each other, we stepped over our plates from where the food was trying to crawl to safety. A minute later we were out the door, free at last.

On the tube to Piccadilly Circus Pru told the American about having sex with Jimi Hendrix. She figured having paid all that money he deserved a treat, but for some reason he refused to believe her, probably because it was the only time she told a truth that night.

The adventure almost ended in tragedy. It nearly killed our friend Dimitrios the Greek. When he heard the story he laughed so hard he hyperventilated and they had to call an ambulance.

Jenny laughed too, but Lisa, hearing herself tell the story, now found it silly and adolescent, like something she had made up. It was an instant of looking backwards and trying to make sense of it, only there was no sense to make, not yet. It was nothing but an amusing story. Was that what the famous sixties, her hiding place, had been reduced to? A source of amusing anecdotes?

Anecdotes only go so far. She had noticed that Canadians did not live on anecdotes, dreaming of the past with no thoughts for the future. They were made of sturdier stuff, these new compatriots of hers. Content stuff. Ironically, while the country grappled with its search for that elusive shy creature, a national identity, individual Canadians knew perfectly well not only who they were, but where and why they belonged. No wonder they were content. Lisa envied them, for she knew she would never become like them, never be of their tribe.

Sensing they were empty offerings, Lisa stopped telling funny anecdotes.

⊨◇⊣

Sonja's daughter Linnea was born in 1976. Sonja called in the middle of the night, breathless with awe over her accomplishment, fully expecting Lisa to wake up the rest of Canada to spread the glad tidings.

Sonja was a mother. Thick envelopes with Swedish stamps began to arrive, crammed with photos of a pretty baby girl with her father's brown eyes. It was hard to imagine Sonja as the devoted slave to an infant. It was a regular propaganda campaign, reminders that Lisa was a proud auntie, enticing her to come home and meet her niece, pointing out how it was her duty as a member of the family, and that she would find herself a happier person for it.

If she came back it would prove that *they* had not won. Sonja's propaganda didn't say it in so many words, but whispered it between the lines.

If it was the birth of her friend's rosy-faced girl child that did it, or something rooting in her subconscious, Lisa dared to think of what had been, dared to look farther back than London, to a past that still lingered. She felt a sudden need to tell a story. Not some flippant anecdote, but a real story, *the* story, and this time in its entirety. But only to Pru. Pru wasn't there to listen quietly, somberly, so she would write to her. Writing it down she could take her time and perhaps make sense of it.

She went out and bought a thick notebook with a glossy cover, and an expensive pen that it felt good to hold. Then she started.

*Dearest Pru,*
*You don't know this, and won't for a while yet, but I'm going to tell you some more stories. Or rather, the rest of the story. You*

won't be reading this as I write it, because it will take time. I'll write it all, a bit here and bit there, at appropriate times. You will read it eventually, a year from now, ten years, twenty years, it doesn't matter. It's not as if I'll forget any of the details.

Suffice to say that you are still the only recipient of my confessions. I will see your beloved aristocrat bitch face before me as I write, pretending I have you near. No, come to think of it, I will see you in profile, staring into the fire, never touching your tea, as you did that first time when we sat on pillows with mirrors in them.

But I will also write this for myself, for Lisa Grankvist McTavish, the thirty-year-old adult, looking back, seeing if it makes sense yet. Melvin once told me (that first time he spent the night at your insistence), quoting Kierkegaard, that life only ever makes sense backwards. I'm hoping that enough time will soon have passed for me to glimpse a small ray of something perfectly rational.

And if it takes twenty years or more before I finish this, always know, beloved Pru, that without you I would never have survived.

She kept writing.

# 24

>>>—▼

**I told you about the night** when Sonja and I were held captive,
about my mother's death, and my stay in Vienna the following
spring. Now I will tell you what happened in between. This is
the important part. What I cannot fathom is how I've managed
to keep it from you all this time.

So I better get started. Suddenly I can't wait to unload it.

I got pregnant, you see. (I kept waiting for you to somehow
deduce that, hoping that you would.) Seven weeks after that
night I could no longer ignore the fact. All the typical symptoms
had manifested themselves. One day I sidled into a bookstore
like a pervert into a pornshop, head down, collar up, and looked
them up in a book to make sure. They were all there. Singly I
could ignore them, but when they presented a united force,
I had to hoist a white flag and surrender. In a way it made sense.
It had been such a horrendous experience it was bound to have
some nasty aftereffects. I looked in the mirror and told myself
the news out loud, to make it official. "I'm pregnant." The statement, though repugnant enough, was far too ridiculous to
take seriously.

My heart didn't beat any faster, I didn't break into a sweat, didn't tremble at the thought. I didn't even bother to tell Sonja, not at first, and that says a lot. I figured, well, let's wait and see if it's serious. Maybe it will go away like a bad case of gas.

Thus, by the end of that September, I was seventeen, orphaned and pregnant. Suffice to say that I felt at a loss.

It was a letter that inspired me to finally make a decision about the pregnancy that refused to ease up. I don't think a day has gone by when I haven't wondered how my life would have turned out, had I not got any mail that morning. For one thing, I would not have you for a friend, and that's an emptiness I can not imagine.

I was having breakfast when I heard the snap of the mail slot. On the hall carpet lay a phone bill and an envelope edged with green and red airmail stripes and two large unfamiliar stamps. It was from Yugoslavia and contained several scribbled pages from somebody called "your friend Juraj."

It was from the man who had helped himself to my virginity. Now he wanted to be my pen pal. The father of whatever was growing inside me, the guy with the tilted eyebrows and the triangular birthmark. Just reading his name was upsetting. Sonja and I were in a constant state of denial about that night. He was not supposed to exist, and here he was, back to violate me with words right in my own kitchen.

I threw the letter on the table and called in sick at work. Then I cried for the rest of the morning. When I finished I got angry, then I threw up. After that, stupidly, I put the safety chain on the door. But it was too incomprehensible. Why did this man with the funny name, this Juraj, think I would want to have anything to do with him? Was he under the impression that we had forged a special bond?

In his letter he assured me that he was "a gut Katholic" and proceeded to give me a detailed account of his family history. Of the men mainly. He didn't have a lot to say about the women, except that his mother was a Slovene from Ljubljana. His great-great-grandfather, who loved his country, had been a proud officer of the Habsburg Imperial Navy, he confided. His grandfather and his father also loved their country very much. They were not only Croats, but also loyal Yugoslavs, and had never been members of something he called *Ustaše*. "Them were Bosnische Kroaten," the letter said. His father and uncle had both joined the "partizans" during the war. They were in the 10th Zagreb Corps. This was, he assured me, not a lie. They were true believers in *Bratstvo i Jedinstvo*. (I've since looked it up. It means Brotherhood and Unity.)

I had no idea what he was on about. His words must have been directed not at me, but somebody he wished to impress. How could any of it possibly be of significance to me sitting in a kitchen in Sweden on a rainy Monday morning?

He went on at great length. His father was from Zagreb, the city he'd grown up in and where his family was still living. Zagreb, he continued, was a very beautiful city. He was sure I would like it. He himself was half Croat, half Slovene, "just like Tito."

My "friend Juraj" wrote about The Mean Hombre and Brother Bear, only he called them by their real names. Ilija and Drago. It made me nervous seeing their names in black on white like that. (It still makes me nervous after all these years.) They were Serbs, he revealed, as if that somehow explained everything. He said they were *Krajišnici*, whatever that meant. Psychopaths, I figured. He must have deemed this explanation sufficient as well, because he left it at that, apart from a conclusive "they are not gut Menschen." He confessed that he had been in Sweden without a work permit, having heard so much about the good life there. In Malmö, eager to partake in this good life, he had stolen from various stores, a fact he wasn't proud of. Because he was staying at Ilija's, The Mean Hombre's, who knew what he had done and who had put him up to it, he had been in no position to behave differently towards me. It was important that I understand that. He would, he assured me, never again associate "mit so bad peoples." He would never again allow such things to happen.

How had he found my address? He had come across it rifling

through my handbag when I was unconscious, or "sleeping very much" as he called it. Would I please write back to him and tell him about myself? Would I forgive him? Would I be his friend? He was perfectly serious.

After reading the letter half a dozen times I fell apart completely. While I was in pieces all over the floor, the molecules that had been me decided to reconvene, only differently from before, so that afterwards I became gradually weightless. Atoms went missing in the reassembly. My head felt like a balloon anchored to my neck, and below it there was no tangible body.

I could not understand why this man had bothered to sit down and write to me (at his kitchen table, perhaps). Or the reason he wanted me to write back. Did he need my forgiveness in order to go on with his life as a "gut Katholic," absolved of all sin? I had no forgiveness to dole out. Whatever reserve of forgiveness I had been born with my mother had used up. I was turning eighteen in a few weeks and I was pregnant with his child.

The next day, after a bout of morning sickness, I read the letter again. The funny thing was, until I got his letter I had experienced no morning sickness whatsoever, now here I was with my head in the toilet, thinking that with a bit of luck I'd throw up the baby. His baby. When I had finished heaving I went back to the kitchen and sat alone at the table with the letter, thankful that my mother was no longer there. I can't begin to describe the peace and quiet that had descended upon what had once been the beleaguered Grankvist household. It was pouring with rain again, but the hanging lamp over the table in the breakfast nook was spreading a cosy glow. I had decorated with a white tablecloth and red and yellow tulips in a vase. Had it not been for the stranger growing inside me, I would have been utterly content with my life.

Having heaved up my insides I was filling up again with a boiled egg and toast. On a Tuesday no less. This was an unheard of luxury. You see, my mother had only allowed us to use the toaster on weekends. Not every weekend, because a toaster was not a toy and should never be misused. And it should always be put away into its box afterwards so it did not get dusty inside, because that would start a fire, and then the whole building would go up in smoke and it would be our fault for demanding toast. (That's why I ate toast every morning whether I felt like it or not, leaving the toaster on the counter, crumbs everywhere.)

I ate toast and thought about my unborn child's great-great-great-grandfather who had been an officer in the Habsburg Imperial Navy. I had never heard of the Habsburg Imperial Navy. He might have made it up, but either way, it had a nice operetta-like flavor, an image of a strutting officer in full regalia of epaulets and tassels, shiny buttons and white gloves, going through life humming melodies by Strauss. I often thought of this on my strolls in Vienna the following April.

As I ate I dripped butter. A drip of butter hit the letter in my hand, and that was the moment I made my decision. No, that's not quite true. I didn't make it. The decision, already formed elsewhere, came flying to present itself, nicely wrapped in plain logic. I still remember feeling a movement in the air as it landed in my head.

The decision was based on a very simple premise: when you plant a seed you are responsible for what grows. (I should know. I became a gardener later and confirmed it time and time again.) Therefore, as this man planted his seed inside me and I was going to give birth to whatever had sprouted from it, his baby (I never thought of it as mine), it was only fair that I returned it to him. Let the "gut Katholic" take responsibility for his own sins. It would be sure to earn him extra points with his God.

Such was my logic. My rapist was going to be a daddy. The thought brought comfort and cheer. Small scraps of meaning found their way into my life and hinted that there might be life after this. It's true what they say, the cliché about revenge being a dish best served cold. At the time I thought of it as chocolate ice cream in a big waffle cone, the kind that that Sonja and I used to get at the fair in the summer when we visited her grandma. They were topped with whipped cream and a dollop of strawberry jam, cold, rich and satisfying. I always felt a twinge of guilt having indulged in such excess.

I was going to need this man's address after his seed had finished growing, so I tucked the letter into the side pocket of my purse. Later that day I sent a postcard to let him know how thrilled I was to have heard from him. I explained that I unfortunately was going away for a while, but surprise, surprise, I might be coming to Zagreb next April, on my way to Greece. If I did, I'd be sure to get in touch. I ended the letter, "If you move, please send me your change of address so we don't lose touch. Your friend, Lisa."

The front of the postcard showed a view of Gustav Adolf's Torg taken in summer, cheerful as can be, all flower beds sprouting red and yellow flowers. In the front was the round fountain with the statue of small boys bathing — peeing actually — water arcing from their little willies. To the left the Mitt-I-City café was clearly visible behind the bushes. I wondered if it would remind him of how we met.

The last time I laid eyes on his letter was in the evening of April 26 the following year, the day before I arrived in England. By then I knew it by heart. I still remember most of the words. It lay scattered in very small, unevenly torn pieces in a garbage bin inside the main entrance to the *Westbahnhof* in Vienna. The grease spots where I had dripped butter were still visible.

# 25

The year Sonja's daughter was born, a little boy in Zagreb turned ten. It felt bewildering to think of that, but Lisa felt strong enough to entertain such dangerous thoughts now she had started to put on paper what she referred to as her confession. She didn't think of this child as her son; he remained a faceless boy with red hair. Sometimes though, seeing boys his age, she would wonder if he played soccer, if his knees were scraped and scarred, if he had dirty fingernails and kept useful worms and insects in his pockets. If he had tried his first cigarette and coughed himself sick. If he wore little rubber boots. If his father loved him. If his red-haired Slovene grandmother loved him.

Later in the year Mimmi wrote to say that she was pregnant again and wasn't it simply too wonderful?

In November Pru, unaware that she was being written to regularly, called with the news that she had got engaged to a suitable victim and was sporting a diamond the size of an ostrich egg. Melvin and Zoe had just broken up. Zoe was tired of white boys.

"What's new with you, Lisa?"

"Nothing much, Pru old girl." She wasn't often that honest. Most time she made things up so Pru wouldn't get bored calling her.

Pru got married in late summer the following year. She sent an invitation to the wedding on embossed paper sprinkled with gold dust, or so it looked. The event was to be held at some unheated mansion, some maze of long-forgotten rooms with wayward ghosts murmuring among the cobwebs. There was to be a marquee in the garden. Gerald, her suitable victim, was filthy rich, needless to say. In their wedding photo he looked fairly human for an upper class twit, apart from the fact that he didn't boast much of a chin.

"Does he say 'I say'?"

"Come to think of it, he does, rather a lot."

"It'll never work out," predicted Lisa.

"Never mind, darling," said Pru. "It'll be a lark anyway."

Lisa and Jenny drank champagne on the screened-in tropical porch, celebrating Pru's wedding and the demise of Elvis, who died on her wedding day.

⊷

That fall Lisa and Len moved again. The toilet kept clogging, and the back door shifted and refused to close. New people moved in downstairs and played thundering music all night, every night. Lisa no longer got much sleep. So much for living in a good neighborhood. She begged Len to have a word with them, but he kept putting it off. One Wednesday night at four o'clock in the morning, she demanded he go forth and do battle, insisting it was a man's job to face the enemy no matter what time of day.

He finally went forth, only to join the party. Unabated the music vibrated the floors. It was after seven the next morning before he came back upstairs. She knew he'd been screwing somebody. She could smell it.

⊷

Lisa's most insightful move during the early years of her marriage was to start school at Mohawk College. She wanted to learn something useful and, not planning a career, she settled on a secretarial course. She had worked in an office in Sweden, but that was a long time ago. Foreign office work didn't count for much in Canada.

It was exciting to be in school again, to go to the cafeteria with classmates who were all a decade younger. It made her feel younger, too. It was a pleasant time, an easy role to fit into.

After the course she got a job as a medical receptionist in a clinic at McMaster Medical Centre and worked as a receptionist for three years before going on to become a medical secretary on the next floor. A few years later she was promoted to administrative coordinator, which was a fancy word for someone who gets to have a private office, look important while delegating the boring bits of the administrative work. Lisa became extremely good at it, did some of the boring work herself, and earned a lot of respect. People liked her. She felt at home in her role.

Life had eased into a comfortable routine. Turning off the alarm, getting up, having breakfast, going to work, feeling the strength of a purpose. Off she'd go like Old Tad of Tad Hall, down the sidewalk, in a straight line to the bus stop.

What had once seemed strange became perfectly normal. She fitted in. She spoke Canadian and used Tupperware. She ate steak and egg salad sandwiches. She belonged, just about.

In 1978 Jenny married a man named Larry who was a systems analyst, whatever that was. He never could quite explain it. He was the kind of regular guy who greeted everybody with a loud, "Hey, hey, hey!" whenever they invited people over for a beer or a barbecue, slapping other men on the back. Eventually they had three equally jovial sons who all learned to shout, "Hey, hey, hey!" before they could talk.

Lisa went to the hospital to admire Jenny's firstborn. As she stroked his dark tufts of hair she thought of another baby. Then she made an excuse for cutting her visit short, and went home.

Len was out and she had the place to herself. She got the notebook out of the locked drawer of her desk, and sat down to write the next part of her story.

# 26

**D**ear Pru, It's been a little while, but the time has come to continue.

I finished at the point where I made a decision about my pregnancy. I then held that decision at arm's length and examined it carefully, turning it this way and that, holding it against the light, but I could find no fault with it. It was appealing from every angle. It looked a finely crafted piece of work, made to last. I became especially smitten with the harmony of its practical justice. The decision became a firm one.

The next step was to disappear before the bulge of my mishap started to raise eyebrows. This might have proved easier said than done. To be able to skip the country without my relatives questioning such a skip, I needed a solid and plausible reason. Something in black and white, an excuse that made my departure so legitimate it shut up all four aunts with a single blow. Luckily there was one thing they had in common, their tendency to automatically curtsey before any authority. But what web of deceit to spin?

That was when I thought of Mimmi. By then she had lived in England a year and a half. I remembered something she had told me in a letter once, and it gave me an idea so brilliant I had to pat myself on the shoulder. I wrote to her at once and asked her for an enormous favor. The reply took only seven days and arrived in the form of an official document. It looked hugely impressive.

Having little time to waste I set the plan in action by arranging a meeting with my aunts. Let me introduce you to them. Aunt Margit is my father's only sister, Gulli and Bojan are my mother's sisters. Aunt Stina is married to Valle, my mother's alcoholic brother, and my favorite uncle.

I invited myself for coffee at Aunt Margit's the following Sunday afternoon, two days hence, telling her to make sure the aunts from the other side of the family were invited too. "I have some wonderful news to share with you." That got her attention. On the Sunday I brought along chocolate cake and fancy pastries, a sure sign that something was up. They were all waiting around the table, panting to find out what was going on. I could tell they had great expectations, Aunt Margit had set the table with the best china. Their questions were predictable. "Have you met a young man?" "Are you getting engaged?"

Bursting with pride, I let the assembled aunts know that I had been accepted at a very prestigious art school in London. Their faces dropped and went blank, then they began shouting all at once. "A what?" "What did she say?" "In London?" "That's abroad, for crying out loud!" That kind of thing. I showed them the letter with its authoritative letterhead. It was in English, of course, which none of them understood a word of. Not that it stopped their protests.

This was not something to be taken lightly, I pointed out. To turn down such a generous offer, such a great honor, was inconceivable, they had to understand that. This was a very selective school.

They didn't bother to pretend to understand what I was going on about. What they did understand was that England was a foreign country and that I had no business going to school there. Aunt Margit, my legal guardian, glared at me and lit another cigarette. She blew a hostile stream of smoke, tapped her finger on the letter and demanded I translate. They knew I was artistic, but this was a euphemism respectable folk applied to people with asocial tendencies and emotional problems. Aunt Stina sighed, "Poor Lisa. She can't help it." This led to the question whether such airy-fairy tomfoolery was something to base one's life upon. What kind of respectable job could such flights of fancy possibly land a person? Aunt Stina's contribution was, "You already have a nice job in an office! What the hell's the matter with you, girl?"

"We're just ordinary people," said Aunt Margit, as if this was a status that must be upheld.

"And what if you marry a foreigner? We'll never be able to talk to him! You'll have foreign children!" That from Aunt Gulli. All queries and opinions were seconded by Aunt Bojan who mumbled something about poor Lisa still being in a state of shock. Aunt Margit started clicking her lighter off and on, staring at the flame, searching for an answer.

But I was right. They did not dare argue with a foreign authority whose language they did not speak.

Instead they poured themselves each a third cup of coffee, stirred in sugar and cream, it being a special day, and shook their heads in unison over poor Lisa's maverick approach to a serious matter like life. In between bites they wondered once again what poor Lisa would ever amount to. They did this amongst themselves, as if I had left for England already.

I, in turn, puzzled over when my name had been formally changed to Poor Lisa, and what they would say if they knew the truth. I was dying to tell them about the foreign child sprouting inside me, if only to see Aunt Gulli choke on the chocolate cake.

Aunt Margit sighed and shook another Pall Mall out of her pack. She lit it and repeated the usual refrain, "If only your dad was still alive." Aunt Gulli bemoaned the situation with a brief glance heavenward, before getting waylaid by more important things, such as, "Say, this chocolate cake is mighty good. Is it from Lindgren's?" I told her what store they were from and she instantly reminded everybody that she had got uncle Henning's birthday cake there the year before. "The one with the marzipan sailboat on it. It was the cutest thing."

Such were my aunts. Their concern was a volatile substance, it evaporated quickly, which at the time was extremely convenient, as I was not emotionally equipped to handle an excess of concern. I felt so weightless with indifference, it was as if gravity were dependent on me giving a damn about the future.

At least the most important obstacle was taken care of. Next came time to get rid of the material possessions in the one-bedroom apartment that had been my one and only home. It was more traumatic than I cared to admit.

You see, back then I was still under the impression that life was heading ruler-straight towards an approaching horizon where, beyond the scope of my vision, hovered a future with my name on it. Best not to be weighed down with bags of tatty possessions that might identify me as someone I no longer wished to be.

I walked around the second floor concrete box that had contained our version of family life in the forced intimacy of one bedroom, a living room, a kitchen, a hallway and a bathroom, five closets and a broom cupboard. This was the sum total of my parents' lifelong achievements, one rung up from the one-room-no-central-heating-no-indoor-toilet world their parents had sprung from. Very little of these material surroundings had been mine. Most objects were reminders only of oppression and thoughts of matricide.

Nothing was of interest, nothing was of any value, neither monetary nor sentimental. Not even the Persian rug in the living room. My father had bought it from a sailor who came knocking on the door late one evening, mentioning a mutual acquaintance. He said he had got it dirt cheap in Istanbul and smuggled it up to Sweden on his boat to make a bit of cash on the side. It turned out to be a nice-looking worthless fake. Nothing was new in our home, nothing was fancy, and it all needed dusting.

I discovered a few treasures that I kept for sentimental reasons, and in case I would some day need proof of who I once was. Remember the herring jar that stood on my mantelpiece in Chiswick? That was one of them. My father's beret that I later wore in Vienna was another. I still have them, as well as his tools and his passport. I still have his teeth too, a Cheshire cat smile wrapped in an embroidered handkerchief. All these years I've been waiting for the rest of him to join his smile.

Next, I announced to the relatives that everything had to go. And no sooner had word gone out than they arrived at my door, en masse. They spilled out of the same bus, like tourists at a tacky souvenir stand, and proceeded to scrap over the loot with the grace of alley cats. I never could figure out why. The worthlessness of the stuff didn't deter them in the slightest. The aunts turned savage and threatened to gouge each other's eyes out, shove gravyboats up each other's butts, over stainless steel cutlery, initialed towels and sheets.

My uncles started out in the kitchen, exuding manly indifference behind clouds of cigarette smoke, taking it easy around the table with a bottle of duty-free whisky they'd sniffed out in the pantry. But as soon as the Johnnie Walker was gone and their cigarettes squashed in the overflowing ashtray, they were seen circling the Grundig TV like a pack of hungry hyenas.

In the bedroom several other male relatives were battling for the antique secretaire. My oldest cousin's husband, a curly-haired man I hardly knew, and whose name continues to escape me, was sporting a victorious smirk that didn't look at home on his nondescript face. I pointed out that I was keeping that particular antique. He snorted, dropped cigarette ash on the rug, and said he didn't want the piece of shit anyway. I gave it to Sonja who still has it. It's apparently worth quite a bit these days. It was just as well that I gave it to her. The nondescript face left my cousin a year later and took up with some Polish woman.

After that I couldn't take it anymore. I went down to the cellar, where I found my father's beret and his tools, then I escaped. I ran all the way to the old water tower, where I stopped to wait for the bus, staring at the tower, thinking of how they used to burn witches where it stands. It was once the gallows hill.

Now, when I think back to standing at the bus stop dressed in my father's dusty beret, eyes swollen and red, clutching an ugly bag full of tools, what strikes me about that "bad part of town," is that it was home. It's where I grew up. Backarna they call it, though its real name is Kirseberg. Backarna means The Hills. If it was dangerous to walk around the streets there, I never noticed. You see, Pru, I belonged in those parts, and that's what I miss. I was never very happy there, but I belonged. I'm starting to think that belonging is more important than happiness as one grows older. In London I was still young, I didn't need a past, I was still creating one. But over here it is as if I have no past. Here I will never run into people I went to school with, used to play with, or live next door to. Here I have no relatives to constantly remind me of my wrongdoing, no aunts to sigh, "If only your father was alive." Nobody here knows that I ever had one.

It's very disconcerting not to have a past.

But there I stood, staring at the tower, with all the primitive fears that had once set those fires alive and well inside me, imagining how they would have burnt me too, had they known.

I remembered those punishing flames when I told you about that horrible night. You sat listening with your face turned towards the fire and didn't interrupt me once. (Oh Pru! You're one of the very best bits of my life.)

I took the bus to Sonja's. Later that night, I told her the truth about the art school and the great-great-great-grandson of the officer of the Habsburg Imperial Navy. She was so stunned her eyes glazed over. Her face went white. For a moment I was convinced she had died and had to poke her to make her blink. When I did, she stood up and started to pace the room. Her lips were bloodless and grim and she hissed through clenched teeth that I was stark raving mad.

Before we went to bed she had mulled it over enough times to concede that I might have a point. This was after I told her about revenge and chocolate ice cream in fresh waffle cones.

In fact, giving the baby to its father wasn't even revenge, I said. Not anymore, as I no longer felt very angry about it. I simply wanted to say to him, "Here, this is yours, you left it in my womb." It's what I told Sonja. It's what I had convinced myself.

"Do it if you think you can get away with it," was her final response. "Just don't think I'm elated about you ruining your life." She regurgitated over and over how devastated and hurt and sick and disgusted and furious she was. She assured me she was going to be a wreck until it was all over. On and on we bickered, letting off steam. We were good at that, like kids getting nowhere, not meaning to get anywhere.

The next day I sat down at the kitchen table to write a letter. There was a piece of tape stuck to the table. (There were bits of tape stuck to everything by then.) The tape read, "Bojan's table — do not touch!" I imagined uncle Weasel, on all fours, nibbling rodent food on it. It inspired me to grab a sharp knife and make a couple of deep ugly gashes in the wooden surface.

Then I picked up the pen and continued my letter to Mimmi. She was already living with Mick in the house on Airedale Avenue at this point. They had met when she was there working as an au pair for some snooty bitch that wouldn't turn on the heat in her room. She left after two months and moved in with Mick. They had been together for more than a year by then.

More important, as you will remember, Mimmi was blessed with a fresh-faced and innocent beauty that was as flawless as it was unassuming. On the day when the good Lord doled out sweetness nobody else showed up, so Mimmi got it all. Her perfect silky skin radiated it. She never bothered with makeup, it was too much work. And then she had that slightly crooked tooth on the left side of her smile. Angled in such perfection it only made her look yet more stunning, don't you think?

Blessed with a remarkable lack of vanity to boot, Mimmi only combed her long hair by pulling a hand through it now and then. That's if it wasn't twisted into a prude bun at the back of her head.

Her method of getting dolled up involved reaching out and grabbing whatever was close at hand in the heap of clothes on the floor that served as her wardrobe. Fashion had never interested her. Remember her tatty cardigan? The odd time she bothered to put on makeup and dress nicely, she was the most gorgeous creature on earth, but even then she couldn't care less.

I thought about all that, and about how I would see to it that Mimmi's irresistible physical charms were not wasted. Mimmi was going to save the day when the time came to smuggle a newborn infant from Sweden to Yugoslavia. It would be her job to put a spell on border guards, a breeze considering her qualifications. I'll tell you why and how later on. I had got out a map and planned a few routes that would work with Mimmi there to help out in an emergency. Her presence was vital. So was Mick's. He had a driver's license and he was going to drive us from Brussels through Belgium, France and Italy to Zagreb, only he didn't know it yet. I'd never met the guy. It was time they both found out what fate had in store for them.

Before I described my clever plan to Mimmi, I thanked her profusely for arranging to send the fake letter from the art school where Mick's sister worked in the registrar's office. I also made sure that, as my life depended on them, I did not expect them to help me without receiving a generous reward. How about a holiday in Venice, for example, gondolas and all?

The following day I quit my job. My colleagues reacted much the way my aunts had when I boasted about my brilliant future.

# 27

↡

**F**or as long as they could manage, Lisa and Len did their best not to grow up. It was as if their marriage were dependent on it. Perhaps it was. In the end, only Len succeeded at remaining in a state of semi-adolescence. Lisa gave in, willingly, and joined the mundane middle-class. This meant a tidier place with good furniture and real hand-woven carpets on the floors. Such indulgences cost money. "You don't spill wine or drop cigarette butts and roaches on these," she said. Len tried to remember.

Once Lisa got used to the material comforts of such an existence, surrounding herself with all kinds of bourgeois fripperies and fetishes, she went a step further. Before she knew it, she was checking out interior design magazines, putting up wallpaper and buying matching area rugs. She was playing house and took inordinate pleasure in it, going to auctions with Jenny and Lauren, buying odd pieces of furniture. She spent four weekends stripping candy-pink paint off an oak dresser to restore the grain.

And one day she found, to her wistful amusement, that she had finally outgrown the rainbow psychedelic décor she had lived in for so long. She looked back on the young person she had once been, as on a child that has flown the coop.

In December 1980, when Lisa and Len had been married for seven years, John Lennon was shot outside the Dakota in New York. An entire generation was in shock. It was the only time Lisa saw Len cry. It was an odd sight.

Pru separated from her husband, Gerald the suitable victim, and opened an art gallery. "I'm now busy pimping art," as she put it. Pru, being Pru, was enjoying herself enormously. "And what's new with you, darling?"

Well, as usual, nothing much. I'm writing you long letters, Pru, Lisa wanted to say. But she didn't. It was not yet time. She wrote another installment instead. Her mind had been on it for a while. Marshall Tito of Yugoslavia had died in May that year. She read about it in the paper, remembering the name, and thought about a teenager in Zagreb who had turned fifteen in March. Whose father was half Croat and half Slovene, just like Tito.

A teenager that was the great-great-great-grandson of an officer of the Habsburg Imperial Navy.

The news had put her in a special fugue state that enabled her to remember the details if only momentarily. Best to put them on paper, should they suddenly fade.

# 28

Dear Pru, after my "acceptance letter" it was smooth sailing. The following week I turned eighteen. Everything regarding my mother's estate had been taken care of. A wooden lawyer named Jonasson, who referred to me as "young miss," handled what there was to handle. The only time I met the man, he summoned up the balance of my mother's life with monotonous formality, shook my hand, and forgot about me before I left the room. Young miss was on "sturdy financial footing — for now" as he put it. My sturdy footing was primarily due to my father's life insurance, which was surprisingly generous. There was also a smaller policy of my mother's. I had been unaware that either existed. Then there was the money from the sale of the apartment. Not a lot, but even so, I was going to need it.

On my birthday Sonja's mum made me a birthday cake with yellow marzipan tulips and eighteen blue candles. "Make a wish!" she cried. So I did. Sonja demanded to know what I had wished, her face full of gloom and mistrust. "You're not supposed to tell," I reminded her. "It's bad luck."

If the wish came true the child inside me would be permanently reunited with his father some time in April the following year. If it didn't come true, I'd no doubt end up chained to the wall in some dank communist dungeon, feasting on cold gruel, dreaming vainly of daylight, like a pit pony.

My aunts were peeved that I wouldn't spend my birthday with them, but they pooled their money all the same and bought me a shoulder bag and a suitcase made of genuine leather.

"Though I think you should have had the decency to spend your last birthday with your family," nagged Aunt Margit. I could tell, by the way she shot smoke through her nostrils straight down into her coffee, that she felt slighted. She kept flicking her lighter off and on and wouldn't look at me. We ended up in one of those absurd conversation you can only have with a close relative.

"Who says it was my last birthday? I'm not going to die, you know."

"You don't know that. You've never been in a foreign country."

"Why would I die because I'm in a foreign country?"

"They have different germs. And you don't know what their hospitals are like."

"I don't know what our hospitals are like either."

I expected to give birth in one in less than half a year, but I didn't tell her that. Aunt Margit lit another Pall Mall and asked if the bags were to my liking, and that was the end of it.

It was high time to leave. I was barely able to hide my condition. I told the aunts that I would be back in three years, promised to write regularly and to visit on holidays. It was shameful the way I lied, but was else could I do? Three of them saw me off to the ferry, unaware that I was only going to Copenhagen for the afternoon.

I went shopping and bought an expensive green winter coat, a demure white cotton blouse and a conservative navy-blue pleated skirt. These were to be my respectable travel ensemble when the time came. After I'd bought some perfume and a battery of Mary Quant war paint, I returned to the ferry station and boarded the ferry back to Sweden. Half an hour later I took the train up to Hälsingborg, in the opposite direction from London.

My friend Barbro from high school had agreed to my not very modest proposal that I hide out with her. She was in her second year, studying Home Economics at a school there, and best of all, she lived alone in a cavernous, echoing two-bedroom apartment that had once belonged to a wealthy aunt of her father's. She was two years older than I, and full of the free-spirited independence and worldliness I had hoped would come natural at a certain age.

I stayed in her spare bedroom until the baby was due the following March, paying more than my share of expenses to make sure she wouldn't resent having me. After the first month (and what a long month it was) I asked her why anybody would want to put up with a moody pregnant orphan unless it was worth their while? Barbro said not to be stupid. She loved having me around because I never made a fuss and, she insisted, I was very brave. I could have told her I wasn't brave at all, only indifferent.

Staying with her was an odd interlude, a suspension of life itself. Every day was unreal. I learned to cook while I was with her and made supper every day. It was playing house. In the evening I often baked a cake and made coffee. We watched TV or sat around talking about this and that. Barbro told me I often cried out at night. It was such a lonely sound, she said.

During the day I tired myself out by walking for hours up and down unfamiliar streets among anonymous faces. I could think of nothing else to do. Roaming aimlessly seemed an appropriate activity during that time of blank non-thoughts and frozen feelings. The child grew inside me, but the larger I got the less I seemed to weigh. I was worried that by the time I reached full term I might soar off like a balloon.

I floated through frosty winter streets in the company of strangers like a pregnant teenage ghost in a green winter coat and an old brown beret, and learned that people don't notice ghosts drifting by when it's cold out, no matter how fat the ghost. They plod right through with red noses peeking out of upturned collars and scarves. The Poor Lisa-ghost had no face, she was invisible. That was somehow comforting.

My favorite spot to haunt was the castle, Kärnan. It was perched conveniently behind the post office, which was the one place where I had managed to become visible. I had business there several times a week, what with making plans with Mimmi and Mick, and keeping in regular touch with the relatives back home. I sent them letters via Mimmi in England. She put them in the envelope I enclosed, and mailed them back to Sweden. I wrote diligently and dutifully to let everybody know that the art school was fantastic, it was what I had always dreamt of. I told them how hard I had to work to keep up. I complained what a long way it was from where I lived in Chiswick to the art school in central London.

When I got tired of drifting around Hälsingborg I took the ferry across the three miles of water to Helsingør and wore grooves in the streets there instead. I joined the ghost at Elsinore castle and together we haunted the grounds. By lunchtime I'd be all haunted out, and would wander down to the hot dog-stand by the ferry station and devour bright red Danish sausages. If the Danish sausage industry experienced a sudden economic upturn that year, it was because of me.

One day the hot dog-vendor finally felt it his moral duty to warn me that if I kept eating *pølse* at such an alarming rate I would give birth to a bright red baby. "And who knows, it might even have two heads." He stared at me with sour eyes, his nose as red as his sausages. Didn't I know that the accumulation of all the chemical dyes in the body could do considerable damage, especially in such amounts? The idea of delivering a sausage-red baby with two heads was appealing, so I ordered another *pølse*.

He was not amused. "Just don't come blaming me for how that baby turns out." He wagged a large sausage-like finger in my direction, mumbling unfavorably about moronic Swedes.

Right then the baby kicked for the first time. How it frightened me.

At Christmas, Barbro made a dutiful pilgrimage to spend the holiday with her family, leaving me behind in her expansive apartment. I felt like Thumbelina beneath those high ceilings with sculpted plaster garlands of a bygone era, imagining how during Christmases past a better class of people had whirled there in merry dance. Men in starched shirts drinking cognac, cruelly corseted women in satin gowns, that kind of thing. Boys in sailor suits, girls in dresses with ruffles and lace, dancing around a Christmas tree decorated with live candles. There would have been mountains of food, champagne and chocolate pralines.

My solitary Christmas was a disparate and silent time doing its own dance, two hours forward, one hour back. I didn't know whether to succumb to the torpor of melancholy or not. I still had to eat though, so I went out and bought a lot of Christmas food, mainly sweet things. Champagne and chocolate pralines. I sat stuffing myself on the couch in the living room. The room was so big, the ceiling so high, that my footsteps echoed even when I wore socks. I had to chew slowly and carefully, or that would have echoed too.

Sometimes during those dark afternoons when the city lay holiday-deserted, I curled up under a blanket and lay very still, wondering if I should suck my thumb and wait for my father to come home. The stranger within me kicked when I did that, reminding me who was the baby.

I promised myself that when I one day got a place of my very own, it would be a single room, small enough that my steps would not echo. A room where I would never feel lost, modest enough that I would be able to fill the emptiness and be of significance. My room in Chiswick was like that. I still miss that room, Pru. I miss the garden even more.

There were moments when hatred hummed in me like a generator. It filled me with so much explosive energy that I cleaned and re-cleaned the apartment three times. On Christmas Eve I sat in the window and stared into the desolate holiday street. Counted how many windows had lit Christmas stars. I could see twenty-four from where I was sitting. Isn't it odd that

I still remember that number?

On New Year's Eve life returned. Once again there was light, once again there was noise. Barbro returned with Sonja and our friends, Helena and Kristina. We had a New Year's party, dressed up and wore silly paper hats, stuffed ourselves with smoked salmon and French bread and drank several bottles of wine. At least they did. They claimed drinking wasn't good for the baby so I was only allowed one glass. (I guzzled several more in the kitchen when they weren't paying attention. It wasn't my baby.)

Sonja had told her parents she was visiting with Barbro, which was true. I had missed her desperately. I couldn't call her on the phone at home. I lived in London and calling long distance was expensive. Seeing her face was such a comfort. Everything became all right for a while. She had brought me a Christmas gift. It was a gold necklace, a heart-shaped locket on a thick chain, the one I always wore in London. I had bought her exactly the same necklace in a shop in Hälsingborg. Neither of us was surprised, but Kristina said it was too eerie how we always did that things like that. Sonja and I cried a bit.

At twelve o'clock, my last year in my own country came to an end. Prime Minister Erlander gave his speech on TV. Outside, the New Year's sky exploded in bursts of color and Sonja cried some more. I didn't dare. Every explosion sounded ominous.

It was very empty when she left.

The days of January and February trudged by in the slush, taking their sweet time. A procession of identical, forgettable days, each one longer than the previous, shrouded in the gray mist that rolled in and never eased. It was dark most of the day. In early February Barbro met a guy named Ingmar and started spending the night at his place. She asked, did I mind? How could I? I wasn't really there.

By February I stopped going out. The front of me barely fit into my coat. The weekends were the bleakest. That's when Barbro was with her new man. I pretended I didn't miss her. I had a window to stare out of. The child inside me was getting heavy. It was nice to sit down.

March came plodding like a wet dog, bedraggled in the rain and the wind. It did little to cheer me up, but by then my plans were at last finalized. After a great deal of debate and weighing of pros and cons, Mimmi and Mick had agreed to help me — mainly because I was paying for everything, but also because they both felt they could use an adventure. Mick in those days, as you may remember, was the kind of lad who was always game for anything that had to do with thwarting authority. He was also, as he put it in a *post scriptum* to one of Mimmi's letters "not fond of dagos." While that referred mainly to Italian football teams, he wasn't fussy. And, Mimmi added, as London had been gray and dreary for so long, a holiday would be just the ticket. Venice especially. She'd do anything to go to Venice, she said. Even the absurdity I had suggested.

Mick had already made arrangements to rent a car in Brussels. They and the car would meet me at *Bruxelles Midi* as soon I let them know the time of my arrival. This in turn depended on when the great-great-great-grandchild of the officer of the Habsburg Imperial Navy decided to join me. The "Croat Kid," as Mimmi and Mick referred to it. If we got caught, the story would be that I was a hitchhiker they had picked up, not realizing that I was a psychotic maniac, or something along that line. That way nothing would happen to them.

By mid-March it was time to transform. My body was getting ready to expel its visitor. As I planned to give birth to the baby in Malmö, so Sonja could visit me, I had to take precautions not to be recognized. Time to take action. I started by having my hair cut short. Not only did this new style look rather elegant, it made me look older, which was an added bonus. It wasn't enough of a disguise though, so Barbro and I spent the evening slopping dark red paste out of a tube onto my scalp. Later that night my stylish hair shone a lovely coppery red. Then I tried out the makeup I had bought in Copenhagen, ladling black stuff around my eyes until they tripled in size. And last, to perfect the disguise, I put on my father's old reading glasses. They made me feel a bit woozy at first, but I got used to it. The difficult part was getting used to the image of the surprised redhead in the mirror. She was a pretty girl, getting a bit round in the cheeks. But she wasn't Poor Lisa.

I finished my makeup and unveiled the new person to Barbro. She said it was creepy, like having a total stranger in the house. I wasn't sure I could get used to it myself. She had such frightened eyes, this strange girl, pleading with me whenever our eyes met in the mirror, as if I was holding her prisoner.

Two days after my metamorphosis Barbro hugged the fat big-eyed redhead good-bye. The redhead took the train back to Malmö.

I had yet to see a doctor. Whatever went on in my uterus had nothing to do with me, you see. It's possible to rationalize any absurdity with a bit of determination. I would be around when whoever was in there decided to come out, but that was it, I was offering it no perks. This was not luxury accommodation. I expected it to kick in protest but it never did. Maybe it didn't speak Swedish.

It was nice to be back, but I felt dejected watching my home-town go about its business without me. I took a taxi to the address of a girl named Yvonne. She was an old friend of Sonja's whom I had known for several years. At age eighteen she already had a two-year-old daughter. They lived in a one-room apartment four blocks from the hospital and she had kindly offered that I stay with her. It got a bit crowded, but her hallway was quite large so I slept there on a foldout cot that squealed under my weight. Every morning I woke up to a noisy little girl patting my stomach and telling me I was a big fat balloon. I kept telling her I knew that already.

I was there for only four days before I went into labor. During that time Yvonne took it upon herself to brief me in gruesome detail on the art of giving birth as an unwed teenage mum. "The maternity ward doesn't roll out a red carpet to the likes of us," she warned. "They prefer if you give birth standing up. You have to bend over and rip out the kid yourself, gnaw through the umbilical cord and get the hell out, so they can go for coffee."

But when the time came, those fiendish nurses went easy on me. I went into labor on a Wednesday afternoon, having my first contraction while fingering tomatoes in the produce section of the local supermarket. I had gone grocery shopping for Yvonne right after lunch and assumed the sudden pains were indigestion, at least until a more severe contraction followed in the frozen food area. I ignored both. A few minutes later I was standing by the sandwich meats, looking at the packages of dark smoked horsemeat that had been my mother's favorite. I was wondering how many horses she had consumed during her miserable life, when a third contraction damn near sent me headlong into the freezer. That's when I put my basket of food on the floor and waddled back to Yvonne's to fetch my bag. The contractions that followed were regular, but less painful, so I decided to walk over to the hospital, taking my time, deferring the future for another few minutes. Bringing a stranger's child into the world seemed such a final and unforgiving act. Afterwards, when I was sent into exile for my sins, nothing would ever be the same.

At the maternity building I explained that I was in labor, and could somebody please lend a hand as I was unsure of the procedure? My indifference and solemn politeness had them worried, but I truly didn't know what else to do. I was an eighteen-year-old girl who knew where babies came from, but was ignorant of all the practical details of bringing them into the world.

And so, dearest Pru, half an hour before midnight on Monday, March 22, 1965, I gave birth to a baby boy. At the time I wondered why anybody would want to go through such an act willingly. It was excruciatingly painful and it took forever. I didn't know what I'd done to deserve it.

When a nurse said, "It's a boy," I said, "I know that," because somehow I had known all along. When they presented the newborn child to me I pretended to faint to avoid having to hold it or look at it, but I did see enough to note that it was not Danish hot-dog-red. Nor did it have two heads, though oddly enough the one little head it was equipped with was covered with tufts of red hair. "He's got your hair," said a nurse when I pretended to come to.

It was difficult being a new mother in a hospital ward. Everyone's eyes were on me. They didn't trust me. I sensed hidden disapproval. They sensed my numbness. Still I couldn't bring myself to muster up the mandatory maternal instinct. It wasn't allowed. Rules were rules.

They wanted to know where the baby's father was. "Oh," I said. "Oh him. He's back in Zagreb. That's in Yugoslavia." I told them that we were going back there to join him as soon as the baby was a bit older. I had just come home to have my baby in a good Swedish hospital where I knew I would be safe among a competent staff. Well, that made perfect sense to all of them. Heads nodded in agreement, little white nurses' caps wobbling.

Sonja and Yvonne came for a visit the next day. Sonja let me know as soon as she stepped into the room that she didn't have the slightest desire to go and see the you-know-what. That's what she called the baby. She threw two of my favorite chocolate bars and a magazine at me, then stood at the foot of the bed angrily tapping a foot. She looked like she expected an apology.

Yvonne said, well, she was popping over to the nursery for a peek. She came back to announce that it was an adorable little sweetie-pie, which thoroughly upset me. It upset Sonja even more. "I told you I wasn't interested!" she screamed and burst into tears.

Yvonne wondered if the baby would have had black hair if I had dyed my hair black. I explained to her that his hair color was the result of my overdosing on Danish hot dogs during my pregnancy, and that it was the accumulation of chemical dye in the sausages had caused his hair to turn red. Yvonne was intrigued. Sonja, red-eyed and huffy, swept out of the room to go for a smoke.

And down the hall in a nursery lay the child that I, Lisa Ann-Kristin Grankvist, had given birth to. Whenever I dared think of that, my mind reared back in panic.

The name on the birth certificate under "father" read Juraj Sterić. The name of a man I didn't know. But it was now official. I had named the baby after its father: Juraj junior. There would be no mistake about whose child this was.

The unnerving bit was that I had to breast-feed this child. It wasn't very common in those days, but I didn't have a choice. There would be no opportunity to heat bottles of milk when we were traveling, and carting along baby formula would be far too cumbersome. These were practical details I had neglected to consider. To tell you the truth, the idea of breast-feeding upset me to such a degree I briefly considered giving the baby up for adoption. Breast-feeding is an intimate affair. I averted my eyes while the tiny stranger suckled my turgid breasts, tried not to feel the soft little mouth on my nipple, but I couldn't help notice that apart from the red hair, it seemed to take after its father. It had an almost imperceptible version of those tilted eyebrows, a minute little dot where a triangular birthmark would one day sprout. It was a relief seeing those telltale signs. As I did not know what went on when I was passed out that terrible night, at the back of my mind had been a dread that they would hand me a small slab of granite and say, "Congratulations! It's a little Mean Hombre."

No, this baby was the son of the man who had written me the letter. And I would reunite the two of them. I would make a necessary detour to Zagreb before continuing my flight into that elusive future where I would wake up and be somebody strong enough to face what she had done with rebel defiance.

It was bewildering how distant I felt from the world around me, how untethered, how weightless still. Everything was unreal, the way it is in dreams where, despite being the dreamer, you have no control over the plot.

On the Saturday I was allowed to leave the hospital. Somebody from the Children's Aid Society would come to visit shortly, I was told. They didn't know I would be long gone by then. Yvonne gave me enough secondhand baby clothes to last, including a big stack of cloth diapers, but said I'd need many more for the trip. This was before the era of disposable diapers. I would be shedding soiled cloth diapers all over Europe. "Babies piss and shit like there's no tomorrow," she cautioned. "Though at this stage they mainly piss a lot."

The following Monday Yvonne had the afternoon off and baby-sat while I went to apply for a passport, another vital detail that had blissfully slipped my mind, never having been outside Scandinavia before. I omitted to declare that I had a baby that would be traveling with me. It would have been a lot easier to acknowledge it, but I had no intention of doing so, because it wasn't supposed to exist. I didn't want the name of a baby that didn't belong to me on my passport. That was the reason I was going to smuggle the baby from Sweden to Yugoslavia. The hiding and smuggling of a small infant seemed entirely appropriate. It was as illegal as the child's conception.

After taking care of that formality, I searched store after store downtown for a suitable picnic basket. I knew exactly what I needed. It had to be large enough to hold a newborn baby, a supply of diapers, and a package of sandwiches. It had to be comfortable and airy. After hunting for two hours, feeling more and more disheartened, my breasts started to leak. I smelled like a dairy when I finally found what I needed at Bredenbergs. It's the kind of store that reminds me a bit of heaven in the central panel of the triptych. I was not one of the chosen, but went in anyway. And sure enough, the wicker basket had a price tag so spectacular it could only have been meant for picnics in the glorious hereafter. On the other hand, it was ideal for what I had in mind. It had two lids that opened up towards the handle across the middle and was lined with checkered blue and white cloth that made the interior a bright and cheerful place. And it was well ventilated. A regular little traveling cot.

On the bus back to Yvonne's I sat with the empty basket on my lap, my soggy bra sticking to my skin. Everything was ready. As soon as I was deemed worthy of a passport I would book a ticket and be off. The mere thought of the approaching journey brought only terror.

# 29



**Len kept screwing around**, seemingly proud of this accomplishment. Lisa spent her free time with her friends or, quite often, alone. She made supper in the evening after work and if Len showed up they ate together, silent or arguing, sometimes making bland small talk like guests staying in the same hotel.

Every Sunday they put on masks and acted out their husband and wife roles, partaking in the weekly family dinner at the McTavish bungalow. Grandchildren kept appearing as the years went by, until there were half a dozen little people running about. These small McTavishes softened daddy McT a wee bit, the boys especially. The girls were sent to the kitchen to help grandma.

Lisa and Len were living in yet another rented apartment. They never got around to buying a house like other couples their age. Len's money went on ever-improved music systems and his car. He had finally seen the light. The rusted Ford had been replaced in 1975 with a brand new something or other. To Len's chagrin, Lisa saved her money. The way he saw it, it would make beautiful sense if she made a down payment on a house. That way they'd own different stuff and there would be no need for fighting if or when they split up. Lisa feigned deafness when the subject came up.

Pru got a divorce from her suitable victim in 1981, reporting that her terminally repressed husband made Prince Charles seem like Frank Zappa on speed. Having recently hobnobbed with His Royal Highness, she knew of what she spoke. Two years later she remarried. Jonathan was fourteen years older than her. Twice she got married and twice Lisa missed her wedding. Two years later, unimaginably, even Pru became a mother. She gave birth to twin daughters, Miranda and Annabelle. "Surprised the absolute hell out of me," she said.

Lisa couldn't imagine Pru as a mother, an infant at each teat. Pru said neither could she, and to please leave her teats out of the equation.

In early January 1984, Pru called to say that Alexis Korner had died of lung cancer. It was a gray day when nothing seemed alive. The father of the London music scene of the sixties, a legend, gone. They talked for a long time, as darkness fell in Hamilton and the clock struck midnight in London, about Alexis, about Les Cousins and Jimi Hendrix.

Pru sounded wistful and sad. "Being a mere mortal is so bloody final, isn't it?"

"Was it really that long ago?"

"I'm afraid so, darling."

There was no news from Sweden until one day in 1985 when a letter arrived from Aunt Bojan to say that Aunt Margit had died from acute leukemia. The past was disappearing, chipped away bit by bit. These days Lisa exchanged only Christmas cards with the relatives so she had had no idea. It was the first, and last, time she called one of them long distance, a frustrating, futile experience. Aunt Bojan found it too intimidating to talk to a person in Canada, never mind that it was her own niece at the other end. Her voice was loud and stilted with formality. They hadn't spoken for nearly twenty years. Perhaps after that many years niecehood lapses. But Bojan managed to get across that Aunt Margit's beloved Evald had been at her side when she passed. Lisa had no idea Margit had still been with the man she had met back in 1965.

"Why wouldn't she be?" Aunt Bojan sounded annoyed.

Well, how the hell should I know? Lisa thought, then hung up and cried.

There was more bad news in 1986. It was on the last day of February. Len had not come home from work, but that was the norm by then, so she had not bothered to make supper. She was preparing her favorite sandwiches instead, egg salad with little green bits, and listening to the news. As she cut the bread into neat triangles, the radio claimed that Swedish Prime Minister Olof Palme had been shot down on a sidewalk in Stockholm. It was too audacious a statement. Obviously she'd heard wrong. Prime Ministers were not mown down in cold blood in the country where she was born.

Times had changed. It was confirmed all too soon that he was dead, and it was with a sense of unbearable loss she realized that the country she had grown up in no longer existed. Nobody back home would know what had happened, it was the middle of the night there. People would wake up in the morning, pick the morning paper off the hall floor and see the big black head-lines. She thought of calling Sonja, but did not want to be the bearer of such devastating news.

She was sitting at the kitchen table before a plate of uneaten triangles, lost in a private sniffle, when Len sauntered in. He stopped dead at the sorry sight of his weeping wife, this tedious woman who was not the one he'd met in London. She could have been, had she ever showed the slightest inclination to please him, but she had always been indifferent to playing that role. He still liked her, it wasn't that, he was just tired of living with her.

"For fuck's sake, Lees! What's your problem now?" He grabbed a couple of triangles and stared at her, self-righteous and scathing.

She told him she was crying because Olof Palme had been

murdered and because she had lost something it had never occurred to her that she could lose.

"Who was murdered, did you say?"

"Olof Palme."

"Who's Pammy?"

"The queen of Switzerland."

"Fuck off."

She looked at the distant face of the man who was husband. He didn't vaguely resemble the man she'd met in London. Neither Lisa nor Len bothered to reflect that this failure of recognition was something else they had in common.

The disappearance of the country that had been hers brought on the heavy memory of leaving it. That night, when Len had gone out again, she got out her notebook, smoothed out the pages and immersed herself in the next part of her confession. The more she wrote, the closer she felt herself getting to some point she still couldn't see clearly. It must be, she thought, the point where it will all make sense.

# 30

Dear Pru, It took seven days to get my passport. After I picked it up I went straight to the train station to book my ticket. It was April 1, which made me a bit nervous, but I already knew the joke was on me. The departure date on the ticket said Monday, April 5, 1965. This was the day Poor Lisa was off to do what had to be done.

Mimmi and Mick were meeting me in Brussels, because it was the most convenient location to convene. The plan was to drive down through France and Italy and cross the border to Yugoslavia, at Opičina, close to Trieste. What we would do once we arrived in Zagreb was a bit foggy, because it was still too daunting to think about the details. Apart from one. Afterwards, when I had done what I was going there to do, I would escape the country as fast as possible, catching a train to Vienna by myself. Mick and Mimmi would drive to Venice for a well-deserved holiday. They would have nothing to worry about. The baby would never be traced to them should things go terribly wrong. My name was on the birth certificate. I would be the guilty party.

Included in the plan, however, was the naive assumption that the father, being such a "gut Katholic," would be thrilled to bits to see the son who was his spit and image. If not thrilled, that he would at least accept responsibility for his offspring. He had planted the seed. That was what I would remind him.

Had I used my handful of working brain cells to full capacity, I might have asked myself why on earth I expected a rapist to do the honorable thing.

I bought a return ticket Copenhagen-London, to avoid the kind of questions that might pop up if I handed the men in uniform a one-way ticket to Brussels. My intention was to avoid having to face men in uniform for longer than necessary. Also, in the back of my mind was the notion that with a return ticket I had the option of going back home in a month if I wanted to. Not that I was planning on it. I had nothing to go back to. I had meticulously seen to that.

Instead I had some dim idea of wandering the globe seeking my fortune, whistling a merry tune, a lucky rabbit's foot and a crust of bread in a spotted kerchief tied to a stick slung over my shoulder, my beret at a rakish angle over unflinching eyes. In storybooks such people, invariably portrayed as brave, cheerful and deserving, find their fortune without fail and live happily ever after, adored by everybody in the kingdom.

I circled the date of my departure with a red marker on the calendar in Yvonne's kitchen. It was hard to miss. Even so, the evening before the big day, when Yvonne said, "Tomorrow's the day, Lisa," it made me flinch. My packed suitcase stood by the door like a dog waiting to go for a walk. It wasn't very large. The baby stuff was in the big shoulder bag and in the basket. The baby would be sleeping on a mattress of soft diapers. I was being very efficient, leaving nothing to chance.

But Pru, I was so frightened.

By daybreak I had already been awake for hours, convinced that I had succumbed to paralysis during the night. My limbs lay dead and stiff and I knew I'd never move again. I heard the earliest of the birds start to trill, I watched the morning light grow brighter through the kitchen doorway. Around five o'clock the newspaper lady shoved the morning paper through the mail slot. I discovered that I could still move, if without grace, and got up. I sat at the kitchen table staring at the first page of the paper for two hours.

Yvonne had taken the morning off and came shuffling into the kitchen around seven to make coffee, full of that forced cheer people resort to when there's nothing to be cheery about. Her daughter sat in the hall singing to the baby. I tried to drink some coffee but couldn't swallow, so I went and stood by the living room window, looking down into the street. It was Monday morning and people were going to work, walking, biking, taking their time, as if this was a day like any other and not the end of the world. The jewelry store up on the corner was opening up, so was the boutique two doors down. Two women stopped to chat. One talked while the other one raised her eyebrows and shook her head. Another day, another workweek. Not a single headline announcing "LISA GRANKVIST LEAVES THE COUNTRY — see details in special issue!"

Yvonne had to hand me the baby to feed. I was in such a state I had forgotten. While she got it changed and dressed, she ordered me to get dressed too, unless, as she said, "you plan to go baby-smuggling in your polka-dot pajamas." That's how pathetic I was. Shortly after nine she reminded me, softly, as if I was terminally ill, "I think it's time. That is, if you're going through with this."

I bundled the baby into its basket, not letting my eyes linger on it. Luckily, it seemed to like the basket. When there was nothing left to do but leave, I said thank you and good-bye. "Everything will be just fine. I'll be back soon, I promise." And with that blatant lie I turned my back to Yvonne and hurried downstairs to the waiting taxi.

I had begged Sonja to come with me to the train station in Copenhagen. I was far too scared to go on my own. She had said she would if I insisted, but that she was scared too. Sometimes she was so frightened she thought her heart had stopped and she was dead. It was a terrible, terrible thing I was doing, said

Sonja. But she had taken the day off and was pacing outside the ferry station, frowning and biting her lip.

We took the big ferry across because it was the slowest one. It would give us time to prepare for the end. I suggested we go up to the restaurant and get a table by a window, thinking a little extravaganza might help lift us out of our doleful mood. The prices in the restaurant were demoralizing compared to the cafeteria below, but there were dazzling white tablecloths, real flowers in the vases, and waiters in uniform. Sonja turned in the door as soon as she laid eyes on the forbidding elegance. It was unnecessary, too fancy for us. Fancy was the frigging intention, I pointed out. It was to be our last supper.

A waiter came gliding up to ask if we wanted a table. He sounded so condescending, I felt a sudden stab of anger. I heard myself loudly request a window table for two, and make sure it's starboard, my good man. I had no idea which side was starboard. (Just as well, he led us to a table on the left side, facing forward.) Sonja sighed. There was a droop of futility in her shoulders as we trailed after the snooty waiter. I insisted I sit facing Denmark so I wouldn't have to watch my country's coastline fall off the face of the earth.

Still bitching and yapping, we ordered beer and open-face shrimp sandwiches. "Isn't this nice?" I said. Sonja didn't say a word. Her eyes were dark and grim, her long thin face pale and pinched. There were two brand-new lines on her forehead. We had had life so neatly planned out and then it had collapsed into one big mess. But it wasn't our fault.

Sonja will worry at the drop of a hat, I reassured myself. She'll be all right as soon as I've left. Until then it was touch and go. She still refused to throw even the briefest glance at the fancy basket. One lid was open, and the baby inside was sleeping soundly. Sonja kept glaring at me, looking betrayed. I glared back, then we stared out over the heaving expanse of gray water for a while before resuming our glaring match. Small bursts of bitchy exchanges flared up, but we never had a proper conversation. At a time like that, what was there to say?

What we failed to understand was that hatred had blinded us differently.

At one point Sonja said, "You can turn around now. Sweden has disappeared." My heart heard her words and fell down dead. I didn't dare turn around, but I sensed the emptiness expand behind me. A desolate wind swept out of it and chilled my back.

I was about order a cup of coffee when suddenly Copenhagen was visible straight ahead. We would be docking soon. I would have to get off the ferry and continue my journey. No catching the next ferry home this time. It made me so frightened I had to run to the bathroom and throw up.

At the ferry station Sonja suggested we save money and take a bus. I hailed a cab. We were driving down Havnegade when Sonja grew a third line on her forehead. I watched an invisible hand etch its curve right above the previous two, while she pretended I wasn't there. By the time we reached the station the line had made itself at home like a permanent shadow.

At the station I needed badly to call Mimmi to hear that everything was going according to plan. The baby was asleep, so I pleaded with Sonja to wait outside with the basket. When she made the expected fuss, I told her to shut the hell up and went into the communications room. This was where I found Bosch revisited. I was in such a state, that from then on I became obsessed with the images from *The Last Judgment*. I saw demons everywhere.

When I had made my call I went back outside and found the basket sitting abandoned on a bench with the flaps closed. There was no sound coming forth.

I discovered Sonja a good distance from the bench, tapping a foot, dragging on a cigarette, staring desperately in my direction. When she saw me, she pointed a long, accusing finger at the basket. "That thing squeaked!" she yelled. I stared at her white angry face, her frightened eyes, and realized how profoundly I would miss my best friend and her flaky ways. In my heart she was all I had left, the only one I belonged to. It was all too horrible. I told her she was the world's biggest idiot, grabbed the basket and stalked off. Hurling feeble insults we went to find the platform where life as we knew it would end and we'd have to grow up.

We located the train to Brussels and London and the carriage with the sleeping compartments. After that there was nothing left to do but wait, not knowing what to say next. The platform was teeming with bodies, but I could focus only on the two of us. Wondering, did I look as young as Sonja? As dejected and sad?

I couldn't stand it. I hoisted my shoulder bag, grabbed the basket in one hand, my small suitcase in the other, and screamed, "Go away!" We stared at each other. I put my suitcase down again. We kept standing glued to the spot. Then Sonja said, "I'm leaving now." The decision came out of the blue, that was her way when she meant business, so I knew it was a firm one. "I'm going now and I'm not turning around, so don't look after me and wait for me to wave. Because I won't, I swear." I said, "Go ahead." Still she didn't leave. We continued to stand there, trying to be strong by arguing.

Then off she went. She was taller than most of the people on the platform. Some people's heads bobbed rhythmically as they moved along, others bounced or nodded loosely. Some were bent as if in sorrow or shame. Sonja's head cut royally through their midst, a proud head upon which a regal crown would not have wobbled, staring straight ahead, getting smaller as she receded into the main building.

The final good-bye was unbearable. I never stopped watching her and, as I knew she would, she eventually stopped and turned around. We looked at each other for a long time while the life that had been ours shattered like glass on a concrete floor. I didn't start to blubber, I would do that later. Nor did I wave. With the great huge unknown beating down on me it would have been impossible to lift an arm. I could only turn my back on what had been and board the train with my cargo. The content of the basket mewled to itself.

My sleeping compartment was the second one down. I had

booked both berths to make sure I would have the place to myself. Safe behind the locked door I lifted the baby out of the basket and put it on the bottom berth to change its diaper. It was soaked, but that couldn't be helped, it was necessary to use diapers sparingly to make them last. The baby's little legs kicked happily in the air. It liked having its bum cleaned. I grabbed a foot and studied it, I'm not sure why. It had such tiny toes, all wrinkled and soft. Inside those bits of flesh were small delicate bones like those of a bird. So defenseless.

I folded up the dirty diaper and put it in the brown paper bag Sonja had brought me fruit in, leaving the apples and oranges on the bed beside the baby while I carried the bag outside and non-chalantly dropped it in a garbage-bin further down the platform. It had to be an inconspicuous maneuver; it was of utmost importance to leave no trace of a baby that didn't exist. Having disposed of the evidence I sauntered back to the carriage, swiftly hopped, ran to my compartment and locked the door. The baby was still there, right next to the fruit, its doll-sized fists opening and closing like little pink flowers.

All that was left to do after that was wait for the train to transport me into my next life. I sat and watched the people on the platform, paralyzed once again. They seemed so far away, all those people. A beautiful woman with a young boy was saying goodbye to an older woman who was probably the boy's grandmother. They were well dressed, the younger woman swathed in pearls and fur. They looked so comfortable and at home in their lives, so sure of who they were. A fat man came waddling with a suitcase in each hand, not looking around. His hat was too small. A young couple with matching backpacks ran by, hand in hand. These people knew where they were going and why. I watched them all pass by. They didn't see me.

Finally the train started to screech, clank and lumber forward. We were on our way. I grabbed the empty basket for something to hold on to.

Imagine, if you will, a young woman sitting rigid on a berth in a sleeping compartment on a train. Dressed in a virgin white blouse, very demure, knees pressed together under a pleated navy skirt, red hair tucked behind her ears to reveal a face transparent with terror. Wearing her father's old reading glasses that make her eyes look huge. Hands, skin stretched tight over white knuckles, clutching an empty picnic basket. On the same berth a small baby, only two weeks old, is kicking its chubby little legs. That is the picture I have carried with me all these years. Sometimes I wonder who that girl was.

When the steward came to prepare the bed I opened the door only wide enough to tell him I had already done so myself. He kindly wished me a good night's sleep and went on his way. As soon as it got dark I removed my pristine clothes and climbed into the upper berth and crawled under the blanket, feeling so lost it stunned me. There was a silence in my head so vast I knew I would never be able to speak again. And sure enough, when I opened my mouth wide no sound emerged. There was nothing there, just the sound of a train wheezing its way through Denmark.

The train arrived at Rødbyhavn. There was a cacophony of metallic crashing and banging as it kept changing tracks. It stopped briefly, only to start all over again with another bout of clanging and screeching. I had pulled the curtains, shutting out the night, but through them I could see lights flashing in the dark. Strange shapes moved about throwing twisted shadows. Having encountered a scene from *The Last Judgment* earlier that day, I knew what was going on, I did not need to look. Everlasting fires were raging in the night. Rødbyhavn was turning into charcoal. Demons were busy slaughtering people in gruesome ways. I could hear them. I knew that come morning, the earth would lay scorched.

There was one detail Bosch had omitted. The cast-out black Madonna and her child arriving by train in the Inferno.

Somebody yelled something in German right outside the window and the baby woke and started to whimper. I climbed down and picked it up to let it nurse, holding its warm little body while it suckled away, still half asleep. A trusting little fist rested lightly against my breast. I glanced at it. That baby loved nursing. Even in the depths of hell it nursed contentedly, poor thing, mistaking me for one of the blessed.

The train scrambled onto the ferry and stopped with a jolt. It echoed in the metal cavern outside. We had now left Scandinavia behind. And, hopefully, the Inferno. Already this was the farthest I'd been in my life. When the train left the ferry we would be on the continent, in a foreign country. Germany.

But we weren't there yet. First we had to cross over to Puttgarden. Confined to a two-berth coffin on a train deep inside the gut of a ferry in the dark of the night, I wondered if in fact I wasn't traveling on the train ferry across the river Styx. When I was little I once saw a picture of a painting of that river in one of my father's books. I don't know who the painter was, but I still recall how when I looked at that boat gliding through darkness towards the unknown, I could hear the rhythmic plop, splash, as the oars hit the water and came up again. It had been the only sound in that empty infinity.

It was morning when I woke up, cosy and warm on the lower berth. The baby was snoozing on my bare chest. I could feel its warm breath on my skin. Appalled at this loss of protocol, I moved the baby, shot out of bed, pushed open the window and stood by it letting the fresh air hit my face.

The train had left the ferry and was rushing through an unknown countryside. It didn't look like the Land of the Dead. Was it Germany or were we in Holland already? If so, where were the tulips and the windmills, the people in clogs and funny hats? It was Germany. Half an hour later the train slowed to a stop at the Dutch border. A man in uniform knocked on the door, leafed through my passport and continued whistling down the corridor. Some tedious hours and a few windmills later, the train arrived at the Belgian border. Once again, the respectably dressed young woman I was had no trouble with passport control. To perfect the look I had pinned a brooch to the starched collar of my blouse. It was a little silver bird, a swallow in flight. It had been a gift from Aunt Margit on my fifteenth birthday. I had never worn it before. A discreet layer of Mary Quant make-up made me look like a grown woman going about her business. My left hand displayed my mother's engagement ring and wedding band, my feet looked reassuringly dowdy in sensible shoes. A mature woman with a return ticket, my passport received but a cursory glance. I was that uninteresting.

By the time we crossed into Belgium I felt claustrophobic, having been locked in a moving box for hours on end with the baby. It was impossible to keep my distance from it. I'd had enough. At one point I contemplated hurling myself off the train into a muddy field where some Belgian farmer would find me with a broken neck, the noonday sun reflecting off the silver bird on my collar. But I knew I couldn't do it.

I only left the compartment to run quickly to the toilet. Soiled diapers were best disposed of straight out the window. I felt guilty about littering three countries in one day, but what was I to do?

We pulled into Brussels at midday. The train slowed to a stop where a sign outside my window read *Bruxelles Midi*. I would at long last be allowed to escape my compartment. So far everything had gone smoothly. It was a small victory, and I dared indulge in maybes. Maybe it was going to be all right after all. Maybe things would work out for the best. Maybe I would find a way to be happy once this was over. Maybe the baby would be happy too. Maybe it would have a good life, maybe I would too.

I left the pile of useless maybes behind with the orange peels and apple cores. The porter, a friendly old man in a white jacket, offered to help me, but I shook my head and pushed past him, struggling with my secret cargo, my suitcase and my shoulder bag.

And there on the platform waited Mimmi and Mick. I was no longer alone. Mimmi was her beautiful self. Mick, who I was meeting for the first time, was wearing a checkered cap with matching vest, both so ugly I couldn't stop laughing. The laughter was relief more than anything else.

The car Mick had rented was a small tin can of a Renault. I was surprised that we actually fit into it. (It was a tight squeeze.) I will always remember Mick's eyes in the rear view mirror, the eyes of a brave and generous stranger, offering me a last chance to back out. I turned down the offer. I don't know if he understood why, but he didn't protest. He was full of concerns, but kept them to himself.

We were off to smuggle a baby across three borders, to give it away to a stranger. Mick's apprehension was not misplaced. But I had already got the baby across three borders, four if you count going from Sweden to Denmark. I had to continue. I was off to unite a father with his carbon copy son. I was not giving the baby away, only returning it to its rightful owner.

I had to introduce Mimmi and Mick to the baby. "Don't let the sight of this small infant fool you," I warned them as I lifted the baby out of the basket. Mimmi, needless to say, squealed with delight and wanted to cuddle it. I handed it to her, babbling my new mantra. "Think of it as a flower. The flower belongs to him who planted it. Right?" It was what I had convinced myself. Now I was trying to convince them. "Right," they nodded. Whatever I said to convince them they agreed with, to please me. "Right," they repeated. "Right."

I leaned forward and hugged their shoulders, again and again, needing to express my gratitude, telling them not to worry, I was doing the right thing. They nodded. I nodded too. Mimmi patted my hand and rubbed her cheek against it.

"I know, Lisa," she said. "I know."

# 31

**Married life had been sliding downhill** for some time, but
suddenly the hill got steeper. When lack of conjugal bliss accelerated and hit bottom, funny enough, it was Len who found
the marriage wanting, Len who had always had his cake while
contentedly munching it too. Munching aside, he one day
arrived at the conclusion that as a wife, Lisa was not right for
what he had in mind. What he had in mind was not entirely
clear; it was more of a feeling he had not felt for some time.

The last five years they had lived in a rented two-bedroom
house in the west end. It was the end of September. Len came
home late one evening, cracked open a can of beer, leaned
against the counter and, turning the tap on and off in an irritat-
ing manner, announced that he wanted "you know, a divorce?"
They had been married for thirteen years according to the
calendar hanging by the fridge. It was a free one from the bank
featuring pictures of heritage buildings. She stared at the calendar with no clear idea where all those years could possibly have
gone. Meanwhile Len repeated his request. He was getting
impatient. Having rehearsed the lines until he knew them by

heart, he didn't want to lose track because his wife saw fit to sit daydreaming. "Did you hear me?"

"What? Yes, I heard you. Just stop fiddling with the tap."

That Lisa had no problem with his need for a divorce for some reason upset him. He sat down at the table and started talking. Trying to reach her one last time. Among the confidences he shared that night was, "You never made me feel special. You never said things like 'Would you like a cup of tea, hon?' or anything like that. Little things like that mean so much."

That's what stunned her the most. It was true, he wasn't lying. But it had never occurred to her make such an offer. She had assumed that her hon was a grown man, and that if he was dying for a cup of tea, he would find his way into the kitchen and capably slap a teabag into a mug. But apparently not. For lack of cups of tea, her marriage — what there was of it — was lost. All these years she had been oblivious to the fact that she was deficient in this most basic of wifely attributes. She had assumed, naive and thoughtless, that cleaning whatever apartment they were living in, doing the laundry, the shopping, the cooking, the dishes, and working full time, had been sufficient.

In this respect, it was fortunate that she could not care less. She had long ago realized that she had to prioritize what she was going to feel bad about. Never making Len a cuppa was at the bottom of the list, right below never having learned to yodel. Perched at the top of this list, like an accusing angel on life's crooked Christmas tree, had long been her basic indifference to her own fate.

The sequence of items on her list was not much of an excuse, she was well aware of that. She knew she was not without blame for the pitiful state of their marriage.

"You don't love me enough," Len explained the last night of their living together, squashing the empty beer can in his hand while doing his English bloke routine. "Not the way I need to be loved."

It was true. She had loved Jimmy Sullivan more in nine and a half hours than she had Len in thirteen years. She still had no idea how Len needed to be loved, but she knew of at least twelve women who temporarily had thought they did, and who had all been forced to admit defeat.

"Len, this may come as a surprise to you, but you're not all that lovable. Nor are you an Englishman. And while we're at it, you look really fucking stupid with that limp excuse for a pony-tail drooping down your back." It was the kind of She-Devil cold anger that made her grow ten feet tall.

Len continued to smile the gentle bloke smile he'd made such good use of, the kind of smile he imagined the follies of mankind would bring to the lips of great gurus and wise men. The kind that made him look toothless.

"You're bitter," he declared. "It's understandable."

Lisa didn't know how to react in the face of such delusions, so she followed her most basic instinct and socked him on the jaw. Not very hard, she was not very strong. It felt good. Len didn't hit her back, which was just as well or she might have gone for him with a sharp instrument.

Now they were no longer pretending, all the repressed contempt that had accumulated for him and his phony ways came bubbling to the surface like foul-smelling gas. Len, if he noticed, ignored it.

"We used to have such dreams, though," he reminisced, rubbing his chin. God knows why. Had he really had great expectations of this hastily assembled marriage? And if so, why had he been so irresponsible?

"No Len, we didn't. *You* used to have dreams. The problem is, having dreams is not enough. You have to pursue them. Dreams are not like dogs, they don't come when you whistle."

"Oh yeah? And what about you then?"

"I guess that's where my lack of ambition differs from your lack of ambition," was all she said, not bothering to explain.

"You're so full of shit!" Len got up and grabbed his jacket. "I'm getting out of here. I'll send for my stuff."

She wondered what movie he got that from. "Nobody says, 'I'll send for my stuff' in real life, Len. That's what people said when they had a house full of servants. You only ever had one servant and I was it. And please put those beer cans in the garbage before you leave."

"Bitch."

"I'm sorry, Len."

"I bet you are."

The next evening Len's friend Josh came by in his van carrying a suitcase and a list. The suitcase was for Len's clothes. The list itemized which of the accumulated belongings Len considered his. It ended with "this week's *TV Guide*."

"I heard you hit him?" Josh was too amused to try and hide it.

"So?"

"Len said, 'I guess she didn't realize how much she loved me until she couldn't have me'." Josh chuckled.

"Christ. And what did you reply to that bit of profound insight?"

"I said, 'It sounds more like she hates your guts.' But you know Len."

"Knowing Len is easy. There isn't much to know."

"You said it."

She offered him one of Len's beers. They sat at the kitchen table and drank beer out of the can and laughed about how things turn out in life. Then they had another couple of Len's beers and ate his stash of sour cream and chive potato chips. It was the longest conversation they had ever had.

Before Josh left, Lisa gave him Len's clothes, stereo and records, the only things Len ever paid for himself. Josh forgot the list on the kitchen table. She tore it up and threw it in the garbage.

Later she called Jenny who wanted to know, not for the first time, why Lisa had not left Len a lifetime ago. Lisa thought about it, also not for the first time.

"It was too much trouble. I never hated him. He was never mean. He was just there, like a roommate."

"You're an idiot," said Jenny. "Come for dinner on Sunday."

Lisa turned down the invitation. She felt uncomfortable

around Jenny's rapidly growing sons. When they were in the same room they took up all the space with their expanding bodies and boundless energy. Worse, Jenny's husband's demeanor towards his wife's friend was growing increasingly patronizing. Lisa had never had children, her husband was screwing around on her. She didn't have what it takes to be a woman. He pitied her for that.

The night Len left was September 26, 1986. That same day excerpts of *The Memorandum* by the Serb Academy of Sciences and Arts were published in a Belgrade newspaper, the first formal indication that the Balkan Peninsula was heading for a holocaust. At the time it was an insignificant faraway event that did not make headlines in the west. There was a small notice about it in the Swedish paper Sonja sent.

The child Lisa had once given birth to had turned twenty-one that spring, no longer a child, but a man. She sometimes thought of that, being the mother of a man.

The following month she surprised herself by turning forty. She celebrated this shocking milestone by cutting her hair short for the second time in her life. This time it made her look younger.

It took another three years for Lisa and Len McTavish to trot off to court for a routine divorce. Theirs was number seven of fourteen that morning. After the *decree nisi*, when the bored judge banged his gavel on his desk, Len asked Lisa if she wanted to go for lunch. The proceedings had given him an appetite. They went for pizza and made jokes about the other couples in the court room.

He never really went away. It was as if he didn't know how, or saw no reason to, hoping that if he hung around long enough she might give in and finally make her hon a cup of tea. Lisa, on her part, never wasted energy on keeping him away. He was an errant roommate that she felt responsible for. The longer they were divorced, the more he kept appearing at her door. She suspected that his other women were getting fed up with him.

By then she lived in an apartment that was hers alone, on the second floor of another duplex in the east end, off Sherman Avenue, only a few blocks from that first sunny kitchen where she had grown herbs. She was to stay there for more than seven years. It was not a single room, but her steps didn't echo. The living room took up the entire front part of the house. One of the short walls consisted of built-in bookshelves with a fireplace in the center. The windows had deep sills full of plants. She had a study, a dining area with a bay window full of more potted plants, and a bright kitchen. At the end of the long hall at the back of the house was a large bedroom with a ten-foot wide south-facing window full of herbs and hibiscus in a variety of colors. Jimmy Sullivan's photo once again sat faithfully on her bedside table. Every morning she woke up to a scent of oregano and rosemary, tarragon and dill, and Jimmy smiling at her. All those years and his smile had not lost its flavor.

Apart from Jenny and their friends, she didn't invite many people to her home. Mostly it was Jenny and nobody else. She preferred to have the place to herself, as though it was an island.

⊨◇⊣

A year after Lisa and Len split up, lung cancer got the better of daddy McT. Very fittingly he was cremated. Lisa accompanied Len to the funeral. She had bought a demure gray silk dress for the occasion and Len said she looked so classy he might want to marry her again. She did not reply.

At the funeral she met half-grown nephews and nieces she hardly recognized and who, although she was no longer related to them, called her Aunt Lisa. How, she mused, did I end up an aunt to adolescents whose names I don't recall?

Mrs. McT blossomed after her husband's death. She dyed her hair an attractive grayish-blond and shopped for new, youthful clothes. Patti and Lucy disapproved of her frivolities, but that didn't faze her. She was on a roll. Exhilarated by her face-to-face encounter with freedom she bought a camera and went on a trip to Mexico. When she came back she signed up for evening classes in pottery and quilting and assertiveness training. A year later she took a course in Italian and as soon as that was finished she was off to tour Italy with her friend Mabel.

Lisa thought about this, and everything else that had happened the last fifteen years. She realized that she had accumulated a Canadian past, full of details she had never paid attention to. But there they were, significant enough that she could say, "Remember when . . .?" To celebrate this surprise, she threw a Tupperware party and served egg salad sandwiches.

Bits and pieces of news from overseas continued to be her reference points, not only to a changing world, but also her own journey through it. Her past lay on a distant shore in that changing world, and it was important to hold on to it. Events in Canada did not have the same impact; it was not where she had grown up. There wasn't the need to stay connected. Though she did miss Trudeau an awful lot. She had considered becoming a Canadian citizen, but decided against it once Mulroney came into power. She couldn't stand the sight of him, nor the sound of his inanities.

In early spring of 1988 a letter from Aunt Bojan found its way to her new address. Letters from the aunts were so rare by then she knew it was bad news. Aunt Bojan was writing to inform her niece that Uncle Valle had committed suicide. He was seventy years old, she wrote, a dried-up husk of a man. "His liver had rotted right through, and he had emphysema."

He had hidden in the walk-in closet and overdosed on Aunt Stina's new prescription of tranquilizers. They found him stretched out with his head resting on his good shoes. "I know he was my brother, and may he rest in peace," wrote Aunt Bojan, "but poor Stina will be far better off without him. It's been hell for her these past few years. You have no idea."

No, Lisa had no idea. She had not been home for twenty-three years.

There was no word about Sigrid the dog.

Aunt Margit dead. Uncle Valle dead. The two relatives she had actually cared about. The Prime Minister murdered. Lisa felt very, very far away.

By November that year, things were stirring in Yugoslavia. In Belgrade there was a "Meeting of all Meetings" that would eventually lead to civil war and the destruction of the country. Nationalism, as blind and deaf as ever, had reared its ugly head. In Croatia something called HDZ, Croatian Democratic Union, became a legal party and called for multiparty elections although there was no doubt about which party would win. This news did not make headlines big enough for her to notice.

Until one day, recognizing the name Croatia on the first page of the paper, she became curious and started to pay close attention. A storm was gathering and somewhere under that dark cloudmass was the child who had turned twenty-four in March that year. A man now, perhaps a father.

I might be a grandmother, she thought, still imagining a small infant in white and green striped terry cloth pajamas, sleeping in a picnic basket on a soft mattress of diapers. Putting aside *The Globe and Mail*, she went to her study and got out her notebook. It was filling up.

# 32

Dear Pru, The trip to Zagreb had started. We were on our way. Off to who knows what in who knows where, to quote Mick. Stuffed in our tin can, we puttered down chaussée this and boulevard that, streets full of Belgians going about their daily Belgian life. They didn't look any different from people at home. There was nothing distinctly Belgian about them. Not that I had the slightest idea what would constitute "Belgian." Neither did the others. We discussed the importance of national characteristics for the purpose of easy identification, and came up with a law whereby, for example, all Belgians would be dipped in chocolate and rolled in brussels sprouts. A practical aide to help distinguish them from their neighbors the Dutch who would be dipped in melted cheese and covered in tulips. (Keep in mind, two of us were still teenagers.) We played this game until we passed the outskirts of Brussels and found ourselves in the countryside, our toy car trundling southeast towards Luxembourg and France at a fair clip. It was a pleasant enough journey through fields of early spring, fields that looked disconcertingly like the fields of early spring in Holland, Germany, and Scandinavia, the same mud and the same lackluster sky that winter had drained of blue.

We had decided to avoid Luxembourg by taking a smaller road down to Longlaville, making it one less border to cross. We chatted about this and that and nothing in particular. "How's Sonja these days?" and "Which one of the Rolling Stones is the nicest?" "Charlie," said Mimmi, when suddenly, out of nowhere, there was a sign for the French border.

Our first border by car. My heart began chasing itself like an idiot dog its too short tail. Mick said not to worry, this will be a mere formality, but he looked tense. Having just fed the baby, I gave it a soother dipped in Mimmi's duty-free gin and some sugar, and deposited it in the picnic basket. According to Mick's grandma there was nothing more efficient than gin when it came to keeping a little nipper content. She had raised seven nippers, so we followed her expert advice. Mimmi handed me the sandwiches she had prepared earlier and I stowed them at the baby's feet for easy retrieval.

These sandwiches were of vital importance. According to my genial plan they were to save our hide in case of emergency. Well, my hide, really. The simple yet elegant strategy hinged on Mimmi, who was sitting in the front seat. Or, to be exact, it hinged on Mimmi's right nipple.

The plan went thus: if the border guards showed an unhealthy interest in the picnic basket, we would immediately decide to have a sandwich. I would nonchalantly flip open the lid at the foot end of the basket, take out the package of sandwiches, open it and hand one to Mimmi. She in turn would reach her right arm back behind her head to grab it, whereby — and here was the clincher — whereby stretching the elastic, her right breast would lift right out of the blouse, rosy nipple hypnotic in its blushing surprise. Mimmi would turn red. Mimmi blushed easily. The men in uniform would forget what they were doing.

Mimmi was looking her most delectable. Her long hair, newly washed, lay in gleaming tresses over her shoulders. She was wearing makeup, all according to plan. Her lips were a soft pouty plum, ripe and ready for kissing. Her border-crossing uniform was bra-less and consisted of a white peasant blouse, low cut with a sweetly ruffled elastic neckline that gave her breasts front row seats. Her skirt was made of the flimsiest of cottons and clung affectionately to her thighs. The effect was incredible. We arrived at the border. The tin can toddled to a stop. This was it. I had to press my lips together or my heart would have lunged out of my throat and splashed into my pristine lap.

All the anxiety soon proved a waste of energy. The border guard's expression revealed only profound indifference. Until he laid eyes on the loveliness of Mimmi, that is. He stuck his snout right in the window and drooled into her cleavage as if it was a vital part of his job description, paying no attention to the passports she held out for him. We could have imported truckloads of screaming contraband infants and this *douanier* would not have batted an eyelid. Mimmi flashed him a smile and he dreamily he waved us on.

I wondered what it would be like own a smile with that kind of power. (I still do.) Mick, feeling compassion, thought Mimmi should have flashed the poor bastard a nipple anyway, just to give him a treat.

"Absolutely not," she said, already busy twisting her hair into a schoolmarmish bun, stabbing it with bobby pins. "I'm saving my nipple for when we need it." She was all prim and proper again, her heaving bosom safely back in the privacy of her shapeless old cardigan.

Feeling incredibly smug, as if this was all a game, we headed for Metz and stopped for the night. When we arrived, our self-congratulatory mood had faded. It was our first night with the baby in a hotel. I was so nervous I nearly fainted at the thought of having to leave the car. Mimmi and Mick were just as anxious. Their backs were stiff and straight. Mimmi had stopped chatting. We found a reasonable-looking hotel somewhere in the center and got out to check in, leaving the luggage and the basket in the car. As it turned out, the hotelier couldn't be bothered with our passports, so it became immaterial whether anybody saw the baby or not. We took it down to the restaurant and let the waiter fuss over it. Of course, everybody assumed it belonged to Mimmi and Mick as Mimmi, a picture of motherhood at its finest, was holding it and cooing at it. I was the sad maiden aunt wearing a brooch on her starched white collar.

The following day was one of glorious spring perfection, so we decided to take our time and relax, pretending to be on holiday. The sun played hide and seek behind white cottonball clouds. Birds swooped in the air, buds burst into bloom, butterflies fluttered, tractors puttered in the fields. We had two roadside picnics. The second one featured a bottle of wine. Stretched out in a French spring meadow, for a moment I forgot why I was there. An early bee buzzed in the pastoral perfection. "Ah, this is life!" sighed Mimmi and before long we were asleep, the baby on the blanket between us.

It was late in the evening when we arrived in Lyons. The city streets lay empty; everybody had gone to bed. It felt safe with nobody about. We found a cheap hotel and had dinner there before going back upstairs to map our route. Going through Switzerland would have been the fastest, but it involved more borders, which was too risky. The Swiss, according to Mick, were a fussy and stuck-up lot that ought to be dipped in fondue and rolled in cuckoo clocks.

The map offered three choices. We could drive all the way down to the coast and cross at Ventimiglia, or turn right and take a narrower road that crossed the Italian border between Larche and Argentera. A third choice would be to cross at Col de Montgenèvre on the way to Turin. Going all the way south was the farthest. The smaller road looked iffy. Mick, who at twenty-two was the oldest and wisest, suggested we try the route to Turin. He claimed to have a good feeling about it. It seemed right. After a couple of bottles of wine everything seemed magnificently logical. We agreed life was bleedin marvelous after all, drank another toast, and went to bed.

The baby, having suckled milk diluted with wine, slept all night.

We started out late the next day, crawling behind a large truck, but even so, the Italian border appeared before we knew it. Three heroes from a Puccini opera came strutting out of the customs building. We watched their approach, waiting for them to burst into song. They were beautifully decked out in uniforms laden with all kinds of frippery and gold buttons and, holding center stage, they were intent upon throwing their weight around. They marched towards us, the first two brimming with purpose. The chubby one at the rear, the runt of the litter, wore a white napkin tied around his neck and was busy chewing on a leg of chicken. It would have been impossible to take them seriously, had we not had something to hide.

"Here come the wops," warned Mick. "This'll be nipple time for sure."

Mimmi squirmed.

The first of the operatic heroes noticed Mimmi and stopped dead. He twirled around and shooed his colleagues away, then strutted over and leaned into the car on Mimmi's side. His eyeballs rolled over her face as he sang out a request for passports in dulcet tones. Purring like a big cat he asked her to *per favore* step outside. Mimmi looked charmed, flashed one of her special smiles, and let her body undulate out of the car. The *commendatore*, savoring the moment, indicated with another elongated vowel that she bend over to unlock the trunk. It was amazing how long he could make a vowel last.

Mimmi followed orders despite the discomfort of his Latin lover eyes fondling her butt. The *commendatore* was so absorbed he never heard the picnic basket emit a very loud fart and a sneeze. "*Grazie!*" he whispered to Mimmi when he'd had his fill. Mimmi, his Botticelli Venus, lowered her lashes in response. The stuff in the trunk went unnoticed. With a *ciao, bella!* he sent us on our way. Mick started the car and said he could think of several things he'd like to dip that particular wop in.

Once again we were safe.

We spent several days trekking through Northern Italy, hither and yon, taking our time, stopping in scenic places, eating pasta and drinking a lot of wine. Mick claimed to have read some-where about a law that said you had to do that in Italy or you'd be deported.

Several times a day I succumbed to anxiety attacks so severe there were brief moments when I had no idea where we were. The wine helped a great deal, mind you, and as I knew nothing about the effect of alcohol in breast-milk, I didn't suffer guilt over that at least. No wonder the baby was so good.

But the closer we got to the Yugoslav border, the more appre-hension overwhelmed us. We kept making excuses to take detours. Then one day the sky turned gray, the weather grew colder and the wind decided to show its nasty side. Ominous dark clouds rolled down from the hills in the north. Studying the clouds, Mimmi sighed one of those delicate little sighs of hers and suggested we drive on down to Venice before heading to Yugoslavia. "The sun is bound to shine there," she said. "We can all ride around in gondolas. I mean, we're so close anyway. Wouldn't that be nice, Lisa? You wouldn't have to miss out on anything."

Absolutely not. Venice was far too romantic. Did she honestly think I would fancy sitting alone on a bench with a basket on my lap while the two of them lay entwined in a gondola, float-ing slowly down some canal towards a burning sunset? With a gondolier lustily belting *O Sole Mio*, or whatever the hell gondoliers belt? No, thank you. We were sticking to our plan. For one thing, we were running out of diapers.

Mimmi apologized profusely.

We headed for Trieste.

It wasn't even lunchtime when we got there. This was the very last stop before entering Yugoslavia, the point of no return. Mick, quick to observe local custom, double-parked the car in the first available spot and got a ticket from a smirking police-man in dark shades before we were out of the car. Mick paid the ticket, and said something in English about Monopoly money and corrupt Mafia lackeys, drove around the block and double-parked on the corner. He left the car there all night, but didn't get another ticket.

We got out and walked about. In a street called Via Roma, a few blocks from the harbor, we found a convenient *Pensione* and booked two rooms, then set out at once to see a bit of the town and kill time. Around the corner from the *Pensione*, as soon as we felt it was safe, we lifted the baby out of the basket and acknowledged its existence. When we stopped at a café with a view out over Golfo di Trieste down the Istrian Peninsula, lots of people came and cooed at the *bambino*. It was the same everywhere. Babies were very popular. Either that or it was because this particular baby was displayed in the arms of the beautiful Mimmi. For a while we felt like celebrities. Little did these people know we planned to give the adorable *bambino* away.

In the evening Mimmi and I started grooming her for next day's performance. Mick had got bored and asked did we mind if he went out for a quick beer? We didn't, so off he went. Mimmi prattled on and filed her nails while I brushed her hair over and over again to make it gleam even though it was gleaming already. We took turns plucking her eyebrows to see if we could improve on that big-eyed innocent Botticelli-look. After that there wasn't anything else to perfect so we lounged around waiting for Mick to come back so we could have an early start.

He didn't turn up until after three in the morning, drunk as a lord, prattling on about football and his new pals. I won't even go into the fight we had that night. Suffice to say we made up before we went to bed. He was wearing a pair of Italian football shorts on his head. Later he removed them and donated them to the baby for good luck.

⌗

It was getting on for eleven the next morning before Mimmi and I were up and about again. We strolled out into a bustling city. People were sitting in cafés, shopping, carrying fresh loaves of bread, cars were honking them out of the way in the narrow streets. There were ships in the harbor, a smell of sea in the air. "I've missed that tang of salt and fish," said Mimmi. She inhaled, breast heaving under her peasant blouse. Men walking by burst into serenade at the sight of her, pressing their hands against their hearts, rolling their eyes. Mimmi, absent-minded, smiled a half-smile but paid no attention. Beside her, I was invisible.

We bought bread warm from the oven, butter, tomatoes, cheese and salami for the emergency sandwiches. They had to be infallibly delicious that day to help save our hide from the communist tyrants. Later, should we get across the last and crucial border safely, we would have them for a celebratory lunch.

When we returned to the hotel Mick had already showered and was standing by the window chain-smoking, his body rigid. The bags were packed. After we'd made our border-crossing sandwiches, we rehearsed the dreaded worst-case scenario one last time. Mimmi knew exactly how to move to make the nipple pop. It all depended on how she lifted her arm. The trick was to stretch it from the elbow to the armpit while leaning back against the seat and sort of lowering her right hip. It had to be a sudden movement, that final stretch. There was no room for error. If that nipple did not pop, I'd be sunk.

The plot was laid for passing through the Iron Curtain. Everything was ready. We had run out of excuses to delay the inevitable, so we headed to where we'd parked the car, secretly hoping it would have been stolen or towed. It wasn't. All too soon we were on our way out of Trieste, nervously debating whether the Iron Curtain extended as far as Yugoslavia. Mick insisted it did, because Yugoslavia was a communist country in Eastern Europe, and thus a part of the East Bloc. Mimmi and I leaned towards the view that as it was less strict, and as anybody could travel in and out of Yugoslavia, it was more of a heavy velvet curtain, easier to push it aside if you needed to let the light in.

"What do you think?" I asked the top of the baby's head. It was nursing, greedy and loud. "You're going home today!" It kept on suckling.

I had no intention of getting my friends into trouble, so, if for some obscure reason the border guard was immune to Mimmi and we got caught, we had a story ready. I was a hitch-hiker Mick and Mimmi had picked up that morning somewhere outside Trieste when they had stopped for coffee. They had kindly offered me a ride after finding out that I was Swedish like Mimmi. They would confess to having been thoroughly shocked to find a live baby gurgling in my picnic basket, but that they had not had the heart to throw me out of the car. Meanwhile I would act confused, unsure of my whereabouts.

Then we were at the border.

I must have screamed out loud, because Mimmi jumped in her seat.

There were two guards on duty. Both looked humorless and programmed. Or maybe we only assumed they did because they were communists. Either way, as soon as they finished with the Mercedes ahead of us, they turned in our direction, approaching our car slowly, one on each side, men on a mission, armed and sinister. Our tin can did not impress them. I stopped breathing. Mimmi rolled down the window at once, stuck her head out and flashed her best smile as she held out our passports, telling them in German that we were on our way to Athens.

Her smile had its usual effect. You could hear their minds grind to a halt and jump track as soon as they glimpsed her. A second later they were both standing on her side of the car, inhaling, expanding their manly chests with essence of Mimmi. The shorter one snorted and his silent-movie mustache vibrated so lustily it nearly soared off his face. Put a man in uniform and he's suddenly convinced that he's not only powerful, but sexually potent.

One would have thought that finding the girl of their dreams, they might ignore their duties, but that was not the case. Perhaps they desired to impress her with their efficiency. Whatever the reason, they were sickeningly thorough. The strutting Italian operetta hero and the drooling Frenchman had lulled us into a false sense of security.

After scrutinizing our documents, and rummaging through the trunk, they gave their full attention to the back seat, studying the basket and myself, with eyes not nearly as indifferent as they were supposed to be. Then one of them raised an arm and pointed to the basket. He opened his mouth to ask something. I stared at his finger.

That was the moment Mimmi decided to throw in the nipple.

Offering her lovely profile to the inquisitors, she asked me in Swedish to pass her a sandwich. I quickly opened the bottom flap of the basket and took out a pack of two sandwiches, opened it and handed her one. Fresh Italian bread fragrant with salami and cheese. She reached her arm back over her head for it, performed that crucial jerking movement, and plop! out popped a breast, its snub-nosed nipple peeking innocently over the elastic of her blouse. And a lovely nipple it was. One of the guards moaned audibly. Mick had to lower his head to hide his grin in the shadow of his cap. Mimmi, face and neck blazing crimson, eyes demurely lowered, tucked her naughty nipple in and offered the officers a cheese and salami sandwich. They declined, shook their heads and waved us on as if they couldn't stand another second of this spectacle.

Less than a minute into Yugoslavia, the baby made a very loud noise inside the basket. It sounded like a celebratory whoop. A few seconds earlier and it would have been fatal. We decided it was an approving whoop, as if the baby could sense that it was on home turf. I hoisted the baby out of the picnic basket and Mick said, "You're happy to be home, aren't you, Croat Kid?"

I nursed it; but at such dangerous moments, with that trusting warm little body against my breast, I always managed to keep my distance. It had been an extremely good baby. It had cooperated one hundred percent. It deserved a chance to be with its dad. Father and son were bound to have a lot in common. I kept telling myself that. I kept telling Mimmi and Mick that too. As usual, every time I opened my mouth on the subject they started to nod on cue. The baby would grow up speaking his father's language. It was all for the best. "Right," they'd nod. "Right."

Having fooled armed authority, we felt pretty cocky breezing along the E93 to Ljubljana, where we stopped and ate our emergency sandwiches by a fountain on a square. The baby's grandmother was born in that city. It was strange to think that some of the people passing by might be related to it.

After lunch we were supposed to head southeast down the E94 towards Zagreb. By then Mimmi's hair was hiding in a tight ugly bun, her body concealed in her beloved cardigan. Reading the map she pointed out that it was only a few hours' drive to Zagreb. That, I said, was too soon. They didn't argue. What about a detour? We could go further south and then head north back up to Zagreb the next morning. If we did that we could drag out our arrival another day. We'd have time to prepare ourselves more. That made sense, so we headed south to places with names like Novo Mesto, Metlika and Karlovac.

We were frightened driving south. Ever so often we saw soldiers, most of them were fresh-faced young men wearing ill-fitting uniforms. They were doing roadwork. A few of them looked at us as we went by. We didn't dare look back.

When we got to the outskirts of the town called Karlovac, we found a cheap place with no running water. We should have driven straight to Zagreb and got it over with, but I wasn't ready. (I would never be ready.) There were soldiers in Karlovac too, and while they paid us no particular attention apart from ogling Mimmi, their presence struck terror in us. We didn't realize at the time that Karlovac was a garrison town.

We spent the evening closeted in our hotel room tossing around ideas about the best way of getting in touch with the baby's father. I had not written to let him know I was coming, afraid to scare him off. Fear put a damper on our inspiration, but in the end we concluded that I should write to him as soon as we got to Zagreb and ask him to meet me at a certain café, or restaurant. Someplace close to the train station. Every city has a central train station. And then, if he showed up, which he had to, I'd pretend to have to go to the toilet, put the basket on the table and ask him to keep an eye on it, and run out the back door, assuming there was one. Once out the door, I'd run straight to the station. Mick pointed out that we first ought to check what time the trains left for Vienna, so we could schedule the meeting accordingly. No point running for a non-existent train, was there?

I was so dim I hadn't even thought of that. "What if the stupid communist train leaves at seven in the morning?" "Never mind," he said "First we have to find out if there is a suitable café somewhere close to the station." There was probably a restaurant at the station, but that would be too close for comfort.

I was worried sick, Pru. We had no idea what we were doing. What if the baby's father didn't show up? What if he was no longer living there? What if he didn't want to see me?

"If he doesn't show up," said Mimmi, ever practical, "we can leave the basket in a church and let God deal with it. These people being Catholic and all. Leave a letter with the father's name and address. That way if this guy doesn't acknowledge his child, the church will see to it that the baby is looked after. They will raise him in an orphanage where he'll learn a trade and grow up to become a useful member of society." She said she'd read that somewhere. It was not an altogether bad idea. "They might," conceded Mick. "Not that I'd ever trust a priest. Or a commie."

The whole time, a voice in my head kept asking, Lisa, Lisa, what are you doing? To which I replied, I don't know.

# 33

In 1989 they tore down the Berlin Wall. That made the headlines. During the early days of euphoria people danced in the streets, as if the state of the world was now approaching some kind of Utopian perfection. Dictators toppled. The Europe Lisa had once known was disappearing. It seemed farther away than ever.

Sonja called to say Andreas was in Berlin for a meeting. According to him it was a nuthouse there.

In early 1991 came more news. This time it was bad. Shortly after their daughter Linnea's fifteenth birthday, Andreas was diagnosed with colon cancer. Lisa spent a fortune on long distance calls. And yet, although she so badly wanted to be with them, she still could not bring herself to go back. Her heart raced to them when she heard, but the rest of her stayed put, making her feel like a coward. Maybe she was a coward. But the time wasn't right yet.

That year, the country where her son lived was marching toward war. Lisa had no idea. Early in the evening of June 25, she was getting ready to go to a dinner party. A friend from work was celebrating her fiftieth birthday. Lisa was in the midst of an agonizing middle-class dilemma, debating whether to wear the black silk two-piece or the long gray skirt with the sleeveless purple blouse, listening to the radio with only half an ear, when it all at once got both her ears. Croatia had declared full independence, as had neighboring Slovenia. The paper confirmed it the next day, asking what would happen now? Lisa thought about the child she had given birth to. The grown man, who perhaps had children of his own. Everything would have to be all right. He would be perfectly safe. So would his children.

Soon young men in that new country were putting on uniforms to go to war. She wondered if there was a red-haired man among them. It was an impossible thought. It made her anxious. It shouldn't have, but it did.

Dark times lay ahead. In late August the Serbs in the Krajina obliterated the entire Croat village of Kijevo, in the mountains near Bosnia, expelling every inhabitant they didn't kill. The world would soon learn the phrase "ethnic cleansing."

By now, Lisa was paying close attention.

In September there were air raids in the Zagreb area and the airport was hit. Then came the siege of Dubrovnik, and, far worse, the siege and months' long destruction of Vukovar. On Lisa's TV screen, drunk Serb soldiers roamed the ruined streets, their pockets full of loot from the buildings they had burnt, shelled and bombed into rubble. Bodies of people and dogs littered the devastation. Here, once again, was the central panel of Bosch's triptych. The world stood by and watched. Almost 6,000 people were killed in Croatia that fall. More than 13,000 went missing. The last judgment was only beginning.

Lisa could not stop thinking of what might have happened to the child she had left there, in the depth of the center panel. He might be dead, or one of the missing. He might be a soldier, killing people.

In November 1993, Bosnian Croat forces destroyed the bridge called Stari most. Lisa stood by the window looking out onto the street where some boys were playing soccer. Stari most. It meant Old Bridge. She recalled the name from the time Mimmi had stopped her on a street in Zagreb, near the old tower up on

Gradec hill, insisting Lisa look at a photo of that bridge, wanting to cheer her up. Smiling her pretty Mimmi-smile. Lisa had wanted to go there and Mimmi had said she couldn't, it was too far away.

⚓

Two days later Sonja called to say Andreas had passed away. Lisa had received many photos of Andreas with Sonja and Linnea over the years; she knew his face well. She had watched him age from photo to photo, but she would never meet the man who had been the love and comfort of her best friend's life.

She thought of Sonja and Linnea dressing in black to say their final farewells. Sonja had said that these days the containers were biodegradable and put in one communal area, as there was no more space. Lisa pictured Andreas' ashes mingling with those of strangers, maybe with those of her father's, until all the departed ones became one, fertilizing the green grass above. There was an odd comfort in that. Then the phone rang and it was Sonja again, for the fifth time in three days.

"I feel so alone." Her voice was small and fragile, so full of disbelief that it sounded like a question. "I was so used to him, you see. We were married for twenty years. It sounds like a long time, but it went by in such a flash. Marriage was such a comfortable place to be."

That all depends on whom you're married to. Lisa didn't say that out loud. She kept quiet and listened to her friend's grief, cried a bit too, inadequate in a place that was feeling less and less like a refuge.

"Are you ever coming home?" Sonja asked.

"Yes," Lisa said. "I am. One day soon. But not quite yet." Remembering Sonja's words the rainy night she first left London. "You've let them win."

"Make it soon. I need you."

"I need you too, Sonja. Believe it or not."

"I'll believe it when I see you."

Lisa looked back on her life, at all she had done and not done, at all the places she had lived, and thought what a rich and textured tapestry it was, so many different colored threads woven into the pattern, like the vests she had once made. Through it ran the distinct chord of survival, sturdier than it looked, rope-like, weaving its way across the strands of bullshit and lies. Some of those strands were weak and transparent, ready to break, others mimicked convincingly a more precious fiber. Alongside the central chord looped the shining, unbreakable threads of friendship, standing out, their texture distinct to her fingertips. And running smoothly through the weave, here and there overlapping the rest, were the black threads of sorrow and despair that sometimes shifted to indigo when the light hit them. They were not out of place, those dark threads, their color adding diversity to the overall composition.

Holding it up to the light she discovered how the monotone background of everyday life brought out the contrast in the pattern. The weave in this tapestry was dense enough that if she wanted to wrap herself in it, it would keep her warm.

No, she thought, *they* had not won. Nobody had won.

And yet, there were silent moments, breaks in the daily routine, when it felt as if she'd spent her entire life in a single room, sparsely furnished, walls unadorned, no tapestry to warm her, waiting for somebody to knock on the door. Wondering who would come knocking?

Meanwhile the notebook was filling up.

# 34

**D**ear Pru, Morning dawned in Karlovac with a glaring bright-
ness that did not reflect our mood. "Well, at least we have
different options to choose from," chirped Mimmi as if options
made all the difference. We squeezed into the tin can and set out
on the last leg of our trip. It was a short leg. There were no more
alternatives, no more detours, no more excuses. Mick gave
me one of his questioning looks in the rear-view mirror. He had
aged since Brussels. I returned a half-hearted version of a fearless smile and a nod of encouragement, wanting to erase the fear
in his eyes. It had no effect, so I said, "I don't know what I'd do
without you two, I really don't."

"Neither do I," said Mick, "but I'm fucking grateful you're not
doing it."

We took our time as usual, feeling increasing paranoia. This
was the day we would arrive at our journey's end. A city named
Zagreb. I kept nagging Mick to slow down until he pointed out
that he was driving in reverse as it was, "what with the bleedin
tractors and all."

We reached Zagreb well before lunch. One minute there was
nothing, the next the outskirts of our destination loomed up

ahead, hitting us in the face, far too ominous and real. Row after rigid row of drab apartment blocks stood erect in fields of mud like the runner-up in a "Most Dismal Suburb in the World" competition. They were not unlike the rows of boxes where they kept the working class where I came from, but there were no trees, no bushes, no playgrounds. They looked newly built, but flimsy, like they were not made to last, so nobody had bothered with any special touches. They shed a gloom that mixed readily with the gloom inside our car.

This was it. Somewhere in this city was the father of the baby. Perhaps he lived in one of those gray apartment-complexes out in the mud, at that very moment looking out the window watching a green tin can scamper by. He might have been one of the soldiers working on the road. Or a student at the university. No, I thought, he'll be at work in a bank counting *dinars*.

I had arrived to hand over a newborn infant to this man, to be raised where there were no playgrounds. He'd be in mud up to his little knees when he learnt to walk. His father would have to buy him tiny rubber boots. Did they have tiny rubber boots in Yugoslavia?

Guilt is so complicated, yet it comes with such ease. Paradoxical, isn't it? (Why am I asking you, Pru? You wouldn't know guilt if you fell over it.)

Mimmi suddenly declared herself carsick and unable to read the map. I felt pretty sick too. Without anybody to direct Mick, we ended up on a wide divided thoroughfare called Proletarskih Brigada, with not a clue where we were going. The road looked so newly built they might have finished it minutes earlier. Mick took an instant liking to the name. The way he saw it, we were all members of the prole brigade. He waved a greeting to his fellow proles. They did not wave back. He made an illegal U-turn and drove down the Prole Brigade in the direction we'd come from.

We were lost, and so scared even the baby started to whimper. I cradled it, ready to give up. Or give in, depending on how you look at it. There were times, you see, when if I did not adhere to the strictest emotional discipline, an uninvited feeling crept up on me, never having stopped stalking me. "Why should this child pay for his father's sin?" it wanted to know. As always, I replied that, paying for a sin was not what this was all about. It had to do with taking responsibility for one's actions. It was about fairness. Nobody else was going to see to it that justice was done, so it was up to me. When I concentrated very hard on that fact, it did seem the right thing to do.

I needed to ignore the stalker, to do something, anything, so I handed the baby over to Mimmi and grabbed the map. I managed to get us onto a street called Sauska cesta that went in what I perceived to be a northerly direction, directed Mick to turn right on a street called Ulica 8 Maja 1945, and got us to the center of the city. The Croat Kid gurgled blissfully in Mimmi's arms. She cuddled it — him — and kissed his red fuzzy top, cooing endearments in Swedish. It's what she did whenever I let her hold him. It never failed. Kisses galore and coochie coo. It had never bothered me before, but now I for some reason found myself resenting it. She had no business kissing my baby. I was getting worked up and irate and was about to tell her off when I managed to stop myself.

Mimmi was just being herself. You remember what she was like? Incapable of not being nice.

We turned a corner and there was the train station straight ahead on the south side of a row of squares. It didn't look like a large central station, more like a big country mansion in a shade of peach. *Glavni Kolodvor* it said above the white columns over the entrance where I would soon make my escape.

We parked close by, out of the way of the many streetcars, and got out, tentatively, expecting immediate arrest. Nobody paid us much attention, so we started out to look for a hotel. There was a big one called Esplanade over to the left, but it looked too posh for us. We crossed the street. Opposite the station, on the south rim of the square, sat a bronze man on a bronze horse, wielding a long stick with a cross on top. He obviously didn't approve of visitors.

The city center looked lovely, stretching to the north where up on a hill the spires of a cathedral rose towards a cloud sitting right above. The square before us was called Tomislavov trg. We walked the length of it to the bright yellow building at the end. (I've since learned that particular shade of yellow is called Habsburg yellow.) Behind it was another square, Strossmayerov trg. We read the names out loud as we went along. On the left hand side was another expensive-looking hotel. It was called the Palace. Two stone figures flanked the balcony above the entrance on the corner, heads bent down. I've always thought of them as angels, but they weren't, they held their hands up on their shoulders, in a position that made their arms seem like wings. They were holding up the window above. Mick declared the hotel too posh as well, but there was a café on the corner, which didn't look very flashy. It was a definite possibility. Far enough from the station, but not too far.

We made a mental note of it and continued on past the next square. Like the previous one it was surrounded by large plane trees. There was a bandstand in the middle. Another possibility? "Meet me on Sunday at the bandstand on Zrinjevac trg?"

We found an affordable-looking hotel a few minutes further north, close to a large square called trg Republike, an open tree-less expanse full of streetcars. The woman in the reception looked us up and down with suspicion and banished us to the top floor. I pretended to have to go to the bathroom so I could go upstairs with the basket right away. She reluctantly handed me a key. For a minute I was sure she would demand to know what was in the basket. To my gratitude the basket kept quiet.

The beds were lumpy, the toilet smelly, and there was no heating. But it was cheap, it would do. Mimmi and I waited in my room with the basket while Mick got the car and fetched our stuff. This was the first hotel where we would be spending more than one night. I locked all the baby things in my suitcase, care-fully hiding all evidence, before we set out for an early afternoon walk to get to know the city where I would leave my baby behind. Before we went out I changed his diaper and put the dirty one in a bag to dispose of.

First we checked out the immediate neighborhood. None of us had expected a city in a communist country to look quite so charming. Then again, it had not become communist until after the Second World War. The charm predated the regime. There were several cafés on the large treeless square, but they were too close to the hotel. The disapproving lady in the reception might see us sitting there bobbing a baby on a lap.

Around a bend on a narrow street leading up the hill to the old city, was a smaller café where two old men sat outside playing chess. A much better place to stop for coffee, it was obscure and dark. We had a lot of time to kill and no idea what to do with it, so we went in and sat down. It wasn't a friendly place, the waiter's face never exhibited a semblance of a smile, but they did serve great Turkish coffee. *Turska kava* it was called.

It was so quiet in the café, we didn't dare talk. Intimidated, we sat and looked out the window instead, at all the people going by. There was an abundance of old ladies about, dressed in black, resembling stick figures. The young women were tall and thin, looking not Carnaby Street, but like they knew how to make the most of what they had. Groups of young men strolled by, all smoking cigarettes. All the young men seemed to go about in cliques.

I knew nothing about the country I was in. I had not bothered to learn anything, I had seen no reason to, yet here I was, sitting in a café, feeling like an outsider, looking like an outsider, wondering if it was such a brilliant idea.

We left the café that first day and continued up the hill to a market place full of fruit and vegetables and flowers and a smell of fish in the air. It looked as if it was about to close down for the day. Dolac market it was called. There seemed to be a lot of people milling about for early afternoon. I caught myself looking for a familiar face, not at all sure what I'd do if I ran into him. Hand him the baby and run? Then, seeing my reflection in a shop window, I realized he would never recognize the worried-looking, nail-chewing redhead that peered timidly at the streets of Zagreb through reading-glasses with unflattering frames.

Up past the market we found ourselves in what was obviously the old part of the city. Strolling along winding streets from long ago, we came upon the cathedral square. In the center, atop a tall column, stood a golden virgin blazing innocence and glory. Below her four angels stood guard. Two stick figures in black were exiting the cathedral, another one was on her way in. "Would this be the place to leave the basket if he doesn't show up?" I wondered. Mick said it looked the right spot. "You better put the basket in the vestry, if you have to go ahead with it," was Mimmi's suggestion. "In case it rains."

"Good idea," I said, while a voice in my head shouted, "No!" I knew then that there was no way I would leave him there all by himself. He would get frightened. "Let's get away from here," I said and crossed the street.

We ambled on. It was such a wonderful place, the old town on the hill. Not far from the cathedral we went through an L-shaped stone gate called Kamenita vrata. In the gloom of the cave-like interior there trembled flames from a small forest of candles, tall ones, short ones, thick ones and thin ones. You could feel their warmth. Old women knelt on the ground, eyes closed, lips moving in silent prayer. Several young people in their midst did the same, looking modern and out of place. A Madonna and her child lived there, alone in their niche, smiling benignly from her painting on the throng of worshippers. The story was that in 1731 a fire had destroyed everything made of wood inside the gate, all except for the wood on which the Madonna and Child had been painted, which lay untouched in the scorched ruins. There she still sat, invincible on her rococo altar, forever to be adored. I needed to get away from her too.

We climbed a staircase to a street higher up. The old town on the hill was called Gornji Grad, informed Mimmi, the diligent tourist. "This area is called Gradec." She was reading out loud from an old book called *Dalmatia* that she had bought for two bob in a secondhand bookstore on Charing Cross Road. That's how we learned about the Madonna inside the gate.

Mimmi went on to tell us that the street we were on had once been a stream over which had spanned a bridge called Blood Bridge, so named because the river had run red after each battle fought there. I stopped listening after that.

After a while, to get my attention, Mimmi grabbed me by the arm and opened the book to a section of photographs. She held it up to my face to force me to stop. "You have to look," she said. It was an order to somebody not behaving, so to please her I obeyed. "This is the country where your baby will grow up," she lectured. "Look at these pictures. They're beautiful. Look at this bridge. Doesn't it look like a picture from a fairy tale? Look at it, Lisa!"

She was right. This was going to be his homeland. Dutifully I studied the picture. Through the arch of a bridge were medieval buildings lining the riverbank. In the distance rose the tower of a minaret. It looked as if the photographer had traveled back in time for hundreds of years in order to take this snapshot.

"Okay, I can see it," I said. It's very beautiful." And it was. Mimmi was delighted. "You see?" she said, bubbling encouragement. "This is not such a bad place. As if I had ever said it was. To be obliging, and to hide my irritation, I suggested we go and see it. She said, no, we couldn't, it was not in Zagreb. Being Mimmi, she apologized for its inconvenient location. The bridge was in a place called Mostar. It was called the Stari most, meaning Old Bridge. The Turks had built it, Mimmi informed me.

"Good for the frigging Turks," I said, because I felt bad. It should have been me buying a book, trying to learn something about this place. Mimmi, unperturbed, showed me more photos of enchanted towns rising like mirages out of a misty sea, deep green forests full of lakes and waterfalls that looked the way I had always imagined the Garden of Eden. There were mountains full of castles and valleys thick with flowers. Was the place called the Bay of Kotor the real thing or somebody's wish of what heaven might be like? I had not thought it possible that a country with a drab communist regime would be allowed to be so stunningly beautiful.

Had we driven through such scenery on the way to Zagreb? I had been too nervous to notice, too preoccupied to care. I began to feel much better knowing I would be leaving my baby in such a fairy-tale part of the world. I thanked Mimmi profusely.

She said, "You're welcome," and treated me to one of her shy Mimmi-smiles, as if she felt she had to seduce me. We passed St. Mark's church and the old Ban's palace. We knew what they were because Mimmi kept quoting from her book, saying it was our duty to inform ourselves. "This was where Tito delivered a speech to a huge crowd on May 21, 1945, talking about a new Yugoslavia where there would be no reactionary nationalism between the republics. A new land of brotherhood and unity."

I remembered those words from the letter. *Bratstvo i jedinstvo.*

Mick paid no attention, he was strolling ahead carrying the baby, patting his bum like a little drum, reciting silly English rhymes I'd never heard before, about cows jumping over moons and Jacks jumping over candlesticks. Mimmi gave up lecturing, caught up with them and joined in. They laughed and skipped about, a happy young family out for a stroll. I walked several steps behind them, feeling left out, pretending not to know them.

The sky was full of clouds, but it was fairly warm. Spring had arrived, there was a gentleness in the breeze. I tried to think of the best way of getting in touch with the baby's father, wondering why I hadn't already done so. Let's face it, it bordered on lunacy to have made it this far without a set plan. But it would have been so much better if I did not have to come face to face with him. That's what held me back.

There were chestnut trees in the secret gardens up in the old town. Unlike the one shrouded in white in the park opposite where I grew up, these were heavy with beautiful pink buds. There were lilac trees in bud here as well, and a market place full of flowers. Just like at home. And yet it couldn't be more different.

It felt peculiar walking around the streets of a strange city, not knowing where the streets led, or what would happen next. Having walked the length of a tree-lined street called Strossmayerovo on the edge of the hill, we made our way down long steep steps by a funicular and walked back down to the new city. On the large treeless *trg* was a large café with a yellow awning. I thought, should I write and tell him, "Meet me in the café with the yellow awning on trg Republike at five o'clock"? Wherever I suggested, first I had to find out about trains. Then I would write. For sure.

I told my troupe that we needed to find out when the trains left for Vienna. Did the trains run on the weekend? I wanted to leave Sunday the latest. If I wrote a letter that day, he ought to get it by Friday. Mimmi said, "Let's go and find out. Then we can plan. I've got a dictionary." And sure enough, she hoisted another book out of her bag to look up the word for train ticket. She thought *vozna karta* might work, and that the word for Vienna was *Beč*, but she wasn't sure how to pronounce it, what with the c having a funny thingy on top. We sent her in to get the ticket anyway, she seemed on top of things. She pointed to her book, flashed her Mimmi-smile and got a ticket. They probably gave it to her with sincere compliments of the management. The destination on the ticket read *Wien Südbahnhof*, the date was for the Sunday which, Mimmi informed me, was Easter Sunday. I'd had no idea it was Easter.

We sat down on a bench and I wrote a brief letter to the baby's father explaining that I was in Zagreb on my way to Athens. Could he please meet me at the café in the Palace Hotel by Strossmayerov trg on Easter Sunday at noon? I had thought about him a lot and had brought along something I wanted to give him. A small keepsake from Sweden. Perhaps we could meet for a *turska kava* and have a chat? I would be wearing black pants and a green sweater. I had cut my hair and dyed it red, but would make sure he would recognize me. Hopefully our meeting would not interfere with him going to church.

"I will be waiting for you at twelve o'clock. I am looking forward to seeing you again under more pleasant circumstances. Your friend, Lisa."

The post office was just east of the station. Mimmi and her

book stepped up to the counter. She pointed to the letter and said two words. The lady held up a finger. Delivery would take one day. He'd get it then, even if it arrived a day late. I had no desire to spend Easter weekend in Zagreb, waiting for the end. It was exhausting living in fear of being caught smuggling the baby in and out of hotels, terrified of him starting to scream at the wrong time. He never did, but what if he had? We would have been in trouble long ago. And what if he got sick? What if he sensed that a change was about to take place? That his mother was going to desert him and never come back?

"I am not his mother. He is not my child."

This is what I told myself.

A thought came to me the next day as I discreetly stole through the hotel lobby with the picnic basket. I had something to thank my mother for after all. It was because of her that I had developed the devious behavior that enabled me to go about this. Living with her had made deviousness second nature to help me hide anything that might land me in trouble, to tread lightly and go unnoticed. I did not feel indebted to her for this, merely grateful that my baby was so cooperative. Docile to start with, it was as if he sensed when it was time to pretend he wasn't there. I put this down to the fact that he was not only very intelligent, but eager to get back where he belonged.

The anxiety of the wait was unbearable. One day we when were walking down the long street which ran along the foot of the hill, we thought we saw the woman from the hotel. Mimmi was beside me, carrying the baby that didn't exist. Luckily it wasn't the same woman; but it could have been, and then what?

Then there was the dirty diaper situation. I'm sorry to go on about something so tedious, but I want you to understand what a constant and primary problem it was. There were a lot of dirty diapers in bins in public places in Zagreb, Easter 1965. Towards the end I had to start washing the last few in the sink in the hotel room. I carried them with me in a plastic bag over to Ribnjak Park, where I spread them on the grass to dry.

$\longmapsto\!\!\diamond\!\!\longleftarrow$

The first night I lay awake agonizing for hours. That's when I made a decision. If the father did not show up on Easter Sunday, I would keep the child that was sleeping peacefully in the basket beside the bed, his red hair soft in the light from the bedside lamp. I would keep my child.

Yes, Pru, I *did* make that decision. Alone in my room, I said the words out loud for emphasis. "I will keep my child." The words had such an unfamiliar flavor, like foreign food full of unknown ingredients.

I already knew I could not leave the basket on the steps of a church, not even in the beautiful cathedral on Kaptol hill in his father's hometown. I would take him with me. The two of us would travel to Vienna and celebrate Easter. I would go to the Swedish Consulate and ask that my child be made official, make some excuse or other. I would buy him a little *Tiroler* hat and tiny *Lederhosen* as souvenirs of his first holiday. I would rename him Johan after my father, turn him into a little red-haired Swede, and warn him about eating Danish hot dogs.

I could only imagine what my aunts would say when I returned from art school after half a year with a foreign baby in my arms.

Thursday went by, but I didn't tell Mimmi and Mick that the Croat Kid might soon become little Swedish Johan. Not yet. But I would when the time was right. The wait was driving me quietly insane, but luckily I never tired of walking around up in Gornji grad, along streets winding out of a mysterious past, onwards to places that would continue to keep their secrets. There was one particular street up there that enamored me. It was by no means the most beautiful one, nor the quaintest one, but it spoke to me in a way that I somehow understood. I found it enthralling. It was the kind of street you sometimes walk down in dreams, wondering how you got there, a street utterly foreign yet strangely familiar. That's why it spoke to me, as if it knew me, too, but couldn't remember where from. On the east side, where it sloped towards the ramparts of the lower hill, it was lined with small houses and gardens hidden behind walls and wrought iron gates. On the other side towered a high wall with ivy cascading down its side. Atop the wall, which wasn't so much a wall as the hillside itself, high above the street, perched several crumbling apartment buildings, three, four stories high. They had long since shed most of their plaster. The few of the red tiles left on the roof were covered with patches of green moss. Each window was an unopened book, each building full of untold stories. All around the buildings stood chestnut trees full of bursting pink buds.

Every day we walked that street at least once, and each day I wondered, would my son grow up behind one of those dilapidated façades? Would this place share with him what it would never share with me? Would he belong? Was that why the street whispered in my ear, Leave the child here, he'll be all right?

He would see to that, wouldn't he? His father, I mean. He would see to that, surely?

Such were the conversations I held with myself.

As we walked about we heard voices from doorways and open windows, voices speaking a language that excluded us. Snippets of music from a radio now and then, sounding old-fashioned to our ears. Once in a while the smell of food would tease us. We'd guess what was for dinner at this house or that, whether it was a special occasion or an everyday meal. The gardens we glimpsed through the wrought iron gates looked inviting, but we knew nobody would let us in.

During the long afternoons we visited the country's past in museums and galleries. Paintings, sculptures, weapons and icons, costumes and jewelry, only confirmed that this was indeed an ancient place that had risen out of a mystical mist full of legends that still lingered. Tomislav, for example, who sat outside the train station shaking his stick, had been a king in tenth-century Croatia.

As time had hurried through the centuries toward the future, through battles and bloodbaths, the country had lost and gained bits along the way. The Venetians left the Dalmatian coast barren, cutting down the trees to build ships. The Turks claimed chunk after chunk and ruled for more than five hundred years. The Austro-Hungarian Empire had run the part we were in, the Italians helped themselves to other bits, *ad infinitum*, until Yugoslavia was created. Now Tito had enforced Brotherhood and Unity and everybody had to pretend to be a proud Yugoslav. We were in a country, or rather a union of nations, with a rich history of unexplained contradictions, full of secrets that would forever remain unknown.

It was a fragmented place that had been held hostage and raped repeatedly.

I learned about Strossmayer, too, the man sitting on his square not far from the Palace café. He was a nineteenth century bishop. Handsome, controversial, intelligent. He had once walked the streets of Vienna. A liberal Catholic who liked to annoy his ecclesiastical superiors, who didn't trust the Habsburgs, and who hated the Hungarians. He believed not so much in Croatian nationalism as in a unification of all Slavic people in the Illyrian peninsula. His middle name was Juraj. I'd named my child not only after his father, but after a great, liberal, forward-thinking man. Sheer coincidence, but even so.

In some museums and galleries I was not able to stay for very long. There was a plethora of holy icons, statues large and small, paintings huge and minute, all of Madonna and child, Madonna and child. Every child had an odd shape, the head too large, the body too long, facial features too old. None of them was as cute as my child. But it was the haloed Madonnas cradling their children that chased me out of there. They glowed with the sort of motherhood that was out of bounds for me. They all stared at me, those damn Madonnas, smug and reproachful from their secure place in some eternal perfection. I had to flee. I feared punishment. Not because I was religious, but because punishment was what I had been brought up on. The certain knowledge that I deserved it had never left me. Come time for the last judgment, Lisa Grankvist was in for it.

By Saturday morning I was buzzing around my room like a bee too dumb to find an open window, hoping that the father of my baby would not have the guts to show up, hoping he was a born coward. He had acted like a big enough coward the last time we met, so it was entirely possible. I didn't have the slightest desire to meet him. Not any more. But I had to, because that was the only reason I was in Yugoslavia. How could I travel that far and not see him?

We spent the morning and early afternoon sitting in cafés, not knowing what to do. "Let's go to the cemetery," said Mimmi, our self-appointed guide, leafing through her book as we were having yet another coffee. Mick didn't fancy hanging out in a boneyard, but we went up on the tram anyway.

The cemetery was the most beautiful place imaginable. Mirogoj it was called. It spread out on the eastern slope of the hill that is basically a foothill of the Medvenica mountains. I needed badly to be alone that day, so I left Mimmi and Mick by the tram stop, said I'd see them in an hour, and walked away fast, through the entrance, in under the trees, just my baby and me.

When I got to the other side I sat down on a wall with the baby in my arms and looked out over the countryside, trying to identify the different parts of this enigmatic Balkan peninsula where my baby would grow up. If his father showed up the next day, that is.

$$\longmapsto\!\Diamond\!\longleftarrow$$

"Are you sure you want to go through with this?" Mimmi asked me again for the very last time in the early morning on Easter Sunday. She hadn't slept either, and looked as frazzled as I did. She hadn't washed her hair for days. Neither had I. There was never any hot water. I told her, my voice feeling querulous and thin, that I had made up my mind, so what did it matter?

"It does matter, luv," Mick butted in. He was looking so mournful by then I hardly recognized him. They were so kind, those two, discreetly offering me another chance to bow out without losing face.

But I wasn't going to. I couldn't. I had written to the father of this child. I would go and meet him. I had to. It was the right thing to do. If he showed up.

I was in an emotional tunnel, too narrow to turn around in, too scary to walk backwards in. I had to continue forward to where there ought to have been a light beckoning, but where I saw only shadows.

Easter Sunday, April 18, 1965, ten o'clock a.m. Eighteen, my lucky number, remember? We were having *turska kava* in the café where the old men played chess. At twelve I had a date at another café.

# 35

Remembering that morning only too clearly, Lisa locked the notebook in her desk, for another while, until the time was right. Then she would finish it. It wouldn't be long now, she knew. The past was gathering speed and the present was slowing down, waiting for it to catch up.

Starting in the winter of 1994, came a sense that life was about to change. It took her gently by the arm, led her into a reflective mood and bade her sit down. More often than not she felt something approaching. There was a wind blowing, the same wind that had chilled her back once, when her country fell off the horizon. After all these years it was blowing again, warmer this time. Writing down the past made her realize that she had described a circle that was starting to close. She sensed herself waiting, expecting somebody to soon knock on her door.

She was lying on the couch reading a book about the Habsburg Empire, now and then looking out on the street. The branches of the tall spruces across the street, always dark and forest-like, hung heavy with snow. Birds were gorging themselves at the bird feeder hanging from the naked maple close by. The sunshine made the snow sparkle, the sky was sapphire blue, a summer sky that had forgotten what season it was.

It was cold out. The city was white. She thought, if seasons were music, winter would be an octave higher than the rest. Winter's chill cuts to the bone, it resonates as shrill and clear as crystal. Something in her northern blood responded to that music.

Once in a while, especially on Sundays when the street lay as still as a photograph, she would nod off like an old woman. Her book would fall to the floor. That Sunday afternoon as she drifted off, she suddenly heard church bells, faintly. They tolled from far, far away, an echo of bells calling to evensong. And she recognized the bells from her childhood, from Kirsebergskyrkan, whitewashed and plain, four blocks from where they once burned witches. From across the decades came the echo, and she woke up, wondering what year it was, recalling another church, much, much smaller.

It was a wooden church that had appeared on the windowsill in the living room the Christmas when she was six. Her father had asked his handyman friend Ivar to make it, wanting to surprise Lisa with something special. She had stood wonderstruck before it, thinking it was surely the most beautiful work of art in creation: a country church, simple and white, with a black-roofed spire and stained glass windows. Inside the church were rows of wooden pews and a simple altar. Beside it hung a tiny blackboard with the numbers of the psalms to be sung. The tower had a bell in it, with a string attached so you could ring it. It rang so clear she was convinced it would attract elves. She knew that on Christmas morning the little church would be full of elves. She would hear the sound of their hymns as she woke up.

Her father plugged the church in and it lit up. It was truly a thing of magic. The stained-glass windows were made of colored paper pulled taut to look real, so solid and hard that she wasn't satisfied until she had poked a finger through one.

It was the sheer wonder of it that made her do it, but she never forgave herself. The hole was impossible to repair.

Her father said, "We'll put some tape over it and turn it around so it won't show and mother will never notice."

Lisa was convinced that it had saddened him all the same. It was horrible that he should think that she didn't care about the magic church where little hand-carved people with red cheeks walked through cotton snowdrifts towards the entrance where the little priest stood waiting, an eternal smile on his face. It ruined her Christmas that year, thinking that she had hurt her father. No elves sang on Christmas morning.

Now that the circle was closing, she saw the lights from that small wooden church, blinking in the approaching night, as if she had traveled no distance at all. When she closed her eyes she stood once again in front of it, peeking through the taped-over window, wanting to shrink until she was an inch tall so she could enter the church, and sit quietly in one of the pews.

It brought to mind other material possessions she now wished she had kept, if only to run her fingers over them in recognition once more, the surface of a Christmas decoration, an old pair of skis, a two-octave accordion, confirming her existence. Needing the end and the beginning to meet, to close the circle that is the pattern of life. Realizing that she should have known all along that she had the power to shape that circle and make it perfect.

One day the bells will toll again, she promised herself, and I will enter that small country church with its windows of colored paper, on a windowsill where the cottonball snowdrifts lie deep. It will be a state of mind, a sense of peace.

The thought of this softened something inside her. She went to her study and got out her notebook. It was time to finish it. It was almost full.

# 36

**D**earest Pru, As church bells tolled, the father of my child did show up. And in the end, when the moment arrived, when the chance of cold revenge presented itself, it was no good. As soon as I saw him, everything changed. I changed.

I would die a little in the process, but I knew I could only go about it one way if I was to go through with it at all. I would have to be honest. I would have to look him in the eye and tell him how I felt. All at once I ran out of the mental and emotional energy required to lie and coldly go through with not telling him what was in the basket before disappearing. I felt no anger, no need for retribution.

This is how it happened. At the appointed time I huddled with my basket behind a large plane tree on Strossmayerov trg, like Little Red Riding Hood ready to offer her basket of goodies to the wolf. Up on his pedestal, over to the left, sat Bishop Strossmayer, whose middle name was Juraj. I wanted to think he was on my side. Peeking around the tree I watched the baby's father arrive at the café. He came around the corner from the street called Ulica Braće Kavurića accompanied by two other young men. Even from across the street I recognized him at once from the way his hair flopped over his forehead. The very sight of him stupefied me. In some far away recess of my mind I had grown used to the idea that he in fact did not exist, and that this was some silly game I was playing. It had done so in tandem with the knowledge that he would show up. Hope is that devious.

His movements were nervous. He kept shoving his hands through his hair while looking around. His two friends kept talking, dragging on their cigarettes. In a minute or less I was going to faint or throw up, or both. This was not a game, because here he was in the flesh, this man, somehow looking more foreign in his own hometown, dressed in a white shirt, a gray suit jacket and black pants. He was about to enter the café, under the watching angels that were not angels, when I heard myself shout his name, resentfully. My mouth had betrayed me.

As he turned around and looked across the street, I stepped out from behind the tree and waved. He stopped and stared. There was confusion mingling with apprehension in his face. He looked like he wasn't quite sure who I was, so I shouted, "It's me, Lisa!" in Swedish to confirm that it was. I felt like an idiot. He turned and said something to his friends who nodded and threw several curious glances towards me clutching my basket, before disappearing into the café. Looking back at me, he threw his cigarette on the ground and crossed the street right in front of a tram. He almost got run over, but he didn't notice. In the café his friends sat down by a window, lit new cigarettes, eyes fixed in our direction.

These are details I will remember until the day I die.

His body movements changed after he became aware of me. He sauntered, not too fast, not too slow, giving the appearance of a man in full control, then stopped a few feet from where I was standing, suddenly unsure of his next step, but with a tentative smile at the ready. Nervously, he took a step forward, stuck out his hand and told me he was happy to see me. His Swedish sounded worse, then again, it had been a while since he had had any use for it. It was never very good to start with. I smelled a faint whiff of alcohol on his breath, though he appeared sober enough. Maybe he was frightened too. I took his hand. It was as damp as mine. How I wished I wasn't there.

"I glad you here," he said as we shook hands, sealing a deal he was still unaware of. We stood face to face for a moment, awkward, saying nothing. He looked older than I remembered him. Shorter too. I could tell he was wondering why I had stopped in Zagreb. This was our conversation.

"So . . . you go to Greece?" he asked.

"No." As I shook my head I remembered what I had written in my letter. "Yes. Yes. But not today, that is. Tomorrow . . . No . . . I . . . I . . ." Telling myself, come on, Lisa, for God's sake! Do it! ". . . I brought you something." I held up the basket, gripping it tightly. My hands were shaking so much by then I almost dropped it.

"For me?" He looked puzzled, as well he might. Women don't usually travel great distances to bring their rapists baskets full of gifts.

"Oh yes, it's for you. You made it." I felt sick to my stomach. It was a good thing I'd had no breakfast.

"I . . . make?" Bafflement fought suspicion in his eyes. They were not as blue as I had remembered them. Now they seemed to reflect the gray of the clouds that had floated down from the mountains as I stood waiting. They had crossed over the old city on the hill and reached the square, blocking out the sun, erasing the shadows of the trees.

Putting the basket on the ground, concentrating hard, I flipped open the lids and lifted out the baby. My baby. No. His baby. The Croat Kid.

"Well . . . congratulations. This is your son." What else to say? I held out the baby to him. He looked so stunned I could have knocked him over with a sneeze. He stood speechless and gaping. Surely he could see the likeness? "Here," I said. "Take him."

"Son?" He pronounced it the German way, *Sohn*, staring dumbfounded at the small baby in its cheerful green and white striped terry cloth jumpsuit.

"Yes, your son. Take him." I might have been shouting. He had to take him. I had a feeling I might faint. But having managed this far I knew I was going through with it. This was meant to be.

His arms lifted, robot-like, and grasped the child. He gazed at it for a very long time, arms straight out as if they didn't bend. The baby dangled between in his hands. I noticed that the father's fingernails were not quite clean. Those were the hands that had once held me in a firm grip, leading me to the outhouse. The hands that had stroked my hair as I lost my virginity.

After a while he remembered that his arms did bend, and he clumsily cradled the baby to his chest. The baby looked unperturbed. The father looked like he'd been hit in the face with a blunt instrument.

"You can see it's your child." I felt defensive, frightened and rigid. "He's got your eyebrows and your birthmark. You can tell."

"Also *rot haar* like has my mother," said the man named Juraj.

"Your mother has red hair?" (So much for Danish hot-dogs.)

"*Da.* Same *haar* like so." He pronounced hair in German too. Then, "Why show child?" He now held it in a manner that claimed ownership. Which, I told myself, was a good sign. "Then go?"

"I have to go." I explained to him. "I'm starting school in London very shortly. But the child stays with you. It's your child."

"You go? Child not?" He was totally befuddled, so I made it all plain to him again, and was honest about it, matter-of-fact, not hostile. Concentrating with all my might I reminded him that he had raped me. He stared at his feet. I said when he had done so he had planted the seed that had grown into a baby inside me. It was the "you reap what you sow" routine I had rehearsed so many times. I don't know if he understood it, but it didn't stop me. "Let's face it," I said. "That's how babies are made. It's your child." He blushed deeply, though whether with anger or embarrassment, I couldn't tell. But he didn't contradict me. There were beads of perspiration on his upper lip, but no words of denial.

I told him my mother had died, that I was alone in the world. He had to take responsibility for what he had done, that's all there was to it. The baby was his. Did he accept that? He didn't reply. Then I told him I was leaving.

"We marry?" he blurted out, without enthusiasm.

I shook my head. "I have to go. So tell me, will you look after your son?" I looked into his eyes. I remembered those blue eyes. Looking closer I realized they were still quite blue, but flecked with gray. The last time I had looked into them he had closed them in shame. Now they remained open and looked into mine where they must have seen a lot of confusion and fear, but in the control of something stubborn and hard. His eyes expressed shame this time too, but something else as well. Not love, for he would never love me, as I could never love him. Call it pride, for lack of a better word. Fatherly pride, macho pride, to this day I don't know.

"He my son." Despite the astonishment in his voice, it was a statement, not a question.

"Yes, he's *your* son," I said. "Will you look after him?" I wondered how sober he was, wondered what on earth I was doing, while knowing I was going through with it.

"Here not so good place for child. Not money. Not good life." He looked embarrassed.

"You don't have a choice. I can't raise your child. You do understand that, don't you?" I couldn't look at the baby. I looked over at the two figures on the balcony above the café entrance. They looked even more like angels from where I was standing. Whatever they were, they ignored me.

The baby's father stared at me, but he didn't reply. Perhaps he was unsure of the right words to use. I tried again. "Will you look after him? Yes or no? There are some Deutschmark in the basket to buy him diapers and things."

"Deutschmark?" That got his attention.

"Yes. Eight hundred Deutschmark." I showed him the money. "It should get you started."

"*Acht hundert* Deutschmark?" He nearly dropped the baby.

"Yes," I said and put the bills away again. He kept asking, "For child?" I kept saying it was, but I was getting impatient. "Answer me, for God's sake! Will you look after your son or won't you? The money is for him. Not for you. You told me you were a good Catholic, didn't you?"

"Is true. You come back? You visit?" He was studying his son's face when he asked, too busy to look at me.

"Yes. I'll come back and visit. When I come back from Athens," I lied. "I will come and check up on you, so watch out. He better be okay. His birth certificate is in the basket. It has your name on it. All his things are in this bag. His name is Juraj, too." And it was. It was not baby Johan. It was Juraj.

"Juraj?" Here he rewarded me with a direct look of surprise. Then he smiled. I saw that he had a tooth missing on the left side of his mouth. I couldn't remember him having a tooth missing.

"Yes. That's his name. Juraj. He's a very good baby. You'll have to get him more milk, though, because I've been breast-feeding. There's a bottle and four cans of formula in this bag. His clothes are in there too. And some diapers. He'll be all right for now, but he'll need more diapers soon. He's a lovely baby." Gibbering as rapidly as I did, I'm sure he didn't catch half of it. He tried to reply, glancing at me briefly again, but I didn't hear what he said, I'd gone deaf. I had to get away before the world fell apart, before the statue behind me crumbled and the bishop toppled on his head and shattered. Before the baby started to cry.

I hoped Mick was standing watch somewhere nearby, as he was supposed to, that Mimmi was waiting at the station with my suitcase.

I dropped the shoulder bag at his feet, then I was running. The baby's father shouted something after me, but I didn't stop, couldn't stop. I bolted across the street right in front of a tram, flew like a mindless goose, wishing I had wings to stretch, down a block of Ulica 8 Maja 1945, turning left at the first corner, then left again, flapping onwards down along the street that led to the station. I heard myself make whimpering sounds. By the time I got to the station I was so out of breath I was choking. My one-way ticket to Vienna was in my coat pocket. Mimmi stood waiting with my suitcase. It was over. Suddenly it was over. The baby was with his father. I no longer had a baby.

Once I saw Mimmi inside the station, I hurled myself into her arms, so violently she lost her balance and stumbled backwards against the wall. I started sobbing and didn't stop. There were just the two of us holding on to each other in a strange country. People stared.

Mick wasn't there yet. His job had been to go for a little walk in the direction of the café, to make sure the baby's father didn't follow me.

When Mick eventually arrived at the station he was trying hard to look unhurried and carefree and not succeeding at all. He reported that the bloke had carried the baby, the bag and the basket to the café where he'd sat down at a table occupied by his two mates, all of them shouting and gesticulating wildly. To say that his mates had looked stunned was an understatement. One of them had just lit a cigarette. "It fell out of his face and into his lap, and he didn't notice, they were that kind of stunned." They were still sitting there. Some other blokes had joined them. While Mick had kept watch none of them had made any phone calls as presumably they would have, had they wanted to contact the police.

"He seemed right thrilled with the nipper, actually. Kept holding him up for his mates to have a look." The baby had not cried, he assured me. It had looked its usual content self. Hearing that, I started to howl again. Mimmi led me out on the platform, hugged me and stroked my hair and patted my back. She, too, was busy sobbing, but then she pulled herself together, and whispered in my ear that if I had changed my mind, now was my chance to fix it. "It's your my baby too," she said. Mick agreed. "She's right, luv," he kept saying. "Now's the time. Go on. They're still at the café."

But I had not changed my mind. It wasn't that. I had known all along that I could not keep what did not belong to me. Perhaps that's where the grief stemmed from, the fact that the baby had not been mine to keep, even had I wanted to. I knew in my heart that I'd been right about that, and that in itself was painful.

But you know what, Pru? I had felt left out. Watching that man holding the baby, cradling it carefully, exuding ownership, ignoring me, I had felt left out. As though, once again, I had been of no importance.

Mimmi wiped my face with the sleeve of her tatty cardigan, smearing it with mascara. She looked odd. Mick looked odd. The shock had numbed our features. But it was time for me to flee the scene. Mimmi hugged me for a long time. "You'll be okay. I can feel it," she said. Mick pressed me against his ugly vest in a paternal hug and asked, "Will you be all right, luv?"

I said that I would. "I'll see you in London in less than a week. We'll do the clubs. I hope you have a great time riding gondolas."

Mimmi promised they'd have my room ready for me, making it sound, reassuringly, like this was not the end of the world, but only the beginning.

I hung on to that.

# 37

**Dear Pru,** I just finished the last bit, sitting here, chewing on
my pen the way I once chewed on my nails, wondering how I
survived it, if I survived. But I did, didn't I?

Having come this far, I want to get this over with, so I'm
going to tell you the rest while I'm at it. There's not much left.
Only fear and paranoia I didn't leave behind. The trip between
Zagreb and the story of Vienna I told you years ago.

Having shed my friends, my baby and the artifacts of my life
to date, I ran down the station stairs, through an underground
passage to Platform Two. I kept stumbling, as though I'd lost my
sense of balance. My suitcase was lighter. The shoulder bag with
all the baby stuff was gone. No more smelly diapers to rinse in
cold water.

The train to Vienna was waiting. I forced myself to get on it,
settled by the window in an empty compartment, hiding behind
the curtain, hoping to have the place to myself.

It was Easter Sunday. Hopefully most people had already
traveled to wherever they were going. To be with family, eat a big
Easter dinner, raise their glasses of slivovitz in a toast. No sooner
had that thought assured my mind, than a voluptuous blonde

opened the door and joined me. She was a tall woman in her thirties, wearing a lot of unfashionable red lipstick that clashed loudly with her pink nylon blouse. The blouse, in turn, did nothing at all for the brown skirt with yellow polka dots. She sat down opposite me and smiled what I interpreted to be a superior smile, before lighting a cigarette. Her blouse had a lipstick stain on the collar. One of her red nails was chipped. Her hair showed black roots.

I was a fine one to talk. Mine was showing blonde roots. My eyes were red, my face blotchy with smears of mascara. I did not smile back. I would not have known how. I wiped my face with the sleeve of my sweater instead. The woman looked on in sympathy.

The train started moving and chugged west for a few minutes, then it slowed down and stopped. They must have found out that I was on board. Any second a gun-wielding posse would storm the compartment. What was the punishment in Yugoslavia for smuggling infants? Would they send me to a Gulag to starve on water and stale crusts of bread? Did they have Gulags? Or would they make it simple and shoot me on the spot?

Two middle-aged men in ill-fitting suits entered the compartment, one after the other. The first man's suit was a size too small, the second one's a size too large. The second one wore a hat. They pretended not to know each other, but it was obvious to me that they were partners, they had secret police written all over them. No one went around looking like that if they were not in the secret police. We were behind the iron curtain, in a communist country. Rules were different here. Besides, the place we had stopped at didn't look like a proper train station. The train had stopped only to let them board because they were coming to get me.

The secret policemen sat down, still pretending to be strangers. They knew their job. The blonde with the ruby lips was briefly ogled by the man in the hat. The other one opened up a newspaper and hid behind it, pretending to read. The blonde closed her eyes.

The train was moving again. I was surrounded. They were

playing some sort of waiting game. Well, it was a long trip; they could afford to take their time. It was more than I could handle.

It took a long time to get out of the city. The train chugged through a few more suburbs, villages on the outskirts of the city. Far away on the horizon sat a mountain, quite alone. On the other side of the train, houses with red tiled roofs dotted tree-covered hills. The river Sava ran along beside the train. The countryside was lush and green. Friendly-looking. After a place called Podsused we crossed the river and it ran on the right of the train, still following. I could see it through the door and the window in the corridor. Once the river stops following me, I'll be safe, I decided.

After Zaprešic-Savska more mountains rose up on the north-west horizon. It was a beautiful panorama, verdant as a rain forest, but it did nothing for my state of terror. It had taken only eighteen years to make a mess of my life and end up on a train climbing the Slovenian hills. The river had not given up.

My mother was right. I was no good. If I tapped one of the secret police politely on the shoulder, would he show mercy this Easter Sunday and put a quick bullet through my head?

And yet, I couldn't help thinking, was it such a crime what I had done? Was it, Pru? Women let their sons go off to war and get killed. All I had done was leave mine with his father. It's not what a good mother does, I know. But I had never meant to be a good mother. I had never meant to be a mother at all.

I got up on shaky legs and wobbled out into the corridor. Stood and watched the view. The train was sliding through a flat valley surrounded by more mountains, greener mountains. A station went by. Savski-Marof Dubova read a sign. No border yet. High hills covered in dense forest drew closer.

Why didn't they apprehend me and get it over with?

I was exhausted, not having slept the night before. Having left my child with a stranger with a missing tooth. Under my sweater my bra was soaked with the milk that had suddenly started to leak. It was feeding time. Would his father remember to feed him?

Oozing milk and paranoia, I went in and sat down with the secret police.

The hills lay green and woolly under the spring sun. Here and there church steeples poked up like witches' hats. Ever so often the river rippled into sight, still following the train on its journey north. At one point it disappeared into the hills only to reappear with a pale yellow village stretched out along its western bank. All the roofs were red, as was the church steeple. The river came and went, still in pursuit, getting wider and wider. It was a bad sign.

We stopped at a place called Sevnica. There were no policemen on the platform. There was nobody around at all, only a woman with two small boys getting of the train. The train kept climbing north beside the river, up into forested emerald mountains. It was cold up there, I had to put my jacket on. But before long we were heading down again into a soft and gentle landscape, the river still disappearing and reappearing, teasing me, playing hide and seek.

Another stop, a place called Celje, a lovely town full of spires and steeples. Here the river danced and skipped as it skirted the town, as if suddenly all excited. Up on a mountain outside the city sat a castle with bits missing.

I left the compartment again and went down the train corridor, weak-kneed, and leaned against a window. Ever onwards chugged the train. Eventually the land began to turn pastoral. Small farms rushed by, little houses and garden plots. How long had I been traveling? According to my watch only two hours had gone by. Two measly, useless hours. Up ahead on the horizon was the silhouette of a mountain range. Was that Austria?

The river disappeared. While I waited for it to return, the train slowed to a stop. We were in a city called Maribor. I remembered from looking at the map that this was the last city before the border. It wouldn't be long now.

The door to the compartment opened and the blonde and the secret policeman without a hat emerged. They made their way towards me. Their plan was to leave the man in the hat as a backup. They were both carrying their bags, playing passengers to the bitter end. I waited, prepared to surrender with dignity. When the man got to where I was standing, I looked him straight in the eye. He ignored me, squeezed by and got off the train. The woman gave me a little nod but didn't waste another smile. I stumbled back into the compartment and sat down.

Out on the platform an older woman opened her arms wide to receive to the blonde, who ran up and hugged her, laughed happily and hugged her some more, twirling her around. I noticed that she had two teeth missing. Was that what her smirk had been about, hiding the gaps? As I watched, the old woman kissed her and patted her cheeks before they hooked arms and slowly, the old woman limping, walked into the white station building. That was all. A woman going home to visit her mother for Easter. Her mother had probably spent the whole day preparing a big dinner.

The hatless man stopped by the kiosk, lit a cigarette and sauntered off. There was still the remaining secret policeman, of course, but he was asleep. Or feigning sleep.

The train rolled on through a rural idyll, between steep pine-clad hillsides, towards the Austrian border. In the south-west a pale afternoon sun kept gliding in and out of gray clouds. I lost sight of the river. Looking out over the green woolly peaks I felt, for the first time, a very, very long way from home.

Passport control at both Šentilj and Spielfeld-Strass was a breeze with a Swedish passport, the uniformed Yugoslav mumbling *molim* and *hvala*, the Austrian nodding *bitte and danke schön*.

The passport belonging to the remaining secret policeman, on the other hand, underwent careful scrutiny on the Austrian side. It was probably homemade. Serves him right, I thought. Eventually he was asked to leave the compartment and go with the customs officer. He never returned. Then the train rolled into Austria and I was safe.

Mission accomplished.

I fell asleep from exhaustion and when I woke up I was in Vienna.

# 38

As the past catches up with the present, the young and the old Lisa stand face to face. The older version, having mellowed, forgives the younger, who only did what she thought was right.

There is no longer a need to run. For the first time in thirty years Lisa releases the imperial teacup from its red box and drinks tea out of it. It is a special, rewarding moment. As she sips tea, the cup warming her hands, she rereads her record of events. Looking back, as Melvin and Kierkegaard once promised, some of it makes sense. What makes sense is that it is not a crime for a misguided pregnant seventeen-year-old girl to believe in justice. It is the insignificant role that justice plays in such sordid affairs that is so mystifying.

⤛◆⤜

One evening a month later, Len drops by, conveniently around suppertime, as is his habit. Lisa has not bothered to cook supper that night, but because she's in a mood bordering on joyous, rippling like the river Sava in springtime, having finished her notebook, she orders a celebratory pizza, an extra large one with Len's favorite toppings, and without anchovies. He accepts this magnanimous gesture as his due and makes himself at home. Puts his feet up on her coffee table and feels good. He likes hanging out at Lisa's, her place is like a real home. Should he ever be invited to sleep over, he'll accept.

Watching him getting comfortable, she asks, "Would you like a cup of tea, hon?" Without batting an eyelid he responds. "Yeah, that would be real nice."

Divorced for six years, they sit in her living room watching TV like any other middle-aged couple killing an evening. Len would rather watch a sitcom, but Lisa insists on watching the news in the evening and it's her TV. Len's ex-wife is a woman who cherishes her habits, if for no other reason than that they are hers.

The evening news is reporting more horrors in the former Yugoslavia. As always a cold hand grabs Lisa by the heart when she watches film clips from that part of the world. These are the images of a medieval nightmare. Only Bosch could have dreamt up Bosnia.

Len asks who the asshole on the screen is. Lisa tells him it's the Bosnian Serb leader, Karadžić, a rabid nationalist mass murderer. Len says the man reminds him of Lucien Bouchard in a dorky wig. "All nationalists are dangerous lunatics," he proclaims. "That's probably why they look alike."

Lisa says Bouchard is not a mass-murderer, but otherwise agrees, which is nice. They have never agreed on very much. Len asks for some more tea. He would prefer beer, but Lisa never has any. Dessert would be nice too.

"Do you have any cookies?"

What was the point of divorcing this man, this needy hanger-on? Don't his women friends bake? Have they all given up on him? Lisa fetches a jar of homemade peanut butter cookies. Content, he digs in.

She should have adopted him instead of marrying him.

There is a news clip about the Croatian Minister of Defense. They say he used to run a pizza parlor in Ottawa. Len finds that hilarious. So does Lisa. This item is followed by an interview with a young Catholic priest from Croatia, who is in Toronto fund-raising for orphaned children. It is interspersed with more images of despair and screaming infants. The priest is in his early thirties. He looks far too fresh-faced and innocent to be a priest. Lisa momentarily recalls a young priest she passed in Mirogoj cemetery.

"Why would a young guy become a priest, for chrissake?" Len wants to know. He sounds offended. "And in a place like that?"

"Maybe he felt the call. Ask your family, they're all religious."

"So? You don't see me in a cassock."

"That would be a sight for sore eyes."

Like two old comrades-in-arms, battle-fatigued, they laugh, surprising themselves. The camera zooms in for a close-up.

Lisa stops laughing.

"I know that priest." She stares at the screen. Her face has grown tense. Her hand, on its own accord, puts her imperial teacup down.

"The fuck you do."

Len doesn't know it, but he's only partially right. Not that it matters. Lisa is no longer aware of his presence. She's leaning forward, hypnotized by the TV, her face white, her eyes dark. Her hands are trembling and fiddling in her lap. It looks like they can't decide whether to join in hasty prayer or start pinching each other. The rest of her does not move.

He looks at her hands fidgeting, never keeping still, trying to find a position, and he wonders if his ex, staring at the priest on the screen, is having a religious experience.

If Len was a different kind of man, one of those frantic hands might reach out to clasp one of his for comfort and reassurance.

Lisa's head is reeling. There are sharp pains in her chest. Somewhere a door has unlocked. The time has come. It's time to get ready. Putting her hands on her white cheeks she draws several deep breaths. When she recovers her speech, she says, in a near whisper, "Len?"

"What?" Len is helping himself to another cookie.

"I'm leaving."

"What do you mean, you're leaving? This is your place."

"I'm leaving Canada. I'm going back to Sweden."

"Yeah? Okay." He turns back to the TV, munches his cookie. If her announcement has upset him, he'll never let on.

Lisa has just made three monumental decisions. The first one she will see to in the morning. After that, as she's just informed Len, she's going home. On the way she will stop in London. Every decision opens the door wider.

Tomorrow she will mail Pru the notebook. It's high time. Then she will call Sonja and tell her the news.

# 39

The day she calls Sonja with the news of her decision is when she takes her first step outside the newly unlocked door. So momentous is this step that she feels a need to look her best. She washes her hair, puts on makeup and perfume before slipping into her nicest dress for this hot date with destiny. Then she pours herself a glass of wine and arranges herself in a suitable position by the phone. When every limb is in position, every hair in its place, she lifts the receiver and dials quickly. Suddenly the news can't wait any longer, it's going to burst out of her any second. And sure enough, as soon as she hears Sonja's voice, out it springs.

"Sonja! I'm ready!"

"Ready for what?" Sonja doesn't sound excited.

"I'm coming home."

"What?" Now she does.

"I'm coming home. It's time."

"Oh God!" There's a long silence, but no thud, so Lisa is fairly sure she has not fainted. The first thing Sonja says when she collects herself is, "Do you like sandwiches?" as if offering a clue to the password that will let Lisa back in the country.

"What?"

"Sandwiches. Open face sandwiches. *Landgångar*. Remember?"

"I remember. Why? What's that got to do with anything? Are you going to make me some?"

"If you want to. But I'm thinking of quitting my job to buy a sandwich shop. I have to make my life different, or I won't be able to go on. It's been so difficult. But I would like a partner. I keep thinking, I wish Lisa would come home. We could work together, grow old together."

"A sandwich shop? You're going to sell sandwiches?"

"Yes." Sonja explains about the shop, patiently, about how she sold the old apartment and moved to a smaller one soon after Andreas died. Linnea lives with her boyfriend out near the football stadium. The sandwich shop is in a central location, only three blocks from where she now lives. "It caters to the lunch trade and closes at six. People who want sandwiches for the evening order ahead of time and pick them up after work."

"A sandwich shop?" Lisa can't get over it.

"Stop repeating that. You sound like a parrot. It's a very busy lunch trade, I'll have you know. Do you know how much you can make in a day with a place like that?" Lisa doesn't, so Sonja informs her.

"That much? In a sandwich shop? People must eat nothing else over there."

"Have you any idea what a *landgång* costs?" Sonja parts with another figure.

"How can people afford that?"

"It's what things cost these days. Then of course there's taxes." She gives Lisa a short lecture about taxes and Lisa thinks maybe she ought to stay firmly put in Canada.

"It's not as bad as it sounds," Sonja assures her. "We can afford to hire somebody part time at least. Linnea says she'll help out. And I have some great plans for the store."

She shares her ideas with Lisa, getting more and more excited as she goes on about how they will travel to different regions of the province to pick out specialties, the adventure of discovering which places make the best sausage, smoked eel, pâtés, pickled herring, regional breads, etc. Her plan is to feature specialty sandwiches that will not be found anywhere else. Lisa gets excited too, with visions of traveling from town to town with Sonja, staying in country inns, sampling pieces of sausage and bread, driving up and down the coast in search of the best smoked fish, growing fatter by the day, until they both look like two happy rotund Aunt Gullis.

They are very appealing visions.

Before she knows it, Lisa has decided to buy half the sandwich shop. She and Sonja have not seen each other for twenty-three years, but that's irrelevant. She's going to Sweden to make sandwiches. With two kinds of cheese, ham, roast beef with remoulade sauce (her father's favorite), smoked salmon, smoked eel, shrimp and eggs. Garnished lavishly with parsley, dill, slices of orange twisted over the ham, lemon over the salmon and the shrimp. Not to mention specialty sandwiches yet to be invented. Taxes aside, it will be rewarding, this new life of hers.

It's late September by the time she's all set. She has quit her job, closed her bank accounts, given notice on her apartment, and has sold most of her belongings. She's not shipping any furniture apart from the brass and glass shelves from her Chiswick island refuge, and the old oak dresser she stripped herself. It's going to be her Canadian memento.

The last weekend she allows herself a solitary farewell walk, as she did in London twenty-two years earlier. The twice-repeated tradition is a painful, self-centered pleasure. Looking at it with different eyes now, she notices how Hamilton has changed over the years. Notices all new buildings, so shiny and futuristic. All the boarded-up shops down on Barton Street.

Heading northwest she walks by Dundurn Castle and the Botanical Gardens, then scrambles around Coote's Paradise where a turtle crosses her path. She gets as far as the hills on the other side of Dundas, where the apple orchards she remembers from years ago have disappeared. She makes her way back to McMaster Medical Centre along the old railroad track and catches the bus to the east end.

Hamilton has become home, another point on a closing circle. She knows she will dream about it and wake up surprised that she's no longer in this third country she has called home for so long. Where she's lived longer than anywhere else, including the country of her birth. Time has passed with ferocious speed on this continent. She has been content here. She will miss it. It's such an easygoing place.

But it is not the land of her tribe.

A week before her departure, Lisa's colleagues at work take her out to dinner at a steakhouse in Burlington. Its outside is lit up like a Christmas tree, its interior dark and gloomy. She orders a giant slab of steak, wanting to finish with the kind of meal she started with. The steaks have shrunk, they're not nearly as big as when she and Len shared a Brontosaurus for their wedding dinner. She still doesn't like cutting through pink flesh, but some occasions call for blood sacrifice. Partaking in a dead animal is a gesture of primitive gratitude to the benign country that has put up with her for so long, has kept her safe, educated her, given her a job, and never once complained that she's not perfect. She's done her best though. She's even tried making crab apple jelly, which turned out to be a pointless substance.

After dinner her colleagues present her with an expensive print, a painting by one of the Group of Seven. They have chosen this print because they feel she ought to take something truly Canadian back with her. Opening her gift Lisa becomes so overwrought they suspect her of putting on a show. It isn't a show, but she doesn't know how to tell them what a perfect gift it is, or why.

The print is one by Lawren S. Harris called *Snow*. It reminds her of lying on the sofa looking out onto the tall spruce trees across the street, their branches drooping under their burden of snow in the tranquil landscape. It reminds her of listening to the

faint sound of bells tolling over the decades. How can she tell
her colleagues that? It was too private a moment, too complicated. She tells them that she has never needed a lot of material
possessions, only a few very meaningful ones. This print is that
kind of treasure. She will hang it in whatever living room will be
hers in the future, lie on another sofa, look at it and hear church
bells echo on a winter's day from long ago.

"We're so glad you like it," they say, unaware of their astute
choice of art.

The next morning she calls Pru and leaves a message on her
answering machine. Pru calls back an hour later.

"Darling! You're finally coming back! I can't believe it!"

"Neither can I."

" I can't wait! Did you know I turn fifty-two this year?"

"Nobody's immune, Pru."

"Don't I bloody know it. The twins are twelve already, cheeky
little brats. They're away at school by the way, so I'm afraid you
won't meet them this time. But you will be back soon again,
won't you?"

"Oh, I will, I will. By the way, Pru, I sent you a package a
week ago. You'll be receiving it any day now."

"Oh, lovely! What is it?"

"A story. The rest of my story. Read it. But promise me not to
mention it when we first meet. Put it aside. Let it wait. I want to
savor the moment of our reunion."

"I promise. Though I'm not all that surprised. I always knew
there was more, figured at some point you'd spill it."

"You were right, Mother Superior."

"No need for snarky name-calling, darling. I'm always right.
Now, promise me . . . don't be different."

"Just older. Much older."

There has been a wailing chorus of people telling her that you
can never go back, although despite their well-intentioned
refrain they have never managed to specify what they mean.
And as none of the doomsayers have ever left anything behind,
never left to go anywhere, how do they know?

Lisa has not listened to their chorus. Nor has she explained that it all depends on one's reasons for going back. It depends on what one's needs are. Hers, as it happens, are profoundly simple.

⊫◇⊣

Len pops over while she's cleaning out the apartment, to see how she is doing, offering to help.

"You want to help? That's a first. Eager to get rid of me?"

Len is not at all eager. Not until she gets bitchy and says that. The truth is, his life will be empty without Lisa, despite her annoying ways. "Yeah, I can't wait," he says. He doesn't tell her that he'll miss her.

"Well, you won't have to wait long." She will always think of Len with a certain fondness. There may be times when she'll miss his predictable presence, his never-spoken-of needs, but she doesn't tell him that. And, as she's well aware, what he really wants that day, is to find out if he can have her CD-player and TV cheap. She donates them to him.

"Thanks, Lees . . ."

"You're welcome."

" . . .We had some pretty good times, didn't we?"

"Yeah, Len. We did."

They hug each other and he goes away looking happy enough.

There is another person she has yet to say good-bye to. It's been a while since she saw Len's mother. Mrs. McT has been her mother-in-law for many years, and, while they are on friendly terms, they are not close. Mrs. McT has been one of the few people who has not tooted the ominous "You can never go back" refrain. When Lisa calls and tells her that she's leaving in five days, her ex-mother-in-law wishes her all the very best. Lisa detects genuine warmth in her voice.

The thaw, since daddy McT's departure from the world and his Naugahyde recliner, has been truly remarkable. The two women chat for a while about this and that, about the weather and air travel. Neither of them mentions Len, their common bond.

"It can't have been very easy for you here," says her mother-in-law out of the blue by way of farewell. It hints of an apology she doesn't owe.

"It's been fine," Lisa assures her. "It really has. I've been very happy here. Canada's been good to me, and I've been good in return. But I have grown terminally homesick. It's something I can't seem to control. I feel this strong need to speak my own language." Does Mrs. McT understand? Would she understand about closing the circle if told?

"I understand," replies Mrs. McT to the unasked questions. "Good luck to you, dear." She's off to her bridge club that evening, a busy seventy-five-year old woman, looking younger every year.

She does not implore her ex-daughter-in-law to keep in touch.

Jenny and Lauren and Diane take her out to dinner at an Italian restaurant on her last night in Canada. The four women are not as close as they were back in the seventies, or the eighties, having veered in different directions, but they do have a past together. That's important. They still like each other, the bond has not broken.

Lisa is staying the night with Jenny. Her friends tell her they're going to save up and maybe come and visit her next year, or the year after. Lisa begs them to do so. She looks forward to showing Sweden off to them, once she finds it again, the way she showed London off to Sonja. Connect her places and her people, shrink the world. "Please come and see for yourselves that the country I come from really does exist. I'll make you sandwiches."

They laugh at the joke. She laughs, too, pretending it is a joke.

Will she one day fill another notebook and send it to Jenny? No, she will not. She will never tell Jenny her story. Because if she does, it will not be about the Lisa that Jenny has known for so many years. It will only serve to confuse her. It will confuse Lisa too.

Two days later Lisa leaves Canada for good, feeling she ought to apologize for her departure and say, sorry, it's nothing personal. But she doesn't.

# England

# 40

Getting on a plane again after all these years is not as horrible as she feared. Then again, the flight is only an hour and twenty-five minutes. A manageable time frame. As the shadow of the plane surfs the East River she gapes at the famous silhouette that is Manhattan, surprised that it actually exists. It looks just like in the movies, this representative symbol of the free world. She gazes down at the almost mythical, invincible image. Walking along one of the canyons between those skyscrapers might be the man she is looking for. Either that or he's somewhere on the other side of the river, in Brooklyn. It was a long time ago, but she still recalls Jimmy talking about Brooklyn. He grew up there.

He better be there, she has less than a day to find him. Tomorrow she continues her trip to London.

She could have stayed longer in New York, but she needs to get the flying over with as soon as possible. Once she reaches the other side she will never cross the Atlantic again unless it's by ship, and that's a promise. So for her New York will never be anything but an airport hotel room and a stack of phone books. It's in view of what happened before she left Canada that she has decided to make this detour. In view of the incident that is going to be the final chapter of her confession, the one she will be telling Pru in person. The one she's still shaken by.

But there are questions. What will she do if she finds Jimmy later that day?

And what if he doesn't remember her?

As the plane lands, she decides to wait and see what happens.

The hotel room is big and clean, tasteful and anonymous. It has a well-stocked minibar, bless it, where she fortifies herself while looking up Sullivans in the phone books she asked to be sent to her room ahead of time. She was expecting there to be a million Sullivans listed in New York, and she's not far off. She would have to settle in New York for a few years to have time to go through them all.

Back she goes to the mini bar. This is going to take time.

What am I doing? She asks this question to the annoying woman in the mirror, who keeps following her around. "Get started," suggests the woman, who always makes Lisa's voice sound sharper.

She begins with the J. Sullivans, tackling the ones in the Brooklyn phone book first. Brooklyn is rich in Sullivans. She dials the number for the first one. No answer. Then the second one, the third, and onwards. The answering machines have voices she doesn't remember as his. Many of them are female. One of them could belong to his wife. The first person to actually answer in person is an old woman. Lisa explains her errand. "I'm looking for a Jimmy Daniel Sullivan," etc. etc.

"Who's dat!" the woman hollers.

Lisa explains that she's in New York briefly and badly needs to get a hold of Jimmy Daniel Sullivan and . . .

"Who's dat!" Louder this time.

"My name is Lisa Grankvist and I'm . . ."

"Who's dat!"

She hangs up. The next person is a man named Joe Sullivan who tells her he knew a Jimmy Sullivan once, no relation of his, mindya, he wouldn't wanna to be related to that two-faced prick. She thanks him for the information.

A woman with a husky voice is married to a Jimmy D. Sullivan and wants to know if Lisa's one of the sluts he's busy fucking senseless. If she is, the woman wants her to know he's got VD, and it would serve her just right if she caught it. It's her sincere wish that Lisa will die in agony.

And so it goes. Not very well.

Twenty-six phone calls and half a minibar later she reaches a man who says, yes, his name is Jimmy Daniel Sullivan. He doesn't sound like Jimmy. Surely she would have recognized his voice in an instant? This sounds like a black man. Her heart puts its leap on hold.

"Are you black?"

"All over, baby."

She makes another thirty-two calls before she finishes the J's, all without luck, then decides to go back and start at A. It's tedious work. Nobody knows the person she's looking for. You'd think a Sullivan would be related to other Sullivans, but apparently not. One speaks only what sounds like Chinese. She hopes the minibar won't run out of fortifying liquids. There are still a few million Sullivans left to pester.

Twelve more calls and she reaches an older man who says, well, his sister married this Italian guy, Bennie Torrelli, know the fella? Lisa confesses ignorance. Never mind, he's sure his sister's oldest daughter's husband, Anthony, is Jimmy's cousin once or twice removed. Lisa asks if this Jimmy has two brothers and a sister who died in a car accident. He says he thinks so, he remembers something terrible happened to them once. He's heard Anthony talk about it.

"You know Anthony? Short guy, did amateur boxing?"

"No, but Jimmy told me about him once. Nice guy, he always said."

"Yeah, Tony's a good guy. Too bad about his knee."

"Terrible. So . . . Mr. Sullivan . . ."

"Call me Mike, little lady."

"So, Mike, would you happen to know Jimmy's phone number? I'm only in New York for the day, kinda. I fly to London . . ."

"I don't know the guy or nothing."

"Oh."

"But I maybe could findya Tony's number. Maybe he'll know, or maybe Melanie will know."

"That would be great!" Her heart begins a beating marathon.

"Hold on, willya?"

"Oh, I'll hold, Mike," she mumbles to the silent receiver, "I'll hold for as long as it takes." He's gone for close to five minutes before he returns with a big reward for her patience. Her fortified head, losing control, starts to spin with premature ecstasy.

"Got a pen, lady?"

"I'm ready." He gives her a number. She's so anxious she can hardly write. Her heart is in her mouth, making it difficult to speak. She might have to spit it out. She manages to thank her kind friend Mike, shoves her heart back down her throat and swallows it, like an aspirin, with the aid of whisky, which she normally can't abide.

She's twenty-five years old.

Then she dials the number and talks to the woman named Melanie, telling her "It was your Uncle Mike who gave me your number. He said it would be all right to give you a ring." Sure thing, that's fine with Melanie, she's not busy and she likes to chat on the phone. She says they don't see too much of Tony's side of the family, not that they been fighting or nothing, it ain't that. But she knows Larry, Jimmy's older brother, because she went to school with Angela, his wife. She's a real nice lady. They moved to Flatbush years ago. She doesn't have their number, but gives Lisa the name of the street she thinks they live on still. Lisa has her spell it out just to make sure. The number is in the book.

She's getting closer and closer to Jimmy.

The minibar has provided great comfort and she's feeling wonderfully relaxed. Had the bar contained cigars, she would be lighting one right about now, celebrating the success of the hunt in her no-smoking room. After a handful of sustaining salted peanuts, she dials and in no time at all she's talking to Jimmy's sister-in-law Angela in Flatbush.

"Hi," she says, stroking the receiver, thinking how incredible this is. "Melanie gave me your number." She goes on to explain, but having Melanie for a reference is good enough for Angela Sullivan. It makes Lisa a friend and confidante. Like Melanie, Angela is talkative. "Larry's out," she says, "he's always out these days, you know how it is." Lisa assures her she does. Angela confides that she's getting kinda pissed off, and goes on about the project Larry's involved in.

Lisa is not interested, she wants to talk about Jimmy. She's so close now she can touch him. As soon as she's able to catch the briefest pause in Angela's monologue she butts her prepared speech into it. "I'm only in New York for the day, so I thought I'd look him up. He was a good friend of my husband's."

"Is that right? Well, now, how about that!" Angela thinks it's real nice of her to call and would have gone on about how precious old friends are, but Lisa manages to cram in another sentence.

"You don't have his number by any chance?"

"Yeah, sure, but he won't be back for about a week, I don't think."

Two very short thoughts flash through Lisa's head. The first one is "Yes! He exists!" and the second one is "Shit! He's not here."

"What a pity." Does she sound as unconcerned as she's trying to? "Is he on holiday?"

"Yeah, sorta. He's off on one of them cargo planes. Left this morning in fact, you just missed him. They were flying up to Alaska, he and Sammy Garcia."

"Oh. He's a pilot!"

"No, *he* ain't no pilot. Sammy is. They've gone fishing up there. Jimmy decided to go along, have a bit of a break. That man works too hard, if you ask me."

"I see. So what's he doing these days?"

"Working at the restaurant."

"He's a waiter?"

"No, honey, he's a chef!"

"He's a what?"

"A chef, dear. At Marcelino's, his restaurant. You didn't know?"

"No, I didn't. It's been quite a while, you see."

"I see. When did you last see him?"

"Oh God, it's been what . . . . Almost twenty years."

"Oh my! That long?"

"I'm afraid so. I don't travel much, or I would have made it to New York before. It's just that . . ." quick, brain, plausible lie required . . . "well, you see, my husband died recently and I thought while I was in New York I'd get in touch with Jimmy. I'm sure he'd like to know . . . . You know how it is . . ."

"Oh honey, I'm so sorry!" Angela's gushing now, she knows how it is, is there anything she can do?

"Well . . ." Lisa sounds tentative, as if considering her offer. "Maybe if you could give me his address, I could just write to him when I get back home. I would have written already but my husband lost his address book a few years back when we were broken into and . . ."

"No problem, honey, you just hold on a sec." She's back in a flash. "I just had to find my list of numbers. You got a pen?"

Jimmy's sister-in-law gives Lisa his address. It's music in her ears. Angela gives her his unlisted phone number too, "in case you're ever back in town."

"I can't thank you enough, Angela." Precious, wonderful Angela. Jimmy Sullivan's flesh-and-blood sister-in-law.

"That's all right, think nothing of it. It's been real nice talking to you."

"Oh! I almost forgot. Jimmy's married, isn't he?"

"Not anymore, honey. They broke up ages ago. But Jimmy's got Stella most of the time."

"Stella? That must be his daughter?"

"That's right. Stella Lisa. His wife wanted to name her Tiffany Gretchen, but Jimmy wouldn't hear of it. Put his foot down. He can do that when he wants to."

Jimmy's a father. And he hasn't forgotten.

"I bet he's a wonderful dad."

"He sure is. He'd do anything for that kid."

"How old is Stella now? She must be . . ." Come on, Angela, fill in.

"She just turned thirteen last month. Teenager."

"Ah, the difficult years." As if Lisa would know.

"You said it, honey. You got kids?"

"Yes, I have a son. He's thirty already."

"Boys are easier, I find."

"You're absolutely right there. So when did they split up? I remember when they got married. Jimmy sent us an invitation." It's astonishing, the ease and elegance with which she can lie after the contents of a minibar.

"Lessee . . . it was when Stella was four . . . yeah, that's right. I doubt if they'd have gotten married if she hadn't been pregnant."

"They split up back in 1986?" Same year she and Len split.

"Oh, yeah, I remember. I think it was in the spring of '82 we got the invitation for the wedding."

"Yeah, that's right. Boy, you're quick! You musta been good at math in school."

"Thanks, I was. They weren't married for very long though, were they?"

"Well, it's hardly surprising. They shouldn't have got hitched in the first place, like I said to Larry at the time, but he told me to mind my own business, it being his family and all. 'Course, Jimmy was always a bit different, as you probably know."

"I suppose . . . I'm embarrassed to admit it, but I don't remember his wife's name. Was it . . ."

"Trudi."

"That's right! I knew it was something German. Was she all German or did she just have a German name?"

"Her dad was German, I ain't so sure about her mom. She died when Trudi was a little girl. But I think she was Italian."

"Yeah? I remember he sent a picture of the two of them from the wedding. She was real pretty, I thought."

"She was all right. Bit of a snob, if you ask me. Thought herself a bit too good for Jimmy's family, if you know what I mean."

"Is that right? That's too bad. I always thought Jimmy was such a nice guy."

"Yeah, he's all right, isn't he? Loves his kid."

"Yes, I can imagine he would. What's he look like these days? I can't picture him older than thirty or so."

"He hasn't changed that much. I guess his hair's a bit thinner. You know, his forehead's grown a bit higher, that kind of thing. Bit of gray."

"Hasn't grown a beer gut yet?"

"I can't imagine Jimmy with a beer gut!" The voice in the phone laughs. "That man eats like a horse and is as skinny as ever. All the men in that family are the same. They say it's their metabolism. I say it's nervous energy. Look at my Larry, for chrissake, can't sit still for a minute. You have to tie him down to sit through supper."

"Is that right? Well, Angela, I shouldn't keep you. It's been a real pleasure talking to you. Thank you so much for your help. And if you see Jimmy, please tell him Jennifer called to say that Harry passed away."

"I'll sure do that, honey. And it was real nice talking to you too. I'm sorry about your husband."

"Thank you, Angela."

Jimmy has a daughter.

When Jimmy got married in 1982 Lisa had already been married nine years. He's a chef and owns a restaurant called Marcelino's. He has a daughter named Stella Lisa Sullivan. What a lot she knows about him all of a sudden. It makes him seem like a stranger. She dials his phone number, holding her breath, waiting to hear his voice on the answering machine. The phone keeps ringing. He doesn't have an answering machine.

Lisa wonders about a great many things it would have been too nosy to ask, lying on her hotel bed amid an assortment of empty mini bottles, feeling elated and kind of sick. Her left hand is gripping a piece of paper with Jimmy's address and phone number. What is she going to do with it? Is it the man she wants back or is it the past? He's a fifty-three-year-old chef, this man, and he's gone to Alaska on a cargo plane to fish. He has his life, his friends, his family. His brother Larry, his sister-in-law Angela, his daughter Stella.

He might have a female companion. She never asked about that.

She sits up.

Christ Almighty.

Jimmy is a real person. The bed in room 41 is empty. No longer burdened by unwarranted guilt she wonders if Jimmy Daniel Sullivan really was the man of her dreams, or if he was the personification of some unexpressed death wish. She doesn't even know why she wonders this, as night falls outside her hotel room and the lights of the myth that is Manhattan glitter across the river. It's just something that strikes her as she sits on the bed and plays with an empty mini-bottle that once contained gin.

# 41

All these hours stuck in a metal tube and she hasn't had a drink. Nor has she died of fear and that's quite an accomplishment. But fear, it seems, has not accompanied her across the Atlantic this time. She feels light, comfortable. The seat next to her is empty and she's been able to stretch out her stiffening joints.

After a brief night it's now morning again. The plane is already soaring over the English countryside, throwing its shadow through tufts of drifting clouds onto irregular little fields, some green, some brown. Here and there are the blots of tiny towns and villages, over there a large city, Birmingham perhaps. Amazing. That's England stretched out down below. The damp old island that used to swing. It still exists.

During her eight years in London she never once ventured outside the city limits. Never once did she travel to the seaside, to Oxford, to the Lake District, to the Peak District, Wales or Scotland. It never occurred to her, she was where she wanted to be. Once Pru asked her to come down to the ancestral pile for the weekend. There was to be a do under a marquee in the garden behind the pile. Lisa declined, thinking she would not fit in with a bunch of horsey-faced toffs. Pru could not comprehend why. For one thing, she said, the toffs in question looked more like overfed boars than horses.

Lisa tried to explain why it was not feasible. Her father had worked in a factory, her mother had been a cleaning lady. Both had quit school in their early teens to start earning a living. Her ancestral pile had been a one-bedroom apartment. "We have simple habits," she explained to her aristocrat friend. "We scratch ourselves in public."

"Oh, spare me for God's sake!" shouted Pru. "What the fuck does that have to do with anything?" Pru's relatives had, over the years, done far worse things in public.

"It has everything to do with it."

"What absolute twaddle!"

"Then why are your parents so outraged that you are working as a waitress?"

"Never mind that. I need you." For a split second Pru had looked vulnerable. It was a side of her Lisa had never seen before.

"You need me?"

"Of course I do, you ninny."

"What on earth for?"

"Oh, I don't know. Never mind, come with me, please?"

But Lisa refused to accompany Pru to the ancestral pile. Afterwards Pru confessed that it had been a ghastly weekend.

There's a ping. The *Fasten Seat Belts* sign has come on. The plane is getting ready to land at Heathrow, descending through a cloud cover that looks like the kind of laundry you have to use plenty of bleach on to get the gray out. The plane sinks through the layer of grime and there it is. There lies good old London sprawled arrogantly to infinity and beyond. Winding through it is the Thames, weaving like a drunk through the urban mass like it owns the place, which of course it does. Already it's pulling at her. Tomorrow she will stand on one of those toy bridges down there and watch the filthy water flow by. Take the tube to Chiswick.

Later today she will go and sit under a plane tree in Green Park.

And tomorrow evening, she will see Pru again. She could see her within the hour, and there's nothing she would love more, but it's too early, much too early. She needs to ease her way into London-mode, find Lisa from Chiswick before she finds Pru.

When the wheels hit the runway she makes a squeaky noise and a woman across the aisle gives her a startled look.

All too soon, here she is, back in London, sitting in a minicab hoping the driver knows where he's going. He doesn't speak much English. "I from Bosnia," he explains. It takes forever to get from Heathrow into the city. Was the air always this smelly? Was there always this much traffic choking the roads? She could have crawled to Mayfair faster on her hands and knees, her suitcase strapped to her back.

There are gleaming new buildings reaching for the sky. She's not sure where she is yet, and neither is the driver, but it's still very much recognizable as good old London, crammed full of people, traffic, and exhaust fumes, trendy cafés, bistros and restaurants, theaters and concert halls, museums, shops and parks. As well as a dreary array of derelict buildings, boarded up stores and graffitied slums.

The streets become cleaner, more sophisticated. Then she knows where she is. She's in Kensington heading towards Hyde Park. She had thought about booking a room in a certain hotel close to Victoria Station, if it was still there. Room 41, hoping they would not have changed the sheets. Shoving such bathos aside, she decided against it in the end. As you grow older, she reprimanded herself, sentimental delusions are like calories, you need to cut down for the sake of your health.

She has booked a room at Fleming's Mayfair Hotel on Half Moon Street instead. The taxi crawls down Piccadilly along Green Park and turns left, and now she knows exactly where she is. *Home* is the sentimental word that comes to mind.

The hotel doesn't look like much from the outside, it's simply a row of Georgian townhouses. The doors in the entrance have glass that she can't see through so she knows it's discreet in an old-fashioned way. Sure enough, the lobby is tasteful and demure, decorated in shades of subdued rose. It has the genteel hush she hasn't encountered since Dimitrios took them to the casino.

Her room faces the street, as she requested. It's expensive, naturally, as Pru recommended it. She wanted Lisa to stay with her, but Lisa declined the offer, needing to be on her own, at least for the first day. Pru understood and suggested Lisa treat herself to a stay in a good old London hotel. She gave her a list of several, including the Curzon around the corner, but Lisa likes the fact that this one is on Half Moon Street where she walked with Mick the last time they met. She's also fond of that name: Half Moon Street. Hopefully, as the hotel is less than a block from Green Park, she might be able to see the trees from her window.

She realizes that she's jet-lagged. Her skin smells of jet fuel and economy class recycled air. The thought that she will never have to cross the Atlantic on a plane ever again inspires her to do a dance on the sidewalk as she exits the hotel on her way down to Green Park, too impatient to wait another minute. A group of Japanese people stare at her and she smiles at them in mid-twirl. They turn their backs and scurry to safety around the corner.

Lisa runs across Piccadilly, through the gates into the park. The leaves on the plane trees have turned, but the grass is as green as ever. She sits down on a bench just as it starts to rain and has time to think only a few dizzy thoughts before she's drenched. It's been so long, she never thought to bring an umbrella. But how happy she is.

How easily she could be mistaken for a sad piece of crazed human driftwood, had it not been for her designer coat and expensive haircut she splurged on before she left.

Back at the hotel she has a shower, then goes to the restaurant for a bowl of forbiddingly dear lobster bisque, before returning to her room and her bed where, within minutes, she's unconscious. It's eight o'clock. Shortly after midnight she's wide awake again, not a bit tired, eager for morning, the incessant noise of jet engines still whirring in her ears, not sure if she's dreaming that unmistakable London night glow in the street outside. She gets up and stands by the window for the rest of the night, gazing down on the deserted street, reconnecting with a lost part of herself.

Up to the left the silhouettes of the trees in Green Park are visible in the dark. A late Rolls Royce drives by and turns right up on Curzon Street.

"I'm back in London. I'm standing right in the middle of London." She repeatedly squeezes her eyes shut for the pleasure of opening them again, knowing it will still be Half Moon Street down below. Smugly at home in body and soul, she remains by the window until morning lights the washed-out London sky again.

꜀꜠꜡

Much sooner than she'd planned, she is hurrying down the steps to the Green Park tube station to catch the Piccadilly Line to South Kensington. It's a bit disconcerting getting on the train. It's new and clean, with a cheerful yellow and blue interior. Smoking is not allowed. What happened to the dirty smelly old trains with the grooved wooden floors?

The first train arriving at South Kensington is the Ealing Broadway, the one, she remembers, that stops at Chiswick Park. This train, too, looks spotless. At least the forest of triplet chimney pots are still in place on every roof going by.

She gets off at Turnham Green. That's her stop, always was. And there's a flower vendor outside the station, just as in the old days. It's not the same one, and the flowers are more beautiful, more abundant than ever. "A lovely bouquet for you, missus?" the vendor says when he sees a woman linger, a deeply sentimental longing in her eyes. The woman smiles and nods like an eager young girl. Moments later she walks away with a large bouquet of blue exotic flowers with some yellow ones mixed in for good measure. She doesn't know what they're called, only that she has to have some.

Carrying her blue and yellow blooms like a bride, she glides down Turnham Green Terrace, which has spruced itself up. Chiswick High Road hasn't changed, not as far as she can tell, though the trees seem bigger, shading the sidewalk. Traffic is heavy.

Dimitrios' restaurant is gone. That comes as a shock. She had fully imagined him still sitting in the booth at the back checking receipts, was hoping to go in and say, hey, remember me? How about an ouzo? Come to think of it, he must be, what . . . in his seventies? Wherever he is.

She has an early lunch in the pasta house where the Greek's used to be, paying a king's ransom for twelve strands of fettuccini in an enormous earthenware dish, sitting close to the window facing the street. It's not the spot where they sat talking to Dimitrios the day they met Pru, but it's close enough. The waiter, who doesn't speak much English, brings a vase filled with water. "For beautiful flowers," he explains with a shy smile. He puts it on the table, which is only marginally larger than the dish.

He gets a generous tip.

Airedale Avenue looks the way she remembers it, though the trees are bigger. At least she assumes they are, it's been such a long time they ought to be. The copper beeches look enormous. She remembers them as rather spindly. The street is lined on both sides, from end to end, with compact little cars, no more than one inch apart. Their owners must be able to drive sideways out of those minute slots. Or never use them at all for fear of losing their place. The absurdity of the dilemmas of modern day life. That too seems new.

Lisa Grankvist, temporarily McTavish, can not control her urges today. First the flowers. Now she walks up the path to ring the bell at Mrs. Billings, as if it is a given that Lisa is welcome, that her old neighbor is still there. Well, the rhodo-dendron bush is. It takes a while before a white-haired old woman opens the door only wide enough to stare at the caller with one myopic eye.

"Yes?" She sounds suspicious.

"Mrs. Billings?" Lisa doesn't recognize the inch of withered face peeking out.

"Yes? Can I help you? What do you want?" The old woman doesn't sound hostile as much as anxious.

"Mrs. Billings, I'm so sorry to come and disturb you like this, but I'm only in London for a few days. You are Mrs. Billings, aren't you?" Lisa is starting to feel incredibly stupid, standing there with her large bouquet, but having come this far, she presses on. "I'm on my way from Canada to Sweden. I'm Lisa. I used to live next door at the Wickses, remember? You taught me all about gardening?"

"Good heavens!" It *is* Mrs. Billings and she *does* remember. The puzzled curiosity does not leave her eyes, but she becomes friendlier and opens the door to reveal another myopic eye and the rest of her face. Now Lisa recognizes her. She's aged, that's all. Time hasn't stood still in Chiswick.

"I just wanted to see if you were still around."

"More or less. I'm not dead yet." Mrs. Billings cackles like she's fooled death more than once in the past week alone.

After that Lisa doesn't know what to say, she hadn't intended to go ringing doorbells, asking the past to come out and play. Instead, she offers the old woman the exotic bouquet as if she were there to deliver flowers. But no, she won't come in for tea. Mrs. Billings seems relieved. She tells Lisa that Mr. Wicks and Bridget up and moved several years back. Got a pretty bundle for the house, Mr. Wicks did.

Lisa doesn't dare ask Mrs. Billings if she's still tending her fuchsias. She wants to get away from there, she feels out of place, she shouldn't have come. "I best move on. I have an appointment for lunch with some old friends. It was lovely to see you again. I'll always remember everything you taught me.

It meant such a lot to me. I just wanted you to know that."

Mrs. Billings seems happy to hear this, flattered to receive flowers, if a bit perplexed that this woman, always a bit odd, should turn up out of nowhere after twenty-two years. She doesn't understand why and is relieved to see her leave.

Lisa should have explained that she was out rooting in her past like a sentimental old sow in truffle-rich woods. Deeper and deeper the sow pokes her snout, past The Flat, the house now restored to its old mansion-hood. She pays her respects and continues up past the green and its striped church spire. The green looks as shabby and littered as ever, but there are a lot of new buildings in the area around Heathfield Gardens. Here she promptly gets lost, and finds herself at the end of Gunnersby Road wondering where she is. She has to retrace her steps carefully, wishing she had a map, feeling profound embarrassment. She used to know Chiswick inside out. It used to be her town. It's important she gets it right.

Back at the green she walks south on the other side, by the estate agent, down Sutton Court Road to Elmwood Road, remembering now, through the underpass still reeking of piss, past the little shop with its façade painted red. She used to buy stamps there. It still has a sign in the window saying Post Office.

                  ↦↤

It takes half an hour to find Burnaby Gardens. Entering from the far end, it looks different, though she can't for the life of her pinpoint why. It simply doesn't match the well-established picture in her head. It's much tidier for one thing. This street too is lined with parked cars. It's very quiet, like everybody's gone away for good.

Then she arrives at the house that was her island refuge for a lifetime not counted in years. She stops before it. It has a smart wooden door with a nameplate above it. The Langleys, it says in curlicue letters.

What does her garden look like these days? The Langleys' garden. Is the apple tree still there? The stone bench? What about her black mulberry tree? She goes and peeks over the narrow side gate. It ought to be visible from there. And there it is! Her very own mulberry tree! It's grown big, strong and proud, as she knew it would. A gust of wind makes its branches wave at her. Like a fool she waves back, overcome by a strong urge to knock on the door to demand visitation rights.

There's only one problem. It's not her tree. She doesn't belong here anymore. Quite possibly she never did. It's a middle-class, over-priced, yuppiefied neighborhood now, quaint and peaceful in the weak midday sun. Quiet, except for a squeaking sound getting louder, coming her way. A stick of a biddie comes tottering up the road, pulling her two-wheel shopping cart, her pale eyes flashing the strange woman a nervous glance. In that glance Lisa instantly recognizes good old Mrs. Mortified. She's shrunk considerably.

"Lovely afternoon!" Lisa brays the words in her best I-say accent.

Mrs. Mortified's eyes flicker, acknowledging the weather report, but that's all. She doesn't reply or slow down. Onwards she squeaks to her garden gate.

Lisa wants to chase after her, beg that frightened dried-up husk to reveal what happened to Ram and his sacred cow. Not that Mrs. Mortified would know. The Langleys might know, but Lisa is not about pester them. They'll be at work anyway.

If she catches sight of her mulberry tree again she'll burst into tears and look ridiculous and menopausal and fifty. She must pull herself together because she's off to the bank next to see about her investment account, which matures next month. A financial institution is a place where you must always keep your cool and speak in a hushed voice, much as in a Kensington casino.

When she passes St. Mary's Grove and sees the red-painted front of The Bedlington Café, she curbs an urge to go in and order beans on toast.

At the bank she's hoping to meet an older version of the bank chap from upstairs at the Wicks residence, but the bank manager is a woman young enough to be Lisa's daughter. She's polite, cool and confident. Lisa is pleased to find that her gambling money and monthly savings, like her mulberry tree, have grown big and strong and healthy. They have turned into £76,958.43. This makes her feel recklessly rich despite the fact that in London today it wouldn't last long. It is, however, enough to buy half a sandwich shop.

On the tube going back to the West End, she tells herself sternly: Lisa, you shall not, I repeat not, go to the pub on that street off the King's Road in Chelsea. And you shall not go past the hotel with room 41. You shall not so much as pass it on the other side of the street. Is that clear?

Lisa does as she's told, though later that day, a phone book in her very close vicinity happens to end up on her lap, where it falls open on the exact page where the hotel would be listed if it existed. It turns out it does, and it gives her an idea. Soon she finds herself writing a letter — no, not a letter — two sentences, to Jimmy D. Sullivan's address.

"I will be in room 41 on the 25th anniversary next January. Will you join me? Love, Lisa."

She's painfully aware how schmaltzy, and perhaps desperate, this sounds, but it doesn't stop her. Her hands seal the envelope and it sits patiently on the table while her eyes stare at it and her brain thinks about how she and Jimmy will soon both be making food for a living. Then her stubborn independent hands tuck the letter in the side pocket of her bag next to his framed photo, and she takes them for a long walk over to Piccadilly Circus, up Regent Street, east along Oxford Street. At Dean Street she turns south and traipses around the littered Soho sidewalks. It feels so good to be back. But Wardour Street has changed. The Marquee isn't there any longer. Nor are the Flamingo and the Whisky a GoGo. It's turned into China Town. It doesn't matter, she wants to dance and sing like Gene Kelly, twirl around lampposts and laugh. She's twenty-five years old. No, twenty. No, eighteen.

At Trafalgar Square a robust woman with long unkempt gray

hair hands Lisa a sprig of wilting heather. She looks like a left-over hippie, a long cotton skirt dragging on the ground, a shawl hanging askew over big round shoulders. Lisa's about to ask her why she's been chosen for this kind, if pathetic, offering when the woman's eyes grow cold. She has a demand. "How about giving a poor gypsy woman some spare change then? Eh?" Her face looms close to Lisa's. It's a round well-fed face. Is the slovenly cow threatening her? She doesn't look vaguely like a gypsy. She reminds Lisa of the blue-faced woman frying people in the center panel of the triptych, her face gleeful, her eyes without feeling. Lisa shoves the sprig of heather back into her demanding claw.

"Aren't you afraid I'll put a curse on you?" It's a threat, not a question. The woman's sneer is contemptuous.

Lisa laughs, and what a superior laugh it is. "You're a bit late for that, lady luck. Just watch *I* don't put a curse on *you*." Smiling an unconquerable smile she strides away, leaving the pseudo-gypsy and her basket of wilting heather.

The woman is putting a hex on her behind her back. Lisa knows that, as she knows that the hex will be useless against her.

Tonight she is going to see Pru.

# 42

**Sitting in a taxi** she suddenly can't wait any longer. She wants to get out and run and get there faster. She's going to see Pru.

They're meeting at the Ivy, a favorite haunt of Pru's. Posh and famous. "Tell them you're meeting me," was her instruction. Tell whom? Lisa wonders in the taxi, anxious and ten minutes late. She was so damn nervous she spilt wine on her new dress, having a glass to steady herself while putting on makeup, intent on the foolish endeavor of erasing the years to look her young self again. Pulling off her dress, she didn't know what to wear, got frustrated and, in a burst of fury, used some atrocious language, out of place in the demure surroundings of the Mayfair Hotel.

The entrance to the Ivy is on a corner. It doesn't look all that flashy from the outside. Lisa reminds herself that this is London, not a Burlington steakhouse with ample parking. The young woman behind the desk in the poky vestibule looks her over politely, as does a gentleman who appears from nowhere as if to bar her way. Their discreet smiles phrase the question it would be impolite to utter: "And who might you be, madam?" In a

Burlington steakhouse they're happy to greet a customer. She's about to tell them that she's meeting Prudence, when a middle-aged man slides out of the restaurant, his movements languid, a man at home where money talks. He stares at her.

"Lisa? Lisa, darling! Is that you?"

She's back in Darling-country. But who is he, this lean stranger decanted into a sleek silk suit, sublime with effortless self-confidence? She stares back. An expectant hush lulls the vestibule.

"Well, darling, if you don't remember me, I won't be offended. And I must admit I would not have recognized you either, old girl, had I not run into Pru just now. Hadn't seen her for eons, actually. She . . ."

"James?"

"Spot on, darling!"

"Christ! It *is* you! I don't believe it! Though you haven't changed that much, James. Apart from shedding your Oxfam togs for Armani."

He smiles indulgently. Lisa thinks that she never knew him very well.

"It's good to see you, Lisa, but I'm afraid I must dash. Late for a play already. Bit of a bother. And Lady Prudence is absolutely dying to see you." His eyes scan the tall slim woman in her tan linen suit, finds nothing objectionable. "By the way, you look wonderful, darling, you really do."

"Thanks, so do you."

"Toodles, old girl."

"Bye, James."

He's off in a cloud of expensive cologne.

Running into James has served one useful purpose. The Guardians of the Ivy have changed their demeanor. Now it's "May we insert our noses into your worthy behind?" and "This way please!" as the door is thrown open to the inner sanctum.

And there she is.

⌐◇⌐

Lisa would recognize her anywhere. Pru, who is turning fifty-two this year, is a glamorous redhead in a simple black dress. She stands up as soon as Lisa walks into the room, regal, watching her long lost friend approach the table. Lisa hears the sound of the voices around her fade as she reconnects with something that was lost a long time ago. Not only with Pru, but herself, the bit that Pru kept. Pru, whose beloved face has gone soft.

They're embracing. They sit down and grin, grins so big it takes a while before they can talk. It ought to have been an awkward silence after so many years, but it isn't, as they knew it would not be. Pru has read her story, Lisa can tell from her eyes.

"Oh, Pru. I've missed you!" She doesn't care that she's crying.

"Darling Lisa! I'm almost sick with delight!" Pru doesn't give a damn either.

"So am I. Why do you think that is? It's odd, don't you think?"

"Haven't got a clue. But you're right, it is odd. How long has it been?"

"Summer of '73. Twenty-two years and a bit."

"Shit! We ought to be strangers!"

"I know." Lisa grins at her some more, cries some more.

Pru grins back. "Well, I'm bloody delighted we're not. Drink?" Her eyebrows move upwards a nanometer and a waiter is at her side.

"You're somebody, eh Pru?"

"Bloody right. You have to be to survive in London these days."

"I just ran into James. I didn't recognize him."

"He hasn't changed much, has he?"

"Not much. Though it occurred to me that I never really knew him."

"Nor I, and I lived with him. Even slept with him a couple of times, if I remember correctly. Rather a private lad, was our James."

"He called you Lady Prudence. You're not really a lady, are you?"

"'Fraid so, darling. But in title only. Don't get hung up on it."

"Shit. Are you serious?"

"I am."

"Christ, Pru, I didn't realize. And you still talk to the likes of me? How long have you been one?"

"Forever, just about. It's a meaningless concept, but it does open doors."

"Meaningless, my ass. Don't lie, Lady Prudence."

"Oh, piss off, you old nag!"

They're back to normal. How easy life can be, how delicious. Before they leave Lisa goes to the ladies' room, ascends up a wide staircase built for stars to descend. Half drunk she tries to exude a star-like quality going down. Nobody pays her the slightest bit of attention.

As they're about to leave the door opens and a cigar enters, followed by a grin and an entourage. A real star.

"Was that Jack Nicholson?"

"What? Sorry, darling, I wasn't paying attention."

They take a taxi to Pru's flat near Sloane Square.

⚓

It's after midnight and they're lounging around half sloshed in Pru's living room, which would be forbiddingly elegant if it weren't such a mess. On a marble-topped table by a midnight blue sofa sit framed photographs of her twin daughters. They have short dark curly hair and don't look anything like Pru, who studies their photos as if intimidated by her motherhood. "Their personalities are different too, thank God," she laughs, "they're a far sight nicer than I'll ever be."

Does she miss them when they're away at school? Sometimes, she says, but mostly she's too busy. There's the odd time when she calls them up on the spur of the moment to see if they really exist. When she does, they're usually too busy to talk for very long.

Pru makes a fire. The two women chat, grow contentedly silent, stretch out, purr, chat some more. "How's Melvin doing? Do you ever see him?"

"Not for ages, he moved to France for some reason or other.

Some woman of his has a house there. He squandered his inheritance, that much I remember. Silly man."

"Did you sell the building with The Flat? I noticed it's been renovated."

"Oh, ages ago."

"And whatever happened to Dimitrios? His restaurant is gone."

"Haven't got a clue, it was a lifetime ago wasn't it?"

It's not yet time to talk about the notebook.

"Pru? Can I ask you something?"

"Ask me anything, as long as it's probingly personal."

"It is. Remember those pretentious twits you used to hang around with after you went back to university? Those dimwitted followers that used to tag along with you to London? The ones that all talked through their noses?"

"Darling! That's not a very nice way to describe my friends, is it?"

"Get real, Pru, it's what they were and you know it. Now answer my question. Why did you so often come to town on weekends with that lot in tow? It's something I've often wondered. It used to upset me. I couldn't stand them."

"Because, whether you liked it or not, and whether I liked it or not, and sometimes I didn't, they were, and they are, my tribe."

"What am I then? I will never belong to your tribe."

"Actually, my pet, you were one of the very few people, apart from Melvin perhaps, that I ever *wanted* to be with."

"Why me? I was so lost when we met."

"Well, surprise, darling. So was I. You just assumed being lost had only one expression."

"I did. You're right. Should I apologize?"

"Don't be bloody stupid." Pru pours Lisa another glass of wine. Pru with her late night face looks softer, older. Somber.

"Were you really lost? I always thought of you as the least lost person on the planet."

"Well, Lisa, you were rather naive. Naive, but never helpless. That's what I always adored about you. Did you know that?"

"No, I didn't. You were always so wild and carefree. And always so sure of yourself. You were my source of strength, did you know that? And how I used to love the way you lied. You had such flair. I could never lie like that, and God knows I've tried."

"Those years were my time out, which, if I remember correctly, was your term. Mind you, I still lie a lot."

"They were my time out too. Sometimes I wish my whole life had been time out."

"Who doesn't? But I'm so very glad we spent it together. That's something. And we shall always be friends, shan't we? We complement each other."

"We always did. I can't imagine growing old without a Pru in my life." Jimmy's face flashes by. It's followed by the face of a priest with blue eyes. Ghosts of the wee hours.

"That's good." Pru senses the time has come. "Shall we talk about your story now?"

"Yes, we shall. Were you shocked?"

"Well, old girl, what do you think?"

"I keep thinking, why didn't I tell Pru this a long time ago?"

"Pru keeps thinking that too. I've read it five times now, imagining you as you looked when I first met you at the Greek's. You wore white ankle boots."

"I remember that day. You came breezing in with a slab of meat wrapped in brown paper."

"You remember that?"

"I remember everything."

"The baby would have been six months old or so when we met, is that right?"

"Yes."

"And nobody in London knew but Mimmi and Mick?"

"Correct."

"Christ, Lisa. I can't imagine what it must have been like."

"I can't either. Not anymore. I was too young to know what I was doing. How else could I have gone through with it?"

"How difficult it must have been. How unbearable."

"Oh, it was unbearable, all right. More than I'd care to remember. That's why I escaped to my island refuge. I was so sure I'd never leave that refuge, forever tend the garden and sit on my white carpet and make clothes. Never age, never go forward. Never remember, yet never forget."

"And the baby was the real reason for all that guilt? The reason you gave up that American?"

"Yes, it was. I convinced myself that morning when I woke up beside Jimmy, that if I gave up the only man I would ever love, I would have paid the price. I would be able to stop feeling bad."

"What absolute nonsense."

"I know. After that I still lost my island, so it was all in vain."

"I hope you're not still carrying that guilt? If you are, I'll beat it out of you, I swear."

"No, it's all gone now. I got rid of it all a couple of weeks ago."

"Just like that?"

"Just like that."

"How on earth did you go about it? You make it sound like it was an item of old clothing given to charity. What made it so easy all of a sudden?"

"It's the last chapter of the story. I thought I had already written you the last chapter, but it turned out I was wrong. There was still a bit to go. Something happened, you see. Something so very strange I have yet to recover."

"What, for God's sake?"

"I ran into somebody after a very long time."

"Jimmy!"

"No. Not Jimmy." She has a hard time saying it.

"Who then, for God's sake!" Pru is getting impatient.

"My son."

Pru knocks her glass over. "Your what!"

"Yes." Lisa sits calm. Her hands lie folded in her lap. Not Madonna-like, but as someone who has arrived at a state of peace with herself.

"How on earth did you know it was your son? Did he come looking for you?"

"No. Len and I were watching the news on TV one night. I never quite got rid of Len, as you know. There were more reports from the Balkans that night. In one segment they interviewed a priest from Croatia. I recognized him at once. The red hair, the eyebrows, the birthmark. He was in Toronto fundraising.

"Are you telling me your son is a priest?"

"Yes. He's a priest."

Pru's disbelief makes her mute.

"He was being interviewed outside a hotel. I could see the name of it in the background, so I called the next morning to see if he was staying there. Then I went to meet him."

Pru remains mute.

"So I shall have to tell you the addendum to my story in person."

"Like the very first one."

"Yes and no. I told you that one like a story. This one I will have to tell you like a two-person play. It's all dialogue, because words were all he shared with me. Well guarded words."

Pru recovers her power of speech. "I think you better get started. Is it traumatic?"

"More traumatic than I know how to describe, though I remember every word that was said."

"It sounds like we'll need chocolate for this."

"I think most definitely."

Pru runs to the kitchen and hurries back with a large box of chocolates, a bottle of chilled champagne and two fluted glasses on a tray.

"You simply have to have champagne with these chocolates. I hope we're up to the late night debauchery. But it's going to be a long night, so what the hell, we'll need it. Leave that other plonk. Let's celebrate your survival." She pours some champagne.

"Cheers, Lisa, my dearest of friends."

"Cheers, my dearest Pru. How I've missed sitting like this."

"I know. Now talk." This time Pru does not turn her face to the fire.

# 43

We were watching the news on TV one evening, Len and I. He'd popped by, as usual. There was a lot about the Balkan crisis, among other things an interview with a priest from Croatia. He was in Canada fund-raising. And I thought, oh, dear God, I know that priest!

He had his grandmother's red hair, you see, and a triangular birthmark beneath his right eye. He also had my chin and my lips, but his father's eyebrows. His blue eyes were only slightly darker than mine, the same shade as my father's.

I couldn't take my eyes off the screen. My mind was reeling. The last time I saw that priest was in Zagreb. He was twenty-seven days old and wore striped terry cloth pajamas. Easter Sunday, April 18, 1965. A gray, cloudy day on Strossmayerov trg.

Eighteen. My lucky number.

I wanted to meet that priest. I don't know why, but I had to. He looked like his father. I had forgotten what that man looked like, but as I watched the priest's face it came back to me. Once again, here was the living proof of what happened during that terrible night. A priest no less. And I thought, what irony.

I needed to see him face to face. I needed to know what he

knew. Only, did I have a right to his story? Did I have a right to know who he was, how his life has been, why he became a priest? I'm still not sure about that. But he was my biological son, whom I had not laid eyes on since that Easter Sunday thirty years before. Now here he was on my TV-screen in Canada.

The time had come. I heard it knocking. For a long time I had felt a sense of expectancy. Whatever it was I had been expecting, here it was. Somewhere a door unlocked. I swear, I heard the click.

Catching another glimpse of the priest I noticed the sign above the doors. It read Metropolitan Hotel. I knew I was going to call the hotel first thing in the morning.

Was I frightened? You bet.

><>—<

The next day, shortly after lunch, I was standing in the hotel lobby waiting for him. It was a big flashy one with a shining marble floor. A wide staircase led upstairs to wherever he was. It had a gilded banister. How could a priest afford to stay in such a pricey hotel? I never did find out.

I had called the hotel first thing that morning and sure enough, he was staying there. I was connected to his room. The phone rang four times. Each time it rang, my heart stopped. I had expected to hear his voice, but it was a woman's voice who answered. She spoke fluent English with only a trace of an accent. She told me she was assisting Father Sterić while in Toronto. I said my name was Lisa Grankvist and that I was a journalist from *The Spectator*, wanting to do an interview. She asked me to wait a moment and she would check his schedule. I heard her talk to somebody in a foreign language. A few minutes later she returned to the phone and said he would be able to see me at two o'clock if that was convenient. He had another appointment at three. He would meet me in the hotel lobby below the stairs. I described myself so he'd know whom to look for.

It was the most peculiar I ever felt in my whole life, standing waiting for that man, and God knows I've felt pretty damn weird at times. I had no idea whether I was going to play journalist and ask a bunch of official questions, or if I was going to blurt out who I was.

Then, there he was, the child I gave birth to, this priest, walking slowly down the staircase, looking very serious. I watched him descend. He was not looking for me; he was walking with his eyes downcast as if deep in thought. The slight bend of his head reminded me of his father staring at his feet.

Not until he reached the lobby did he raise his head and look my way, as if he already knew where I was standing. He was a tall man. He made his way towards me, and I thought, yes, those are his father's eyebrows, his father's triangular birthmark, his Slovene grandmother's red hair. That's my chin. And he has definitely inherited my lips. Like mine, they were not smiling.

Oh Pru, how astonishing it was.

I stood rooted to the spot, listening to myself breathe as he walked slowly towards me. How blue his eyes were. The blue of my father's eyes in the face of a stranger.

His face was stern, a bit sanctimonious even, when those eyes looked into mine, and very much on guard. Soon he stood before me, formal and stiff, and I heard his voice ask me a question.

*You are my mother, yes?* His first words, a near accusation, uttered in that soft Slav accent. They floored me.

*Yes,* I confessed when I found my voice. *How did you know?*

*Your name is on birth certificate.* It was a cold and factual statement.

*I'm sorry.* I didn't know what else to say. I'd completely forgotten about the birth certificate. If I had still used the name McTavish, he would not have known who I was. I looked at him. His gaze was quizzical and unwavering. He stood waiting to hear what I could possibly want. I remembered he had another appointment at three o'clock.

As I gazed at his face I felt I ought to want him to want me for his mother. I sat down on the sofa behind me, feeling faint. He joined me.

Funny isn't it, him being a priest, when I once considered leaving the picnic basket on the cathedral steps up on Kaptol Hill? I thought, should I tell him that?

↦◇⇥

When I looked into his eyes, the eyes of this reserved Catholic priest, the eyes of the man who is my son, something happened. It was extraordinary. I suddenly remembered what the flowers were, those flowers that grew in the courtyard by the bicycle stands back in Sweden. Early that morning, just before this priest was conceived, when his father led me to the outhouse. Do you remember when we talked about that? The innocence of the beauty of flowers? Not until then did I remember that they were red peonies. Their image leapt into sharp focus and they bloomed again, big and round. I could once again see individual red petals, some curled at the edges, starting to wilt, others in their first fresh bloom. A tall cluster of them in the middle of the little courtyard, surrounded by bicycles. Their misplaced perfection.

My face must have revealed that some unexpected revelation had struck me.

*Something is matter?* He looked vaguely concerned, though I had a feeling he didn't like me. Well, why on earth should he? He no longer looked me in the eye, he was very much on his guard.

*I just now remembered something,* I said. *An irrelevant detail.*

*I make you remember?* He seemed puzzled.

*Maybe. It's difficult to say. But behind the building where your father raped me was a small courtyard. That was where the out-house was. When my friend and I had to go to the toilet they allowed us to put on our dresses, then a guard led us down to the outhouse. Your father was my guard.*

He didn't want to hear that, he got angry. Was he angry with me or his father? *Only now you remember?* There was such bitterness in the question.

*Yes,* I said. *In the middle of the yard was a small flower bed surrounded by bicycle stands and bicycles. It was full of flowers.*

*I could never remember what kind of flowers they were that grew there. Until now. They were red peonies.*

He didn't understand, and repeated the name. *Bee-yonnies?*

*Peonies.* I described them and he nodded. He mumbled they have those in his country too.

⚓

By then I was positive he didn't like me. God knows he had little reason to. I was his mother and I had given him away. That was how he saw me. Only I was never his mother. I was the woman who gave birth to him. A man forced his way inside me and planted his seed and my virgin soil was fertile ground. That's what happened. That never changed. But this bee-yonnie was not my flower.

How many times had I told myself that over the years?

I wanted to tell him the same thing, but I couldn't.

Still, it bothered me that he didn't like me. As a priest, surely he ought to like everybody? He should have blessed me and forgiven me my sins, it was his job. He should have made the sign of absolution or whatever it is priests do. Exorcised the demons.

When I told him so, he blushed. There was a flash of lightning in his eyes. *You are not Catholic woman*, he said. He made it sound like a crime.

It was my turn to get angry. *That's irrelevant. I got pregnant. I gave birth to you. Then I returned you to your father. It's the least you can do.* Why did I suddenly sound so belligerent? I don't know.

Our eyes met. It was a head-on collision. I thought, I don't know this priest. This man. I'm not sure I'd even like him if I got to know him. He's his father's son. He's a Roman Catholic priest. What could he possibly know about women? Has he ever had sex? I honestly don't know why I thought that, but before I knew what I was doing, I asked, *Are you a virgin?* I shocked myself.

He stared at me. I sensed outrage. *I not discuss this matter. I am priest.*

*I was a virgin when your father raped me. Did he tell you that? If he had been the Holy Ghost you might have been Jesus Christ.* Thinking, what on earth am I saying! What is the matter with me? Why do I feel so angry?

Perhaps it was not so much anger as sadness, a sadness with a hard edge. I remembered the Saturday afternoon before Easter Sunday, sitting with the twenty-six-day-old baby by a graveside at the cemetery in Zagreb. I told the baby then that I was the wrong Madonna, he had a right to know, but he was asleep at the time and didn't hear me. No point reminding him now.

The man who had been that baby was shocked. It was shock tinged with embarrassment. *Please!* He whispered the word. *You come to punish me for sin of father?*

*No. No, that was honestly not my intention. I'm sorry. I . . . I don't know . . . But why can't you forgive me for my sins?*

*I not see this way,* he said. He was stubborn. But so was I.

*I bet you've forgiven your father, heart and soul.*

I was acting like an eighteen-year-old.

Then our eyes met again.

*My father was good man,* he said. *Also he was good father. I love him very much.*

*Did he raise you?*

*When I am child. My father go to jail when I am six years old.*

I calculated that that would have been in 1971, the year I met Jimmy Sullivan and sacrificed a chance at happiness. *What did your father do to end up in jail?*

*He not did bad thing. He join Maspok. You know what was this?*

*No, I don't.*

*It was organization. Nationalists wanting free Croatia. Tito put everybody away.*

*I thought your father liked Tito. He was half Croat, half Slovene just like him.*

He shook his head at that. *Tito become like madman.*

*I read somewhere that he was like a huge tree. Nothing could grow in the shadow of its branches.*

*This is correct.*

*How long was your father in jail?*
*More than one year. I live with grandparents. We have good life.*
He was getting increasingly defensive.
*What's he doing now? Your father?*
*He dead. You want know how he die?* The question reached me on a cold breeze. He looked distant.
I said, *No.* I did want to know, of course I did. I wanted to find out how he died, out of simple human curiosity, but didn't feel I had the right. *Did he work in a bank?*
*In bank?*
*Yes. When you were a baby, did he work in a bank?*
*I not remember. He go to university. You give to him money. This he tell me.*
*That money was for you, not for him.*
*He know this. University not cost money. He study for to get good job. Then later join Maspok.*
*Are you a nationalist too? Is that why you're here? I mean, why would a Yugoslav priest come to Canada?*
*I am Croat.*
*Actually you're half Swedish, one quarter Croat and a quarter Slovene.*
*No.* His voice was dead firm on this. *I am Croat. Where I live you are Croat, Slovene, Serb or Muslim. I am Croat. When this alone is reason to cut neighbor throat, you must be what are you. If not, other people do decision for you.*

It was quite a little lecture, yet he was not expecting me to understand it. As I didn't, never having lived in a world where people get out of bed one day and decide to slaughter their neighbors for being different. What this priest was talking about was utterly alien to me. So was the priest himself.

This was not the little baby in the green and white striped terry cloth pajamas that I had handed over to his father in Zagreb. This was a man from a part of Europe that had been, and still is, ravaged and torn apart by its own people. Millions have been displaced, their towns and villages torched in a continuing conflagration of hatred.

We were both Europeans. But I didn't understand. Did he understand?

He confessed that no, he did not, and that it was a source of great sorrow.

No doubt he was a brave and proud man. But he was not my son. I had not shaped him. I had no claim to him. Every event that helped make him what he is today, I knew nothing about. He was my flesh and blood, but apart from DNA there was no connection.

So we sat in a moment of apprehensive silence. I saw before me the picture Mimmi had showed me in her secondhand book as we walked among the old buildings up in Gornji Grad in Zagreb. Mimmi who had cooed at this man and kissed his little nose and call him sweetie. What would he say if I told him that?

I said, *I saw a picture of a beautiful bridge once. It was when I was in Zagreb to return you to your father. It was called Stari most.*

*I know this bridge. But is not in Zagreb. Is in Mostar. Over Neretva river.*

*That's right. It was built by the Turks in 1566.* My brain hoards some curious facts. *The Bosnian Croats blew it up couple of years ago.*

*Yes.*

*Why did they do that?*

*I not know. Every country has many fools.*

Amen to that, I thought.

It says in the Bible, "Blessed are the merciful, for they shall obtain mercy." I had a feeling this priest was not one of the more merciful of God's servants. At least not as far as runaway teenage moms were concerned.

*Why did you become a priest?*

*I wish serve God.*

*Why? What did God ever do for you?*

*He return me to my people. This is for reason, perhaps. To help, but not kill.*

God did not return him. I did, because I didn't want him. At least I thought I didn't.

*You're only thirty years old. You can't have been a priest for very long.*

*Only few years.*

*Are you happy?*

*Happy?* Here he looked at me like I was a complete idiot. *Yes. Happy. Are you happy?*

*Nobody in my country is happy these times. Is not possible. Everywhere around has been too much death.*

I was an idiot. *I'm so sorry. I wasn't thinking.*

He studied me as if he was about to say something I would not like to hear, but he changed his mind and looked over towards the reception desk, to the elevator, at his watch. Leaning his elbows on his knees, he started rubbing his temples.

*I forgive you,* he said eventually, not looking up, and I suspect, to get rid of me. He didn't say it like a son. He didn't say it like a father either. He uttered the words like a tired man under pressure. It was slightly mechanical, a hair's breadth away from a sigh. A "go forth and never come back" kind of deal. I half expected him to make the sign of the cross. This man who, whether he liked it or not, was the product of his father's sin.

*Thank you. But you know what? I no longer need your forgiveness.* I stood up. It was amazing how little I felt all of a sudden. Or rather, how well I coped with feeling too much. *It wasn't your forgiveness I needed, you see. I realize that now. It was my own.*

This father, son and holy ghost of my past stood up as well. He looked surprised, but it was surprise mixed with mild disapproval. I realized that he felt superior to me. It was a very judgmental person standing before me.

I got upset. He had no right to feel that way. *You should thank me,* I pointed out to him. *If I had kept you, you wouldn't be a priest helping your country.* As if mine had been an unselfish act. It was my turn to blush.

*I will not thank you,* he replied, revealing the child within. Realizing this, he blushed, too.

I desperately scanned his face, his rather handsome face, for a sign that might have revealed the small child I gave up, a sign that might have helped me know him, love him even. He noticed and asked what I was looking for, so I told him. I had to, I didn't want to be dishonest. He replied that he understood, but confirmed there was nothing there.

And he was right, there wasn't. Under his cool surface I sensed a sturdy stubborn spirit. He may have gotten that from me.

*You never was my mother*, he said. It was an accusation as well as a reminder.

Some priest this was. But he was right.

*I didn't want to be your mother*, I hit back. *I was raped. I returned you to the man who planted you in me. It was that simple.* It wasn't that simple at all, but I didn't elaborate. It was none of his business. I looked at him again. He looked at his hands. I decided to leave and made for the exit. I did not say goodbye. Before I got to the exit I heard his voice behind me.

*Excuse me, please!*

I turned around. His mouth was giving nothing away, but there was something in those eyes that were my father's shade of blue.

*Yes?*

*You did right thing*, he said, not quite meeting my eyes. *Is all right.*

*Does that mean you forgive me?*

*Perhaps.* He was struggling to. Maybe one day he would. *Where I come from is not so easy to forgive.*

He turned away from me then and I left. I didn't look back.

I walked for quite a while afterwards. At some point I ended up on Yonge Street close to Bloor. When I passed a restaurant I went in and ordered coffee. A white cup and saucer, a splash of coffee on the saucer. I didn't touch the coffee, like that time long ago when the priest was already germinating inside me.

Thirty years earlier I had covertly escaped my country with a small baby in a basket. Recently I had made a vow to go back